Praise for *The Extraordinaries*

An Indie Bestseller!
An Indie Next Pick!

"Uproariously funny, this razor-sharp book is half a love letter to fandom, half self-aware satire, and wholly lovable."
—Sophie Gonzales, author of *Only Mostly Devastated*

"The most down-to-earth book about superheroes I've ever read. I laughed, I cried, and I had a smile on my face the entire time I was reading it."
—Mason Deaver, bestselling author of *I Wish You All the Best*

"If you're looking for a book to read and then reread several times before the next Spider-Man movie releases, this will be perfect."
—*BuzzFeed*

"TJ Klune is doing powerful work that inspires and impresses. He is a gift to our troubled times, and his novels are a radiant treat to all who discover them."
—*Locus*

"Hilarious, sweet, and absolutely super!"
—*Kirkus Reviews*

"Klune's deliberate use of traditional comic book themes, such as masking one's identity, mirror common struggles faced by neurodiverse and LGBTQIAP+ youth; this thoughtful approach urges readers to embrace their true selves."
—*Shelf Awareness* (starred review)

"Just what teens who devour the CW's DC shows and Marvel's films need to tide them over as they await new seasons of superhero television."
—*BookPage*

"Klune's romp is irresistibly readable. . . . Readers will be delighted!"
—*Booklist*

"There's plenty in this lighthearted, superhero-interested teen dramedy for kids who feel like they're sometimes on the outside, including the positive representation of a teen with ADHD."
—*Publishers Weekly*

"Hand to teens involved in fandom, writers of fanfiction, lovers of superhero stories, and queer romance readers."
—*School Library Journal*

TOR BOOKS BY TJ KLUNE

FOR YOUNG ADULTS
The Extraordinaries
Flash Fire

FOR ADULTS
The House in the Cerulean Sea
Under the Whispering Door

THE EXTRAORDINARIES

TJ KLUNE

TOR
TEEN

A TOM DOHERTY ASSOCIATES BOOK
NEW YORK

THE EXTRAORDINARIES

Copyright © 2020 by Travis Klune

A Tor Teen Book
Published by Tom Doherty Associates
120 Broadway
New York, NY 10271

www.tor-forge.com

Tor® is a registered trademark of Macmillan Publishing Group, LLC.

The Library of Congress Cataloging-in-Publication Data is available upon request.

ISBN 978-1-250-20366-3 (trade paperback)
ISBN 978-1-250-20367-0 (ebook)

Our books may be purchased in bulk for promotional, educational, or business use. Please contact your local bookseller or the Macmillan Corporate and Premium Sales Department at 1-800-221-7945, extension 5442, or by email at MacmillanSpecialMarkets@macmillan.com.

First Edition: July 2020
First Trade Paperback Edition: July 2021

Printed in the United States of America

0 9 8 7 6 5 4 3 2 1

*For the neurodiverse who think big and dream even bigger:
you are a superhero, and your powers are infinite.
Never let anyone tell you otherwise.*

Fic: This Is Where We Scorch the Earth
Author: ShadowStar744
Chapter 67 of ? (IT KEEPS GETTING LONGER!)
267,654 words (LIKE A LOT LONGER!!)
Pairing: Shadow Star/Original Male Character
Rated: PG-13 (Rating might go up, but I don't know if I would be good at it, ugh)
Tags: True Love, Pining, Gentle Shadow Star, Violence, Happy Ending, First Kiss, Maybe Some Smut if I Can Talk Myself into It, But Who Knows

....

Chapter 67: Caught in a Storm

Author's Note: Hey! Sorry I haven't updated in a while. I was having computer problems, and then my summer was really busy. I also had writer's block, which is the worst. I didn't mean to leave it on a cliffhanger for four (!!!) months, but your comments asking me when I was going to update next gave me the inspiration I needed. Thanks for that! I can't promise when the next chapter will be out, because I'm starting my junior year (ugh), and I'll probably be really busy. Hopefully, it won't be too long. And sorry for any mistakes! My beta reader is apparently "busy" (whatever that means), and I'm not very good at editing. Just point out anything wrong in the comments, and I'll try and fix it. Thanks!!!!!!

Nate Belen wasn't a damsel in distress, even if he was currently tied up on top of a bridge waiting for Shadow Star to save him. As he regained consciousness, awareness seeping in, all he felt was pain. He groaned lowly. Everything hurt. His neck. His legs. His right hand.

And his heart.

His heart hurt worst of all.

Because it had been broken into tiny shards.

The words that Shadow Star had growled at him echoed in his head.

I care about you, Nate, but I can't be with you. Nova City needs a hero. And I have to be that hero. I can't take the chance of my enemies finding out how much I care about you. They could use you against me. This is over.

A single tear tracked its way down Nate's face. Not that he was a crier! No, he didn't cry over anything. He was strong and brave and *never* cried.

Except when his stupid superhero almost-sort-of boyfriend broke up with him.

"I see you're awake," an evil voice said.

Nate opened his eyes.

And gasped.

The wind whipped through his thick hair. He tried to struggle against the binds wrapped around his body, but it was no use. He was trapped.

At the top of one of the spires on McManus Bridge, the biggest bridge in *all of Nova City*.

Birds flew by. The stars were bright overhead. And in front of him, black cape billowing, was Pyro Storm.

His mask covered his face, leaving only a slit for his mouth. His eyes were covered in red lenses. His costume was tight—black with red piping—and showed off his strong, muscular body. He had an eight-pack. His chest was really strong. His thighs were thick. His boots were killer. On his chest was a symbol that caused the good people of Nova City to cower in fear: a tornado made of fire.

Nate felt his heart start to race, but he would never let Pyro Storm see he was scared. No way. He struggled against the binds that held him. "What do you want with me?" he snapped courageously at the supervillain.

Pyro Storm tilted his head back and laughed. "Oh, Nate. It's not *you* I want."

"Then why am I here?" Nate asked heroically.

Pyro Storm flew a little closer to Nate, eyes narrowing behind his mask, cape billowing. "You know why."

"I have no idea what you're talking about."

"I think you do," Pyro Storm retorted. "Everyone knows to whom your heart belongs. And since I have captured you with my diabolical scheme, we both know who will come to your rescue. He always does."

Nate felt a trickle of sweat drip down his forehead. "He doesn't care about me."

Pyro Storm shook his head. "You're wrong about that. You mean everything to him. Even though he could have anyone in the city, man or woman, he has chosen *you*. You must be something extraordinary for him to have fallen the way he has. And now I know how to strike at him. How to get him to his knees."

"You'll never win," Nate snapped valiantly. "Villains were only made for one thing: to be *defeated*."

"Wow," Pyro Storm said, sounding really impressed. "Did you think of that all on your own?"

Nate nodded. "Yes."

"That was pretty great. I can see why he likes you as much as he does."

And then a voice growled, "You shouldn't have touched him."

"Shadow Star!" Nate gasped.

Because, *yes*, it was. Shadow Star had come.

He looked as amazing as he always did. He wasn't as buff as Pyro Storm, and his costume wasn't as obscenely tight, but he still was the most handsome Extraordinary that Nate had ever seen, even if he couldn't actually see his face, given that it was hidden behind a black mask that covered his entire head except for his mouth. His costume glittered like a starry sky, and no matter what the haters said, it absolutely did *not* look like it was sequined. Instead, it was as if he were covered in tiny jewels.

Shadow Star had once pulled Nate close, and just when Nate was sure he was about to be kissed for the first time in his life, Shadow Star had turned and run, climbing up the side of a skyscraper quicker than Nate could follow.

But he was here, now, hanging off the spire across from Nate by one hand, his other hand a fist as it dangled toward the river hundreds of feet below. Shadows grew around him like they were sentient, thick bands of tentacled darkness that whipped back and forth. Nate wished he knew Shadow Star's secret identity more than anything else.

"Ah," Pyro Storm said, turning to face his greatest nemesis. "I see you got my message, Shadow Star."

"I did," Shadow Star said, his voice a deep rumble that made Nate shiver. "Though I'm sure the city would appreciate if you sent me a text instead of burning it into the side of the mayor's office."

"Had to make sure I'd get your attention," Pyro Storm said.

"You have it, though I'm not sure you want it." Shadow Star glanced at Nate. "You all right?"

Nate nodded. "I . . . I'm fine."

"I'll get you down."

"That'd be nice."

"I need to talk to you."

Nate didn't know if that was good or bad. "O . . . kay?"

Shadow Star stared intensely at him. Or, at least Nate thought he was staring intensely, given that he couldn't actually see Shadow Star's eyes. He wondered if they were blue. He hoped they were. A cerulean blue, like an exotic ocean. They were probably beautiful and hot and full of anguish and pain at the sight of Nate trapped by Pyro Storm.

"Wow," Pyro Storm said. "You could totally cut the sexual tension out here with a knife. Are you guys soul mates? Because you seem like you're soul mates."

Shadow Star turned away, staring off into the distance, full of quiet angst and strength. "I don't know if I can believe in love. I've been . . . hurt. In the past."

Pyro Storm nodded. "Oh, I get that. It sucks, right? But sometimes, you have to move on from whatever hurt you in the past. Or *who*ever."

"You don't know what you speak of, villain," Shadow Star said, clenching his fist. "It's not as easy as you think it is. Loving someone whether they're an Extraordinary or not only brings sorrow."

Oh, the quiet power Shadow Star had. Nate's stomach twisted painfully. "It's worth it," he said. "Because without love, we have nothing."

Shadow Star glanced at him before looking away. "It's not you, Nate. You have to know that. I don't care that you have ADHD that you think makes your brain all screwy, or that you get terrible migraines. Even when you let your dad down last year with bad grades, I know you tried.

You try. You try harder than anyone else I've ever met. It's one of things I . . . I . . . ." He shook his head. "Nate. I have so much to tell you. Things I should have told you long ago. But I'm scared of letting someone in, letting someone get close. To see the man behind the mask."

"I see you," Nate said fervently. "All of you, mask or not. Which is why I will do what I must to keep you safe."

Pyro Storm was distracted as Shadow Star began his hero's lament, saying that he'd ignored his heart since he'd learned they were made to be broken. Pyro Storm didn't see that Nate had managed to get one of his arms free. He was up really, really high, but he wasn't scared. Nothing scared him.

Nate leapt from the bridge spire directly onto Pyro Storm's back. The villain shouted in anger as Nate wrapped his leg around his waist, reaching between them and pulling the cape up and over the villain's head. "And *that's* why you don't wear a cape, you dick," Nate growled awesomely, like a badass.

Pyro Storm cursed as he struggled to find his way out of his cape. Nate tried to hold on as best he could, but Pyro Storm was bigger and stronger. Nate couldn't avoid the elbow that Pyro Storm threw back at him. It struck the side of Nate's face. Nate saw stars.

He let go of Pyro Storm.

And began to fall.

"Nate!" Shadow Star screamed.

To be continued . . .

....

Comments:

ExtraordinariesSuperFan 14:45: OMF GOD! This was AMAZING! But why did you have to leave it on ANOTHER CLIFFHANGER???!!! AAAAAAAAAAAA

PyroStarIsLife 15:13: I kno u said u didn't want to hear about it n e more, but I think Pyro Storm and Shadow Star are in love. They have so much tension!!!! They should kiss and see if they like it. Nate would understand!

MoltenMagma 16:04: How much longer is this going to go on? You've been writing this for almost a year. I just want Nate and Shadow Star to finally get together. This is already the longest work in the fandom.

ExtraordinaryGurl 16:14: JLKHGSLKDHT!!!! I LOOOVE IT SO MUCH. THIS IS MY FAVORITE FIC ON THIS ENTIRE SITE GAAAAAAAAAAAAAAAAAHH-HHHH

ShadowStarIsBae 16:25: Why does Nate suddenly have ADHD and migraines???? That's never been brought up before. Noah Fence, but this is REALLY improbable. How did Nate get out of his binds? How did he jump on Pyro Storm? I like this, but you need to have it be realistic if you're going to talk about real-life Extraordinaries.

FireStoned 16:36: SHADOW STAR IS STRAIGHT. HE LOVES REBECCA FIRESTONE. STOP MAKING HIM GAY, IT'S WEIRD. HE'S NOT GAY. NOT EVERYTHING NEEDS TO BE GAY ALL THE TIME. I DON'T UNDERSTAND YOU SLASH SHIPPERS. STOP MAKING THINGS GAY!!!!!!!!!!!!!!

ReturnOfTheGray 17:15: Sorry I couldn't beta this. Stuff came up. But you did good. I really liked it. Tho, you really talk a lot about Pyro Storm being more muscular than Shadow Star. What's that about? Text you later.

1

Nick Bell stared at his phone as he shifted on his bed in his room. "Not gay," he muttered to himself. "He has *sequins* on his costume." He thought about deleting the comment, but others were already responding to it, coming after FireStoned with a vengeance, so he decided to leave it up. Whoever FireStoned was, they'd learn fast that one absolutely did not comment on a ShadowStar744 fic like that. After all, Nick was one of the most popular writers in the Extraordinaries fandom (even if he'd had to use the screen name of ShadowStar744 since Shadowstar1–743 were already taken, those bastards), and slash would always be more popular than the hetero nonsense FireStoned seemed to want. *Straight people,* Nick thought as he shook his head. He'd never understand them.

The other forty-two comments, though. They weren't too shabby. Especially for a shorter chapter that ended on the thirty-second cliffhanger in a row. Thank god his fans understood. They were the only reason he'd continued writing what could be considered a quarter-of-a-million-word masturbatory ode to Shadow Star. Without them, the fic probably would have ended a long time ago, or worse, been one of those unfinished works that turned into a cautionary tale for new people in the fandom. He could deal with the occasional idiot like FireStoned.

He switched over to Tumblr and reblogged a few things, thumb twitching over a rather risqué drawing of Shadow Star in an evocative pose that was both physically impossible *and* erotic, but decided against it. Ever since his dad had discovered what Tumblr was and that his son had accidentally posted a drawing that apparently *no one under the age of eighteen should be looking at,* he'd kept things clean. It was the only way that Dad had let him keep his Tumblr page at all, even after the powers that be decided showing something as inconsequential as nipples could be considered pornography. That, and his dad had demanded the password. Nick had nightmares of his father logging on himself and posting to all of Nick's followers that he'd be grounded if anything remotely explicit showed up on his page again, just like he'd threatened to do.

Nick had been mortified.

Which, of course, was made worse when Dad frowned, and as if it were an afterthought, said, "Also, I feel like we need to discuss how it's a naked man on your page, Nicky. Unless it's just supposed to be artistic. I don't get art."

What Nick said next weren't words, not really. They were a combination of sounds better suited to a nature documentary on the mating habits of elks in the Pacific Northwest. His brain had shorted out as he'd tried to come up with a logical explanation as to why he'd decided to reblog a picture of Shadow Star with a comically large bulge that made him look like he needed to seek medical attention immediately.

His father waited.

Finally, Nick said, "Yeah. So. Um."

And Dad said, "Right. Have you had sex?"

"*No*, Dad, oh my god, why would you even—"

"Do you know what condoms are?"

"*Yes*, Dad, oh my god, I know what condoms are—"

"Good. That means you'll use them if, and when, you decide to have sex. Which won't be for a very long time."

"*Yes*, Dad, oh my— I mean *no,* I'm not having sex, why would you even say that?"

"If it were with a girl, I'd be telling you the same thing. Wrap it, Nicky. Always wrap it before you stick it anywhere." He tilted his head and squinted at his only son. "Or if it's stuck in you. It don't matter to me one way or another. What's that called? Bottoming? I don't care if you're a bottom or the other one. Use protection."

Nick had gone into a full-blown meltdown: synapses firing, eyes bulging, breath caught in his chest as he started to hyperventilate. His father had been there, of course, as he always was when Nick lost his mind a little bit. He sat next to Nick, wrapping an arm around his shoulders and waiting until his son's head started to clear.

They didn't say much after that. Bell men weren't the greatest when it came to *feelings,* but Aaron Bell had made it clear, perverts were everywhere, and that while some of the people Nick interacted with online might be nice, they might also be men in their late forties still living in their mothers' basements, waiting to lure in an unsuspecting sixteen-year-old for nefarious deeds like making their victims into hand puppets or wearing their skin.

And while Nick didn't think that would happen to him, he wasn't sure. He was a cop's kid. He knew the statistics, had grown up hearing stories of some of the terrible things Dad had seen on patrol. He didn't want to end up as someone's hand puppet, so he didn't reblog porn anymore, no matter how tasteful it was.

(Which meant he'd also had to scrub his *other* Tumblr page which was considerably more adult, but the less said about that one, the better.)

And that was how he'd come out to his father at the age of fifteen.

Because of Extraordinary porn.

He'd been so young, then, so naïve. He was sixteen now. A man. Perhaps he was a man who once bought a pillow off Etsy with Shadow Star's face on it. He had tracked the delivery at the top of every hour, making sure that the moment it was on their doorstep, he was the one who got to the door first. It wasn't that he was embarrassed by it (even if it was now hidden under his bed), it was just . . . there'd be a lot of questions, and Nick hadn't been in the mood to answer said questions.

(It does need to be said that three days after receiving the pillow, he kissed it—even though he knew it wasn't exactly normal.)

But Nick was still a man. He'd promised to make good decisions this new school year, a clean slate for both of them. New day, new dawn, blah, blah, blah.

He was shoving his feet into his beat-up Chucks when there was a knock at the door. That too had been part of their agreement. Nick would be trusted to have his door closed if he was responsible enough to do his own laundry so his father wouldn't see any evidence that Nick had been . . . *exploring* himself. Nick loved his dad, but his singular talent for making Nick's life excruciating was something that needed to be addressed.

"Breakfast," Dad called through the door. "You better be getting ready, Nicky."

Nick rolled his eyes. "I *am*."

"Uh-huh. Stop your Tumblring and get your butt downstairs. French toast waits for no man."

"Be right there. And it's not *Tumblring,* you philistine. God, it's like you don't know anything at all."

He heard his dad's footsteps retreat down the hall toward the stairs. The floorboards squeaked, something they'd talked about fixing for years. But that was . . . well. That was Before. When things had been right as rain and everything had made sense. Sure, his dad had worked too much back then too, but she'd always been there to rein him in, telling him in no uncertain terms that he *would* be home for dinner at least three times a week, and they would eat as a family. She didn't ask for much, she pointed out. But it was understood by all that she wasn't asking.

Dad still worked too much.

Nick pushed himself off the bed. He turned his phone to vibrate (muttering about Tumblring under his breath) and crossed the room to his desk to slip it into his backpack.

She was there on his desk, as she always was, trapped in a photograph. She smiled at him, and it hurt, even now. Nick suspected it always would, at least a little bit. But it wasn't the ragged, gaping hole it'd been two years ago, or even the constant ache of last year. Seth, Jazz, and Gibby didn't walk on eggshells around him anymore like they thought he'd burst out crying at the slightest mention of moms.

Dad had taken the photo. It'd been on one of their summer trips out of the city. They'd gone to the coast of Maine to this little cottage by the sea. It'd been weirdly cold, and the beach had been rocks instead of sand, but it'd been . . . nice. Nick had moaned about being away from his friends, that there wasn't even any Wi-Fi, and could his parents possibly *be* any more barbaric? His father laughed, and his mother patted his hand, telling him he'd survive.

He hadn't been too sure about that.

But then, he'd been thirteen, and so of course he'd been overly dramatic. Puberty was a bitch, causing his voice to break along with a group of zits that had decided to nest against the side of his nose. He was gawky and awkward and had hair sprouting everywhere, so it was in his very nature to be overly dramatic.

Only later did Nick find out his father had taken the photo.

It'd been halfway through the trip, and they decided to find the local lighthouse that was supposed to be scenic, which was code for boring. It'd taken a couple of hours because it was in the middle of nowhere, and the paper map she insisted on was absolutely useless. But then they nearly drove past a sign half-hidden by a gnarled old tree, and she shouted, "*There!*" Brightly, full of excitement. Dad slammed on the brakes, and Nick laughed for the first time since he'd set foot in the state of Maine. She looked back at him, grinning wildly, her light hair hanging down around her face, and she winked at him while his father grumbled and reversed the car slowly.

They found the lighthouse shortly after.

It was smaller than Nick expected, but there was something exhilarating about the way Jenny Bell threw open the car door as soon as they stopped in the empty parking lot, waves crashing in the background. She left the door open, saying, "See? I knew we'd find it. I *knew* it was here."

The Bell men followed her. Always.

The frame of the photograph was oak and heavy. He had taken it from his mom's nightstand without a second thought. His father hadn't said a word when he'd seen it on Nick's desk the first time. It was something they didn't talk about.

One of the somethings.

She smiled at him every day. She must have seen Dad with the camera, because she was looking right at it, her head on her son's shoulder. Nick's head was turned toward the sky, his eyes closed.

They looked too much alike. Pale and green-eyed and blond with eyebrows that had minds of their own. There was no doubt where he'd come from. Dad was big, bigger than Nick would ever be, tan skin and dark hair and muscles on top of muscles, though they were softer than they used to be. Nick was skinny and all gangly limbs, uncoordinated on his best day, and downright dangerous on his worst. He'd taken after her, though she'd made being a klutz endearing, whereas he was more likely to break a table or a bone. She'd told him she'd met his dad by literally falling on top of him in the library. She'd been on a ladder, trying to get to the top shelf, and he happened to pass right on by the moment she slipped. He'd caught her, Dad would say, and *she'd* say, sure, right, except you didn't because I landed on you and we both fell, and then they'd laugh and laugh.

Nick looked like her.

He acted like her.

He didn't know how Dad could stand to look at him some days.

"I'm going to do better," he told her quietly, not wanting his father to hear. The fact that he spoke to his mom's photo would probably get him back to the psychiatrist, something Nick was desperate to avoid. "New Nick. You'll see. Promise."

He pressed his fingers against his lips, and then to the photo.

She kept on smiling.

Dad was in their small kitchen, an old dishrag thrown over his shoulder. He'd taken off his uniform at some point after he'd gotten home from the night shift. Breakfast was their time—unless Dad had the day off. It was usually all they got for weeks. It'd get even harder now that school was starting again, but they'd figure it out. After the events of last spring, they were working together as a team.

The table had already been set, plates and silverware and glasses of juice. And, of course, the oblong white pill with the cheery name of Concentra. "Concentra will help Nick concentrate," the doctor had told them with a straight face. Dad had nodded, and Nick had somehow managed to keep his mouth shut instead of saying *something* that probably wouldn't be appreciated.

Dad kept the pills locked up in the safe in his room. It wasn't because he didn't trust Nick, he'd told him, but he knew the dangers of peer pressure, and he didn't want Nick to get caught up in the world of drugs and dealing them under the bleachers on the football field.

"Thank you for not letting me become a drug dealer," Nick had said. "I felt the pull toward a life of crime, but you saved me."

Nick picked up the pill now, Dad turning to watch him with an eyebrow arched, and he swallowed it, chasing it down with a sip of orange juice. Gross. He'd just brushed his teeth, and now he had a mouthful of the plague. He grimaced as he stuck out his tongue, raising it up and down, showing that he'd swallowed the pill.

Dad turned back toward the stove and the growing stack of French toast.

An old TV sat on the counter near the fridge, turned to the news as usual. Nick was about to ignore it until the perfectly coifed anchor announced they were going live to Rebecca Firestone, now on the scene.

Nick's attention snapped to the screen as he grabbed the remote off the table and turned up the volume.

Nothing else mattered. Not the bitter aftertaste of the pill. Not the fact that his father seemed to be making enough French toast to feed a family of thirty-four. Not the fact that Nick was pretty sure he'd forgotten to put on deodorant after his shower. No. All that mattered was Rebecca Firestone. Because if Rebecca Firestone was on, that meant one thing.

Shadow Star.

There she was, makeup expertly applied over glowing white skin, brown hair cut pixie-short, eyes wide and teeth Hollywood white as she smiled at the camera. In the background, police cruisers lined the sidewalks, lights flashing. "Thank you, Steve. I'm standing here on the corner of Forty-Eighth and Lincoln in front of the Burke Tower, where last night, a brazen attempt at a break-in occurred." The screen cut away, showing the gratuitous skyscraper rising high above Nova City. "Sources tell me that a group of armed militants attempted to parachute onto the roof of Burke Tower. Though their intentions remain unclear at this point, their plans were immediately vanquished upon landing when they were met by Nova City's own Extraordinary, Shadow Star."

"Immediately vanquished," Nick muttered, making a face. "Because that rolls right off the tongue. Get an editor, Firestone. You're an embarrassment to your profession."

The screen returned to Rebecca Firestone. She was smiling widely, her cheeks flushed. "I was able to speak with Shadow Star off camera earlier this morning, and he told me that while the militants were prepared, they didn't get much farther than attempting to gain access through the ventilation system. All seven were incapacitated in a matter of moments and have since been handed off to Nova City's finest. No civilians were injured."

Nick absolutely did not swoon. And if he did, it had nothing to do with Rebecca Firestone. She was the gnarled barnacle attached to the wonder that was Shadow Star. Most everyone thought there'd been something between them at one point. And even though Nick knew Rebecca Firestone was nothing but a nosy jerk who lived to play the role of a professional damsel in distress, Shadow Star was always there to rescue her, no matter what she did to get herself in trouble.

Nick was not a fan of the self-proclaimed intrepid reporter. She was obviously using Shadow Star to make a name for herself in the cutthroat world of reporting on Extraordinaries. Maybe Shadow Star tended to give her exclusives he never gave anyone else, and *maybe* there'd been that one picture where he'd saved her from a burning building, Rebecca clutched in his buff arms, her face in his neck. And yes, Nick had printed that photo and used it as a target for the dartboard in his room, but he wasn't jealous. He was just a firm believer in journalistic ethics.

"With me now, is Nova City's Chief of Police, Rodney Caplan."

The camera panned left, and a large Black man stood next to Rebecca Firestone, sweating profusely, his caterpillar mustache wilted. His uniform was straining at the stomach, and he reached up to wipe his brow before attempting a smile that came off as a grimace.

"Cap looks like he could use a vacation," Nick said without looking away from the TV.

"We all do, kid," Dad said. "Maybe next time he comes over for dinner, you can tell him that. See what happens."

"I did last time. He laughed at me."

"That's because it was a dumb thing to say."

"Positive reinforcement," Nick reminded him.

"Right. Sorry. It was a dumb thing to say, but you used your words. Proud of you."

"Thank you."

"What can you tell us, Chief?" Rebecca Firestone asked.

"Absolutely nothing," Cap said. "In fact, you already know more than you should. Probably more than we do."

Rebecca Firestone barely faltered. Some might say she was professional; Nick was not one of those people. "This is the third major criminal operation we've seen in the last five months attempt to gain access to Burke Tower. Granted, they have all failed thanks to Shadow Star, but—"

"Not *thanks* to Shadow Star," Cap said, glaring at the camera. "Thanks to the hardworking men and women of the Nova City Police Department. We absolutely don't need these costumed vigilantes flying around with their capes and their powers, trying to—"

"Shadow Star doesn't wear a cape," Nick and Rebecca Firestone said at the same time.

Cap turned to stare at Rebecca Firestone.

Dad turned to stare at Nick.

Nick ignored him.

Rebecca Firestone said, "Isn't it true that Shadow Star has—"

"For all we know, Shadow Star is responsible for these crimes," Cap said, mustache drooping farther as he frowned. "As a way to increase his profile. These groups could be working for him. A setup to make him look like the hero. Nova City was safer before the Extraordinaries reappeared, and I will do everything in my power to see all of them behind bars."

"Yes," Nick said. "Invite Cap over again. I have some things I'd like to discuss with him."

Instead of responding, Dad reached over Nick's shoulder and switched off the TV. It was an effective rebuttal. Nick was impressed. Annoyed, but impressed. "I was watching that."

"Breakfast," his dad said, like Nick hadn't spoken at all.

Since Nick was supposed to make this a better year, he didn't argue, at least not out loud. The retort in his head was fierce and devastating.

"Why weren't you there?" he asked, pulling at the chair and sitting down.

Dad scrubbed a hand over his face as he sat on the other side of the table. "If I tell you that I was, you get to ask me two questions, and two questions only."

Nick gaped at him.

Dad put two slices of French toast on his plate.

"But—I want—you can't just—"

"Two questions, Nicky. Make 'em count."

His father was amazing. Gruff, but kind. He was good at what he did. When he laughed, his eyes crinkled, the lines around his mouth deep, and that made Nick happy, though it didn't happen as often as it used to. He was courageous and just, and sometimes, Nick didn't know what he'd do without him.

But he could also be the biggest jerk. Like right now. "Seven questions."

"No questions," Dad replied, handing Nick the butter.

"Six questions!"

"I'm bored with this."

"You're terrible at negotiating. How am I supposed to learn how to adult when my parental figure refuses to work with me?"

"Life sucks, kid. Take what you can get."

"*Fine.* Two questions."

Dad pointed his fork at Nick. "While you eat. You took your pill. You need food in your stomach."

"I'm supposed to wait thirty minutes before—"

"Nicky."

"What did they want?" Nick asked through a mouthful of French toast.

"I don't know. I didn't talk to any of them before they were taken downtown. Cap told me to go home because he knew it was your first day of school. Said to remind you there's an empty cell with your name on it if there's a single grade below a B minus on your report card at any point this year."

"I wonder if the mayor knows that officers in his police department are threatening minors."

"He does," Dad said. "And he supports it completely. You get one more question."

Like he didn't know what Nick was going to ask. "Did you see him?"

"Yes," Dad said, mopping up a disgusting amount of syrup.

Nick waited.

Dad said nothing.

Nick could play this game.

On second thought, he absolutely couldn't. *"And?"*

"Is that another question?"

Nick barely stopped himself from throwing his fork at Dad's head. "Why are you like this?"

Dad grinned at him. "Because your adolescent angst brings me joy as a parent."

"Dad!"

"Yes, Nick. I saw Shadow Star. I even talked to him. In fact, I got his autograph for you. And his phone number. He gave it to me after I told him about your crush on him. He said he'd love to go out on a date with you, because he thought you were dreamy when I showed him a picture of you—"

"Please tell me I was adopted," Nick begged. "It's the only thing that could possibly salvage the wreckage that is my life."

"Sorry, kiddo. You came from my loins."

Nick groaned and dropped his head to the table. "Why did you have to phrase it like that?"

Nick felt a hand on the back of his neck, squeezing gently. "Because I think it's adorable when you get flustered. Especially when talking about your boyfriend."

"He's not my boyfriend," Nick muttered into the tabletop. "He doesn't even know I exist."

"Probably for the best. He'd most likely be scared away when he saw the Tumblring you do about him. Nobody likes a stalker, Nicky."

Nick knocked his dad's hand away as he sat back up. "I am *not* a stalker—"

"No, I didn't see him. None of us did. And he's lucky we didn't, or we would've arrested him on the spot. Damn Extraordinaries. All they do is—"

"Make your job harder, yeah, yeah. I know. You say it all the time. But, Dad. He can climb walls and control shadows. I don't think you fully grasp how amazing that is."

"Oh, I fully grasp it, all right. But he needs to let us do our jobs. Life isn't like one of your comic books, Nick. This is real. People can get hurt."

"He's one of the good guys!"

Dad scoffed. "Says who?"

"Everyone."

Dad shook his head. "This isn't black and white. It's not about heroes and villains. Shadow Star is as much a pain in my ass as Fire Guy—"

"Pyro Storm, and don't you dare compare them like that. Pyro Storm is Shadow Star's archnemesis, and the fate of Nova City hangs in the balance as Shadow Star fights for us against the tyranny of—"

"They're douchebags who wear tights they bought at a thrift shop."

Nick glared at him.

Dad shrugged.

Nick decided to be magnanimous. "I'm going to pretend you never said that."

"What a blessing."

Maybe not *that* magnanimous. "This is the worst start to a school year ever."

"Speaking of."

Yeah, that was his fault. He should've seen it coming. "We're not going to do this again."

"I think we are," Dad said, sitting back in his chair and crossing his arms. Nick saw the bags under his eyes, the wrinkles on his forehead that hadn't been there a couple of years ago. He felt a sharp pang in his chest. He forced himself not to look at all the ghosts that still haunted the kitchen: the spice rack neither of them had dared to touch, her favorite towels hanging off the front of the stove, the ones with little cats embroidered onto them. "Just so we're on the same page."

Better to get it over with. "I'll pay attention."

"And?"

"I'll do my homework every night."

"And?"

"And if I'm having trouble, I'll ask for help."

"And?"

"And if things start to get too much, I'll tell you."

"Why is that?"

Nick barely restrained from groaning. "Because it's easier to stand together than it is to struggle apart."

Dad nodded slowly. "Good." Then, "I know it's been tough, Nick. And I wasn't the best person to be around."

Alarmed, Nick said, "That's not—"

Dad held up his hand, and Nick subsided. "I made mistakes—mistakes I shouldn't have. I made you a promise to do better, and I'm going to keep it. I may need you to remind me every now and then, but I know you will. And you know I'll do the same for you. We gotta be a team, kid. It's . . . it's what she would have wanted. You know that as well as I do."

Nick nodded, not trusting himself to speak.

"Good. Pound it out." He held up his fist.

God, his dad was so embarrassing.

Nick fist-bumped his father anyway. It would've been rude to leave Dad hanging.

2

Gibby and Jazz were waiting for him at the Franklin Street metro stop when Nick stepped off the train. They sat on a metal bench, pressed close together. Gibby was glaring out at the milling crowd as people were herded toward the stairs to the street above. Jazz blew a bright pink bubble, twirling her dark, shaggy hair in her fingers. Her phone was in her lap, earbuds attached, one in her ear, the other in Gibby's.

Gibby had decided she was a baby butch a while back, which led to her shaving her head and wearing a wallet chain. She made sure everyone knew that if they called her Lola, they were getting a boot to the nuts. Anyone who hadn't thought she was serious was corrected when a brainless jock had winked at her and she had done just that. He'd had to sit on an ice pack for a couple of days. Gibby got detention for a week.

It'd been worth it, or so she claimed. She said the world needed more Black dykes, and she wasn't going to take shit from anyone anymore.

Nick decided then he'd support her 100 percent in every decision she'd make from that point on. It helped that she looked good with a shaved head, something Nick would never try, given that he'd end up looking like a bobblehead.

Jazz's bubble popped when she saw him approach, and she smiled prettily as she sucked her gum back into her mouth. "Nicky. I saw a pigeon eating a burrito on the train. I was going to take a photograph of it because I thought it was artistic, but then a homeless man wearing an orange coat kicked it and ruined the shot."

Nick bumped one of his Chucks against her chunky shoes that

probably cost more than the entire contents of his bedroom. "Kicked the burrito or the bird?"

She shrugged. "Both, I think. Then I was going to take a picture of the homeless man, but he started peeing in the corner, and I decided it was a good idea to switch cars rather than suffer for my art."

"You're a regular van Gogh."

"For what it's worth, I like all your parts where they are," Gibby said, squeezing her knee.

"I would give you my ear if you wanted," Jazz said, blue eyes wide as she snapped her gum. "But then my face wouldn't be perfectly symmetrical." She frowned. "Maybe that wouldn't be so bad."

"Uh-huh," Nick said. "Fascinating. Really. So, Gibby, you survived the Summer of Love. Congrats."

She'd been gone for the last few months, her parents deciding that their family needed to rent an old van and travel the country under the guise of touring colleges, but in actuality, they were commune-hopping as they'd both embraced a midlife crisis head-on (Gibby's words) and believed they made better hippies than they did accountants. Apparently, they thought the free love community needed more Black people.

Nick didn't know what to do with any of that, so he'd patted Gibby on the arm in June and told her to have fun.

He'd managed to avoid a boot to the balls. Barely.

Lola Gibson was fierce that way.

Her girlfriend, Jasmine Kensington, hadn't been pleased at the idea of Gibby being gone for so long. It certainly hadn't helped her anxiety that Gibby was in her senior year and would be graduating, heading off into the big, wide world before she did. Jazz told Gibby she wasn't allowed to fall in love with some flower child who wore skirts made of hemp that she later smoked. Gibby had agreed immediately, not bothering to correct her girlfriend that most flower children didn't smoke their clothes.

Nick thought they were disgustingly sweet. Or sweetly disgusting. It really depended on the day.

Gibby had gotten back a week ago, but Jazz had made it clear in no uncertain terms that she'd get all of Gibby's time before school started. Which was fine, seeing as how Nick had been busy trying to finish up the latest chapter of *This Is Where We Scorch the Earth*. They had their priorities, and he had his.

Besides, hanging out with Jazz and Gibby while they reconnected after a months-long separation would have probably meant watching them make out and whisper lovingly in each other's ears, and Nick wasn't masochistic enough to bear witness to that for any length of time. He loved his queer girls. He just didn't want to watch them swallow each other's tongues, which was why he'd given them their space. He was selfless that way.

"Summer of Love," Gibby repeated. She didn't sound amused.

Nick took a step back to protect his nuts. Her boots looked new. He didn't want to take the chance they were steel-toed. Also, her wallet chain was bigger than the one she'd had before, and he wasn't versed well enough in lesbian to know if that signified anything.

Gibby rolled her eyes. "If I ever have to sit in another drum circle again in my life, I'll likely end up a mass murderer."

"Pick a school yet?"

Jazz frowned. Gibby glared. Nick took another step back.

"I haven't decided," Gibby said through gritted teeth. "But thank you for caring about my future and bringing it up right at this very moment."

"Yeah," Nick said. "I tend to speak before I think. I'll just—"

"I can take it," Jazz said earnestly. "I mean, sure, I'll probably cry and then my makeup will be ruined and it'll be all your fault, but I can take it. I have lady balls."

"I know you do," Gibby said. "But I haven't made any decisions yet. You'll be the first to know."

Jazz seemed placated for the moment. Nick wondered how long it would last.

But then Gibby smiled at him, and he realized he should have kept his big mouth shut. Lola Gibson had three smiles: the loving one she gave to Jazz, the one she had when she was trying not to laugh, and the one when she was about to be a magnificent dick. He'd borne the brunt of that last smile many times before, and it never failed to make goose bumps sprout along the back of his neck.

"So, Nicky," she said, and Nick gave very serious thought to ducking into the crowd and disappearing forever. "Speaking of the Summer of Love, how's Owen doing?"

Nick scowled at her. "I have no idea what you're talking about."

"Uh-huh. And how's Seth?"

He scowled deeper. "I still have no idea what you're talking about."

Jazz, never having learned how to read a room, said, "I thought Owen and Nick broke up? Remember? Nick said Owen was a dumbass, and Owen was his usual self and said he couldn't be tamed by one person, and then Seth said *he*—"

Gibby slapped a hand over Jazz's mouth, cutting her off.

Nick knew he was blushing, but he powered through it. "What did Seth say?"

They ignored him in favor of having a silent conversation involving narrowed eyes and wiggling eyebrows. It went on for far longer than Nick was comfortable with. Finally, Jazz nodded as Gibby dropped her hand back to her own lap.

Jazz said, "I mean, I don't even know what we're talking about right now. Did I tell you about the pigeon and the burrito? It was a breakfast burrito." She squinted up at him. "And a huge pigeon."

Nick crossed his arms. "It was *months* ago. We weren't—it wasn't like we were even boyfriends, or anything. Owen was . . ."

Nick didn't know quite how to finish that sentence. In fact, most of the time, he didn't know how to describe anything about Owen Burke. Oh, sure, Owen was hot and popular, and everyone seemed to worship the ground he walked on given that he somehow had the gravitational force of a super planet. All he had to do was grin devilishly, and most everyone (queer or not) would end up doing whatever he wanted.

Including Nick, much to his dismay.

Before Christmas break last year, Owen had appeared at their lunch table, smile wide and toothy, looking devastating in a leather jacket that had probably once been the finest bovine in the field. They knew who he was, of course; everyone did. He came from big money (perhaps the biggest of all), his father being Simon Burke, CEO of Burke Pharmaceuticals. Seth was convinced it was a front for something nefarious, but Seth always thought everything was a front for something nefarious. Including Owen.

Nick, though. Nick had been . . . well. Not *enamored,* not exactly. But he'd been fifteen years old and hormonal, and Owen was probably the hottest guy in school, and for some reason, had decided to make Nick the focus of his attention.

Therefore, Nick proceeded to make an ass of himself on a regular basis.

Jazz had been confused. Gibby had been annoyed. And Seth?

Seth had withdrawn. Just a little at first, but it should have been enough to set off Nick's internal alarms. But Nick had been sucked in by Planet Owen, and it wasn't until Seth became downright hostile—something Nick hadn't expected from his best friend of nearly a decade—that he'd gotten a clue something was off. It was never to Owen's face (Seth was far too pure for that), but when it was just Seth and Nick, and Nick mentioned Owen for the tenth time in thirty-six minutes? Yeah, Seth could be hostile.

"It was nothing," Nick finally said. "I barely even saw him this summer. I was too busy."

"Uh-huh," Gibby said, sounding bored with the entire thing. "Stalking an Extraordinary takes up a lot of time, I suppose."

"I'm not *stalking* him—"

"Hey, sorry I'm late."

Nick turned his head, and one of the best people in the whole wide world appeared next to him, pushing up his thick glasses, which had slid down his nose as they always seemed to do, a curl of his black hair hanging down on his forehead. Seth Gray, the person Nick trusted more than anyone else. He was wearing his usual baggy sweater, with a collared shirt underneath that was tucked into one of his many pairs of chinos. And today, for whatever reason, he had decided to wear a *bow tie,* and Nick didn't know what to do with Seth's bow tie that didn't involve wanting to reach out and straighten it for at least three hours, while whispering he was too good for this world.

He kept his hands to himself.

Except—"Did you get taller?"

Seth blinked owlishly at him. "Since you saw me a couple of days ago? I don't . . . think so? I mean, it's possible, I haven't measured myself in a few hours, but—"

"You seem like you're taller."

"Oh." Seth looked away, reaching up and tugging on his collar. "Um. Thank you?"

"Oh my god," Gibby mumbled. "This still happens?"

"I think they're precious," Jazz whispered to her.

Nick ignored whatever they were talking about. He was still stuck on the fact that he and Seth were almost *eye* level now, which caused him a level of consternation he wasn't prepared for. Not when Seth had always been pale and chubby with curly hair that should have been illegal for how perfectly messy it always looked. But he'd been *shorter* than Nick and—

"Are you wearing lifts?"

Seth shifted like he was nervous. "No, I'm not wearing lifts. Maybe you're getting smaller."

"I'm not getting *smaller*. That's not a thing."

Seth started to say something, but it was swallowed by his yawn.

Nick frowned. "Are you tired? Why are you tired? You look tired. Did you not get enough sleep last night?"

Seth reached out and squeezed his shoulder. "I'm okay, Nicky. Just a late night."

"Doing what?"

"Tossing and turning. Anxious about today, I guess. First day back and all. You know how I get."

Nick did. Sometimes, Seth worried too much about nothing at all, and it frustrated Nick to no end, because it meant there was something making Seth feel bad that Nick couldn't tear apart with his bare hands.

Gibby stood, pulling Jazz up with her. "As fun as it is to watch you two do . . . whatever it is you're doing, we're going to be late."

"I can't be late," Jazz said, putting her earbuds back into her bag. "Daddy said if I show up on time for the entire first month, he'll buy me the Alexander McQueen skull-embellished pumps I need to continue to exist."

"Sounds fake, but okay," Nick muttered, as he followed his friends toward the subway stairs.

The streets of Nova City were crowded as they made their way toward Centennial High School, home of the Incredible Fighting Wombats. Traffic was backed up, yellow taxis honking their horns as if it would get the gridlock to move forward. Jazz and Gibby walked in front of them, hand in hand, Jazz talking animatedly while Gibby glared at everyone who bumped into them.

Seth and Nick walked side by side, shoulders brushing together. Nick was trying to surreptitiously see if Seth did, in fact, have lifts on, but they looked like the same terribly endearing loafers he always wore.

"What?" Nick asked, having missed what Seth was saying.

"I said, I'm sorry I didn't have time to beta read the chapter before you posted it." Seth tugged on one of the straps to his backpack.

"It's fine. It was pretty much perfect already."

Seth snorted. "I guess."

That wasn't the glowing praise Nick had expected. "You . . . guess?"

"It was fine, Nicky."

Nick chose to believe him. "I saw your comment. You said stuff came up. What stuff?"

"Oh," Seth said. "Just. You know. Stuff."

"Uh-huh. That sounds believable." Nick was struck with an absolutely horrendous thought, though he couldn't figure out *why* it was absolutely horrendous. "Did you have a date or something?"

Seth started coughing explosively.

Nick patted his back like any good friend should.

"No," Seth managed to say, wiping his mouth. "Why would— who would I—"

"I dunno, man. Maybe you've got a secret girlfriend. Or boyfriend." That left a weird taste in his mouth.

Seth had come out to him first when they were fourteen, telling Nick he thought he was bisexual. Nick, in his attempt to be cool and accepting, had squeaked and fallen off the park bench where they'd been feeding kettle corn to birds. It'd taken longer for Nick to figure out his own queerness, but then *he'd* been the one with a boyfriend (ish) first. It wasn't a queer race, but that had to count for something, right?

Seth had been scarce over the summer, much to Nick's consternation. What if he'd met some Luxor Avenue debutante or a burly mechanic with oil stains on his fingers? Nick read alternate universe fanfiction. Stuff like that happened all the time.

"Are you still a virgin?" Nick demanded rather hysterically. "We were supposed to tell each other when we had sex for the first time. We promised."

Seth blinked at him, eyes wide behind his glasses. "I didn't have sex. What are you talking about?"

"I don't know," Nick admitted. "You're as tall as me and it's freaking me out."

"I can't control that!"

"Well, *try*. I'm supposed to be the statuesque one here. It's all I've got going for me, Gray. You know this. That and my uncanny ability to tell heart-wrenching love stories based on real people, which is probably borderline unhealthy." Speaking of stories. "Did you see that evil wench on the news this morning? God, she was practically salivating over Shadow Star. Someone should tell him he needs to get a restraining order against her."

Seth sighed. "I doubt there's anything going on between Shadow Star and Rebecca Firestone."

"I know that. You know that. We all know that. But does she? Because I don't know if she does. She wore extra lipstick today like she thought it was going to make her look more attractive. Just because Superman has Lois Lane doesn't mean Rebecca Firestone gets to play the plucky reporter who needs to be saved all the time. And besides, everyone knows Superman is in love with Batman. Even though *someone* decided their ship name should be SuperBat rather than the golden opportunity that is ManMan. I mean, come on! How iconic would ManMan be? SuperBat sounds like something found in a dirty cave underneath a swamp." Nick frowned. "What are we talking about?"

"Honestly? I have no idea. You were on Shadow Star, and then Firestone—"

"*Right*. Firestone. She gets all these exclusives with Shadow Star, though no one knows why."

"Let me guess. You have a new theory."

"You're damn right I do!" Nick crowed. "And this one could totally be true." He dodged what looked like a wedding party, who apparently decided that standing in the middle of the sidewalk for photos on a Monday morning was the right thing to do. He groaned as he stepped in a puddle filled with dirty water. The would-be bride glared at him. He wished her many happy returns. She wasn't pleased.

Seth pulled him along before a woman in a white dress and veil decked him. "Unlike the last one where you thought she was Pyro Storm, even though Pyro Storm is obviously a guy. Speaking of Pyro Storm, I think we need to talk about your descriptions of him—"

"No, but this theory is most likely probably true," Nick said. "What if she knows his secret identity and is, like, holding that over him? That would explain why he talks to her and tells her stuff. Because she's *blackmailing* him."

"Evidence?"

"I don't have any. I'm postulating. I'll figure it out eventually. It's only a matter of time."

Seth seemed dubious. "How're you going to do that?"

"I have no idea. But I'll come up with a plan. You'll see. It'll be epic."

Seth sighed. "Every time you say that, my palms get sweaty. Can't you just let this go?"

Nick stared at him suspiciously. "Why? Do you . . . do you like her?" It was the most terrible of thoughts. Nick had never felt so betrayed in his life.

"What? No."

"Because if you did, I would support your feelings toward her." This was a lie, and one that Nick didn't feel bad about.

"That would have been more believable had you not said it through gritted teeth. No. I don't like her. I don't even know her."

"Oh, thank god," Nick said. "Because I don't know if I'd be able to survive something so awful. You deserve someone who isn't an Extraordinary groupie."

"I feel like the irony is lost on you."

"About what?"

Seth shook his head. "Never mind. Maybe you shouldn't try and plan anything. Focus on school. That kind of stuff. I can help you—"

"You sound like my dad."

"Well, you did promise him. And junior year is going to be hard enough as it is. Wouldn't it be easier just to follow the rules and have everything be nice and peaceful and calm?"

Why, yes, yes it would. But . . . "Calm makes me twitchy."

Seth's face softened. "I know. And twitchy, somehow, always leads to calamity."

"It's not like I mean for it to. It's just how my mind works."

"How's the Concentra?"

Nick shrugged, unable to bring himself to meet Seth's gaze. "I don't know. It's whatever. It doesn't matter." He hated talking about it. Having a disorder made him feel . . . disordered. It wasn't fair that on top of all the other crap he had to deal with, his brain constantly felt like it was being electrified. Some people were born to be an Extraordinary. Nick was born to have a million thoughts in the space of a minute that often led to splitting headaches. It wasn't fair.

"It's going to be okay," Seth said quietly, reaching out to squeeze Nick's hand just once before letting it go. "It'll take some time to get used to it."

Ever the optimist. It was one of the things Nick loved most about Seth, even if it could be annoying in the long run. Seth was a good person, better than Nick would ever be. But for some reason, he'd stuck by Nick longer than anyone else. Which, of course, led Nick to following a strand of thought that led to— "You can't like Rebecca Firestone. She's the worst."

Seth grinned, that sharply sweet smile he only seemed to have for Nick. "You're an idiot."

Hearing that from anyone else, Nick would've been pissed. But Seth wasn't like anyone else, which meant Nick knew he wasn't being a dick. "Yeah, well. Just so we're clear. I wouldn't like it very much."

"I'll keep that in mind, Nicky." He bumped his shoulder against Nick's. "We good?"

"Yeah. We're—"

"Are you losers going to stand there all day? We're going to be late. We still have to go through the metal detectors that are supposed to make it so we don't die in class."

They both jumped, looking over to see Gibby and Jazz staring at them from the steps to the school. Nick hadn't even known they'd arrived already. Thank god he had friends so he didn't need to be more aware of his surroundings.

"You ready for this?" Seth asked as Gibby and Jazz started climbing the stairs.

Nick took a deep breath and nodded. "Ready. This is going to be the best year ever. Wait and see."

3

"ongratulations, Mr. Bell. You've received the first detention of the year. And it's only six minutes into second period. That must be some kind of record."

"But I'm trying to work on my story! I'm having *ideas*. You can't stifle my creativity!"

Mr. Hanson, who was seven hundred years old if he was a day, said, "That's all well and good. Except this is trigonometry, and I distinctly remember you avoiding summer school by the skin of your teeth, so it would be in your best interest to pay attention."

The class snickered around them as Nick sunk into his seat. He opened his mouth to invite Mr. Hanson to give examples of when something as ridiculous as trigonometry would ever be used in the real world, but he remembered the promise he'd made to his dad and decided against it. He was already going to get it if Dad found out about getting detention on the first day. Luckily for him, Dad was on shift tonight and would already be gone by the time Nick got home. He'd text him later to tell him he was hanging out with friends to cover his bases.

A couple of people seated next to him whispered back and forth while glancing at him, laughing quietly.

Nick flipped them off.

The girl gasped.

The guy glared at him.

Nick felt better.

Until he heard his phone vibrate in his backpack a moment later.

Most everyone had to turn their phones off completely during class. Nick was one of the few exceptions. After Mom had—after *that*—Nick had been prone to spiral rather quickly, thinking about all the things that could happen. She was supposed to have been safe; she was a lawyer for heaven's sake. Sure, she dealt with some of the worst types of people, but she was always all right. She knew how to take care of herself. If anything, it was his father who put himself in harm's way every day.

And so *After*—because there was an After just as sure as there was a Before—Nick couldn't stop thinking about how dangerous Dad's job was.

One day, sitting in freshman English, he'd spiraled. One moment his blood was rushing in his ears, and the next, he was lying on the floor, curled up into a ball, trying to remember how to breathe, thinking thoughts of *what if what if what if*. Because *what if* something happened to his dad? *What if* he never came home? Nick would be alone. There was no one else. Cousins, maybe, out west, but he'd never met them. Would he have to go with them? Who would take care of him if the *what if* became something real?

The haze of sheer panic hadn't begun to clear until he'd heard a familiar voice at his ear, telling him to breathe, just breathe, that everything would be okay, Nicky, everything was going to be okay, breathe, breathe, breathe.

It was Seth, of course.

Somehow, he'd known.

Later, when his dad had come running into the school, a haunted look on his face that had yet to fade in the few short months since his wife's death, it was decided that Nick would always have access to his phone, just in case. He'd have to keep it on vibrate so it wouldn't disrupt the other students, and he couldn't abuse it, but he could keep it switched on in the event of an emergency.

The memory of the day his father had come for him was sharper, now. Even though he knew Dad was at home asleep, his heart still managed to trip all over itself as he reached for his phone.

Making sure Hanson wasn't watching, Nick set it on his leg and looked down.

OWEN, the screen read.

He turned to glare at Owen, sitting a few desks over.

Owen waggled his eyebrows right back in that devastatingly handsome way he did.

He thought about ignoring it. It would be the smart thing to do. And Nick was smart. At least four people thought so.

Owen nodded toward Nick's phone.

Nick sighed.

He swiped open the text.

PAY ATTENTION.

He hated Owen Burke. Mostly.

Sometimes he liked him. He liked the way his skin tingled when Owen had kissed him, had liked the way Owen could make him laugh. He didn't necessarily like Owen as a *person,* but that was because Owen was an ass who didn't seem to care who he stepped on to get what he wanted.

Owen had girlfriends, pretty ones with manicured nails and extensions, and then, somehow, he had Nick one night while it was just the two of them eating bad tacos from a hole in the wall with the disturbing name of Gato Grande. Nick hadn't known how he'd ended up alone with Owen, because he'd been positive Seth had been there too, and Owen had said Nick had salsa verde on his face. He'd reached out with his thumb to wipe it away, and then, for reasons Nick wasn't quite sure of, they'd been kissing.

It was . . . nice? Sort of. Nick had never been kissed before and didn't think his first time would be when he was still swallowing a mouthful of chorizo. His brain mostly shorted out, and when Owen pulled away, that devilish smile on his face, he'd felt himself blush furiously.

"So," Owen said, and Nick had wondered how his jaw was so chiseled for someone barely a year older than himself.

"So," Nick squeaked.

And so began the Great Romance of Nick and Owen.

Jazz had been confused. Gibby had been annoyed. Seth hadn't liked any part of it, if the sour expressions on his face had meant anything.

Which was why when it ended a few months later, Nick hadn't been *that* upset. It wasn't as if they went on dates. Sometimes, they would go out as a group and Owen would put his arm around

Nick's shoulders, but that was usually as far as it went. A couple of times, Owen tried to take it further, but Nick remembered his father sitting in front of him with a condom in one hand, a banana in the other, and a gigantic bottle of lube on the table between them, and the idea of anything remotely sexual happening had gone right out the window.

He'd never forgiven Dad for that, especially since he'd made it clear he'd already known what condoms were. It didn't help that he'd forever be haunted by the way Dad had accidentally used too much lube and the banana had squirted out of his hand and landed on the floor. The sound it made when it hit the ancient linoleum would be something he'd have to go to a support group for when he reached his midthirties.

The Great Romance of Nick and Owen came to an end as quickly as it started. ("You're a great guy, Nicky, but I'm a wild animal who can't be caged." "Oh my god, you are *not*!") Nick hadn't been too upset by it because whatever else Owen had been to him, he was still a douchebag. Nick expected Owen to fade away back to where he'd come from, telling the other hot people that he'd bagged a Normie, but he'd stuck around.

The phone vibrated again.

SERIOUSLY. STOP LOOKING AT YOUR PHONE.

Nick struggled not to smile.

He scowled at Owen instead.

Owen was wearing red pants today (who *did* that?) and a loose white V-neck shirt that stretched down to the middle of his chest, revealing long miles of tan skin. His light hair was made up of angelic locks that Nick did *not* like to put his hands in, no matter what anyone said. He'd been vacationing somewhere exotic like Greece or Daytona on the family yacht. Before he'd left, he'd leaned over and kissed Nick on the cheek as he said goodbye. Nick had shoved him away. Seth had stared at both of them but said nothing.

STOP IT NICKY. YOU'RE GOING TO GET IN TROUBLE.

"*Mr.* Bell," Hanson trilled from the front of the classroom. "Are we trying for two detentions on the first day?"

Everyone turned to stare at him.

"No," Nick mumbled, sinking even lower.

He heard Owen laughing quietly.

God, he hated Owen Burke.

hate Owen Burke," he announced as he sat at the lunch table in the cafeteria. "In case you were all wondering."

Gibby snorted. "I distinctly remember you sitting in that exact spot with his tongue down your throat at one point last spring."

Seth started choking. Nick patted him on the back while wishing death upon Gibby. Regardless of what his report cards said, he was fine at multitasking.

"It looked very wet," Jazz said, snapping the lid off her Tupperware to reveal a perfectly plated caprese salad with a small jar of olive oil and a twist of salt and pepper wrapped in parchment paper.

Nick thought he had bologna. He hadn't checked when his father had handed him the brown bag, but it was most likely bologna. Which, to be fair, was better than the Pimiento Loaf Disaster of last April that had almost killed Nick, no matter how much Dad had thought he was overreacting.

"Not one of my best moments," Nick admitted, pulling open his backpack until he found the wrinkled bag smooshed between two textbooks he needed after lunch. The chips were mostly powder now, but the sandwich wasn't pimiento loaf, so life was pretty okay. "I got detention."

"Already?" Seth sighed, pushing his glasses back up his face. "It's only been half a day. What did Owen do to get you detention?"

"Absolutely nothing," Nick said, biting savagely into his sandwich. "I was being creatively stifled by Hanson again. Why he needs to teach multiple grade levels is beyond me. I've decided he exists solely to make my life miserable. But if I think hard enough about it, I can figure out how to blame everything on Owen. Therefore, it's Owen's fault, and I hate him."

"Nah," Owen said as he appeared, sitting next to Gibby and

across from Nick. "You like me." He reached over and grabbed one of Seth's carrot sticks. Seth didn't stop him, but his scowl deepened.

"I do not," Nick retorted. "You vex me. And I don't like being vexed. If anything, I would rather be the opposite of vexed. Whatever that is."

"Delighted," Seth said.

"Yes, *that*. I would rather be delighted."

Owen winked at him. "I delight you."

"You don't. You're wearing a leather jacket in September. Nothing about you delights me. You—"

"Kensington, just who I wanted to see. You look good. You thought about my offer to take you out and show you a good time?"

The tables around them quieted.

Gibby started to get up, but Jazz reached over and touched the back of her hand. Gibby sat back down with a huff, turning to glare at the Heteroh-hell-no standing next to the table in a letterman jacket with a perfect smile on his face. Nick didn't know his name off the top of his head, but it was most likely something douchebro like Derek or Westley. All the straight jocks looked exactly alike to Nick, and he didn't care to try to differentiate between them.

"You should probably run," Seth said to Derek or Westley as Jazz finished drizzling the olive oil over her caprese salad.

Derek or Westley narrowed his eyes as he looked down at Seth and dropped a hand on Jazz's shoulder, squeezing gently. "Oh, really? And why exactly would I do that, you weirdo?"

And *oh*, did that make Nick mad, but he knew better than to intervene. Jazz had this, even if Derek or Westley didn't know it yet.

Jazz stood from the table slowly, running her hands down the front of her skirt, brushing away the wrinkles. She smiled up at Derek or Westley. He grinned cockily down at her. "Not that it's not hot," he said. "Two girls, or whatever, even if one of them is butch. I think you need to explore your options, you know?"

Nick really didn't understand straight people. They didn't seem to have any sense of self-preservation.

"Do you?" Jazz asked sweetly. Well, it *sounded* sweet, but Nick had seen one too many shows on Animal Planet about how lionesses hunt. And since lionesses hunted in groups, Derek or Westley was up to his neck in shit. "Maybe show me what I'm missing?"

He reached down and grabbed her hand. "It'd be my pleasure. And then if there's time for it, it could be *your* pleasure too. I'm not selfish."

"Oh, man," Nick said. "You shouldn't have said that."

Derek or Westley glanced at Nick, eyeing him as if he were some kind of bug. "What'd you say?"

It'd been a long time since he'd heard Jazz make a near-grown man scream. Usually, she'd let them off with a warning, but Derek or Westley was grosser than most, so when she turned her hand and snapped it around two of his fingers, twisting them viciously and bringing his arm behind his back, Nick couldn't find it in himself to feel all that bad. He took another bite of his sandwich.

Derek or Westley cried out in pain as his head fell to the lunch table right next to Jazz's caprese salad. Gibby pulled the Tupperware away, just to be safe.

"Thank you, baby," Jazz said. "I appreciate that."

"You asshole," Derek or Westley managed to say. "Let me—ow, ow *ow*!"

"Now, here's how this is going to go," Jazz said, apparently able to ignore the fact that everyone in the cafeteria was staring at her. You didn't mess with Jasmine Kensington, especially not during lunch. And if you did, you certainly didn't insult her friends at the same time. "You're going to apologize. And after you apologize, I will let you go. If any of that sounds too much for you, we'll see how far your fingers can bend before they snap."

"You can't—"

"That wasn't an apology," she said, and Nick didn't know it was possible for fingers to be facing the direction Derek or Westley's were. He should have paid more attention during anatomy.

"Okay! Okay! I'm sorry!"

"And you will never touch another person without their consent again."

"I *won't*."

"Or call my friends any derogatory names. Because that's rude."

"So rude!" Derek or Westley cried.

"Good," she said cheerfully. "If I find out that you do, we'll have to see if you can live a normal life without your testicles. Do we have an understanding?"

"*Yes,*" he groaned.

"How wonderful. You can leave now. I'm done with you."

He groaned again as she let him go. She shoved him away from the table before sitting back down primly, spreading the cloth napkin—which had undoubtedly been packed by one of the maids in her parents' employ—in her lap. She picked up her fork and was about to slice into a fat tomato, when she looked around the cafeteria. "You may continue eating."

Everyone quickly turned away from her as Derek or Westley all but ran toward his friends, who would most likely talk about how evil the queer table was.

"That's better," Jazz said. "I don't like it when people interrupt my lunch. I'm hungry, and I'm going to eat all of this."

"I love you so much," Gibby said, sounding awed.

"As do I," Nick said, because it was true.

Seth nodded. "Me too."

"Eh," Owen said, "I could go either way—what the hell, Gibby? You didn't have to kick me!"

"Wasn't her," Seth said. "And you were being stupid. Ergo, you deserved to be kicked. Repeatedly. In the face."

Owen winced as he rubbed his shin. "You wound me, Seth."

Seth smiled at him. "Do I? I feel just awful about it."

"Oh, I bet you do."

"We'll have to see about that, won't we?"

Owen's eyes narrowed. "I'm sure we will."

"Are you guys flirting?" Nick asked, glancing between the two of them. Nick didn't necessarily know how to flirt, or even really what it looked like. It had taken Owen kissing Nick for him to even understand that Owen might have liked him in the first place. He figured he'd have time to learn how to flirt at some point, but in the meantime, he couldn't be sure what he was witnessing.

Seth gaped at him.

Owen scoffed. "He wishes."

"I do not!"

"What would it matter to you if they were?" Gibby asked, a strange glint in her eye.

Nick . . . didn't know how to answer that, not really. If he was going to say exactly what he was feeling at that moment, it probably would have come out as a strangled snarl, so he kept his mouth shut.

Jazz sighed. "You can lead a blind man to water, but you can't make him fish."

"That's not even remotely how the saying goes," Gibby told her.

"It's not?" Jazz frowned. "Then how does it go?"

"I have no idea, babe. But that's definitely not it."

"Huh," Jazz said. She ate another piece of perfectly sliced tomato.

"I hate you," Nick said, finally remembering how to form words. "You are the absolute worst thing in the entire world."

"Careful there, Nicky," Owen said, leaning forward on his elbows. "I might get the idea you still have feelings for me."

"He doesn't," Seth said.

Owen took another one of his carrots and bit into it with his perfect teeth, grinning at Seth. "That right?"

"I've decided we're going to talk about something else," Nick said, because he didn't like the way Seth and Owen were staring at each other. If this wasn't flirting (and Nick was pretty sure about that now—mostly), then it was something else, and he did *not* want this to turn into a repeat of last spring when things were awkward for everyone involved. The Great Romance of Nick and Owen hadn't been the best of days. Sure, Owen could do this weird little twisty thing with his tongue, but Nick didn't think that was the foundation for a long-lasting relationship. "I assume you're all aware of the latest Shadow Star news."

Everyone groaned.

Nick ignored them. He was used to it by now. "Once again, he defeated villains who attempted to commit crime in our fair city. I think we need to start another online petition for a solid gold statue to be erected in his honor."

Gibby snorted. "Speaking of being erected in his honor—"

"Didn't the last one only get seventeen signatures?" Jazz asked. "And yours were twelve of them, signing it with different names."

"Right," Nick said. "But that was before I ascended in popularity with *Scorch the Earth*. As of this morning, I have the most viewed story in the fandom. And since I'll probably let the power of being popular in a fandom go to my head, that means I should be able to get what I want."

"And you want to start another petition," Owen said, sounding bored.

"Yes. And we could—wait a minute." Hold the motherfreaking phone.

"Oh no," Seth moaned. "That's his realization face."

"We should probably have more boundaries than we do," Jazz said as she squinted at Nick.

What had Rebecca Firestone said this morning? Something about— "Burke Tower."

That got their attention. "What about Burke Tower?" Gibby asked, glancing between Nick and Owen.

"It's where the gunmen were going," Nick said excitedly. "They were trying to break into Burke Tower. It was on the news this morning!"

"No, Nick," Owen said. "It's—"

Nick stared at Owen with wide eyes. "Owen Burke. Burke Tower. They were trying to break into your *father's* building. And Shadow Star was there."

"Absolutely not," Owen said, shaking his head. "You leave me out of this. I have nothing to—"

"You have to get me the security tapes! So I can watch them over and over again for my own personal reasons that don't involve anything weird."

Seth put his face in his hands.

"You *are* weird," Owen said. "And why do you think I would have access to the tapes?"

"Uh, because it's your father." What about this did he not understand? It seemed easy enough to Nick.

Owen snorted. "Right, because he listens to anything I say. I don't even remember the last time I saw him."

That caught Nick off guard. Owen Burke rarely let anything slip through the facade of douchedom that he'd perfected.

"Oh," Nick said, suddenly uncomfortable with this tiny sign that Owen might be human after all. "That's . . . too bad." He wasn't very adept when it came to comforting people he'd made out with. Or, at least, that appeared to be the case. He'd never made out with anyone else. He wondered if he needed to find someone else to make out with and then have them talk about their damaged relationship with their family to make sure.

"Gosh. Thanks, Nicky. Really."

Nick tried to recover. "Didn't you go yachting with him in Greece or Daytona?"

"Isn't Daytona in Florida?" Jazz asked. "How exotic."

"We were supposed to," Owen said stiffly, picking at the peeling lunch table. "But he backed out at the last minute, so it was just my stepmom and her assistant who is also her boyfriend. And we weren't in Greece *or* Daytona. It was the Bahamas."

"Whoa," Nick breathed. "Rich people problems."

Owen shrugged. "It's whatever. I don't care."

Nick didn't think that was quite the truth, but he was nothing if not pragmatic. "Maybe this could be a bonding experience for you and your dad. You know, going over the tapes and then making copies for me. Then you can go outside and toss a football back and forth. Or something."

"Not going to happen."

Damn. He'd been so close. "Fine," Nick said with a weary, put-upon sigh. "I guess I can accept that answer. Though, if you change your mind, I'll support you completely."

Owen cocked his head. "Why do you care so much?"

Nick felt the others staring at him. Nick didn't like where this was going. "About?"

"Shadow Star. Pyro Storm. Extraordinaries." He said the last word with a curl of derision. "It's like you're obsessed with them. They're not that great."

Oh, hell no.

"You really shouldn't have said that," Seth muttered.

"Not that great?" Nick said shrilly. "Are you out of your mind?"

Owen blinked. "They're not—"

"Let me tell you something, *Owen*."

"Uh, never mind. I take it back."

"Nope," Gibby said, grabbing Owen by the arm as he tried to get up. "You started this. You're going to sit here and accept your punishment. Be thankful lunch is over in fifteen minutes."

Nick was already revved up. "Extraordinaries are incredible. They can do things that us mere mortals can only dream about. They have secret identities and superpowers and look really good wearing costumes that would probably get a normal person cited for indecent exposure. And Shadow Star is the best one of them all. He fights for truth and justice and doesn't take crap from anyone."

"Big whoop," Owen muttered.

Nick was pretty sure the only reason he didn't reach across the table and slap Owen upside the head was because he'd already gotten one detention and didn't want to risk another. "You shut your whore mouth," Nick snarled at him.

Owen reared back. "Whoa."

"Yeah," Seth said, smiling quietly. "He's . . . exuberant."

That was probably an understatement, especially since Nick was just getting started. "Not that cool? They can manipulate shadows and fire and pose on tops of buildings while the sun sets behind them!"

"He's given this a lot of thought," Gibby told Owen.

Nick nodded furiously. "I have. And Shadow Star is brave and gives ice cream to orphans and helps little old ladies with their shopping. He rescues puppies from puppy mills, and one time, he marched with Black Lives Matter because racists are stupid and he hates them so much."

"Yikes," Gibby said.

"I don't know if he did any of that," Seth said. "That might have been fanfiction, Nicky."

"Whatever," Nick said. "Even if he didn't *actually* do any of that, I know he would, because that's the type of person he is. He helps those who can't help themselves. He keeps Nova City safe, and he is strong and neat, and if you ever say anything bad about him again, I'll drop-kick you into the Westfield River, and I won't feel bad about it at all."

"Isn't the Westfield River the one with all the sewage that smells like sadness?" Jazz asked.

"Yes," Nick said fiercely. "I'll do it. You just watch me."

"Hmm," Owen said, and Nick hated that sound.

"*Hmm?*" he demanded. "What's this *hmm*?"

"Dunno." Owen gave him a smug look. "Sounds like you have a bit of a crush on Shadow Star."

Yes. Nick absolutely had the world's biggest crush on Shadow Star. When he was by himself and no one could hear him, he would whisper "Mr. and Mr. Nicholas Shadow Star" into his pillow, but Nick had it under control. He did.

But when his crush was mentioned out loud?

Nick felt his face turning red, tongue thickening in his mouth. His first instinct was to deny, deny, deny, but that would be betraying everything Shadow Star stood for.

So instead, he managed to say, "Uh. Er. Glugh. Blargh."

Seth stared at him with a strange look on his face.

Owen smiled the way he did when he was about to be a dick. "Eh. I suppose he's all right. But if we're going to talk about cool Extraordinaries, we should probably talk about Pyro Storm."

Which . . . okay. That was fair. Even though Pyro Storm was *technically* a villain and caused mayhem and chaos with his dastardly deeds, he was still Shadow Star's archnemesis, and had to be acknowledged. Plus, he had really muscular thighs, and often posed in ridiculous positions while cackling maniacally. Nick had to appreciate the thighs and the cackling. It seemed like a lot of work. Nick's own thighs were sticklike, and when he tried to cackle, he sounded like a chicken watching the eggs it'd laid being turned into omelets.

"I'll allow it," Nick said begrudgingly. "Pyro Storm *is* cool, even if he's a bad guy."

Owen arched an eyebrow. "Why does anyone have to be bad? What if we're all misunderstood?"

Nick glared at him. "You really can't believe that. It's black and white. There's no in between. Good is good. Evil is evil. One is a jerk who burns things because he's a pyromaniac or something. The other is a paragon of virtue who saves people and controls shadows and climbs walls." That was Nick's favorite part, and it should be everyone else's.

"Pyro Storm does control fire," Owen said. "And Shadow Star is all about the shadows. One is dark. The other burns it away. It's poignant, if you think about it. Opposites."

"You're so dumb," Seth muttered. "Life isn't a comic book. Extraordinaries aren't everything. So what if they can do things others can't? That doesn't make them more special than the rest of us. It doesn't work like that."

Owen leaned forward, elbows on the table. "Then why don't you tell us how it *does* work, Seth? Seeing as how you apparently know better than the rest of us."

Nick didn't quite know what was going on. Were they still flirting? God, he hoped not. "Maybe we should—"

Owen flashed that dangerous grin again, all teeth. "It seems our Seth here thinks all this Extraordinary stuff is dumb. How do you feel about that, Nicky?"

If there was one thing Nick hated aside from having to console someone whom he'd made out with or being faced with his crush on an Extraordinary, it was being put on the spot. His brain tended to misfire more often than it didn't, and he was feeling a little dizzy. "Um. Well."

Everyone waited.

Instant flop sweat. "You both made good points," Nick said hastily. "And while I normally am so on board with picking sides, I don't know that I can, at this moment in time, without more data."

Seth stood abruptly, glaring at Owen, who smiled lazily up at him. "I have to go," he said through gritted teeth.

And with that, he grabbed his backpack and headed toward the exit.

Nick stared after him, wondering what the hell had happened. Since when did Seth feel so strongly about Extraordinaries? Normally, he indulged Nick's diatribes about them, but to get this upset? It wasn't like him.

"Go after him," Gibby snapped. "You can't let him walk away like that."

Owen snorted. "He's throwing one of his fits. Let him be. He'll get over it. He always does."

"Do you remember that time about ten minutes ago when I nearly broke that jock's fingers?" Jazz asked him sweetly. "I can show you what would have happened if he hadn't apologized, if you want."

Owen paled.

"Go," Gibby said to Nick, jerking her head in the direction Seth had gone.

"Going," Nick said. He shouldered his backpack as he stood, glancing down at the others.

Owen winked at him.

Nick flipped him off before following his best friend out of the cafeteria.

4

When Nick was six years old, he met a boy who was sitting on the swings by himself. Nick was new at school and didn't know anyone. He was wary of the other kids because they were loud and got finger paint on everything, and Nick *hated* finger painting.

There were two sets of swings. One looked brand new and everyone was shouting around it, taking turns, and the chains squeaked to the point where it sounded like they were screaming. Nick wanted absolutely nothing to do with it.

There was another set of swings toward the rear of the playground. These swings were ancient. The seats were made of cracked plastic, and the chains looked like they belonged in a castle dungeon. But it was quiet, and it helped Nick's head to clear and gave him a moment to think since no one ever used those swings.

Except on this day, there was another kid there, sitting on one of the swings, the tips of his shoes barely scraping the ground. He was chubby, and he wore a sweater and khakis. He was eating from a pudding cup. For a brief second, Nick thought about trying to find somewhere else to make his head stop spinning.

But then the boy looked up at him, and he had a smear of chocolate on his upper lip that resembled a sticky mustache, so Nick said, "Hi."

"Hi," the boy said quietly.

Nick had never introduced himself to anyone before. He'd always had his mom or dad there to do it for him. But they weren't here now, and Mom said he had to be brave like Wonder Woman and Thor, and so he squared his shoulders and said, "My name is Nicholas Bell. It's very nice to meet you."

The boy stared at him.

Nick frowned, unsure if he'd gotten it wrong. He'd thought it had sounded just like Mom and Dad did when they said it, but the boy was looking at him like he was speaking another language entirely.

"Um," Nick said. "So."

The boy looked behind him. Nick did too. There was no one there.

The boy turned back around. "Are you talking to me?" he asked in a small voice.

Nick nodded. "I think so."

"Okay. I'm Seth. Seth Gray."

It was a nice name. Nick kicked at the dirt. "Those other kids were loud."

"I know. S'why I'm over here."

Nick felt relieved at that. "I don't like loud kids."

"Me either."

"Or finger painting."

The kid made a face. "It gets *everywhere*."

"Right? S'not cool."

"Not cool," the kid echoed.

"Can I swing with you?" Nick asked nervously. He thought it was going well, but one couldn't be too sure about such things.

The boy nodded, licking his pudding mustache away.

"Awesome," Nick said.

"Yeah," the boy said, watching Nick climb onto the swing. "Awesome."

Nick tried to start swinging, but he wasn't very good at it yet. Mom said he'd get there, but it would take practice. He gave up after a few seconds.

"I can't swing either," the boy said.

"It's hard," Nick agreed. "My dad is a policeman, and he says that he couldn't swing until he was, like, eight or something."

The boy looked amazed. Nick liked that. "He's a policeman? With a *badge*?"

Nick shrugged, playing it cool. "Yeah. I get to wear it sometimes." Nick absolutely did not get to wear it, but it was fun to pretend he did. "He has a utility belt like Batman does." Nick tried to kick his legs and swing again but failed. "He's pretty much Batman, now that I think about it."

"Wow," the boy said. "That's awesome. My aunt is a nurse. And my uncle fixes buildings and is a meter maid. He says he's a meter butler, because girls are maids."

Nick frowned. "Boys can be anything girls can. And girls can be anything boys can. My mom says that sometimes, boys can even be girls."

Nick thought the boy's eyes were going to pop out of his head. "That's so cool."

"Yeah," Nick said. "I know. Cool. Why don't you live with your mom and dad?"

"They died," the boy said, dipping his plastic spoon into the pudding cup. "When a train crashed. I was with them, but I don't remember."

And since Nicholas Bell was six years old, he didn't understand the concept of death. It was too big for him to grasp, so he said, "Oh. Was it a big train?"

The boy shrugged. "Maybe. Probably the biggest train."

That was enough to confirm it for Nick. "We should be best friends. Forever."

The boy looked at him, spoon hanging from his mouth. "Forever?" he said through a mouthful of pudding.

Nick nodded solemnly. "Forever."

And from that point on, he never left Seth's side.

Here he was, ten years later, vexed by his ex-sort-of-boyfriend, chasing after his best friend after they'd argued over Nick's Extraordinaries obsession, an ache in his chest that he couldn't quite explain. He didn't like it when Seth was upset, he never had. It didn't happen very often, but when it did, Nick felt like hunting down and killing whatever caused it. Nick decided a long time ago that Seth needed to be protected at all costs. He wore bow ties and loafers and could recite the Greek alphabet backwards, and there was no one like him in the world.

He should've punched Owen before he left, even if Nick wasn't exactly sure what they'd been arguing about. He thought it was about Pyro Storm being a villain. And yes, that was true, but he was a *cool* villain. He was Shadow Star's archnemesis, which meant he had to be respected. Both of them had appeared suddenly out of nowhere shortly after . . . well, After. There had been other Extraordinaries Before, but they'd been nothing compared to Shadow Star and Pyro Storm. Even if Cap and the mayor thought they were a menace—in fact, all Extraordinaries were a menace, according to Cap—no one could deny how cool they were. If they tried, they were wrong. Period.

Still, he should have done more. Seth deserved as much.

Seth was at his locker when Nick found him, banging his head against it repeatedly, muttering, "Stupid, stupid, stupid." Nick reached up and put his hand between Seth's forehead and the locker, so when Seth tried to hit it again, he met a bony hand instead.

"Hey," Nick said. "Do you want me to kill him? Because I will." He was very serious about this. He'd learned how on the internet before Dad had tightened the parental controls. He just needed to find some sharks.

Seth sighed. "No. Then you'd go to jail. I'd visit you, but it wouldn't be the same."

"Probably. But then I could get a teardrop tattoo and be all bad-ass. That might be worth it." Nick frowned. "Unless there was a big guy named Enormous Gregory who wanted me to keep my hand in his pocket at all times. I don't know if I could do that."

Seth stared at him. "Your brain."

"I know, right? It's—whatever. It's what the Concentra's for." Nick looked away, tapping his fingers against the locker, quietly hating that he always needed to be moving.

"There's nothing wrong with you," Seth said, and Nick felt even worse for not sticking up for him. He needed to be a better friend. Seth always had his back, no matter what. Nick should've done the same.

"Maybe," Nick mumbled. "Takes some getting used to. I feel a little whacked out, you know? But the doctor says that's normal, and it'll even out eventually, kind of like with the ones I had to take before. Except they won't make me a cracked-out zombie like last year."

"Good," Seth said, and Nick could hear the smile in his voice. He glanced at Seth, still a little startled they were eye level. "I thought I was going to have to take out Cracked-Out Zombie Nick with a headshot."

"It's the only way to kill 'em," Nick agreed.

"I'm glad your brain is okay."

Nick was absurdly touched. "Yeah." He took a deep breath. "You can't let Owen get to you, man. He wants to get under your skin."

Seth's smile faded slowly. "I know. It's part of his charm."

Nick rolled his eyes. "I wouldn't call it charm."

"You sure fell for it, though." And then Seth immediately blanched, as if he couldn't believe those words had come out of his mouth.

"Dude," Nick breathed reverently. "That was hardcore. I'm impressed. Holy crap."

Seth rubbed the back of his neck. "I didn't mean—"

"Yeah, you totally did. You can't take it back now. That'd be weak."

"O . . . kay?"

Nick nodded. "Also, that was kind of mean. And maybe my feelings are hurt."

"The truth often does that."

"Okay. Like. Who *are* you? I mean, I'm sorry and everything, because you're right. I should have said more. But also, what have you done with my best friend? Oh my god, are you Bizarro Seth? Like Batzarro the World's Worst Detective? If you are, tell me now, so I can figure out how to get normal Seth back. I mean, it's cool if you're Bizarro Seth, but I really like my Seth the way he is."

Seth squeaked.

Nick squinted at him. "Uh—you okay?"

Seth nodded furiously, his face red. "Y-yeah. I'm cool. Cool, cool, cool."

"Good."

"I'm not Bizarro Seth."

Nick's eyes narrowed. "That sounds like something Bizarro Seth would say."

Seth took a deep breath and let it out slowly. "I promise. I'm . . . *your* Seth."

Nick grinned and put his arm around Seth's shoulders. "Fantastic. I believe you. What were we talking about again? I can't remember."

Seth shrugged, but he looked better, which was the only thing Nick cared about. "It doesn't matter. It's all good now."

Nick felt Seth's arm wrap around his waist and give him a brief side hug, and all was right again with the world. "You've got AP History next, right? My class is right next to yours. Let's walk and talk. I've got some ideas for how Nate Belen will be saved that I wanted to run by you. You got a few minutes?"

Seth did.

Maybe today hadn't turned out so bad after all.

It was pouring down rain when Nick was finally released from the prison known as after-school detention.

"Dammit," he mumbled to himself, staring out the front doors of the school. He could hear shouts and the squeak of sneakers on the gym floor down the hall, and a sharp blast of a whistle, but other than that, only the rain.

He hadn't even thought to check the forecast this morning. He'd been too distracted by wishing Rebecca Firestone would cease to exist.

The train station was a few blocks away, which meant Nick was going to get wet. He hated getting wet.

He closed his eyes tightly and thought as hard as he could for the rain to stop, just in case he'd somehow developed Extraordinary powers while in detention and could now control the weather.

He opened his eyes.

It was still raining.

He could wait it out, but according to the weather app on his phone, it was going to rain for at least two more hours, and he didn't want to be at the school any longer than he had to be. He made the decision that since he was a man, he could stand getting his hair and socks wet.

He pushed open the door.

His hand was immediately soaked.

And it was *cold*.

He closed the door again.

Nick was about to slide to the floor to wait it out when he heard his name called from behind him. He turned to see Gibby walking down the hall, hand raised in his direction.

"Oh, thank god," he said. "I thought I was going to die here. You've got an umbrella, right? Wait, what are you still doing here?"

Gibby punched him in the shoulder. He didn't almost fall down, no matter how it looked. "Jazz had cheerleading practice. I was watching to critique her performance later."

Nick rubbed his shoulder as he grimaced. "You were perving on her from the stands and got kicked out again, didn't you."

Gibby shrugged. "She looks hot in the uniform. I'm allowed to stare. There also might have been some gloating since the football team was running drills in the gym."

"You're incorrigible."

"I'm dating the cheerleading captain. I'm allowed to be."

"So gross," Nick muttered. "Can we leave now? This place is sucking out my soul, and I don't want to be here until I'm required to come back tomorrow. And hearing reminders from you that I'll be alone forever isn't helping."

"I can't believe—you know what? Nope. I said I'd stay out of it, and I'm going to. I don't know how the patriarchy ever succeeded. You're all so stupid."

"Stay out of what?" Nick asked, confused. "Did Owen say something to you? I swear to god, I'm going to punch him in the *pancreas*. I don't—"

"I'll leave you here without a second thought."

Nick believed her. Gibby was a woman of her word. "Shutting up now."

"I don't think that's actually possible."

Nick sighed. "Yeah, I don't have a neurotypical brain. I'm lucky that everything I say is awesome and I have a couple of people who actually like me."

"Barely," she said, though Nick could see her fighting a smile. "Let's blow this Popsicle stand, daddio."

And like a couple of cool cats, they did exactly that.

The train was delayed.

"Why?" Nick asked, looking toward the ceiling of the station. The tile was dirty, and something that looked like it'd once been a hot dog was hanging from one of the grates over the fluorescent lights. "What did I ever do to you? Aside from all those things I did?"

"Looks like it's a problem farther down the track," Gibby said, frowning down at her phone. "Says it'll be twenty minutes. Which in Nova City Transportation Authority speech means they have no idea what's wrong, something's probably on fire, and it could be up to an hour."

It had definitely once been a hot dog. Nick could see dried mustard and everything. "My socks are wet."

"Yeah. Your life is a tragedy in four acts. Want to wait or do you wanna hoof it down to Market Street and get on the Silver Line?"

"That's eight blocks!"

"I'm aware."

"In the *rain*."

"Your powers of observation are your greatest skill."

He didn't know why someone had thrown their half-eaten hot dog into the light. It was one of the millions of stories that happened in Nova City every day that he'd never get to hear. "My socks are wet," he said again.

"So you've said. Make up your mind, Nicky."

It was stifling down in the station. People were milling around angrily, everyone staring at their phones with similar scowls on their faces.

Nick hated crowds.

And honestly, the hot dog was perturbing him more than he cared to admit.

"Fine," he said, knowing he sounded grumpy but unable to do much about it. "If we have to."

Gibby wasn't the type of person to deal with his crap. It was one of the reasons he liked her so much. She rolled her eyes at him, letting him know exactly what she thought about him, and then grabbed him by the arm and pulled him toward the stairs.

But when they reached street level, she made sure to stand close so they could both be under the umbrella.

Nick and Seth had been ten when Lola Gibson quite literally punched her way into their lives.

It'd been two against four, and Nick was positive the on-duty teacher looked the other way right when they'd been cornered. Seth shoved Nick behind him, the top of his head barely to Nick's chin, like he thought he'd be able to protect him from the beating they were about to get.

Granted, Nick probably deserved it, given that his mouth moved before his brain managed to convey it was a bad idea to laugh obnoxiously when David Carlucci swung at the tetherball and missed, falling face-first into the metal pole.

David Carlucci and his goons were *sixth* graders, which meant that Nicky was going to die.

But then Seth was there, standing in front of him, all four foot ten of him, like he thought he'd be able to stop them from getting their asses beat.

And right when Nick was about to open his mouth again, there'd been a flash of black braided hair, heralding the arrival of Lola Gibson, some girl Nick and Seth were peripherally aware of but had had no contact with previously. She stood in front of Seth, hands on her hips, wearing jeans and a hoodie with a skull and crossbones on the back.

David Carlucci told her to move. Lola Gibson responded by punching him in the mouth, splitting his lip. David Carlucci recoiled before snarling, eyes narrowed as he started toward them again.

Lola Gibson opened her mouth and screamed, which, at the

time, became the loudest sound Nick had ever heard. He was suitably impressed as David Carlucci and his goons took a step back. Nick, never able to keep his mouth shut for long, was about to tell them off when a teacher came running over.

Lola Gibson burst into tears, sobbing that these *boys* were trying to hurt her and her friends, and she was just a little *girl*, and they were trying to hit a *girl*, and—

David Carlucci and his gang of prepubescent misfits were led away on a one-way trip toward the vice principal's office where Nick was convinced they'd be drawn and quartered for their crimes against humanity.

As soon as they were out of earshot, Lola Gibson immediately stopped crying.

"I like you," Nick told her seriously. "I've never said that to a girl before."

Lola Gibson narrowed her eyes at him. "I will hit you just as hard."

"I take it back."

"Good."

"Your tie is blue," she said to Seth.

"Thank you," Seth mumbled, because he didn't do very well with new people.

And that was how Nick and Seth met Lola Gibson.

She never left after that. Even when she went to high school before them, she still hung out with them almost every day after school and on weekends.

It was the summer between Nick and Seth's freshman and sophomore year that she shaved her head and demanded they call her Gibby. Since Nick and Seth liked their faces in the shape they were in, and because they respected their friend, she was Gibby.

People didn't get their friend group, not that Nick really cared. He didn't understand most of them, so it was fair. They were the queers of Centennial High (and though they weren't the *only* ones, they were the most visible). They were the nutjobs, the weirdos. Seth was too smart. Nick was too loud. Gibby was too butch, and Jazz had once been like everyone else before Gibby had put her lesbian magic all over her and taken her to the dark side. Or at least that was what Jazz had heard one day in the girl's bathroom. Gibby had laughed so hard that she cried, something Nick and Seth had never seen before, and were amazed by.

Then came Owen and . . . well. The less said about that the better, seeing as how the Great Romance of Nick and Owen was a by-product of Owen's arrival, and no one wanted to relive those days. Though Nick hadn't said it out loud, he wondered if Owen had put his lesbian magic all over Nick. That seemed to be the only explanation as to why Nick would have let Owen touch his nipple that one time.

They weren't popular, but that didn't matter. He loved his people very much.

It's not as hard as she's making it out to be," Gibby said. They were huddled close underneath the umbrella. "I know she's worried, but why can't she believe me when I tell her that everything is going to be okay?"

Nick shrugged. "You're graduating. Going on to bigger and better things and leaving us all behind. I mean, I get what you're saying, but I can see where she's coming from too."

"I care about her. A lot."

"I know." It was touching, though Nick would never say that to Gibby's face because she'd never let him hear the end of it. "And she knows it too. But you have to admit, she's got a point. Things change. And you're young."

She scowled. "I hate it when that's the excuse. That me being in a relationship at seventeen isn't the same as having a relationship when I'm older. Plenty of people marry the person they dated in high school."

Nick nearly tripped. "You want to *marry*—"

"Oh my god, *no*. That's not what I meant. I'm saying that being young doesn't mean we're stupid."

"What happens when you turn eighteen and she's still underage? What if her parents try and give you crap for that?"

Gibby rolled her eyes. "It's fine. Her parents like me. And my parents think she's—and I quote—'the bee's knees.' Whatever the hell that means."

Nick frowned. "I don't understand hippies."

"No one does."

"Especially when they're also accountants."

"It's confounding in ways I don't even want to think about. We were the only Black people at every commune we visited. We were weirdly treated like royalty."

"Can I give you some advice? Not about the royalty thing. I'm too white to ever give you advice about that. About Jazz."

Gibby stared at him while they waited at an intersection for the light to change. "You? *You* want to give *me* advice?"

"I feel like I should be offended, but I don't quite know why."

"Oh, you should be. This'll be good. Lay it on me, Bell. Give me advice."

Nick thought for a moment. Then, "Respect her fears. You may think they're unfounded, but they're still what she's feeling, and that's valid. Reassure her if that's what you want. And if you don't, make sure she knows you still care about her, but it's better to end it now than further down the road when it would hurt more."

"That . . . wasn't bad," Gibby said, sounding begrudgingly impressed. "Where did you come up with that?"

"I'm very self-aware," Nick said smugly. "I see everyth— *Ow*, who put this freaking *fire hydrant* here?" He glared down at it as he rubbed his knee.

"That's better," Gibby said, pulling him back under the umbrella. "The world is right again, and all is well."

"Whatever. I gave you good advice, and you know it."

"True," Gibby said. "But I've always felt like the best advice is the one you can also follow yourself."

"What?"

She bumped his shoulder with hers. "What about Seth?"

Nick blinked at her. "What *about* Seth?"

"Really. That's what you're going with?"

Were they speaking the same language or . . . ? "I don't know what you're talking about."

Gibby sighed. "Oh, lord. Okay. Let's try this a different way. Nicky."

"Gibby."

"What happens when you graduate and you and Seth go to different schools?"

"Not going to happen," Nick said immediately. "Seth and I already have plans to go to the same school where we'll share a dorm the first year, and then move off campus the following years. When we graduate, we'll get an apartment in the city where I'll spend four years on the force before leaving to open my detective agency-slash-bakery. Seth will become a famous author who writes true crime stories that won't actually be true because they'll have dragons in them, or he'll be a lawyer that wins every case since he'll be the voice for those who can't speak for themselves."

Gibby gaped at him.

Nick looked over his shoulder, but there was nothing of note behind him. He turned back to Gibby. "What?"

"You just . . . how can you . . . If I hadn't made that promise—" She shook her head. "I swear to god, if I'm not there the moment you have the biggest realization of your life, I'm going to cry foul and make you do it all over again."

"Are you okay?" Nick asked seriously. "Because you're not making sense. Did you have a stroke? Can you feel the side of your face, or is it numb?"

He reached to poke her cheek, but quickly backed down when she snapped her teeth at his fingers.

They'd made it four blocks when it happened.

Nick said, hey, let's go down this alley, because it's a shortcut.

Gibby said that going down alleys when it was dark and raining was never a good idea.

Nick called her a chicken. He might have even folded his arms at his sides and said *bawk bawk,* though he wasn't proud of it.

Gibby threatened violence against his genitals.

Nick demurred.

But then Gibby stomped toward the alley, and later, Nick would tell himself that it was all her fault, that if she'd stuck to her guns, they wouldn't have run into two goons with leather jackets and knives that looked like swords but were actually only switchblades.

"There was a hot dog stuck in the light on the platform," Nick told her as they made their way down the alley. The rain pounded down around them. "I can't stop thinking about why it was there."

"Someone threw it up there."

"I know that, but not that kind of why. Not the why of action. The why of reason. Why did the owner of that hot dog decide to do that? It makes absolutely no sense."

Gibby snorted. "Sometimes, people do things just because they can. There doesn't have to be a reason. It's all chaos."

"Anarchists, man. I'll never understand them."

"It's not about—"

"Well, well, well. What do we have here?"

No one who started a sentence with *well, well, well* ever wanted to do something nice. Nick turned slowly to look over his shoulder.

Two men stood behind them. One of them had a mustache. It was wet from the rain and hung under his nose like a drowned rat. The other was balding, the strands of his comb-over plastered to his head, rainwater dripping off his earlobes.

Nick froze. They didn't look like they had a gun, but all he could think about was his mother's last moments, something he'd stressed over time and time again. He'd never been given a clear picture of what had happened, only being told by Cap that it had been quick, something so uniquely terrible that it didn't help as much as Cap thought it would. Nick was brave, yes, but he was also in a position to know that sometimes, people didn't come home no matter what they'd promised him.

He almost tripped when Gibby shoved him behind her, hands curling into fists. He swung his backpack around to his front, going for the mace that Dad had given him. He'd wanted a Taser, but Dad had figured he'd end up electrocuting himself, which— while rude—was probably accurate. But given the way the universe worked, Nick found everything *but* the mace as he dug through his bag, including lip balms, a used straw, and an old sandwich that needed to be disposed of immediately as it posed a health risk. He was panicking, and it was only getting worse. He looked up from his bag out to the street behind the men in the alley. He could see people scurrying by on the sidewalk, umbrellas up, faces down toward their phones.

And it *sucked*. Even though Nick had lived in the city all his life, he'd never been mugged before. Because he was wired the way he was, he'd fantasized about what he'd do if the situation arose. In these fantasies, he'd be brave, taking no shit from anyone. He wouldn't need to be saved because he'd save himself. But faced with this cold reality, he could barely function, becoming more and more desperate when he couldn't find the goddamn mace.

"Everything," Mustache Man snapped, causing Nick to inhale sharply. "We'll take the whole bag. Both of you. Now."

"And if we don't?" Gibby asked, because she was more of a badass than Nick could ever be.

"No," he whispered in her ear. "Give them what they want." He could picture it, clear as day: Dad receiving yet another phone call that would send everything crashing down around him. He couldn't let Dad go through that, not again.

She didn't look at him. "We're not going to give them anything—"

Male Pattern Baldness pulled out a knife, popping out the blade with the click of a button. In the grand scheme of things, it wasn't the biggest knife Nick had ever seen. It was maybe five or six inches. Small, really.

But Nick knew it wasn't the size that mattered.

It was what could be done with it.

He gripped Gibby's shoulders, trying to make his legs work so he could step around in front of her. He was sweating, and his heart was racing, but he tried not to let it show on his face. You didn't show fear in the face of a predator, especially when said predator had a knife.

Scratch that. *Two* knives, because Mustache Man *also* pulled out a knife similar to the one Male Pattern Baldness had. And because Nick wasn't always in control of his thoughts, he wondered if they were dating, and had picked out his-and-his matching switchblades. He cursed himself for being a romantic even when he was about to be stabbed.

He leaned his forehead against the back of Gibby's neck, struggling to breathe, his bag pressed between them, trying to gather the tattered remains of his courage. In his head, he could picture it: He'd shove Gibby behind him, his shoulders squared, and he'd tell their muggers to go to hell. His dad had been a cop for longer than Nick was alive and had instilled in him a sense of duty. Of honor. You protected those who needed it. And not that Gibby needed it, exactly, but the principle was the same.

It was something Shadow Star would have done. He was a hero, and he wouldn't take crap from anyone.

He could do this. He could *do* this.

"Okay," Nick said slowly as he raised his head. "No one needs to get hurt." He stepped around Gibby, meaning to stand in front of her, but she grabbed his wrist, holding it tight. They were shoulder to shoulder. He heard Dad's voice in his head, whispering that it was easier to stand together than it was to struggle apart. He slid his hand up until Gibby's fingers latched onto his own. He squeezed her tightly.

"Then hand everything over," Mustache Man said, jabbing the knife toward them. "And maybe we won't consider seeing what your blood looks like on the pavement."

All in all, it was a very believable threat. Nick absolutely didn't want to see what his blood looked like on the pavement. Even if he was brave (ish), it was outweighed completely by the fear of being stabbed. Nick did not want to be stabbed. He did not want Gibby to be stabbed.

"Okay," he said, hating how his voice wobbled. Gibby heard it too, inhaling sharply, her grip hard enough to cause Nick's bones to grind together. "Please. Don't hurt us. We'll give you whatever you want."

"That's better, kid," Male Pattern Baldness said, mouth twisting in a sneer. "Maybe next time, learn to keep your gob shut."

"There won't *be* a next time," a deep voice growled from somewhere above them.

Nicholas Bell froze because he knew that voice.

That voice had starred in many a fantasy, alongside those in which Nick had saved himself. Sometimes, that voice would whisper in his ear as its owner held his hand, telling him he thought Nick was cute, and they should go on a picnic or to the boardwalk and make fun of all the tourists paying fifteen dollars for cotton candy. *That* voice had also been his muse in the writing of his magnum opus, the ever-growing tale of love and sacrifice, of hot superheroes and supervillains in skintight costumes, starring a young, handsome man named Nathaniel Belen, mild-mannered and innocent until he fell for the protector of a city and thus put himself in the crosshairs of the war between good and evil.

That voice belonged to someone Extraordinary.

Nick took a step out from under the umbrella. He turned his face toward the sky. Rain fell onto his cheeks.

And there, perched on the side of a rent-controlled apartment building, was Shadow Star.

His black costume was slick with water. It glittered in the low light that filtered out from one of the windows of the building. The star symbol was stretched across his muscular chest. The lenses over his eyes flashed, and his mouth was open, teeth bared as he snarled down at Mustache Man and Male Pattern Baldness.

Nick's mouth dropped open, but no sound came out. He'd had dreams that had started like this, and in those dreams, he'd say something witty and hilarious, causing Shadow Star to laugh (something Nick didn't think he actually did, given that he needed to spend his time brooding about darkness and the diseased heart of the city). But for the life of him, Nick couldn't say a word, his brain misfiring at the sight of the Extraordinary he idolized to what was most certainly an unhealthy degree. Eventually, a sound *did* fall from his mouth, but it was a breathy sigh. Not his finest moment.

Mustache Man took a step back like he was getting ready to run. Male Pattern Baldness gaped up at Shadow Star, mouth opening and closing.

Mustache Man turned and—

Shadow Star raised his hand, and from underneath his wrist, a bright light burst into life, illuminating the alleyway, casting shadows where none had been before. Nick blinked against the flash, turning his head away to shield his eyes. He looked back in time to see Mustache Man make it two steps before his own shadow rose up from the ground, grabbing him around the ankles, flipping him up and *over* until he landed on his back with a bone-jarring crunch. He stared, dazed, up toward the sky, blinking slowly in the rain.

Male Pattern Baldness didn't try to run away.

Instead, he darted toward Nick and Gibby, knife still clutched tightly in his hand. Nick scrabbled backward, pulling Gibby with him, causing them both to stumble into a small, ancient dumpster against the side of the building, overflowing with what smelled like weeks-old Chinese food. The umbrella fell to the ground, and they were instantly soaked.

Nick held his hands up, annoyed that he was about to die right in front of *Shadow Star of all people,* already preparing an angry diatribe he was going to snarl at God and Jesus and some apostles when he got to heaven, if that was where he ended up.

Male Pattern Baldness had almost reached him when Shadow Star flipped down between them. He landed gracefully in front of Nick, crouched low in the way only superheroes seemed to do, one hand against his chest, the other raised away from his body. Male Pattern Baldness tried to stop, but the pavement was slick, and he slid through discarded newspapers and what looked to be the remains of either curry or a diaper.

Shadow Star wrapped a hand around his throat, using his other hand to knock the knife away before it'd even become a threat to him. The man's eyes bulged and he said, *"Urk,"* like he wanted to speak, but couldn't quite do so around the grip Shadow Star had on him.

Nick had never mustered as much willpower as he had right then to keep himself from reaching out and touching Shadow Star's back. It was only a couple of feet away, and it'd be *so easy,* but in the end, while he might have had a rather significant crush on the Extraordinary, he was also respectful of one's personal space, and would not touch someone without their permission, even if it seemed like Rebecca Firestone did it all the time.

"You made a mistake," Shadow Star growled at Male Pattern Baldness, bringing their faces so close together, their noses almost touched. "One that you'll regret." His voice was deep, almost like it was being modified somehow to disguise it, but Nick also thought there was a great possibility that was how he *normally* sounded. He tried desperately not to sigh dreamily right then and there, especially with Shadow Star actually growling like Nick had made his character do in the fic. Screw everyone who didn't think art imitated life.

Male Pattern Baldness said, "*Blargh*," and then Shadow Star threw him against the side of the building, and he landed in a pile of trash, where he stayed, the only movement the slow and steady rise of his chest.

Shadow Star turned toward Nick.

It was at this moment that Nick realized two very different things:

First, his underwear was wet from the rain, and having wet underwear was worse than wet socks.

Second, this was the moment he'd been waiting for ever since he'd seen Shadow Star for the first time On the news three months to the day since Before had become After—a blurry cell phone video that showed him backflipping off the top of a bridge, landing in front of a man who'd been ready to end it all and jump into the Westfield River. Nick had, at last count, watched said video 647 times in the last two years. Granted, since then, there'd been other, clearer videos of Shadow Star (hell, he'd even been interviewed, though it'd been with Rebecca Firestone, but Nick had become an expert at muting the video whenever she spoke), but that had been Nick's first, and therefore his favorite.

So, yes. Nick's underwear was wet, and his crush on this Extraordinary could apparently grow even bigger when he was standing right in front of him. He needed to act cool. It was not every day one was rescued by the superhero of their dreams.

The problem with that was Nick didn't necessarily know how to *be* cool. Oh, sure, he understood the objective concept of it, but Nick was an awkward sixteen-year-old boy who wasn't always in control of his mouth. Which was why instead of being cool and saying *Thank you for saving us, you're so neat, my name is Nick, and I'm glad I'm not dead right now,* he blurted, "I have a pillow with your face on it!"

The only sound that followed Nick's slow, mortifying death was the rain on the pavement. And Gibby saying, "This is painful to watch."

Shadow Star offered a hint of a smile, and Nick did his best not to stare, though he was failing spectacularly. "Are you all right, citizen?"

He couldn't believe Shadow Star was actually talking to him. "I don't do anything weird with the pillow, in case you were wondering," and oh god, *why couldn't he stop talking about the stupid pillow?*

Shadow Star said, "Oh. That's . . . good."

"Yeah," Nick said. "It is. Like, so good."

"Right," Shadow Star said slowly. He glanced over Nick's shoulder at Gibby, then looked back at Nick, who couldn't help noticing they were almost eye to eye. Add in the fact that Shadow Star looked so much younger up close, and Nick couldn't tell if he was smitten, or if he was about to faint. "Are you both all right?"

"Aside from the emotional trauma that will probably rear its head when I'm thirty-seven and working at my cubicle in a dead-end job that I hate, just fine," Nick babbled, unsure why the words coming out of his mouth were the ones his brain deemed necessary to speak out loud.

"I'm fine," Gibby said mildly. "Any trauma I might have had is being washed away by the tragic comedy occurring right in front of me."

Shadow Star took a step toward them, gaze fixed on Nick. For his part, Nick remained where he was, though he doubted he could have moved even if he wanted to. Shadow Star's mouth twisted slightly, and Nick tracked the movement with laser-sharp focus. They were—speaking objectively, of course—nice lips. Perhaps the nicest lips he'd ever seen.

Shadow Star leaned toward him, and though Nick had no idea what the hell was going on, he was so on board with this unexpected turn of events, because it looked like Shadow Star was going to kiss him.

Holy shit. Yes. Yes. *Yes.*

This was what he'd written fanfiction for. He understood at that moment that Shadow Star had seen through Nick's failings as a human being and had somehow already fallen in love with him right back. He didn't know how it'd happened (especially so *quickly*— maybe Nick was cooler than he thought), but he was already picturing a house in the suburbs where he'd go to book club meetings and say things like, "Yes, *Pride and Prejudice* is an old book about stuff, but I didn't get a chance to finish it because Shadow Star took me out to dinner last night at a fancy restaurant that had separate forks for the salad."

Life was glorious.

Except.

Except it wasn't a kiss. It was Shadow Star bringing his left leg up toward his chest, then kicking it out behind him. The moment Nick thought was supposed to be the second first kiss of his life was actually Shadow Star's foot striking the newly risen Mustache Man in the chest, knocking him back.

And yet, Nick's lips didn't get that message until it was far too late. He kissed the side of Shadow Star's head, right on his mask. It tasted of wet rubber.

Gibby made a sound like she was choking behind him.

Nick widened his eyes in terror as Mustache Man slammed against the wall, slumping down on top of Male Pattern Baldness.

Shadow Star lowered his leg. "Did you just . . . kiss my head?"

Nick forgot how to human. To his horror, he fell back on old habits with the sound he made: that of an amorous elk in the Pacific Northwest, bleating and terrible.

Gibby, struggling to breathe, said, "Why is nobody else here to witness this?"

Gathering what was left of his wits, Nick said, "Um. No?"

"Oh," Shadow Star said. "Because I could have sworn you kissed the side of my head."

"Nope," Nick said, thankful that it was still raining, so no one could see that his entire body was on its way to being covered in flop sweat. "I didn't do that. That would be weird."

"A little," Shadow Star said.

"And I respect your agency," Nick said.

"Thank . . . you?"

"You're welcome," Nick said, wishing that Pyro Storm would appear right at that very moment and try and destroy Nova City so Nick could perish in a wave of fire. It would be easier than trying to get through the next two minutes. He glanced up quickly. Nothing. Apparently, supervillains only cared about death and destruction when Nick wasn't making an ass of himself. Goddamn Pyro Storm.

Shadow Star pointed his thumb over his shoulder. "I should probably take these guys down to the nearest precinct."

To which Nick said, "Yes, I know how the law works. My dad's a cop. So. Ten-four."

Gibby sounded like she had somehow transformed into a rather large manatee and was trying to sing the song of her people, a sonorous wheeze that lasted far longer than Nick thought was necessary.

"Is he?" Shadow Star said politely. "That's great. Nova City's finest do good work. You must be proud of him."

"So proud," Nick said. Then, "I have your poster in my room. Can I have your autograph?"

"You want me to come into your room and sign your poster?" Shadow Star asked, eyes widening behind his mask.

Yes. Absolutely. Nick wanted that more than anything in the world, but he could see why that sounded a little creepy. "Uh. No? No! Those were two independent thoughts that sounded like they were one. Ha ha. That would be weird, right? Inviting you over to my room when you don't even know me. Did I tell you my name? It's Nick. Not that that means you know me now. I'm very complex underneath. Like, what you see isn't what you get. Not that you're trying to get anything! Ha ha. You can autograph my . . . something."

"Like your boobs," Gibby said.

Nick nodded. "Yes, like my boo—" Pyro Storm could show up anytime now. That'd be just great with Nick. Hopefully, he'd take out Gibby first. "*No,*" he said forcefully, causing Shadow Star to jump back as if he was startled. "Not my b— That's . . . I don't even have—" The ground didn't open up and swallow him whole, no matter how hard he wished it. "I have *paper*. And a pen. You can use that."

"It's raining," Shadow Star pointed out.

"You're so smart," Nick said in awe.

Then Gibby was standing next to him again, a smile on her face that Nick knew he should be terrified of but couldn't muster the strength since he was still dazed. She put the umbrella over them and said cheerfully, "There. That's better. Now you can sign Nick's something without it getting wet. Even though Nick probably already is."

"So wet," Nick agreed.

Gibby manateed again. Nick promised silently that he'd have his revenge against her in this life, or the next.

He took his backpack from Gibby, reaching in to find his notebook. He managed to get it out without much struggle. He couldn't find his Spider-Man pen, but Gibby was there to help him as his hands were shaking. She handed Shadow Star a pen before turning around and motioning that he could use her back as a surface to sign his name. Nick was instantly jealous because *he* wanted to feel the pen pressing into his skin when Shadow Star wrote on the paper. But he still had at least a little of his wits about him, so he was able to stop himself from shoving Gibby away and taking her place.

Shadow Star put the paper on her back and signed his name. He looked like he had nice hands under his skintight gloves.

"There we go," Shadow Star said. "If that's all—"

"Oh," Gibby said as she stood upright again. "We can't let you go without getting a picture. Right, Nicky? Don't you want a picture with Shadow Star?"

Nick's brain short-circuited.

He said, "I. Can't. Think."

"Yeah," Gibby said. "He wants a picture."

"Okay," Shadow Star said. "But just one. I need to get these guys behind bars before they wake up." He turned his face toward the sky. "And the city is calling for me. I need to keep her safe. There is a shroud of shadows over her."

"Oh my god," Nick whispered. No one could ever tell him again that fanfiction wasn't a realistic artistic expression, not with Shadow Star spouting off lines from Nick's imagination.

Gibby rolled her eyes. "Yikes. That was . . . I don't know what that was. Nick, you want to use your phone for—"

Nick shoved his phone at her. He hadn't even realized it'd already been in his hand. He didn't even care that it was getting wet. Nothing else mattered at this moment.

She stepped back, taking the umbrella with her.

Nick was rained on immediately. That was fine. Wet *everything* was fine because he was standing next to Shadow Star. It could have been raining acid, and he wouldn't have complained.

"Okay," Gibby said. "Get close, you guys."

Nick squeaked but managed to cover it up with a cough. He scooted sideways until he was firmly pressed up against Shadow Star. He didn't turn to look at him so he wouldn't accidentally kiss the side of his head again.

"Nick, you look like you're in pain. You need to smile."

Nick smiled.

"And now you look like you're about to eat baby animals. Dial it back."

Nick dialed it back.

"There we go," Gibby said. "Shadow Star, you don't need to smile because you're brooding and deep or whatever."

"Exactly," Shadow Star said. "I breathe the shadows of the dark, and—"

"Everyone say *I think Nick is super cute!*"

"I think Nick is super cute," Shadow Star and Nick said at the same time.

Gibby took the picture as Nick realized what had come out of Shadow Star's mouth.

"You said I'm super cute," he said in awe, blaming puberty for the way his voice cracked.

"That's not—that's what she told me to say." Shadow Star sounded flustered. "I'm not—"

"So you *don't* think he's cute?" Gibby asked.

Yes, that. The most important question that had ever been asked in the history of humanity. Nick waited on pins and needles for Shadow Star to either confess his love or break his heart.

Shadow Star did neither. Instead, he said, "The dark heart of the city pulses beneath my feet. Its blood is calling for me. I have to go."

And with that, the lights burst to life on his wrist. He pointed them at Mustache Man and Male Pattern Baldness. Their shadows grew on the walls behind them. Shadow Star grunted, and the shadows reached down and grabbed the would-be muggers, pulling them up the side of the building. Shadow Star crouched low before springing upward, landing on the wall, dark shades holding him against the brick as he ran after the criminals. He disappeared over the rooftop and was gone.

Nick stared up after him, blinking the rain away.

"You're welcome," Gibby told him, shoving his phone into his hand. "Now, can we go? Watching you get a boner in an alley that smells like feet is not how I expected to spend my afternoon. I need a shower."

5

The first thing he did when he got home was lean against the door and run a hand through his wet hair.

The second thing he did was laugh hysterically.

The third thing he did was run up the stairs to his room and hug the pillow with Shadow Star's face on it.

The fourth thing he did was pull out the autograph.

It read,

> *Nicholas Bell,*
> *Always remember to keep to the shadows!*
> ★☆★ *Shadow Star* ★☆★

The fifth thing he did was lie back on his bed, a smile on his face.

The sixth thing he did was sit back up and dig through his bag furiously until he found his phone.

There it was, saved in his photo album next to at least thirty pics he'd taken in front of the bathroom mirror, trying to track if he was gaining any muscles in his arms from the few times he'd tried to lift weights (five-pound barbells did *nothing*).

Shadow Star glowered at the camera as he stood next to Nick, who looked as if his smile was trying to eat his face. Or at least Nick thought he was glowering since it'd be what he did, but he couldn't be sure. Shadow Star's face was almost completely covered by his mask, with only his mouth visible.

Nick stared at it for a good thirty-six minutes. The picture, not Shadow Star's mouth. Mostly.

Then he clutched the phone to his chest and sighed happily. He had to tell everyone.

Except he couldn't tell everyone.

Right? He couldn't, because it would get back to Dad that he'd been in an alley after leaving school late. And he was only at school late because he'd gotten detention. On the *first day*. And he promised his father he'd do better. That and the fact that he'd almost been stabbed in the face with a knife, and Dad probably wouldn't let him do anything by himself ever again, much like he hadn't let Nick go into a bank by himself since—

Well. Since his mom had entered a bank a few months after their trip to the lighthouse. Four minutes after she'd passed through the doors, three men wearing armor and carrying guns followed.

Six people died that day. A security guard. Two of the gunmen. An elderly man named Bill who came in at least three times a week to make a deposit, but usually used it as an excuse to chat up the pretty bank tellers. A woman named Ella who was meeting with her broker.

And Jenny Bell.

Nick looked at the picture on his desk.

She was there like she always was, her head on his shoulder. "I met him," he said quietly. "Mom, I met him."

She was smiling.

But she was gone. Nick knew that. She wasn't real, not anymore. And he needed to tell someone, right? A person couldn't go through a life-changing event of monumental proportions and *not* tell someone.

That was why best friends existed. For moments exactly like this. He called Seth.

"You've reached Seth's voicemail. I'm probably busy. And nobody calls anyone anymore unless it's an emergency. Send a text. Unless it's an emergency."

"This *is* an emergency," Nick hissed after the beep. "What could you possibly be doing right now that you can't pick up the phone when I call to tell you something that will forever alter the course of my history? Seth! I demand you call me back immediately! The only way I'll forgive you is if you're taking a nap because you were so tired earlier today. Also, I hope you're having a good afternoon and that you didn't get rained on too much because I know you get sick easily, and I don't like it when you're sick. This is Nick. Bye."

He thought about calling Jazz, but she was probably still shaking her groove thang, or whatever it was that cheerleaders did.

He didn't need to call Gibby, because she'd been there. And also because she'd told him before they parted that he was *not* allowed to call her about this tonight because she didn't want to hear him gushing about Shadow Star for the billionth time.

He almost called Owen, but that was probably a bad idea. Owen still made him feel weird when they talked on the phone, and he wasn't in the mood to hear Owen do that dumb flirting thing he did.

Instead, he put the phone beside him and stared at it, thinking as hard as he could at it so Seth would call him back.

It didn't work, and fifteen minutes later, Nick had the beginnings of a headache.

He picked the phone back up, looking at the photo of him and Shadow Star for longer than was healthy.

He texted his dad, letting him know that everything was five-by-five and that he was doing his homework, even though homework on the first day of school was the equivalent of Christmas getting canceled and being replaced by a mayonnaise enema. He thought it was dramatic enough so Dad wouldn't know he'd already done his homework in detention.

He stared at his phone some more.

He thought about posting the photo on Tumblr. It would set the fandom on fire and would add to the validity of his fic. After all, he'd breathed the same air as Shadow Star now, which meant he understood the Extraordinary better than anyone else in the fandom. *Do it. Just do it.* Let them all see he wrote from experience, which was what every author worth their salt should do.

He overthought it. It might be using his position as Shadow Star's most incredible rescue to increase his popularity, and he never wanted to use Shadow Star for anything.

Well. Maybe for a few things that shouldn't be said out loud because in all seriousness, Nick was sort of a prude when it came down to it.

His phone still hadn't rung. His stomach rumbled.

"Fine," he growled, his voice almost like Shadow Star's. "I'll go downstairs and forget how I have no one to tell this to, even though I'm never going to be the same again."

He needed new friends. But the idea of trying to make new friends sounded terrible, so he decided to keep the ones he had, even if they did things like not call him back when he wanted them to.

He stood from the bed and was about to head down the stairs when his phone lit up and started ringing. He dove for it immediately.

"Did you get my message?" he asked breathlessly. "You're not going to believe what happened to me. Like, it was the greatest thing that has ever happened to anyone in the history of ever. Not even the advent of the Industrial Age can compare. You'll never guess. Okay. Start guessing."

The person on the other end of the phone sighed. "Do I even want to know?"

Nick pulled the phone away from his ear in horror.

The screen said DADDIO.

He gave very serious thought to hanging up right then and there. And running away. He'd have to get a new identity. And a job on a barge. He'd grow a beard, and when someone tried to get close to him, he'd shut down and become distant because he could never know the touch of another.

But since he couldn't be sure he even knew what a barge was exactly, he put the phone back to his ear and, trying to act like absolutely nothing had changed, said, "Hey, Pops. What's the haps? What's the 411?"

There was a beat of silence. Then, "What did you do?"

"Nothing," Nick said quickly and believably. "I have no idea what you're talking about. All I'm doing is sitting here at home where I'm supposed to be on a school night, doing my homework. Soon, I'll go downstairs and eat something healthy and go to bed early since everyone knows children need a good night's sleep in order to function—"

"Nicky."

Nick sucked in a sharp breath of air. "Yeah. Sorry about that."

"I left you your pill on the counter. You need to take it, okay? You sound a little wired."

And didn't that just put a damper on things. "I'm not—"

"Nicky."

"I'm allowed to be excited and happy," Nick muttered. His headache was getting worse.

Dad made a sound that was either annoyed or exhausted, Nick didn't know which. It hurt either way. "No one's saying you aren't. In fact, you being excited and happy is one of my favorite things in the world. But I want to make sure we're being safe about it. I'm not trying to take that away from you."

"It feels like it. Sometimes." Nick picked at his comforter. He knew Dad was right. The adrenaline of the afternoon was already working its way out of his system, and he felt himself crashing.

"You trust me?"

Of course he did. There was no one he trusted more. "Yeah."

"Good. And you know we're working on me trusting you again. You've done a lot of good lately, Nicky. I'm proud of you. I want you happy above anything else. And I know how you get, sometimes. It's okay to be that way. But if we can make it better for you, then we should do that, right?"

"Yeah."

"Now, what's the greatest thing to have happened to anyone that not even the advent of the Industrial Age can compare to?"

"Um," Nick said, because regardless of what else he was, Nicholas Bell was a terrible liar, and his father was a living, breathing polygraph machine. "Well, you see—"

Nick heard a voice in the background. Then, his dad said, "Dammit. Sorry, kid. Call came in. I've got to go."

And even though Nick knew it was his job, his heart still thumped terribly in his chest. "Okay. Be careful. Text me when it's done."

"Will do. Do your homework. Take your pill. I love you, and I'll see you for breakfast."

"Love you too."

And then Dad was gone.

Nick stared at the pill on the counter as the lasagna turned in the microwave.

"I'll take you," he told it seriously. "But this is only temporary. You better not get used to it."

The pill didn't respond, but Nick didn't expect it to. If it had, he probably would have run screaming from the house.

The microwave dinged.

Nick picked up the pill and put it in his mouth. He grimaced as he dry-swallowed it. "There," he mumbled. "Hooray."

He believed his dad when he'd said all he'd wanted was for Nick to be happy. He really did. It was just—sometimes, Nick's happiness led to Nick's excitement which transformed into things becoming a little too much for Nick to handle. It'd been explained to both of them in terms Nick could understand that his body was like a cell phone: the more apps he used and left open, the quicker the battery drained. Or, even worse (because apparently the doctor *lived* for metaphors, the quack) his brain was a Ferrari, built for speed, except it had the brakes of a bicycle.

Nick had always been a little . . . different. At first, it was chalked up to growing pains. But then there'd been days when focusing had been next to impossible, and his mind had been racing, and he hadn't been able to sit *still*. His parents were told he wasn't *applying himself,* that he was *disruptive* and *always felt the need to be the center of attention.* Nick had been only eight when he'd tearfully told his parents that no, he *didn't* want to be the center of attention at all, because that meant everyone stared at him, and treated him like he was a freak. He didn't know why he couldn't stop. He didn't want to twitch or move all the time, didn't know why he talked more than he listened, but he wasn't doing it on purpose.

After he'd been diagnosed with ADHD, things had made so much more sense. His dad had growled that the school should have known better, and there was talk about transferring him somewhere else, but Nick had *begged* them to stay. He couldn't leave all his friends, he told them, though he really only had the one. But the idea of not seeing Seth every day was unbearable, and he wouldn't allow it.

Before the Concentra, it'd been Adderall used to pump the useless brakes on his Ferrari brain, but Nick hated the way it made him feel. It brought things into razor-sharp focus, and while that wasn't so bad, it made his headaches worse, and made him feel strangely hollowed out if he missed a dose. And before the Adderall, it'd been some other drug, and before *that*, something else entirely. ADHD was a bitch of a thing, the reality implied in the name. Nick's attention had a deficit, and he was hyperactively disordered. The Concentra was supposed to be better. The transition had been a bit rough, but Nick had gotten through it. Mostly.

But he understood the cell phone battery metaphor—the bicycle brakes on his Ferrari brain. He really did. There were days when everything felt like it was dialed up to eleven, and he didn't know how to stop it, no matter how hard he tried. For the most part, he'd accepted that some people were born to be Extraordinaries, and some people were born to be medicated so they didn't spin out of control. Fair? Not really, but Nick was learning that his brain could do things that others couldn't. In a way, he had his own superpower, even if it was called a disorder.

He took the lasagna from the microwave, the plate hot in his hands. When his dad had days off, they'd spend time together cooking, making meals for the upcoming weeks that could be frozen and saved for later. Lasagna was Nick's favorite, his dad made it just right with sausage and spinach and the perfect amount of cheese.

He turned on the tiny TV in the kitchen before going to sit at the table. An afternoon soap was on, a dazzlingly beautiful woman telling a man with an eye patch that she'd had her conjoined twin removed for a *reason,* and he'd have to make a choice, either her or her sister.

"Get your man," Nick said as he picked up his fork. "Don't let him walk all over you."

He had a mouth full of noodles when the conjoined twin love triangle was interrupted mid-scene by Action News, the red graphic shooting across the screen, screaming BREAKING! BREAKING!

The camera focused on evening anchor Steve Davis, who looked as if he'd never met a form of plastic surgery he didn't want to try at least once. He shuffled the papers in his hands and smiled a perfect smile. "We're interrupting your regularly scheduled broadcast to bring you something . . . extraordinary. We go live to Rebecca Firestone, out in the streets of Nova City. Rebecca?"

The screen cut away to Rebecca Firestone, looking as perfectly put together as she had that morning. She was holding an umbrella in one hand and her microphone in the other. "Thanks, Steve," she said. "New footage this afternoon of a daring rescue. A passerby recorded Nova City's very own Shadow Star apparently working overtime. Not only did he foil the attempt at the break-in at Burke Tower in the early hours of this morning, but he found the time to help stop an attempted mugging. Action News has this exclusive look at what happened."

The screen cut to the alley where Nick had been standing only a couple of hours before.

There was Shadow Star kicking ass and taking names, knocking down Mustache Man and Male Pattern Baldness with special guest stars Nick and Gibby standing in the background.

Nick sprayed lasagna all over the table.

"No," he said, sauce dripping down his chin. "No, no, no." Because if this was on the news, then that meant there was a chance his *dad* would see this.

Nick practically crawled over the table to get closer to the screen.

It wasn't as bad as he first thought. Whoever had taken the video had been standing on the sidewalk on the opposite side of the street, and it'd been raining hard. The video wasn't that clear. Shadow Star was obvious, for sure, but Nick and Gibby were mostly obscured by the umbrella and the rain.

Rebecca Firestone's voice came over as the video continued to play. "As you can see, two young people were obviously frightened and in distress, unable to take care of themselves."

"What?" Nick said, outraged. "They had *knives*. One had a mustache!"

Since Rebecca Firestone couldn't hear him, she wasn't deterred. "But they needn't have worried. Shadow Star was there to prove that in Nova City, even the smallest of crimes don't go unpunished. Whether it be a major break-in at a large pharmaceutical company, or the rescue of what appears to be two helpless young children—"

"I'm not a child! Why are you *like* this?"

"—Shadow Star has proven once again that he will do anything he can." Nick could practically hear the smarmy smile on her face when she continued. "And it looks as if one of the children was quite starstruck by our resident Extraordinary."

The blurry scene zoomed in, showing Shadow Star kicking Mustache Man just as Nick leaned over and kissed the side of his head.

Nick groaned, banging his forehead on the counter. "Why? Why? Whyyyyy?"

The screen went back to Rebecca Firestone, and sure enough, her smile *was* smarmy.

"Though the identity of these two children is still unknown, it appears these damsels in distress were saved, and needed to thank their hero with kisses and even a selfie. Steve?"

Steve Davis appeared back on the screen. He chuckled. "Did that child really kiss the side of his head?"

"It appears so," Rebecca Firestone said. "I'm sure Shadow Star took it in stride. He's used to being adored."

Steve Davis laughed again. "I bet he is. You'll need to ask him how he deals with his fans the next time you speak to him."

"Oh, you can bet on that," Rebecca Firestone said. "Back to you, Steve."

"And there you have it," Steve Davis said, and Nick wished it was the future so he could be older and look back on this and chalk it up to nothing but the angst of being a teenager. "Shadow Star once again saves the day and gets a reward he probably never saw coming. We'll have more on this story tonight on Action News. Now, back to *Love Hurts A Lot*."

Nick turned the TV off, wondering what he'd have to bribe Cap with in order to make sure the entire Action News team was arrested immediately.

He was wiping up the noodles he'd spat on the table when his phone rang again.

He froze.

It was most likely his father.

His father who, even though on patrol, had somehow gotten word of what was shown on the news. His life was over. He had no reasonable explanation for what had transpired, and Dad was never going to let him hear the end of it.

He picked up the phone.

The screen read BFF SETH.

Oh, thank god.

Except he was *angry*. "Am I really a damsel in distress who gets to be made fun of even though I did nothing wrong?" he snapped in lieu of a greeting—as one does when mocked by Rebecca Firestone.

A pause. Then, "What?"

"I am *not* a damsel in distress! Not that there's anything wrong with that. I'd make a pretty good damsel, but that's not the point."

Another pause. Another "What?"

Before Nick could get himself too worked up, he hesitated. "Why does your voice sound weird? Did you get caught in the rain and get sick? Didn't you listen to my voicemail? Don't get sick, especially when you were already tired. Your body's immune system will shut down, and then you'll get a cold which will turn into pneumonia, and what will happen to you *then*? You'll miss school, and I'll be all alone—"

"I'm not sick," Seth said quickly, and his voice sounded normal again. "I had something stuck in my throat."

"Oh. What was it?"

"What was what?"

"What was stuck in your throat?"

"Um. A . . . waffle."

Nick frowned. "A waffle."

Seth cleared his throat. "Yep. Breakfast for dinner. You know how it goes."

"Your aunt doesn't make waffles. She said she doesn't trust food with uniform divots."

"She, uh . . . got over that?"

Then Nick had a terrible thought. "Are you on a date?"

"*What?* No! Why would you think that?"

Nick looked at the remains of his lasagna. He wasn't very hungry anymore. At least his headache was already starting to fade. "I don't even know. It's been . . . I've had a weird day."

"I'm not dating anyone."

"Oh. That's good."

"It is?"

Nick shrugged, though no one could see it. "I guess. But it would explain a lot if you had a secret boyfriend or girlfriend for all those times this summer when you disappeared randomly and didn't answer your phone."

"I told you. I was volunteering at the animal shelter. And don't you say what I know you're going to say—"

"You're far too precious for this world," Nick said. "You're like a Disney princess except real."

Seth sighed. "You're so annoying. Now why are you a damsel in distress or whatever?"

"Because Gibby and I were attacked by a group of super soldiers in an evil alley who wanted to take my virginity, and Shadow Star swooped in and saved us, and I played it cool and got his autograph, but then someone recorded it, and it was on the news, and Rebecca Firestone was being so freaking *smug* about it."

The longest pause of all, followed by the loudest "*What?*"

"Right?" Nick groaned. "I finally had Shadow Star standing right in front of me, and I swear to god, Seth, I was trying to play it cool, but then I spazzed out and accidentally kissed the side of his head, and it went downhill from there."

"I don't know what to do with any of that."

Nick scowled. "Well, you need to figure it out! Seth, I told him about the *pillow*."

"Yeah," Seth said. "I bet that didn't come off as creepy or anything."

Nick slumped dramatically in his chair. "Right? But you know how I am around people I like. I get—"

"Stupid?"

"Hey!"

Seth snorted. "You did the same thing with Owen. At lunch, earlier."

"That's because he was freaking me out!"

"About what? You don't get like that with me."

Nick blinked. "That's because you're Seth. You're my favorite person in the world after my dad. I don't need to be stupid around you. You already like me as I am."

"Eh. Mostly."

"Don't be mean," Nick said. "I've had a traumatizing day."

"I'm sure. A group of super soldiers, was it? And they wanted to take your virginity?"

Nick sighed. "It was two men and they were trying to take my bag. One was balding, and the other had a get-into-my-ice-cream-truck-little-boy mustache."

"Maybe you should have given it to them."

"But it's mine."

Seth sounded aggrieved. "Shadow Star can't always be there to help you, Nicky. Or any Extraordinary, for that matter. What if something happens again, and no one's there to save you?"

Oh, that wasn't irritating or anything. "I can take care of myself."

"It's not about— You could have been hurt. What if one of them had gotten you with the knife before Shadow Star stopped them? You need to be more careful."

"Way to victim blame, man," Nick said. "It's not like I asked for this to happen. Why can't you be happy for me? I got to meet Shadow Star."

"I just—" Nick knew Seth was gnawing on his bottom lip. Seth did that when he was trying to think about what to say. "I need you to be okay. I don't want anything to happen to you."

Nick knew loss. He did. He knew what it meant when something happened that shouldn't have, when life was wholly unfair and took and took and took. Sometimes, he was so wrapped up in himself that he forgot Seth knew about that too, probably better than anyone else. It was why they could be the way they were with each other. That and the fact that Seth picked Princess Daisy when they played Mario Kart because he didn't believe in the patriarchy and didn't complain too much when Nick cheated with the red shell like a dick.

"I'll be careful," Nick said, because Seth needed to hear it. "I promise. And besides, it wasn't as if there actually were super soldiers. It was two goons with—" Nick frowned. "Wait. How did you know they had knives? I didn't tell you that."

Seth hesitated. "Pretty sure you did."

"No," Nick said slowly. "I was saving that part for the dramatic reveal toward the end."

"Oh. Uh, I thought you said knife. My bad. Must have guessed. Didn't mean to ruin the dramatic reveal. Sorry."

"Good guess, then," Nick said. "Because they *did* have knives. But they were more like machetes. And they came at Gibby and me and demanded our belongings, but I pushed Gibby behind me like a man does—"

"Gibby is stronger than the both of us."

"Oh, right. Good point. And I'm totally equal opportunity, because I'm a feminist. Also, I lied because I was behind Gibby. Anyway, so there we were, standing side by side and they demanded we hand everything over, and I said *no way,* and Gibby said *I know karate* probably, and when we were about to save the day because I am *not* a damsel in distress no matter what Rebecca Firestone says, Shadow Star came and beat them up, and his voice was so deep and strong."

"And you got his autograph?" Seth asked, sounding strange. "That must have been . . . cool."

"Oh, it was. Hold on. I'm going to go upstairs so I can read it to you. And then I'll send you the picture that Gibby took of us where Shadow Star said I'm cute, or something similar."

"Okay, but I can't talk long. I've got homework, and I'm going to try and go to bed early tonight."

Nick took the stairs two at a time. "You should have done what I did and gotten detention. It's the perfect place to do homework."

Seth sighed. "I'll keep that in mind for next time."

Nick ran back into his room and found the paper that had once been held by Shadow Star. "Okay, are you ready for this?"

"I wait with bated breath."

"It says, *Nicholas Bell: Always remember to keep . . . to the . . . shadows . . .*" Nick squinted down at the paper.

"Wow," Seth said. "His catchphrase and everything. That sure is . . . something."

"Yeah," Nick said slowly. "Except . . ."

"Except what?"

"I didn't tell him my full name."

Silence.

Then, "Well, you must have. He wrote it."

"No. I didn't. Don't you think I'd remember every single word I had with Shadow Star? Because I *do*. I remember everything. From telling him about the pillow to denying kissing the side of his head when I totally did, it's all in my brain like the world's most awkward fantasy come to life. Seth, I only told him my name was Nick."

"Maybe he saw it on something inside your bag?"

"No," Nick said, sitting on his bed in shock. "He was never *in* my bag. Seth. Oh my god. Do you know what this means?"

"I don't . . . think so? Should I?"

"Seth. I've figured it out. I know."

"Oh boy. I can't wait to hear this."

Nick barely heard him, lost in what could only be the truth. "It makes so much sense. I've always thought we had some kind of connection. But now I know why. I don't know how I didn't see it before. Seth. It's like—it's like he's read my fic. I think he has a Tumblr account and has read my fic! What if he was a commenter and I *didn't know it*?"

"Yep," Seth said, sounding amused. "There it is. It's moments like this I realize you still haven't lost the capacity to surprise me."

"I get it now," Nick said, standing and pacing back and forth in his room. "I mean, of *course* that's exactly what happened. He's probably standing in his Shadow Lair right now—"

"His Shadow *what*?"

"His Shadow Lair," Nick explained patiently, because he knew that if this was causing his own head to explode, it must be doing the same to Seth. "Every superhero has a base of operations, and Shadow Star has the Shadow Lair. It's where he broods in the shadows and stores all his gear while practicing fighting. You know this. You beta read my fic. I described it in great detail, so much so that you told me I didn't need sixteen thousand words to make it clear to the reader he lives in a wet cave. Keep up!"

"How could I forget," Seth said dryly. "You might be overthinking this one, Nicky. Just a smidge."

"No," Nick said. "I'm thinking clearer than I ever have before. Nate Belen was rescued in my fic, and so Shadow Star thought he had to rescue me. But then Rebecca Firestone said I was a damsel in distress, and so maybe *that's* what he thinks because they have a platonic understanding that is in no way romantic or sexual since that's gross. Seth, what if Shadow Star thinks I'm only going to be in danger and that he has to come rescue me all the time?"

"I don't think you have to worry about that."

"You're right," Nick said, coming to a decision he should have made a long time ago. "Because I'm not going to be a damsel in distress."

"Well, for one, you're not a damsel *anything*—"

"I'm not going to be someone who needs to be rescued all the time. The best love interests for superheroes are always other superheroes because they understand the journey and what it takes to survive. Seth, I know what my destiny is. I know what I have to become." Here it was, right in front of him, and he couldn't believe how simple it was.

"I'm not going to like this, am I?"

"I need my own origin story," Nick announced grandly. "I'm going to become an Extraordinary."

"Nicky, *no*."

"Nicky, *yes!*"

Fic: This Is Where We Scorch the Earth
Author: ShadowStar744
Chapter 68 of ? (HOLD ON TO YOUR BUTTS!)
267,924 words
Pairing: Shadow Star/Original Male Character
Rated: PG-13 (Rating will *definitely* go up)
Tags: True Love, Pining, Gentle Shadow Star, Violence, Happy Ending, First Kiss, Maybe Some Smut if I Can Talk Myself into It, But Who Knows

Chapter 68: The Destiny of Nate Belen

Author's Note: Surprise! I bet you all didn't expect there to be such a quick update. But let's just say that I found myself with some . . . inspiration that was certainly . . . inspired by a certain someone who . . . inspires me. Someone who might have done a backwards kick and then didn't really make a big deal about a pillow. (YOU KNOW WHO YOU ARE!!!!) If that . . . person . . . is reading this, I hope you enjoy it. Sorry this is so short! I'm laying the groundwork for what will become something AMAZING.

Nate leapt from the bridge spire directly onto Pyro Storm's back. Pyro Storm shouted in anger as Nate wrapped his leg around his waist, reaching between them and pulling the cape up and over the villain's head. "And *that's* why you don't wear a cape, you gigantic jerk," Nate growled awesomely, like a badass.

Pyro Storm cursed as he struggled to find his way out of his cape. Nate tried to hold on as best he could, but Pyro Storm was bigger and stronger. Nate couldn't avoid the elbow that Pyro Storm threw back at him. It struck the side of Nate's face. Nate saw stars.

He let go of Pyro Storm.

And began to fall.

"Nate!" Shadow Star screamed.

But what neither of the Extraordinaries knew was that Nate Belen had been waiting for this *exact moment*. It was all part of his plan. He didn't *need* to be rescued, even though he knew Shadow Star couldn't help himself. Nate understood that even though Shadow Star had tried to push him away, they were connected in ways that defied explanation. There was a bond between them stronger than steel, more powerful than a laser beam shot from the world's biggest ray gun.

But Nate had a secret of his own.

You see, Nate too was an Extraordinary.

And it was time for the world to see what he was capable of.

He heard Shadow Star crying out his name. Pyro Storm was cackling maniacally. But Nate wasn't some damsel in distress.

He was more.

And right before he hit the water, his power unfurled and everything went white.

TO BE CONTINUED!!

....

Comments:

ExtraordinariesSuperFan 18:16: WHAT IS HAPPENING. WHAT IS THIS. WHAT IS THIS TWIST. WHY ARE YOU DOING THIS TO ME.

PyroStarIsLife 18:26: They should let Nate die & then Pyro Storm & Shadow Star should get married & have bebbies & live in a farm & sell organic produce uwu

Lobster16 18:54: Wait, what? When did Nate become an Extraordinary? Hasn't this whole thing been about him not being an Extraordinary? I'm so confused. He's been captured seventeen times in this entire fic, and not once did his powers ever come out. This really messes with the continuity. Why not have Nate reveal himself to be an Extraordinary back when Pyro Storm took him captive at the zoo in chapter 16? Or at the street fair in chapter 19? Or even in chapter 24 when Nate was randomly a DJ at a bar mitzvah for reasons that were never explained?

MoltenMagma 19:12: Yeah, you're making this up as you go along, aren't you. I dunno how much longer I'm going to read this. Nothing about this makes any sense. Like, why does Nate suddenly have powers *now*? It's dumb.

ExtraordinaryGurl 19:19: AKSHDHDKD!!!! I DIDN'T SEE THIS COMING AT ALL. YEAH BOY! GAAAAAAAAAAAAAAAAAAAHHHHHHH

ShadowStarIsBae 19:30: I'm with MoltenMagma. This doesn't make any sense. I mean, it's cool and all that Nate won't get captured (again— for the millionth time), but when did he become an Extraordinary?

FireStoned 20:45: WHY ARE YOU STILL INSISTING THAT SHADOW STAR IS GAY AND IN LOVE WITH THIS LOSER? HE IS STRAIGHT. NOT EVERYTHING IS GAY BECAUSE YOU WANT IT TO BE. THE RAINBOW DOESN'T BELONG

TO THE GAYS. GIVE IT BACK AND MAKE SHADOW STAR STRAIGHT AGAIN.
STRAIGHT PRIDE!!!!!

ReturnOfTheGray 21:21: SHADOWSTAR744, NO.

ShadowStar744, *yes.*

6

"Okay!" Nick exclaimed to no one in particular, seeing as how he was alone in his room at six o'clock in the morning. "Think. Think. First things first. When one decides to become an Extraordinary, one must throw away all they know about their lives in pursuit of their dream."

And—though he tried not to focus on it too much—when one is being love-stalked (possibly) by the world's best Extraordinary, one must come up with a plan that ensures the ensuing origin story is for the ages. This part threatened to overtake his thoughts, but since he was certain of his newly formed plan, he only considered the love-stalking for thirteen minutes.

The *problem* with deciding to have an origin story and becoming an Extraordinary is that there were so many different ideas on how to go about it. This, of course, made Nick immediately overwhelmed, given the enormity of the task.

It didn't help that he couldn't talk to his father about this. He didn't want Dad to worry, especially if Nick ended up needing to do something dangerous in order to become Extraordinary. It wasn't that he was necessarily concerned about his own well-being, but more so that he didn't want his plans to be curtailed before they even began. What Dad didn't know wouldn't hurt him. Hopefully.

He pulled out a notebook from his bag and sat on the edge of his bed, toes digging into the carpet. He tapped his pen against the blank page before deciding on the perfect way to begin. He wrote:

IDEAS FOR BECOMING AN EXTRAORDINARY

It was a good start. Nick was impressed with himself. It showed initiative and follow through. He'd set his mind to something, and by god, he was sticking with it! He'd gotten the hard part out of the way and now all he needed to do was fill in the rest. Easy.

"Okay," he mumbled. "You got this, man. I believe in you. How can you have the best origin story so that Shadow Star doesn't see you as a liability and instead judges you on your *lay*-ability?"

He blushed, because he was still a prude and because puns were the lowest form of humor.

Shadow Star would probably be gentle. And romantic. Like, flowers and junk. Candles. The long ones they got at fancy restaurants in movies. Nick could deal with that. Boys could give boys flowers, right? It wasn't only for girls. Nick didn't know for sure. Which meant he had to look it up on his phone. He felt badly for all the generations that had come before him, unable to access queries immediately such as if it was okay for boys to give other boys flowers.

Two minutes later, he was somehow reading a Wikipedia article on the Women's Cricket World Cup, unsure of how he got there.

"Focus," he hissed to himself, putting his phone back in his backpack. "If you're going to commit to this, you need to do it right. Think, Bell."

It couldn't be that hard, right? Sure, it wasn't quite clear on how Extraordinaries got their powers. They made up such a tiny percentage of the population that no one was even really sure where they'd come from. Many believed that Extraordinaries were born, not made, a twist of genomes that was almost like a defect. Others claimed they received their powers through government testing.

The first verifiable Extraordinary was a man in California in 1947, near the dawn of nuclear power. He'd been super strong and had gone by the name of the American Patriot, his costume essentially one gigantic flag of stars and stripes. But, as it turned out, the forties had been filled with misogyny, racism, and homophobia, and the American Patriot had had some terrible ideas about what constituted being an Extraordinary, so much so that he only fought to promote the power of straight white men. He'd lasted as a hero for sixteen days before deciding that a life of crime as a villain paid far more than doing good.

Which led to the reveal of a *second* Extraordinary, Primate Girl, a young woman with really large forearms and gorgeous body hair who ended the American Patriot's reign of bank-robbing terror by punching him so hard, authorities found his jawbone three miles away in a tree outside an orphanage. Thankfully, the children of the orphanage had been on a trip to the zoo and did not see the jawbone before it was removed. Nick thought that if he'd found a random jawbone, it'd mess him up for life.

Primate Girl was somewhat celebrated for her actions; unfortunately, it was still the forties, and public opinion was that a woman's place was in the home, caring for her family. Primate Girl, much to Nick's glee, publicly announced she would retire immediately and marry the first man who could beat her in an arm wrestling contest. Seventeen men volunteered. By the end, Primate Girl remained unmarried, and the men were treated at area hospitals for injuries sustained while attempting to prove their masculinity.

From there, more and more Extraordinaries appeared. Oh, they were still rare, and most cities never had one. But they were emboldened by Primate Girl's actions and began exhibiting their powers, mostly in the name of truth and justice. Regardless of what feats they were capable of, they all had one thing in common: They always hid their identities, which made it next to impossible for scientists to get their hands on them for study. There'd been a call in the late sixties and early seventies to require Extraordinaries to reveal their true identities to the public and submit for testing, but it'd died before gaining much traction. Hippie protests had seen to that. Extraordinaries were so few and far between that they inspired awe rather than fear, for the most part.

Even Pyro Storm had his own groupies. And it wasn't like he'd actually done anything *too* evil. Aside from being Shadow Star's archnemesis, the worst thing he'd done was somehow make all the traffic lights in Nova City turn green at once, causing thousands of fender benders and a complete gridlock in the streets that lasted for seventeen hours. Granted, he'd used that time to try to steal priceless artwork from the Nova City Fine Art Museum, but his attempt had been foiled by Shadow Star, so everything was fine. At least, that was what Rebecca Firestone had reported.

And it wasn't like they were the only Extraordinaries in the world. There was a man in Berlin who could shoot ice from his eyes. There was one in Portland, Oregon, who was capable of creating portals that could take him easily from one side of the city to the other. There was one in Tallahassee who had the skin of an alligator, though there were some people who thought it was a rather aggressive fungus. There was a nonbinary Extraordinary in Tokyo who could create fireworks with their mind, and another in New Zealand who controlled herds of sheep with a single thought, which she displayed proudly.

So maybe they weren't exactly like the comic books Nick read, but that was okay. He didn't need them to be. The Sheep Herder was good for the economy, apparently. Which, while not exactly glamorous, was still pretty cool.

But Nick didn't want to be just pretty cool. If he was going to be an Extraordinary, then he was going to be the best one that ever lived. Which brought him back to his list and finding out how to become Extraordinary in the first place. Origin stories needed to be organic. In a lot of the comics he'd read, heroes were put into impossible situations that led to them gaining their powers. He just needed to find a way to be in the right place at the right time.

The internet, for one of the first times in his life, failed him in that regard. There were too many theories, and none of them seemed to be based in any kind of reality. Most seemed to be stuck on the idea that Extraordinaries were born and not made. If that were the case, Nick was screwed even before he got started. And since that wouldn't do, he chose not to believe it. Besides, it smacked of pure-blood bullshit, and Nick wasn't here for that at all. Anyone could do anything, so long as they put their minds to it. Or so he hoped.

No one really knew where Shadow Star or Pyro Storm had come from when they appeared roughly two years earlier. They were unique in that their powers seemed to be stronger than others before them. Nick had never heard of another Extraordinary that could control shadows like his hero could. And while there had been others with pyrokinesis like Pyro Storm, none had the strength he had. Not only could he actually control fire, he could create it with his mind out of nowhere, which, if it weren't so rad, would be terrifying.

The Nova City Fire Department had come out against Pyro Storm last year, claiming he had the potential to make their jobs harder, but then everyone had gotten distracted when Shadow Star had saved a bus filled with elderly people on their way to a time-share seminar from crashing into a gas station after the driver fell asleep at the wheel. That had been a good day for the Shadow Star fandom.

But they weren't the first heroes Nova City had seen, were they? No. Anyone worth their salt knew that Nova City once had its streets protected—in a strange time known as the turn of the twenty-first century—by a different Extraordinary, one who'd gone by the name Guardian. This Extraordinary appeared out of nowhere, their costume sleek and cerulean blue from head to toe. They'd started small, stopping muggings and break-ins with their telekinetic powers before taking on larger tasks, such as diverting the terribly named Men's Rights Parade so the marchers all ended up falling into the Westfield River. Most hadn't known what to make of Guardian—no one even knew if they were a man or a woman, given that their costume hid what lay underneath—but they'd cautiously cheered the hero on. Then, for reasons no one could explain, Guardian had disappeared in the early aughts, never to be seen again. Either they'd been killed in their regular lives, or they'd decided Nova City didn't need saving. It wasn't until the coming of Shadow Star and Pyro Storm that the city once again had Extraordinaries of its own.

Which, unfortunately, did little to help Nick in his quest. The photographs of Guardian were blurry, out of focus, only catching the hero's boots or the back of their head, covered in a mask. Guardian had never sat for interviews, had never given grand and exciting speeches about being the savior the city needed. They'd kept their head down, fighting for the forces of good until they didn't. They were just . . . gone. Nick didn't understand how someone could *stop* when they could move things with the power of their mind.

"What are you doing?"

Nick looked up, startled at the voice. He blinked when he saw he was in the Franklin Street station. He hadn't even realized he'd left his house. Autopilot was a scary thing, especially for one such as Nick. He had a vague memory of taking his pill and choking down burnt toast, but that was all.

Seth stood in front of him. He was wearing a sweater vest over a collared dress shirt. Instead of a bow tie, today he had a checkered ascot, his curly hair sticking up every which way. If anyone else had worn an ascot in front of Nick, he would have—well, probably not said anything because that would be a dick thing to do. People could dress how they wanted. But they wouldn't be Seth, that was for damn sure.

"Why are you looking at me like that?" Seth asked suspiciously.

Nick felt his face grow hot. It wasn't—okay. *Objectively,* he knew Seth was attractive, and yes, maybe the fact that he dressed like he was a junior senator who vacationed in Connecticut in the fall and went winter skiing in Vail was . . . something. But it wasn't anything. Seth was his best friend. And it was always bros before hoes. Not that he or Seth were hoes or anything. In fact, now that he thought about it, he didn't think Seth had actually had a boyfriend or girlfriend, unless he'd actually been keeping one from Nick like Nick had accused him of. Which, if that was the case, it was fine.

(It was absolutely *not* fine, but he already had a lot on his plate and the fact that he wanted to sigh at his best friend for actually having *pennies* in his loafers wasn't making things easier.)

"No reason," Nick said awkwardly as he scratched the back of his neck. "You look . . . nice."

Seth blushed. "Oh. Um. Thank you."

Nick scuffed the toe of his ancient Chucks on the dirty station floor. He wanted to say more—possibly even compliment Seth on his fashion decisions—but he couldn't make the words come out.

"What are you writing?" Seth finally asked.

Nick looked down at the notebook in his hand, filled with his chicken scratch. He held it flat against his chest so Seth couldn't read that he'd written MR. NICHOLAS SHADOW STAR in the margins. "Nothing."

"Nicky."

"It's *nothing*."

"It's always something," Gibby said, appearing out of nowhere like a lesbian ghost bent on proving Nick wrong. Before Nick could stop her, she grabbed the notepad out of his hand, looking down at it. Jazz hooked her chin over Gibby's shoulder, reading what Nick had written. Even Seth leaned over to take a look, which lessened the appeal of the ascot, given that he was an opportunistic betrayer.

"Nicky, no," they all said at the same time.

"Nicky, *yes*," he snapped, grabbing the notepad back.

"Does this have to do with what happened yesterday?" Jazz asked. "You know, the whole Nick being scared and needing to be rescued by Gibby and then by Shadow Star."

Nick turned slowly to glare at Gibby.

She shrugged. "Needed to sound heroic for my lady."

"By throwing me under the bus?"

She patted his shoulder. "Your contribution was noted. And that's exactly how it happened, so shut up."

Jazz nodded. "You screamed at the muggers in a high-pitched voice that you were going to tell your dad."

"Literally none of that happened," Nick said. "And frankly, I don't have time to tell you what really happened because I'm busy. And not with what you think! It's time for school."

Jazz looked at his notepad again. "Mr. Nicholas Shadow Star. Nicky, I don't think that's how last names work. Like, at all. If anything, you'd be Mr. Nicholas Star." She smiled. "That sounds like it should be your porn name. I approve."

Nick needed new friends.

"—and *furthermore*," Nick said as he sat at the lunch table, apropos of nothing, "I feel as if I'm being judged for wanting to be something different than I already am. Gibby, when you shaved your head and asked that we call you Gibby instead of Lola, did we argue with you about that?"

"Is he still on this?" Gibby asked Jazz. "It's like he resumed a conversation we were having hours ago as if no time had passed."

"He finds the little things important," Jazz told her. "I like that about him."

"You would," Gibby muttered. Then, "No. Nick, you asked if you could be the one to shave my head after it grew out again, and then decided I should have racing stripes on the side to see if it would make me go faster."

"Exactly," Nick said fiercely. "And as a side note, I'm still upset you didn't let me do any of that. It would have been awesome. And, Jazz, when you decided you wanted to take self-defense classes because men can sometimes be disgusting and not know the meaning of the words *back off, you sumbitch,* did I not support you in that regard?"

Jazz smiled at him. "You did. You even went with me to the first class and got your butt kicked by a sixty-three-year-old grandmother."

"She felt really bad after and made me pie," Nick agreed. "But it was a purple plum pie, and that's disgusting, so I had to throw it away. But it was the thought that counted. And *Seth.*"

They all turned to look at him.

His ascot was slightly askew. Nick didn't know how to handle that.

Jazz sighed.

Seth blushed.

Gibby coughed pointedly.

Nick shook his head. He couldn't get distracted. "What were we talking about?"

"How you threw away pie from an old lady," Gibby said.

"That's right. Seth, when you decided you wanted to wear ties to school for reasons that no one quite understands, who was the one who helped you look up how to tie a Windsor knot on the internet and then let you practice on him for an entire month until you got it right?"

"You were," Seth said, looking down at the table.

"With minimal complaint!"

"For the first twenty minutes."

"Which was twenty minutes more than it should have been!" Nick exclaimed. "You know I can't sit still for that long without going out of my mind. Why on earth did you need to learn how to do a full Windsor? The only thing that made it bearable was when you found the one called the Nicky knot and insisted on wearing that one more than all the others."

Gibby and Jazz turned slowly to look at Seth.

Seth didn't acknowledge them, finding something extremely interesting to pick at on the table. It looked like dried ketchup.

"The Nicky knot," Gibby said. "Seriously."

"Yeah," Jazz said. "Seriously."

"I liked the way it looked," Seth muttered.

Gibby snorted. "I bet you did."

Nick didn't have time for their vagueness. "And now that I've given you all examples of specific times I've been a good friend and supported you with something, I'm asking that you do the same for me and respect my decision to become an Extraordinary."

Jazz opened up her Tupperware. She pulled out what looked like quinoa tabbouleh with sliced avocados. Nick couldn't be sure how he knew what quinoa tabbouleh even was. "How are you going to do that?" she asked. "Not everyone can be an Extraordinary. If they could, there'd be millions of them. I'd be one."

"What would your superpower be?" Gibby asked.

Jazz shrugged. "Flying. Or maybe growing orange trees. You know I like the way orange trees look."

Nick frowned. "That's not a—"

Gibby shook her head in warning. "You do that, babe. I bet they'd be the best orange trees."

"Of course they would," Jazz said. "And then I'd harvest the oranges and make orange juice with so much pulp, it would be like chewing rather than drinking. And then I'd donate it to people who can't afford orange juice."

Nick wanted to protest—because *what?*—but he had to stay on their good side so he could have their complete support in his new endeavor. "That sounds . . . so great. Good for you."

"Thanks," Jazz said, beaming at him.

"I'd want to be able to make my hands turn into swords," Gibby said, stealing an avocado slice from Jazz. "And then I'd stab everyone who pissed me off."

"Very effective," Nick said. "Bloody and violent, but I can dig it.

Sword Hands, they'd call you. Look out, bad guys! Here comes Sword Hands, and she's gonna stab your throat."

They turned to Seth, who didn't seem like he wanted to take part in the conversation, if the look on his face meant anything. He just needed a little motivation, and in another life where Extraordinaries didn't exist, Nick could have been a motivational speaker.

"Your turn," Nick said, bumping Seth's shoulder. "You got this, man."

Seth sighed. "I dunno. Maybe I don't want to be an Extraordinary."

Nick was scandalized. He said, "But—" and "Are you—" and "How could—" before deciding on "*Why?*"

Seth shrugged, but didn't look up from his lunch box in front of him. "It sounds like it'd be hard work, you know? More than you think it ever could be."

Nick didn't understand. "But—it's about being brave. It's about helping people!"

Seth jerked his head up, and his jaw was clenched, his eyes narrowed. Nick had never seen that expression on his face before. A chill ran down his spine.

"Helping people," Seth said, laughing quietly, though it didn't sound like he found anything funny about it. "Sure. There's that. Once you decide to go public and help people, you *always* have to continue helping them, no matter what. You can't help one person and not another, right? And what happens when there are multiple people who need help, but you can't get to all of them at once? Who do you choose? And when you *do* choose, how can you live with that choice if one of the people you didn't help gets hurt? Or worse."

Seth was getting upset. Nick didn't like that at all. When Seth got upset, it made Nick twitchy and want to maim whatever had caused it. "Is this about what Owen said? Don't listen to him, man. It's just a game. You don't need to—"

"It's *not* a game," Seth snapped, slamming his hands on the table. Nick struggled not to move away. "And even when you try your hardest to do good, there are always going to be people suspicious of your motives. Wondering what you're *really* trying to do. And it doesn't help that there's going to be some jerk who appears out of nowhere and thinks he's your archnemesis, and does his best to make everything worse."

"But—"

Seth shook his head. "And it's lonely. That's the one thing you don't expect. How lonely it is. Because you can't tell anyone about it. You can't tell your family because they wouldn't understand. You can't tell your friends because they could become targets, and you don't want them to get hurt. So you keep on going by yourself, hoping one day it will get better, and the *only* thing that's in your head is why you started to begin with. Why you put on that stupid costume in the first place. The promise you made to yourself. And some days, that's almost not enough."

Silence fell over the table.

Gibby was staring at Seth strangely, and looked like she was going to open her mouth and say something, but Nick got there first. "Whoa. That . . . was . . . *amazing*."

Seth's eyes widened. "What?"

"No, seriously. That was perfect. Holy crap, Seth. Did you think of that off the top of your head? Oh my god, we need to collaborate on a fic together. Why didn't you tell me you had an imagination?"

Seth groaned, putting his face in his hands.

"Did you guys hear that?" Nick demanded, looking at Gibby and Jazz.

"I think so," Jazz said, squinting at Nick. "We're sitting right here."

Gibby didn't say anything. She continued to stare at Seth, brow furrowed.

Seth groaned again.

"Yes, I know," Nick said, reaching over and putting his arm around Seth's shoulders, pulling him close. Seth came willingly enough, and Nick was pleased. "It's shocking when you discover the depths of your creativity. Believe me, I would know. It happens to me on a daily basis." He smacked a kiss on the top of Seth's head. "By the way, I'm stealing everything you said as my backstory when I become an Extraordinary if I want to be the brooding kind. I haven't decided if I'm going to do that, or go the happy, sarcastic, kick-ass way."

"You don't know how to brood," Seth mumbled.

"Aw, isn't this cozy," Owen said, tossing his bag on the table, almost knocking Jazz's quinoa tabbouleh into her lap. She glared up at him, and Nick wondered if Owen was about to go through the rest of his life without his fingers. Thankfully, Gibby put a hand over Jazz's and squeezed, keeping her from getting up. Owen was too busy staring at Nick and Seth to see how close it'd been. "You two are so adorable, I can't even stand it. Seriously. Stop. It's disgusting." He sat down, the bench creaking beneath him.

Seth pulled away, even though Nick was loath to let him go. It felt . . . nice, sitting like that with Seth. "You just missed Seth being so badass," Nick told Owen.

Owen rolled his eyes. "First time for everything, I suppose."

That didn't sit well with Nick. It never did when someone talked badly about Seth. "That's not fair. He's badass all the time. More than you could ever be."

Owen winked at Nick. "I highly doubt that."

"You have sunglasses on top of your head."

"And?"

"You just came from class. Which means you're inside. Which means you look like an idiot."

Seth snorted.

Owen shrugged. "Or I look good no matter what I'm doing."

"Men are terrible," Jazz told Gibby.

"I'm glad you think that way," Gibby replied. "Means more of you for me."

Owen reached over and stole one of Seth's sugar snap peas. Seth looked like he was going to say something but swallowed it down instead as Owen continued with his nonsense. "Why are the dorks being all touchy-feely with each other? Not that I care."

"Right," Gibby said. "You don't care so much that you asked anyway."

Owen grinned at her, razor sharp. "I'm pretending to be interested. It's what friends do." He glanced at Nick. "And exes, I suppose."

"Where did you come from?" Jazz asked suddenly.

For a moment, Owen's facade morphed into a look of surprise, before it cooled again. "I have no idea what you're talking about."

"You weren't friends with us. With any of us. And then all of a sudden, you were here. Why?"

Owen bit into the sugar snap pea, teeth crunching it cleanly. "You knew me before they did. My parents are donors to the same charities your parents are. We saw each other all the time."

"Rich people stuff," Gibby whispered to Seth and Nick.

"Right," Jazz said, gnawing on her bottom lip. "And I remember seeing you at our country club, but we never talked. Well, except for that one time when you asked if I wanted to go back to your house and see your bed."

Gibby's eyes narrowed.

For the first time since Nick had known him, Owen almost looked scared. "Yeah," he said hastily. "That wasn't one of my better ideas. But if you could tell your guard dyke that it was *before* her, that would be great."

"It was," Jazz said, putting her hand on Gibby's arm, much to Nick's consternation. He wanted to see what Gibby would have done. He thought it would have been gory. "And I wasn't the only one he tried to get with."

Owen shrugged. "What can I say? I've got a big . . . heart. Ain't that right, Nicky?"

"Ugh," Nick said. "You know, you've got the whole attractive thing going for you, but what most people don't know is that you're also terrible. It's really not the best combination."

Seth laughed.

Owen narrowed his eyes at Nick. "You didn't seem to think I was terrible when I put my tongue down your—"

"Gibby, *no,*" Jazz said.

"Gibby, *yes,*" Nick muttered, but Gibby let Jazz pull her back down to her seat.

"Look," Owen said. "I don't know what you want me to say. You guys are losers, and I happen to like losers." He looked at Seth. "Everyone at this school is so . . . fake. You guys keep things interesting. Isn't that right, Seth?"

"Right," Seth said through gritted teeth.

Nick was almost positive they weren't flirting, but that didn't explain the tension. He knew Seth hadn't been thrilled when Owen announced that he and Nick were an item, but he'd said as long as Nick was happy, nothing else mattered. Nick hadn't seen much of Seth during the Great Romance of Nick and Owen, but he figured that was because Seth was busy. And Nick had also been busy, but it'd been the type of busy that made his lips chapped.

Looking back, it was obviously temporary insanity; that was the only thing that made sense.

"So, that's why I'm here," Owen said. "Because gosh darn it, I just like you all so much." He reached across the table and pinched Nick on the cheek. "Doesn't hurt that you're all so cute."

Nick smacked his hand away. "I hate it when you do that."

"I know," Owen said, eyes glinting. "But I like it when you're flustered. Now that that's all settled, would someone fill me in on what was going on before I got here? Something about Seth being cool, or whatever. Which, honestly, doesn't seem possible."

For a moment, Nick thought about changing the subject entirely. He knew his ideas were . . . well. Sometimes they were out there. And he was going to soldier on even if he had to go it alone, but he didn't want someone like Owen making fun of him. Because Owen could be all right sometimes, but he could also be mean. Nick had never had it directed toward him, not really, but he'd seen Owen be vicious before, and it'd made him uncomfortable. And while he didn't think Owen would give him crap for wanting to be an Extraordinary, he didn't want to risk it.

But it was taken out of Nick's hands when Jazz said, "Gibby and Nick were almost mugged yesterday, but then they were saved by Shadow Star. And now Nick wants to be an Extraordinary because he thinks it'll get Shadow Star's attention." She frowned. "I still don't know how that's going to work."

Owen leaned forward on the table, and that sharp smile was back as he stared at Nick. "Really? You don't say. Shadow Star. How fortuitous that he happened to be there at that exact moment."

"It wasn't a big deal," Nick said, glancing away. "Just, you know. I got his autograph, or whatever."

Owen threw his head back and laughed. "Oh, Nicky. Never change. I'm sure it was painfully awkward and so, so sweet. But why in the hell would you want to be an Extraordinary? It seems like such a big responsibility." He reached out and traced his finger along the back of Nick's hand. "Think you could handle it?"

Nick pulled his hand away. "I'd be good at it."

Owen sighed. "Right. I bet you would. But still. Being an Extraordinary is so yesterday. I can't imagine anything more boring. Oooh, superpowers. People expecting you to do something for them all the time. It'd be aggravating."

"Not everyone is a jerk like you," Seth said coldly.

"Eh," Owen said. "I can think of about a billion things to do with my time that would be better." He glanced at Nick. "But that's what you want, huh?"

"Well . . . um. Yes?"

Owen reached up and rubbed the back of his neck. On anyone else, Nick would think it a nervous gesture. But on Owen, it seemed practiced, as if he *knew* how it was supposed to look, bicep flexing, looking up at Nick from under his eyelashes. He wondered how many people had fallen for it. Hell, *he'd* fallen for it. And sometimes, maybe he still did. He was a teenage boy, after all, and Owen had big arms and at least three abdominal muscles. Of course he fell for it. "If that's what you want, I suppose I can do what I can to help you—"

"No," Seth said suddenly, making Nick jump. "You don't need to do that. Because I already decided *I'm* going to help him."

"And me," Gibby said.

Everyone looked at Jazz.

She had a mouthful of quinoa tabbouleh.

Gibby elbowed her in the side.

"Oh," Jazz said, a piece of avocado falling from her mouth. "And me."

"So, you see," Seth said smugly, "Nick doesn't need your help. We've got it covered."

"Wow," Nick breathed. "My heart is so full. It's like my birthday except better."

Owen rolled his eyes. "Right, well. Good luck with that. Nicky, if you really want to find out how to become an Extraordinary, you come find me. I'll show you things these guys won't even begin to tell you."

And with that, he got up and walked away. Nick had to admit it was a pretty epic exit.

It didn't hurt that Owen looked pretty okay in those jeans.

But Nick didn't have time to think about that now. He had *support*.

"Okay!" he said, grinning so wide, his face hurt. "Operation Turn Nick into an Extraordinary and Live Happily Ever After with Shadow Star in a Villa Off the Coast of Italy Where We Feed Each Other Grapes by Hand is underway!" He paused, considering. "I might need to work on the name of the operation, but you get the idea. Let's do this thing!"

The bell rang.

"After school gets out," Nick said hastily. "Because education is important, and my dad will murder me if I don't get at least a B average. I have to go. My class is on the opposite end of campus. Bye!"

7

Even though Nick had the support of his closest friends and an operation planned (at least in name only), it wasn't until the weekend that he was able to get things going. Not because he didn't *want* to start sooner (oh lord, did he) but because apparently junior year meant the teachers decided there should be at least forty-six hours of homework every night. Nick often wondered what happened in their childhoods to make them want to grow up and make his life miserable.

Not only did they ask for essays and warn of evils-to-come such as pop quizzes, they were also telling the students they needed to start thinking of their *futures*. Nick didn't know how to explain that he was trying to do just that, but they were getting in his way. Sure, they were talking about things like colleges and vocational schools, and Nick was more focused on being able to conduct electricity through his fingertips, but still. It was easier to think about being an Extraordinary than it was to think about getting older.

Then Dad had a rare Saturday off, so they'd gotten pizza from Tony's for an early lunch, sitting outside on the ancient tables, watching people go by, making up stories about who they were and where they were coming from and where they were going. It was something they'd done since Nick could remember. And Before, Mom had laughed and laughed at some of the stuff they'd come up with. She'd said they were the most creative people she'd ever known, and that she thought Nick would grow up to be an author one day.

It'd taken time After to—it hadn't been easy. Nick had been confused and angry and scared, and Dad had been hollow-eyed and barely speaking. There were times Nick hadn't seen him for days, their schedules so opposite, it was like they were merely roommates, and there'd been a moment when he'd been unable to sleep, his thoughts racing, thinking that he *hated* his father. He'd *hated* him for not protecting Mom even though he'd been nowhere near the bank when it'd happened, hated him for leaving Nick alone when he needed him the most. Hated him for not being strong enough. Hated him for saying, no, Nicky, no you can't see her, kid, you can't, it's better off you remember her as she was. Then she came home in an urn, nothing but a pile of ashes that Nick couldn't believe had once been his mother. They'd spread the ashes near the lighthouse, neither of them speaking.

It had gotten better, albeit slowly. Nick knew Cap had something to do with it, because suddenly Dad was home all the time, saying with an awkward shrug that it was a forced vacation. It'd lasted a few months, and they'd had to learn how to be the two of them in the same space where there'd once been three.

Things were better now, leading to days like today when it was just the two of them. They got back to the house, leftover pizza in a cardboard box. And there, sitting on the front steps of their old row house, was Nova City's chief of police himself.

"Huh," Dad said, glancing down at his watch. "He's early."

Nick was suddenly nervous. The last time Cap had been here had been right before the *forced vacation,* and though Nick had been upstairs, he'd kept his ear to the floor, hearing words like *I don't have a choice here, Aaron,* and *you were out of line* and *you punched a* witness, *for Christ's sake* and *you're lucky you're not getting fired. It's a demotion. Beat cop. I went to the mat for you, Aaron. I can't keep you in Homicide. You're a good cop. But you went too far here. You need to think of Nick. Take the offer. It's better than having nothing at all. It's either this or you look for a job in private security.*

Yeah. So the last time Cap had been here hadn't been the best.

Which was probably why Nick started breathing heavily, his fore-head sweating.

"Nicky?" he heard his dad ask, concern in his voice.

Nick swallowed thickly, his fingers twitching at his side, always moving. "Is he—is he here to—"

To give bad news, he was trying to say, but couldn't get the words out.

Dad was in front of him, balancing the pizza box in one hand, and his other on the back of Nick's neck. "What are you—oh. *Oh.* No. No, Nick. He's here to have a beer and watch the baseball game. I know your friends are coming over, or I would have invited you to watch with us."

Nick nodded, trying to work his muscles loose. "Sorry," he muttered. "I wasn't thinking."

Dad shook him gently. "Nah. That's just it. You *were* thinking. And that's okay. It's my fault. Completely slipped my mind that he was coming. I should have told you. I'm the one who's sorry."

Nick winced. "You don't need to apologize."

Dad sighed. "Yeah. I think I do. I know you're trying, kid. I see that, and I appreciate it. And I need you to know that I'm trying too, okay? My fault. Won't happen again."

Nick felt weird, off-kilter. "I'm not fragile."

Dad rolled his eyes. "I know. I figured that out the first time I dropped you on your head and it made a little dent. You didn't even cry."

Nick glared up at him. "What do you mean, *the first time*? There was more than once?"

"Being a parent is hard. Kids are slippery."

"Baseball is stupid."

"You were adopted. Didn't even cost anything. You were in a box filled with free kittens outside of a bodega. We almost went with the calico."

"You're not funny," Nick mumbled, though that was probably a good idea for an origin story. He could be Calico Man . . . or something. "I don't know why you insist on thinking you have a sense of humor. Oh, hey. Idea. I'll watch the baseball game with you and Cap, and you won't complain if I have a beer."

"Sure."

Nick's eyes widened. "Really?"

"No."

"But you—oh my *god.* Okay, what if I had just a sip?"

Dad sized him up. "You'd have to stay for all nine innings. Longer, if it goes into overtime."

Nick threw his hands up. "Nothing's worth that. I refuse. Baseball sucks."

"You really don't know how to negotiate, do you?"

"I haven't had to learn, because you usually give me every-thing—I mean, no, Father, whatever are you talking about?"

"Uh-huh. I'm on to you, kid."

"As you should be," Cap said, groaning as he rose to his feet. "Keep an eye on this one. He's either going to do great things or turn to a life of petty crime. Jury's still out."

"Most likely petty crime," Nick told him. "Because then I'd get to see your pretty face every day."

Cap reached out with a big hand and ruffled Nick's hair. Nick scowled.

Cap grinned at him, his mustache looking as if his lips were spreading wings. Nick hoped one day he would be capable of epic facial hair. He'd tried to grow a beard over the summer, but he'd somehow only gotten one weird, gnarly hair coming out of his chin. He thought about keeping it but realized it probably wouldn't do if he ever met Shadow Star.

Good thing, then, since the alley rescue happened. Shadow Star probably wouldn't have posed for a picture if he'd had that chin hair.

Dad shook Cap's hand. "Come on in. Sorry we made you wait."

"No big deal," Cap said, grunting as he climbed the remaining steps. "I was early. Missus made me walk. Doctor's talking her ear off about *controlling cholesterol levels,* which means that I have to choke down whatever nasty concoction she found on the internet." He glanced back at Nick. "You don't know any vegans, do you, Nicky?"

"No, sir."

"Good. Keep it that way. They can't be trusted. But what she doesn't know can't hurt her, right? A beer sounds good right about now."

"She already called me," Dad said from the kitchen. "I picked up low-calorie beer for you."

"That woman," Cap muttered. "Meddles in everything. Still gay, Nicky?"

"Yeah. They say I'll never be rid of it. Apparently, my body is riddled with homo—"

Cap waved a hand at him. "Yeah, yeah. I hear you. You're lucky. You can get yourself a man and not have to deal with all this nonsense."

Nick frowned. "I don't think that's how it works."

"Maybe I'll give it a go," Cap said, rubbing his mustache. "My secretary says your dad is dreamy, whatever that means. Think I got a shot?"

Nick stared at him in horror. "Why would you *say* that?"

"So I could see the look on your face," Cap said, shaking his head. "Oh, Nicky, don't ever change."

Dad came out of the kitchen, two beers in hand. He paused in the entryway to the den, eyes narrowing. "Do I even want to know?"

"Having some guy talk," Cap said, patting Nick on the back. "Ain't that right?"

"You can't marry Cap," Nick said to his dad. "Not only is that a conflict of interest for your job, it's gross. He can't be my stepdad!"

Cap laughed, bending over and slapping his knee.

Dad gaped.

The doorbell rang.

"I'll get it," Nick shouted, hurrying toward the door where hopefully his salvation awaited. He didn't want to see Dad and Cap cuddling on the couch.

Seth was standing on the tiny porch, shuffling from side to side. He wore khakis and a wool pullover that looked really soft.

"Why do you still ring the doorbell? You're here almost as much as I am."

"It's polite," Seth muttered, shoving his way past Nick into the house. "Just because you tromp into my house—"

"Excuse you, I don't *tromp*. I don't even know what that is!"

"—doesn't mean I do the same. My aunt says hi, by the way. She wants me to remind you that she needs you to come over and eat all her cookies so she can make more."

Nick closed the door behind them. "Why don't you eat them?"

He'd seen Seth polish off an entire batch of peanut butter cookies in one sitting. Granted, that had been a few years ago, but still. It was impressive. The peanut butter farts later that night hadn't been as impressive. Nick had almost died.

"I don't eat much of that stuff anymore," Seth said.

"Oh. Why?"

"Don't want to."

"Huh." Nick eyed him up and down. He still looked like Seth. Yeah, he was taller, and maybe his face was thinner than it'd been before, but— "There's pizza, if you want it. Leftovers. Dad and me went to Tony's."

"Nah," Seth said. "I had boiled chicken and spinach for lunch."

Nick made a face. "That sounds terrible. And speaking of terrible, Cap is here, and I think he's going gay for my dad."

"I don't . . . what does that even *mean*?"

"Right? I have no idea! But they're on a date, and—"

Seth glanced toward the living room. "Isn't Cap married?"

"Well, yeah. But that doesn't mean he can't have a side piece."

Seth's head snapped back toward Nick. "You just called your dad a side piece."

Nick felt the blood leave his face. "Oh my god."

"Why would you say that?"

"I don't know!"

"Ugh," Seth said, face in his hands like he couldn't get the image out of his head. "Ick. Gross. No. No."

"Are you two done?" Dad called from the living room. "It's funny how you think we can't hear every single word you're saying."

"Wow," Nick said. "Glad to know you think eavesdropping is okay. Rude."

"I'm a cop, kid. I see and hear everything."

"And I'm a law-abiding citizen. I know my rights. You need to have probable cause to do—"

"He's going to make a good cop," Cap told Dad. Then, "Except maybe we won't give him a gun."

"He's not even allowed to have a Taser," Dad muttered.

"Whatever," Nick said. "I don't want to interrupt your weird man date. We're going upstairs. Seth, come on." He was halfway up the stairs with Seth trailing after him when his dad called his name. He peered over the banister.

Dad was looking up at him, head resting on the back of the couch. He seemed loose and relaxed, and it made Nick happy for reasons he couldn't quite explain. But then he said something so confounding, Nick didn't know what to do with it. "Keep the door open, okay?"

"Uh. Okay? Why? It's Seth."

"Nick."

"Oh my god, *fine*. Then *you* should keep *your* door open because it's Cap and . . . okay, that doesn't totally make sense since you're in the living room, but the point remains the same."

"Regret saying that yet?" Dad asked Cap.

"Not even a little," Cap said, grimacing after sipping his beer.

"Have fun with your boring sport that takes forever for anything to actually happen!" Nick hollered as he made his way to the second floor.

"They all wear tight pants," Dad called after him. "Seems like it'd be right up your alley."

Nick tripped on the stairs. "Ow, you son of a— We just had a discussion about how you're not supposed to try and have a sense of humor!"

"I made you, didn't I?"

"Whatever," Nick grumbled, rubbing his shin. He glanced back at Seth. "You coming?"

Seth was flushed, but then, their air conditioning was on the fritz again, so Nick didn't question it as Seth stared up at him. "Are you actually going to reach the top of the stairs anytime soon?"

Nick scoffed. "I don't know why people think you're not sarcastic. It's all I hear from you. It's like you're two separate people sometimes."

"You have no idea."

Nick threw open the door to his room and dramatically collapsed on the bed, giving his shin time to heal. He didn't think it was broken, but it was probably a close thing. He needed to stay off his feet if he was going to go through with becoming an Extraordinary. He had to be in tip-top shape to pull this off.

"What is that?" Seth asked, eyes wide.

"What?" Nick looked to where he was pointing. "Oh, that's my idea board. I read on *Cosmo* that having an idea board helps to make planning easier."

"Why were you reading articles on *Cosmo*?"

"I don't even know. One moment, I was reading about diamond mines in Latin America, and the next, I'm following step-by-step instructions on making an idea board on *Cosmo*."

"I don't think you know how you get to some of the places you do."

Nick shrugged. "That's pretty much the story of my life. You sound like you're judging me. And *Cosmo* said that people who judge my idea board aren't going to be supportive in the long run. Also, I took a quiz on *BuzzFeed*, and apparently, my ideal sandwich has Manchego on it and I should be an airline pilot. I don't even know what Manchego is, and I don't know if I want it on my sandwich. And planes have too many buttons that I'd have to press."

"It's a Spanish cheese made from sheep's milk," Seth said, studying Nick's idea board.

Nick frowned. "I don't know if I want to eat cheese made from sheep. And I feel like we need to talk about dairy in general. Who was the first guy that decided to squeeze the thing hanging off an animal and drink whatever came out? Because you *know* it was a guy. A woman would never be that dumb. Do you think he was dared to do it by his caveman friends? Like, they started with cattle and then worked their way to a saber-toothed—"

"Nick."

"Right," Nick said, relieved. "I don't know how much longer I would have gone with that." He pushed himself up from the bed, testing his weight on his grotesquely injured leg. It barely caused a twinge. Maybe his power could be super healing. "It's pretty amazing, right? If *Cosmo* has proven anything, it's that I have the best ideas to put on idea boards."

And he did. Nick could humbly admit that his idea board was a thing of beauty. It was a corkboard that used to hold up pictures and articles of Shadow Star that he'd kept hidden in his closet and absolutely did not pull out when no one was home and sigh dreamily at it.

(It was. It was that same board. He'd taken down the Shadow Star stuff and placed it in a shoebox on a shelf, next to the autograph.)

Now, there was a sheet of paper at the top of the board emblazoned with: OPERATION TURN NICK INTO AN EXTRAORDINARY AND LIVE HAPPILY EVER AFTER WITH SHADOW STAR IN A VILLA OFF THE COAST OF ITALY WHERE WE FEED EACH OTHER GRAPES BY HAND. The font was small because that was a lot of words.

Underneath, there were printouts of all the world's greatest superheroes. Spider-Man. Superman. Batman. Wolverine. The Hulk. Wonder Woman. Shadow Star. Psylocke. Captain America. Midnighter. Batwoman. Flash. Rorschach. Northstar. Krypto, though he was a dog, and by that point, Nick had been printing off everything just because he could.

"What do all of these beings have in common?" Nick asked.

Seth waved a hand at the board. "Aside from Shadow Star, they're all fictional?"

"What? No, that's not—well, *yeah,* that's true, but that's not—ugh. Why do you have to be so literal all the time?"

"I'm literally telling you what I see."

Nick rolled his eyes. "That's because you have no imagination. You're lucky you have me."

"I know," Seth said, and he was so earnest about it, Nick's palms got a little sweaty. "But maybe tell me why."

"Because I can see things that others can't. Like big-picture stuff." Nick looked at his creation. "It's not *only* fictional characters, though. See?" He went to the board, pointing at different pictures he'd printed off. "Primate Girl. The American Patriot, though he was a dick. The White Rhino because that dude could destroy anything he charged at. Guardian, because they're mysterious and cool. The Galavanter, though she was pretty much like a kid's birthday party clown who could expel helium from her lungs, but who am I to judge?" He frowned. "Okay, maybe I went a little overboard with it. But you know that's how my brain works. I can be a little crazy, sometimes."

Seth scowled at him. "I don't like it when you say that. You're not crazy. You're fine the way you are."

His mom had told him the same thing. And now that she was gone, it was Seth who understood him more than anyone else in the world, had seen through the tornado of words that was Nick Bell, even when they were just kids. Yeah, other kids had given Nick crap for being all over the place, but Seth had been overweight and gotten it almost as bad. Nick was too young then to understand the idea of cruelty, but he knew people could be mean, even if they couldn't really explain *why* they were doing so.

It'd gotten easier when Gibby came along. And the other kids had grown up too; what had once been bullying became indifference, and Nick and his friends essentially faded into the background. They still got shit every now and then, but if Nick had his way, they wouldn't have to worry about anything like that again. No one would mess with them if he was an Extraordinary.

"Maybe that's my superpower," Nick said, trying to dispel the annoyance on Seth's face. "Maybe because my brain is wired different, it'll lead to ESP or the ability to explode things with my mind. I'm probably already at the next stage of human evolution, which means that I'm better than almost everyone else."

The look on Seth's face faded, though not as much as Nick would have liked. "You *are* better than everyone else."

Nick's hands were really clammy today. He wiped them on his jeans. "I'm glad you see that. It makes our friendship easier when you can recognize how awesome I am."

Nick was almost proud of how quickly things became awkward. He didn't think it'd ever happened this fast before.

He coughed and waved at the board. "So, ideas!"

Seth looked back at Nick's creation. "You don't have Pyro Storm up there."

"Well, yeah. He's not a hero. He's a villain. I don't want to become a villain. I don't know how to laugh maniacally or do something nefarious. I'm far too pure. The only reason I have someone like the American Patriot up there is to remind me of how *not* to be."

"But you always talk about how muscular Pyro Storm is."

Nick was scandalized. "I do not."

"Uh, you realize I beta read for you, right? You talk about his thighs all the time."

"That's because his costume accentuates his assets," Nick said, moving until he stood next to Seth in front of the board. "But you can look nice and still be a douchebag. They're not mutually exclusive."

"Like Owen."

"Exactly."

"But you still—"

Nick slapped a hand over Seth's mouth. "We shouldn't talk about it if we don't have to. Consider it a lapse in judgment that'll never happen again."

Seth arched an eyebrow at him.

And since Nick was fluent in Seth eyebrow-speak, he said, "I'm serious. Never again. I don't care how good he looks in those red pants he owns. Been there, done that."

Seth shoved Nick's hand away. "Those pants aren't *that* great."

"Yeah, try saying that again when you're staring at him from behind—why are we even talking about this?"

Seth scowled at him. "Because he flirts with you all the time, and sometimes you look at him like you don't know if you want to punch him or kiss him."

"Again, not mutually exclusive. But he broke up with *me,* remember? And it wasn't like we were ever really dating to begin with. We were . . . I don't know. Make-out buddies, or whatever." Nick winced. "Wow. That makes me sound easy."

"I know. We were all there to witness it."

Nick shoved Seth. "Don't be weird. Just because you haven't kissed anyone—"

"What makes you think I haven't?"

"—doesn't mean you get . . . to . . . tell—wait, what?"

"What makes you think I haven't kissed anyone?" Seth repeated.

Call it, Doctor. Time of death: 1:37 in the afternoon. Cause? Seth Gray. A strange, twisted knot in Nick's chest began to tighten, his hands still sweaty. Rationally, Nick knew that it was possible that Seth could have someone who wanted to kiss him. And if he *really* thought about it, of course people should want to kiss Seth. He was funny and smart, and when he smiled, it was like literal sunshine. He could recite pi to the 126th digit, owned a bonsai tree that he'd managed to keep alive for seven years, once climbed a fire escape to rescue a trapped cat near the park, and when Nick was sick with the flu a few years back, Seth had brought him his homework, medicine, and the latest issues of Marvel's attempt at an event series that was supposed to change the face of the world but in actuality had made Captain America look like a Hydra agent, which made Nick's illness worse until he was convinced he was going to die.

Add in the fact that Seth wore bow ties and ascots, so *yes*, someone would want to kiss him.

In fact, who wouldn't?

Well shit. What the hell was he supposed to say now? He went with the first thing that popped into his head. "Oh. That's . . . nice."

Seth shrugged as if he hadn't just dropped a bomb on him. "I suppose."

"So . . . nice."

Seth squinted at him. "You okay?"

Nick nodded furiously. "Fine. Great. Wonderful."

"Good. So, idea board?"

Focus. Focus. Don't think about Seth's— "Um. Right. So. Idea board. I'll . . . talk about it. Because that's the thing to do. Right now. With you. And I—okay, I can't do this. Who did you kiss?"

Seth patted Nick's arm. "I don't kiss and tell."

"What?"

"It doesn't matter."

That terrible thought struck Nick once again. "Do you have a secret girlfriend and/or boyfriend?"

"No, Nicky. I don't have a secret girlfriend and/or boyfriend. I already told you that."

Nick stepped closer, staring at his friend. He leaned forward until their faces were inches apart. Seth's breath smelled like toothpaste. Nick's probably smelled like pepperoni, which, in retrospect, probably wasn't the best thing to be breathing on someone, but there wasn't time to worry about that now.

Seth didn't move away. His eyes widened a little. He licked his lips. He had nice lips. Really nice. Nick didn't know why he hadn't noticed that before.

Nick whispered, "Then who did you—"

"Your dad told me the door needed to be kept open," Gibby said from behind them. "I laughed at him, but now I see why."

Nick screamed as he jumped, almost falling to the floor.

"I didn't know his voice could go that high," Jazz said, looking over Gibby's shoulder. "He could be a diva. Or make a living doing impressions of a cat getting strangled."

"I don't think that's a thing."

"Anything is a thing if you want it to be," Jazz said, pushing past her girlfriend and into Nick's room. "My grandma told me that. And *she* married into nineteen million dollars, outlived her husband who cheated on her with a badminton instructor named Edward, and then turned it into thirty million."

Gibby sighed. "I'll never understand that kind of money."

"Neither does she," Jazz said. "Which is why she's given half of it away to save the whales. She really does like the whales."

"Speaking of whales," Gibby said, eyeing Seth and Nick deviously. "*Moby-Dick* and all that."

Nick blinked. "What are you talking about? That book was terrible. I've never read it, but I did see the Chris Hemsworth movie that was based on it, and even he couldn't make me care."

"Seth?" Gibby asked sweetly. Well, sweetly for *her*, which meant it wasn't that sweet.

"Shut up," he mumbled. "I have no idea what you're talking about."

"Uh-huh."

Nick didn't know what Gibby was doing now, but it was distracting, and he couldn't have that. "Did you bring me what I asked you for?"

Jazz sat on the edge of Nick's bed, putting her Coach purse on her lap. "Well, here's the thing. I found one in the backyard shed where the landscapers keep the tools. I got dirt on my forehead. It was wonderful. I felt like *Indiana Jones and the Temple of Doom.* And in the back, I saw a gigantic web. Like, the biggest I'd ever seen."

Nick shuddered at the thought.

"Ah," Jazz said, watching him. "Now I know why you couldn't get one by yourself. I didn't know you were scared of spiders."

"I'm not *scared* of them," Nick retorted. "I would just rather they didn't exist near me at any point in my life."

"Spiders are good for the ecosystem," she said, and Nick wondered why anyone would think she wasn't smart. "They eat the bad bugs." She reached a hand into her purse.

"I'm with Nick on this one," Gibby said, taking a step back. "I don't want that thing near me."

"Why did you have Jazz bring you a spider?" Seth asked.

"Because I need it," Nick replied. "It's Phase One of Operation Turn Nick into an Extraordinary and—"

"You really need to come up with a better name," Gibby muttered, studying the idea board. "And would you look at that. Shadow Star's picture, front and center. How interesting. Wouldn't you say that's interesting, Seth? Shadow Star, being front and center?"

Seth glared at her. "I have no opinion about it one way or another."

Gibby snorted. "Are you sure about that? Because if I were you, I'd—"

Jazz pulled a specimen jar out of her purse. "Okay, but you all rudely interrupted my story and didn't let me finish. That's not nice. There was the gigantic spiderweb, but—"

"Got it!" Nick crowed, snatching the plastic jar out of Jazz's hand. The thing inside that was most certainly *not* a spider scrabbled along the side of the jar, and Nick almost shrieked and threw it across the room. Somehow, he was able to call upon all his bravery at once and resisted. Instead, he set it down on his desk next to the idea board and backed away slowly.

"What is that?" he asked, and his voice wasn't high-pitched, no matter what anyone might say otherwise.

"If I can *finish*, maybe you'll find out," Jazz said, mouth twisted down. "As I was saying, I didn't see a spider, but I did see something else. It was caught in the web, and it was *struggling*. I felt really bad about it, so I saved it from the web like Indy saved himself from having his heart ripped out of his chest." She frowned. "Can you believe that movie is only rated PG?"

"That's because other than R, another rating didn't exist," Seth said. "That movie was partly the reason they came up with—"

"What is it?" Nick said, shoving Gibby toward the jar. "I think it hissed at me."

Gibby glared at him before taking a step toward his desk. "It's . . . It's a . . . It's a . . ."

"Cricket," Jazz said. "Obviously. What are you going to do with it?" She had a tiny compact mirror out and was puckering her lips at her reflection.

Nick stared at her. "You brought me a cricket."

She closed the compact. "At great risk to my life. I don't think you sound very grateful."

Nick remembered the way the jock's fingers had bent awkwardly and said, "No, no. I am. I don't know if it'll work with a cricket. I don't even know what a cricket *does*."

"We don't even know what you're trying to do," Seth pointed out.

Ah! Nick's moment to shine! "Spider-Man was bitten by a radioactive spider, right?" he said excitedly. He couldn't wait for the forthcoming praise to be lavished upon him. "As shown by the fact that they've rebooted the movies four hundred times—he's in Oscorp and breaks off from the convenient tour group and gets bitten on the hand by a spider that's a part of unsanctioned experiments. Which, if you think about it, potentially opens up the multibillion-dollar company to a lawsuit in addition to turning Peter Parker into a superhero, but I digress. Also, I feel bad for Andrew Garfield. He was a good Spider-Man trapped in terrible movies. Sure, the new guy is good, but poor Andrew. His hair is so curly."

"I'm not going to like this, am I?" Seth muttered.

"No, because you're going to *love* it. Now, I don't have access to radioactive isotopes. I don't even know where you can get them. I tried looking online, but apparently you can't just buy them whenever you want. I should mention that I've probably been flagged for that search by the CIA or the NSA, but we'll worry about that later."

"I can't wait," Gibby said dryly. "The idea of you having anything radioactive should be reason enough for its limited access."

Nick ignored her. "So, I thought, what can I possibly do to get myself a radioactive spider? Then I figured it out." He paused for dramatic effect. "I'll nuke it in the microwave."

He waited for thunderous applause.

He got thunderous silence.

Maybe they hadn't understood. "The spider. It'll go into the microwave. For science."

"What," Gibby said flatly.

"Microwaves use RF radiation," Nick explained patiently. "And that's a form of electromagnetic radiation. Which is *radiation*. Right? And so when the spider is exposed to the radiation, it will become radioactive and bite me, and I will become a Spider-Man rip-off. And I promise up front I'll avoid the weird emo-dancing Tobey Maguire tragedy that made no sense. I don't even know how to dance, so we should be good there."

More silence.

He understood that it was complex. People had a hard time understanding the way his brain worked. Most days, he was on a completely different level, though he tried not to think that way too much because that made him sound like a conceited dick, and he really wasn't.

So he gave them time to process, because he was a good friend.

Jazz spoke first. "Okay. I can see it. Problem. It's not a spider. It's a cricket."

Nick tried not to glare at her. "And whose fault is that?"

She shrugged. "Maybe next time say thank you when someone gives you something."

"Thank you for not getting me what I asked for."

"You're welcome. So, you won't be Spider-Man. You'll be Cricket-Man. And your superpower will be rubbing your legs together to make noise late at night when everyone is trying to sleep to remind them you exist and are very annoying."

"Yes," Gibby breathed. "Yes to this. Yes to all of it. Oh my god, *yes*. This is so stupid. I can't wait. White people are *freaky*."

Nick closed his eyes and took a deep breath. One part of the article on idea boards told him that people might not initially grasp the concept, and that he needed to be patient. Great ideas were often born of frustration, which was a feeling he knew well. When he'd calmed himself down with a breathing exercise he'd also found on *Cosmo* (in addition to finding out sixteen ways to please a man that involved things he was *not* prepared to read), he opened his eyes. "I appreciate your support," he said evenly. "Does anyone else know what crickets are good for?"

"They eat plants and sometimes meat," Gibby said, though it sounded like she was struggling not to laugh. "And that chirping sound is used to scare away other males, and to find a mate." She grinned smugly at Seth. "I wonder what would happen if Nick chirped with his legs."

"This is the dumbest conversation we've ever had," Seth muttered.

"They can jump really high," Nick said, trying to find a way to salvage this debacle. "So, my superpower could be that I jump over things." It wasn't ideal, but he could work with that. Leap tall buildings in a single bound? Completely original.

"And your chirping could be a supersonic sound wave that knocks people through walls," Jazz said, eyes wide. "Once you landed from jumping really high, you could lie down in front of the bad guys and rub your legs at them."

Gibby cackled, her arms clutched around her middle.

"Okay," Nick said, pushing through his annoyance. "This isn't so bad. Mostly. Next step. I would be Cricket-Man. And since I'll be shipped with Shadow Star, we need to discuss our ship name." That was the part he cared about the most.

"CricketStar," Gibby wheezed, bending over.

"ShadowCricket," Nick decided, because Gibby was the worst. "It's . . . okay. I mean, sure, it could be better, but still. It sounds like—Gibby, I swear to god if you don't stop laughing, I probably won't do anything about it, but I *could*."

Gibby continued to laugh, because everyone knew Nick's threats were empty, no matter how much he bared his teeth.

"So, let me get this straight," Seth said. "You want to take this cricket and put it into the microwave. You want to nuke the cricket and then have it bite you."

"Yes," Nick said, grateful he had a best friend like Seth who understood him. "That's exactly what I want to do. Thank you, Seth, for being the way you are. It's truly—"

Seth sighed. "Nicky, I don't know why I need to explain to you how many things are wrong with that."

Nick frowned. "What are you talking about?"

"First, crickets don't bite people."

"Wrong," Jazz said, looking down at her phone. "According to this website on crickets called CricketsAreCool.com, it's rare, but they do." She wrinkled her nose. "Though apparently they carry a significant number of diseases. But it's okay! None of them are fatal to humans. If anything, maybe that will be a part of your superpowers. In addition to shock-wave legs, you'll be able to make people moderately ill."

Gibby lay on the bed, tears streaming down her face as she rocked back and forth.

"*Second,*" Seth said through gritted teeth, "if you put a bug in the microwave, it'll die."

"Not if I only make it for five seconds or so," Nick said. "I think."

"Third, isn't torturing animals the first sign of becoming a serial killer?"

That gave Nick pause. "Huh. I hadn't thought of it that way. But it's a bug that scares me, so therefore, it's inherently evil. I don't think crickets qualify as animals because they don't have souls or feelings. Like, you hear about dog ghosts and tiger ghosts, but you never hear about bug ghosts, right? Also, to become a serial killer, I think you have to wet the bed with alarming frequency and have had a head injury at some point in your life."

"You wet the bed at my house when you were seven and tried to tell me you got juice in the middle of the night and accidentally spilled it on the bed."

That set Gibby off all over again as Nick stared at Seth in horror. "You monster! And it *was* juice!"

"Juice that smelled like urine," Seth retorted.

"Why didn't you tell me you didn't believe me?" Nick demanded. "All these years, I thought I'd gotten away with it. What other secrets are you keeping from me?" He pointed at Seth, finger trembling. "Does this have to do with your secret girlfriend and/or boyfriend? It's like I don't even know you anymore."

That made Gibby stop laughing. She immediately sat up just as Jazz's mouth dropped open. "Your secret *what*?"

Seth crossed his arms. "I don't have—it's not like that. I don't—ugh."

"We were talking about kissing," Nick said.

"You were?" Jazz asked. "Oh my god, finally. Tell me everything."

Nick blinked. "Wait, what? I told him I'd kissed Owen, and then *he* said he'd kissed someone, but wouldn't tell me who."

"Oh," Jazz said, shoulders drooping. "That's . . . not what I thought this was going to be about. How disappointing."

"Who did you kiss?" Gibby asked Seth. "And also, followup: What other secrets do you have that you're not telling us about? Maybe something you've kept hidden in the—"

"Will you excuse us for a second?" Seth asked, and before Nick could stop him, he'd grabbed Gibby by the arm and pulled her from the room.

"Strange," Jazz said in the silence that followed. "I wonder what that's about."

"You really don't know about Seth kissing anyone?" Nick asked, glaring at the empty doorway.

"Would it matter if I did? He can do what he wants. Why do you care so much?"

"We tell each other everything."

She fanned out her fingers in front of her, checking her red polish. "Really? That's the only reason?"

Nick looked at her blankly. "What other reason is there?"

She sighed as she dropped her hand. "I thank my lucky stars every day I'm not a man. So much bluster for nothing."

"We can be pretty stupid," Nick agreed. "But I still have no idea what you're talking about."

"I worked really hard to get that cricket."

He glanced at the jar. The cricket was hopping up and down. He felt bad. "I know."

"And now you want to put it in the microwave."

"That's the plan."

"I don't want you to be a serial killer. Torturing animals and wetting the bed. A decade from now, I'll be interviewed for some news show, and I'll cry on camera and everything when I have to say no one saw it coming. Why would you do that to me, Nicky? Do you *want* to see my makeup ruined on national television from your maximum-security jail cell?"

Damn her. She knew exactly what to say to get through to him. He didn't know why he was so surprised, but maybe that was part of it: Jasmine Kensington—perhaps more than any other person he knew—could cut through to the heart of the matter with the simplest of ease. He hadn't known what to expect from her when Gibby first brought her over to their lunch table, announcing in no uncertain terms they were dating, and that was the way it was going to be. He'd fallen prey to his own misguided characterizations, initially believing Jazz was nothing more than a somewhat empty-headed yet totally hot cheerleader. He'd been wrong in that regard and kicked himself for being so quick to judge. It'd taken time, sure, but change often did. They were three, and then they'd become four, but it wasn't until this past summer when Seth had been busy almost every day and Gibby was out of town doing hippie things that Nick got one-on-one time with her and saw the splendor that was his friend.

It'd been slightly awkward at first, texting her to see if she wanted to hang out. She'd immediately responded yes thank you ur cool, and though Nick thought she was an excellent judge of character, he'd worried they wouldn't have anything to talk about that didn't revolve around Gibby or Seth. Or worse, Owen.

But she'd surprised him, as was her way. She wasn't the smartest person in the world, yet she never claimed to be. She was happy just . . . being. Nick didn't understand it, not really, but he thought maybe he didn't have to. She didn't expect him to be anything but who he was, and Nick could count on one hand the number of people who were like her.

And it *had* been awkward, at least the first few days. He'd worried he'd say something stupid that would end up somehow ruining her relationship with Gibby, and then he'd have to face *her* wrath, which terrified him down to his bones. It wasn't until Jazz had called him on a Tuesday morning mid-June to tell him she'd bought them both tickets to the latest superhero movie with slow-motion explosions and men and women in skintight uniforms that he'd realized that maybe they weren't so different after all. They'd spent the entire six-hour run time of the movie cackling at the ridiculousness of it in an empty theater, throwing popcorn at each other, and getting sticky with melted Junior Mints, shouting at the screen whenever something implausible happened for the sake of plot. Nick had gone into the movie with someone he considered a friend. He'd left with a bestie he would do anything for. If that made him easy, well. That was just fine with him.

(Which he proved to be true the next day, when she invited him to go along while she took her mother's toy poodle—Maria Von Trapp, an awful name for a dog, in Nick's estimation—to the groomers. The dog did not like Nick. This was made clear when it bit him on the hand and then pissed on his shoes. Jazz had made it up to him by buying him ice cream. Nick considered them even, especially when she didn't look at him in horror when he poured chocolate syrup on top of a pile of sour gummy worms, as most people did.)

"No," Nick mumbled to Jazz now, especially since he didn't like seeing anyone he loved cry, even if it meant his plan was pretty much ruined. It hurt too much when he couldn't find a way to fix it. "But what if I promise not to serial murder anyone? And besides, I've never had a head injury—"

"Concussion," Gibby said as she came back in the room. The laughter was gone from her face, and Seth trailed in behind her looking troubled. "Seventh grade. You got hit in the head while playing dodgeball because you were like an awkward baby gazelle and didn't understand how to dodge."

Nick scowled at her. "That game is so archaic. It's a middle school torture device meant for thinning out the herd. And it wasn't *that* bad of a concussion. I only had to have three follow-ups and my vision was blurry for a week and—crap."

Seth nodded solemnly. "And a cricket in the microwave will complete the trifecta. Because no matter what you think, it'll be torture for the bug, and it will die, Nicky. You can't do that to the cricket. If anything, think of the backlash if you were ever found out. Say it worked. What happens when PETA hears about your origin story? They'll come after you, even though they're hypocritical monsters."

"But," Nick said weakly, "people eat crickets in some cultures. You can get them covered in chocolate and everything."

"Yes, but they don't get tortured. What if they do have a soul? Do you want that on your conscience? And what happens if it comes back and haunts you? Do you really want a ghost cricket around forever? It'll probably chirp really loudly next to your ear and eventually drive you crazy. I don't want my best friend to go insane because of ghost crickets."

Nick looked forlornly at his idea board. *Cosmo* hadn't said anything about a rebuttal when one of your ideas could potentially make you a serial killer and/or cause you to be haunted by a ghost cricket. It should have come with a warning.

He knew he needed to be the bigger person here. He picked up the specimen jar and went to the window in his room. He pushed it open, the sounds of the street below pouring in. He didn't know how people could live in the middle of nowhere. It'd be too quiet. Nova City was like his mind, always moving. It was comforting, in a way.

"Okay, little guy," he said to the cricket, "today's your lucky day. You got a stay of execution. Be free!" He unscrewed the lid to the jar and flicked his wrist toward the window.

Except the cricket landed on the windowsill, and then immediately turned and jumped straight at Nick. Given that it was the size of a small Buick, he screamed and took a stumbling step back. It landed on his arm. He waved it wildly, trying to get it off before it could maul him.

He succeeded in that regard, but at great cost. The cricket launched itself at Gibby, who made a noise as if she got punched in the stomach, trying to push herself back on the bed and hitting her head against the wall. "No," she moaned. "Oh god, no."

The cricket landed on Nick's pillow. With a warrior's cry, Nick picked up a textbook off his desk and threw it at the cricket, only to hit Seth in the arm when he tried to reach for the bug himself.

"Ow!" Seth cried. "Why did you throw a book at me?"

"I didn't! You got in my way!"

"You're all useless," Jazz said, rolling her eyes. She stood, smoothing her skirt. She reached down and slid off one of her heels, flipped it over in a deft move, and then smashed it against Nick's pillow.

It was quiet, after.

She lifted her shoe.

There was a black, wet smudge on Nick's pillow.

"There," Jazz said, lifting her leg and sliding her heel back on. "Now that that's over with, I saw pizza downstairs, and I think I've earned a slice. If you'll excuse me."

Her hair streamed behind her as she exited the room.

"I'm sorry, Nick," Gibby said, staring after her girlfriend.

Nick sighed. "It's fine. It's just a bug—"

"No. Not about that. I'm sorry that I'm now aroused on your bed."

"Ack! Gross! Get off, get off, *get off!*"

8

"If I'm going to be haunted by ghost bugs, it will be all your fault!" Nick called as he watched Jazz and Gibby walk down the sidewalk from his house. Gibby flipped him off. Jazz waved. Those crazy kids. He hoped they made it.

Dad and Cap were in the kitchen, munching on leftover pizza. "Don't tell my wife," Cap warned him through a mouthful of sausage. "I'll arrest you, and you'll never see the sun again."

"That's police intimidation," Nick said. "I have a Tumblr with almost six hundred followers. They'll hear about this, mark my words."

"What did he say?" Cap asked Dad.

"Teenager speak," Dad said. "It's like the message board at the station."

"Oh." Cap looked at Nick. "You a snitch now?"

"You're damn—"

"Nick."

"—darn right I am," Nick said. "Gotta bring down the corruption within the Nova City Police Department. I'll be a hero."

"Speaking of being a hero," Dad said, "that was an awful lot of screaming you did for a bug."

"Jazz should have kept her mouth shut," Nick mumbled. "I'm going back upstairs so I don't have to watch two old men being weird."

"Keep the door open!" Dad called after him.

"Why are you even—? You know what? I don't have time for your nonsense." They weren't *leave the door open* friends. Seth was obviously kissing other people, much to Nick's consternation. As he climbed the stairs, he thought about all the times Seth had been busy lately or hadn't picked up the phone when Nick had called. He'd later say he was busy with volunteering, or he was doing chores for his aunt and uncle, or that he was doing prep work for the upcoming school year like a nerd, but what if . . . what if he'd . . .

What if he *did* have a secret girlfriend and/or boyfriend? That didn't sit well with Nick. Why would Seth lie about something like that?

Nick hadn't been lying when he said they told each other everything, juice/urine notwithstanding. They'd been friends forever. There was barely a time Nick could remember when Seth *hadn't* been a part of his life, especially when Before had become After. Those were hazy days, days where Nick couldn't figure out how to gather the shattered pieces of his heart to begin trying to put it back together. Days when instead of his mind running on a billion different tangents, it was strangely white, as if absent of everything that made him who he was. He was in a fog, vaguely aware that he should be angry, but unable to latch on to the rage his father felt.

For weeks After, the house had been filled with cops and detectives, their wives and husbands and partners bringing more food than could ever be consumed. Nick didn't understand the idea of casseroles for mourning. Eating was the last thing he wanted to do. People tried to coax him, but Dad had hoarsely told them to leave Nick alone. Nick tried to be grateful, but Dad's eyes were hollow, as if all his insides had been scooped out, leaving nothing but a shell of skin and bone.

Gibby had been there, and she'd hugged him and kissed him and told him that it would be okay. She smelled good and Nick had clung to her, but it wasn't exactly what he'd wanted. It wasn't exactly what he needed.

Seth *was* what he needed, though, and he'd been late, but then the door had burst open, and he'd stood there, cheeks flushed, chest heaving, eyes wide as he searched the living room until he found Nick. Nick made a wounded sound, wanting to get to Seth as soon as possible, but unable to move his arms.

Seth knew, though.

Somehow, he'd gotten Nick upstairs and put him to bed, climbing in behind him and curling around him protectively. Nick remembered thinking that he was safe, then. He was safe, and though everything Before would now be After, Seth was there with him.

He had cried, then.

Seth had whispered in his ear for the longest time, breath on Nick's neck, telling him that he was sorry, he was sorry this had happened, that he would do everything he could to make sure nothing like this ever happened again. He didn't know how yet, he told Nick, but he'd figure it out.

It'd taken a long time for things to get better.

There was still that ache in Nick's chest, a feeling that a piece of him was gone and would never come back. Nick knew he would probably always feel that way. He was allowed, the therapist had told him. Dad had forced him to go, and though Nick thought it was stupid, he'd gone with minimal complaint because Dad had almost looked hopeful. Nick was allowed to feel as he did because that was the nature of grief. He was young, and his mom being taken from them was unexpected. He would work through it, and it would get easier. Eventually.

And it had, surprisingly. He thought about her every day, spoke to her picture in a way that was probably unhealthy, but no one could take that from him. It wasn't like he thought she was *actually* listening, it just made him feel better, saying stuff out loud that he might not say otherwise.

"Okay," Nick said as he entered his room. "Phase Two of—"

And he stopped.

Seth looked up at him almost guiltily.

But Nick couldn't be bothered with that.

Because Seth had rolled up the sleeve to his oversized sweater almost to his bicep. Not only did Nick not expect to see a muscular forearm with thick veins running along the hard curl of his bicep, he most certainly didn't understand the *bruising* on Seth's arm.

Some of it looked old, mottled green and a sickly yellow.

But some of it looked *new*, the skin red and purple.

Seth quickly pulled down the sleeve of his sweater. "Hey," he said, averting his eyes. "Gibby and Jazz get off okay?"

"What happened to your arm?" Nick demanded. "Did I do

that with the book? I'm so sorry. Crap, Seth, that looks like it hurts—"

"It's fine," Seth said, smiling, though it didn't seem to reach his eyes. "It's fine. I just bumped my arm a little while ago. You didn't hurt me at all."

"Bumped your arm," Nick repeated dubiously.

Seth nodded. "Oh, yeah. You know how I am. Clumsy me. Tripped over my own feet and fell into my closet door. It's not a big deal. Barely even feel it."

Now, Nick knew he wasn't the smartest person in the world. His strengths lay in such places like idea boards and fanfiction and taking care of his dad because no one else would. But he was the son of a cop. He had a bullshit detector ingrained in his head. "Some of that looked newer than the rest."

Seth's smile faded a little. "I bumped into a lot of things."

Nick nodded slowly. It wasn't—he *knew* Seth's aunt and uncle. They were good people. Kind and caring and thought the world of Seth. He didn't think they were the type to hurt anyone, much less Seth. Or so he assumed. "You can tell me anything. You know that, right?"

Seth looked away. "I know, Nicky. I tell you everything I can."

"That."

"What?"

"What you just said. You tell me everything *you can*. What does that mean?"

Seth sighed. "Look. I'm working through some stuff right now. It's not bad. I promise. Once I figure it out, you'll be the first one I come to, okay?"

That didn't sit well with Nick. "Is someone hurting you?" he asked, hands curling into fists at his sides. "Because I swear to god, if someone is hurting you, you better tell me who it is so I can knock them into next week. If it's your secret girlfriend and/or boyfriend, that's not cool. Like, at all. You don't need to—"

Seth choked out a laugh. "I'm not being abused. I don't have a secret *anyone*."

Nick stared at him suspiciously. "You promise."

"Yeah. I promise."

"But there is something happening."

"Something is always happening, Nick. I don't think I've ever heard you scream like you did when the cricket jumped at your face."

"Shut up," Nick muttered. "It was attacking me. I did what I had to in order to defend myself."

"At least Jazz was here to spread it all over your pillow."

Nick groaned. "I'm going to have to do laundry because of her. I hate doing laundry."

"Later, though, huh? I feel like it's been a while since we've been able to hang out, just the two of us. Wanna read comic books and be stupid for a little while?"

Nick grinned at him. "That sounds awesome. We should go way back and read the Onslaught arc again. That's one of my favorites."

Seth looked relieved for reasons Nick didn't understand. "Sure, Nicky. Sounds good."

It wouldn't be until much later that Nick would realize how neatly Seth had deflected him.

It's been a while since Seth was over," Dad said that night when it was just the two of them. Cap had said he needed to get home to the missus, and Seth was going to have dinner with his aunt and uncle. He'd looked like he was going to say something else while standing on Nick's porch, but then he'd shaken his head, smiled, and said he'd text Nick later. Nick watched him walk down the sidewalk until he couldn't see him anymore. "Everything all right?"

"Yeah," Nick said, walking to the couch where his father sat. Dad had his socked feet propped up on the old coffee table. He looked relaxed, something Nick thought he needed to do more. "At least, I think so."

Dad arched an eyebrow. "What do you mean?"

Nick thought for a moment. Then, "It feels like he's keeping something from me. I don't know. I thought maybe he was dating someone, but he says he's not."

Dad snorted. "Kid, I can pretty much guarantee that he's not dating anyone else."

"Why?"

"I think he's got everything he needs already. He's just . . . biding his time, I guess. Waiting for things to become clear."

"What things?"

"Yeah. He's definitely waiting, all right."

Nick scowled. "Why is everyone always speaking in code around me?"

"I'm allowed to because I'm an adult and also your father. It's my job to be maddeningly vague."

"Well, you're doing a good job at it."

"Thanks, kid."

Nick hesitated. "The dad stuff too."

Dad smiled. "You're not so bad yourself. Wanna watch a dumb movie where things blow up in slow motion? I'll even make some popcorn, if you want."

Nick really wanted to get upstairs and start planning Phase Two of becoming an Extraordinary, but he thought maybe that could wait. There was an empty space on the couch next to his dad, and things blowing up in slow motion sounded pretty good. "I'll go put on some sweats and meet you here with the popcorn in five minutes. But god help you if there's butter or salt on it. You're not getting any younger."

Dad rolled his eyes. "You drive a hard bargain."

"Someone in this house has to."

"Deal. Get your butt moving, Nicky. We've got big plans."

Nick moved his butt.

Before he left his room to head back downstairs, he reached over and touched his mother's smile. "We're okay," he told her. "Today, we're okay."

And if that night, while lying in bed and staring at the ceiling, Nick thought about the veins in Seth's arms, well.

That was nobody else's business.

Monday mornings were bad.

Monday mornings when his dad had to work late were even worse.

But Monday mornings when his dad had to work late and Nick managed to sleep through his alarm?

All in all, it was not the greatest start to the second week of school.

"Dammit," he grumbled, trying to shove his foot into one of his Chucks while attempting to descend the stairs. There was a moment when Nick was sure he was about to tumble head over heels, but he managed to catch himself on the banister.

Because the only thing that would have made this Monday even more terrible would be if he'd fallen and broken his neck.

His phone beeped as he shouldered his bag and headed out the door, locking it quickly behind him. He pulled it out to see messages from Seth and Gibby, asking where he was. He apologized profusely to a woman pushing a stroller as he bumped into her while he typed a response, telling them to go on without him. He was already going to be late, and he didn't want them to run the risk of getting in trouble too. If he hurried, it shouldn't be too bad, but there was no way he was going to get there before the final bell rang. There was also an alert on his phone with a headline that new information had come in about a scuffle between Pyro Storm and Shadow Star in the early morning hours of Saturday, but Nick didn't have time to read it, no matter how much he wanted to. He saved the link for later.

For once, the trains were running almost on schedule, which helped, but by the time he made it to Franklin Street, he was fifteen minutes late. He thought about skipping first period entirely, but that would mean a phone call would be made, and Dad had learned rather quickly to have the calls sent to his cell phone and not the home phone where Nick could intercept any messages, especially if he switched the ringer off. It had been one of those things they'd talked about over the summer, one of the things Nick had promised he would be better about.

He decided to bite the bullet and stumble into class late. Maybe his teacher would believe the excuse that there'd been a fire on his train or a body on the tracks. It happened all the time, right?

The school was in sight. He could do this.

He was about to head for the steps when a limousine pulled up in front of the school, black and sleek, the chrome bumper glinting. Nick wondered who the hell had the kind of money that they needed to take a *limo* to school. Unless there was some important speaker today, like the mayor.

As soon as the limo came to a stop, one of the rear doors flew open, and Owen Burke stepped out, a stormy look on his face, mouth twisted in a snarl. Nick had never seen Owen look so furious before.

"You stop right there," another voice snapped from the car, and for a moment, Nick thought Owen would keep on walking.

He didn't.

His hand tightened on the strap of his backpack, and his scowl deepened.

A man climbed out of the limo. He was immaculately dressed, his expensive suit obviously tailored, his dress shoes probably costing more than Nick's entire wardrobe. He wore sunglasses, though it was mostly cloudy. His silver hair was styled short and tight against his head, and he cut an imposing figure.

Nick had only met Simon Burke once before. He'd gone to the Burke house (*house* being a bit of a misnomer—Nick didn't think any dwelling with eight bathrooms and a cleaning staff of six could qualify as just a *house*) toward the beginning of the Great Romance of Nick and Owen, unsure if he should take off his shoes. Not that he even wanted to do that because he was pretty sure one of his socks had a hole in it.

Nick had felt wholly out of place standing on marble floors, walls decorated with art that probably sold for millions but looked as if it had been painted by a particularly furious color-blind two-year-old. It was made worse when a man in a suit had taken Nick's bag and coat without a word, hanging them in a closet that looked as if it were bigger than the top floor of Nick's house.

Owen had obviously not been expecting his father to be home, and when he'd come into the foyer, cell phone firmly attached to his ear, brows furrowed angrily, he'd barely given his son a glance. Nick had wished he could just sink into the floor, but seeing as how he hadn't figured out how to do that yet, he had stood as still as he could. Which meant tapping his fingers against his side and bouncing on his heels.

It looked as if they were going to ignore each other until Simon Burke had turned toward his son and said, "I won't be home until late. Your mother has a charity . . . something, so you're on your own. Sophie's in the kitchen. She'll—" And then he'd caught sight of Nick.

Nick knew he didn't make the best first impressions. He was too twitchy, too awkward, and it didn't help that when he tried to smile while stressed, he looked as if he were about to be ill. There was nothing he could do about that, no matter how hard he tried. So, when Mr. Burke turned back to his son and asked, "Who's your little friend?" Nick said, "How do you do, your lordship."

Owen groaned.

Mr. Burke turned slowly to Nick again. "Beg pardon?"

Nick winced. "Um. Sorry. I don't know what to call you. I've never been in a house this big before, and I'm worried that I'll break something. Not that I plan on it. Your priceless heirlooms are safe with me."

"Right," Mr. Burke said, and the expression on his face looked as if he were speaking with an increasingly quarrelsome sloth. "See that you don't. I'd hate to have to sue your parents. I'm sure they wouldn't be pleased to have to deplete the meager account they call a college fund for something so . . . avoidable."

"Right," Nick said hastily. "Agreed."

"You can leave," Owen said, sounding irritated. "We're not going to do anything."

"I highly doubt that," Mr. Burke said. "At least it's a guy this time. I won't have to worry about any unwanted . . . complications." And with that, he'd turned toward the door, barking into his phone.

"Complications?" Nick asked after the door had closed again.

"Doesn't matter. Let's go up to my room."

That was Nick's only interaction with Simon Burke of Burke Tower and Burke Pharmaceuticals and Burke Fill-in-the-Blank.

He wasn't a fan, though he could totally see where Owen had

gotten his . . . Owen-ness. Both were cool and aloof and more than a little scary. They were also both hot, though Nick would *never* admit that out loud. He wondered if fear boners were going to be a thing for him for the rest of his life. He hoped not.

But seeing Simon Burke again, here, now, in front of his school, snapping at his son, certainly didn't do much to raise Nick's opinion about him. He thought about heading to class and trying to get to his seat before he could get into more trouble, but that would mean passing in front of Owen and his dad, and he didn't want their attention on him.

So he waited.

Owen turned toward his father. "What do you want?"

"What I *want* is for you to lose the attitude," his father said angrily. "You think this is a game? I don't know where you get off believing you have the run of the household, but you better course-correct that line of thought right now. Coming and going at all hours of the night like you're not just a *child* is—"

"What do you care?" Owen retorted. "It's not like you're ever there to begin with. What does it matter if I am?"

Something fierce crossed Mr. Burke's face. "You watch your tongue, Owen. It would be very easy to take everything away from you. I *made* you. You would do well to remember that. Especially since I could just as easily *unmake* you. Everything I've given you, gone in a flash. And where would you be, then?"

"You wouldn't," Owen said, voice barely above a whisper. "You need me."

Mr. Burke scoffed. "Try me. I promise you won't like what I do. Know your place. Don't make me remind you of it. I have plans for Nova City, and I won't see them derailed. It's the principle of causation. Everything you do affects me. Think, Owen, before you act. Are we clear?"

"Crystal," Owen said bitterly.

"Good." He looked over his son's shoulder up at the school, his mouth twisting in disdain. "I don't know why you insist on this place. There's a private school much closer to home that would do more for someone of your station."

"I like it here."

Mr. Burke nodded slowly. "Good to know. Because this too can be taken away. Remember that."

Owen looked like he was going to argue more, but instead, he deflated. "And my medicine? I need it."

"Not right now," Mr. Burke said. "You've had enough for the time being. Go. You've already made me late as it is."

With that, he climbed back into the limo, slamming the door behind him. A moment later, the limo pulled out into traffic.

Owen watched it disappear.

Nick waited.

And then Owen turned and looked directly at Nick.

Dammit. He thought he'd been so careful not hiding behind anything and staring at the two of them.

"Enjoy the show?" Owen asked, though his tone wasn't as harsh as it'd been with his father.

Nick sputtered. "I didn't—I wasn't trying—man, what happened to your *face*?"

There was a splotchy bruise on Owen's jaw, spreading up toward his right ear. Owen reached up and pressed into it, hissing slightly and pulling his hand away, leaving the skin white until it turned back to purple. "Got punched."

"Who punched you?"

Owen smirked at him. "Careful, Nicky. You're beginning to sound like you care, and we can't have that, can we? I already broke your heart once. Don't think we need to do it again."

Nick scowled at him. "You didn't break my heart. I was barely invested. It was a fling."

Owen reached up and patted Nick's cheek. "Sure it was. I know I'm hard to get over. Don't you worry your pretty little face over me. You should see the other guy."

"Does this have anything to do with why you didn't come to my house and help us with my plan?"

Owen shrugged. "That, and your plan sounded terrible. You want to get it right, you come talk to me. Otherwise, you can keep on doing what you're doing."

"I can do it by myself."

Owen studied him, a strange look on his face. Nick felt like squirming. "I bet you can. We'll see, won't we? Any chance you wanna ditch the rest of the day? I don't know that I want to be here right now. Whaddya say? For old time's sake."

Nick shook his head. "I can't. I'm already late, and I promised my dad that—"

"Right, right. Dear ol' Dad. You're supposed to be a good boy this year, aren't you? Well, far be it from me to aid in the corruption of Nicholas Bell even more than I already have. Run along, Nicky. Go be a good boy. Time waits for no blah, blah, blah."

Nick started to turn toward doors of the school, but then he hesitated. "What about you?"

Owen looked surprised, and his face softened slightly. Gone was the cocky swagger he wore like a shield. This unmasking was something Nick had only seen a handful of times before, mostly when it was just the two of them, hands roaming to dangerous territories, lips chapped and swollen, and Nick could have sworn that Owen was almost fond of him. "You worried about me, Nicky?"

"I worry about all my friends."

"Yeah. You do, don't you? I'm fine. Just need a *me* day, I think. Some self-care." Owen reached up and squeezed the back of Nick's neck. And then the mask slid firmly back in place, a cocky twist to his lips. "Get inside, Nicky. Before I think you're waiting for me to take you away from this place."

With that, Owen spun on his heels, whistling brightly as he headed down the sidewalk.

Without thinking, Nick called after him, "What medicine was your dad supposed to give you?"

Owen didn't look back.

Nick watched as he disappeared into Nova City.

There was a text from his dad as he headed toward the cafeteria. Got an email from the school. You late today?

Nick groaned. Of course he already got told on. yeah alarm didn't go off my bad only missed 20 mins of 1st period

A moment later: We talked about this Nick.

yeah just an accident sorry won't happen again

See that it doesn't. Love you.

u too

His dad was disappointed. Nick could tell even through those few short words, and he hated it. Sure, he'd been up late the night before researching what his next steps should be on his journey to become an Extraordinary, but still. It wasn't going to be like last year. Dad had tried to put it all on Owen in the end, telling him that Owen was a bad influence, but Nick hadn't let him. Nick had made his own decisions, however bad they might have been. Owen had been more than a willing participant, but it wasn't like he'd pressured Nick into anything.

Dad had called earlier today, apologizing for waking him, telling him he was going to be late, and he'd sounded tired. He'd been almost short with Nick, telling him to go back to sleep before hanging up. He hadn't said why he was going to be late, if it was overtime or if it was because something had happened that he couldn't get away from. The life of a cop was unpredictable, especially when it came to the hours. If something happened right before they got off shift, they had to stay until they could be relieved.

It hadn't helped that Dad had been demoted. Nick knew what that meant. Going from detective back to beat cop was a harsh pay cut along with the bruised ego. There'd been insurance money and a payout from the Nova City Victims' Fund for what happened in the After, but Dad put all that money away for Nick, telling him it was for a future he deserved.

His dad worked hard. That much was clear.

So of *course* Nick wanted to become an Extraordinary. Yes, it would mean getting to team up with Shadow Star and most likely falling in love and having a superhero-themed wedding with cake that had yellow frosting, but it also meant he could potentially keep the city safer.

And doing that meant his *dad* would be safer.

He wouldn't have to worry as much, and Cap would see just how good of a cop Dad was and make him detective again, something his dad had loved with everything he had.

Plus, that would be extremely altruistic of Nick, which meant Shadow Star would see how selfless he was and then they could go on a date before the whole rest-of-their-lives thing.

So when Nick got to their table in the cafeteria, his friends looked up at him, and he said, "Phase Two is a go. I repeat, Phase Two is a go." And he felt *good* about it. Following fickle whims could sometimes turn out okay. Nick believed that with all his heart.

Jazz smiled.

Gibby shrugged.

Seth sighed.

Nick made a mental note to have them work on their reactions to his good ideas. After all, an Extraordinary was only as good as the people who supported him. And since these were his people, they needed to be at their best.

What am I looking for again?" Seth asked the following Wednesday afternoon. They sat in the library at the school, homework spread out and forgotten in front of them, waiting for Jazz to get done with cheerleading practice. Gibby had declined the offer to join them, telling Nick she'd rather sit in the bleachers and watch her girlfriend. Nick was sure that *watch* meant *leer*, so he hadn't pushed her on it.

"Meteors," Nick told him, scrolling the screen on his laptop. "We need to find out what the chances of the next one falling near Nova City will be. I feel like it should occur on a regular basis because space has a lot of rocks in it, and Nova City is really big."

"Your logic is undeniable," Seth said. "I don't know how anyone can argue with you based on rational fact."

"Right? Yet people still try. It's weird. It's like they don't understand anything I'm saying. It's why I have you. You get me better than anyone else. You're a Nick Whisperer."

Seth coughed roughly.

Nick looked over his laptop at Seth, who was blushing furiously as he swiped his thumb over his phone. "You okay?"

Seth nodded. "Just swallowed a bug."

"Ugh. Gross. Make sure you don't kiss your secret girlfriend and/or boyfriend without brushing your teeth first."

Seth looked up, eyes narrowed. "Are you going to let that go?"

"Probably not for at least three more days."

"Three more days," Seth mumbled. He looked back down at his phone. "Why do we need a meteor?"

"Because. If one of them comes from a distant planet, chances are it will have alien goo on it, and I'll be able to eat said alien goo. Which, by the laws of nature and our lord and savior Stan Lee—may he rest in peace—will give me superpowers and I'll be able to become an Extraordinary." It was foolproof.

"You've certainly thought this one through with your regular amount of planning."

"Wow. Sarcasm. Exactly what is *not* needed at this very moment."

Seth sighed. "I do wonder if your life is sometimes not based in the real world."

Nick frowned. "Weird. That's not the first time someone has said that to me. I wonder what that means."

"That maybe life isn't supposed to be a comic book?"

"It's not?"

"No, Nick. I don't—" He shook his head like he was frustrated. "I know you want this. I get that. But have you thought far enough ahead about what it could mean? Say on the off chance this *did* work. Have you any idea what would happen next?"

"Yes. I've thought everything through. It'll mean that Shadow Star will want to date me and I can help my dad with—" He looked away. "Just . . . don't worry about it. I'm doing this because it's something I want to do. That should be enough, right?"

"Help your dad with what?"

Yeah, Nick hadn't meant to say anything about that. He was still dealing with the shift in his worldview that maybe becoming an Extraordinary didn't need to be just about himself. And since he was still pretty new to the whole *being mostly selfless* thing, he wasn't sure how to deal with it yet. "It's nothing. Forget I said anything."

"Nicky."

Nick was getting annoyed, and he didn't know why. "Why can't you let me have this?"

Seth set his phone on the table. "I didn't say you couldn't. I just want you to be safe."

Nick rolled his eyes. "I'm always safe."

"That's not always true. I seem to remember that time you wanted to see what happened when you held a flame in front of a can of hairspray."

"Yeah, that fire was certainly bigger than I expected it to be. I can't believe my dad didn't notice one of my eyebrows was more singed than the other."

"Why on earth do you think you'll be able to find a meteor with alien goo?"

Nick shrugged. "Why not? It's just one of the avenues I'm exploring. I'm spinning a lot of plates right now, Seth. A lot of fingers in pies. So many—"

"I get it."

"Good. That makes things easier."

Seth picked up his phone and began tapping the screen. "What are you researching? Because I gotta admit, I don't think we're going to find a meteor anytime soon. Apparently, they don't fall from the sky with any regularity. Imagine that."

"Hmm?" Nick said distractedly. "Oh, I'm just trying to find blueprints for the nearest nuclear power plant so I can break in and then get exposed to gamma radiation and maybe Hulk out a little or something. Do you know how much radiation a normal human can take before they get tumors in their eyeballs?"

Seth didn't respond.

Nick looked up.

Seth was gaping at him.

"What?" Nick asked, looking behind him to see if something was on fire. It wasn't. He turned back to Seth. "What is it?"

Seth took a deep breath and let it out slowly. "You want to break into a nuclear power plant and expose yourself to radiation?"

"Yeah. Genius, right? Since the whole cricket-in-the-microwave debacle—which, again, was it *really* so hard to find a spider, Jazz?—I got to thinking more about it. After Chernobyl and Fukushima, the plant and animal life there genetically mutated. Yeah, it was because of a nuclear meltdown, but I figure if I can get just a *minuscule fraction* of what they got hit with, I can probably mutate a little." He frowned. "Granted, I'd want to avoid any loss of life because getting what I want shouldn't mean hurting someone else, so it can't be *exactly* like Chernobyl and Fukushima, but keep in mind, this is a work in progress."

There was a moment of silence. Then, "Sometimes, I don't know if you're really smart or completely insane."

"It's a fine line," Nick agreed. "There are a couple of nuclear power plants within a few hundred miles, but not a single one of them puts their blueprints online."

"Wow," Seth said faintly. "It's almost like they don't want someone getting inside."

Nick scowled at his laptop screen. "I'll figure it out. We just have to have faith that someone made a mistake and put clear, detailed instructions online on how to break into a power plant and get a safe blast of radiation that will give me superpowers and not make my testicles explode. Should be—"

Seth's phone beeped in his hands.

Nick looked up again.

Seth's expression tightened. His brow was furrowed, his mouth in a thin line. He looked tougher than Nick had ever seen him before. It was . . . shocking. For a moment, Nick almost thought Seth looked *dangerous,* but that was ridiculous.

"Is everything okay?" Nick asked slowly.

Seth stood abruptly. His chair scraped against the floor, bumping into a shelf of books behind him. One of the librarians glared at them. "I have to go," Seth said, shoving his books back into his backpack.

"What? What do you mean, you have to go? We're busy! You're supposed to be helping me—"

"I'm sorry, Nicky. It's—there's been a break—an emergency at the animal shelter. They put out a call to all volunteers. Apparently it's a pretty big deal."

Nick squinted at him. "An . . . animal shelter emergency?"

Seth nodded. "Flooding, because of the rain. They have to move all the animals, and they need all the help they can get."

"I thought you stopped working there after school started."

"I did," Seth said, slinging his bag over his shoulder. "But they need me. I have to go help them. Can't let the animals drown, right?"

Well, no, because that would be evil. "Need help?"

"Nah, don't worry about it. I'll handle it. Keep doing what you're doing."

That sounded fake, but okay. "I . . . guess?"

"I'm sorry," Seth said, but he was distracted, like he was already somewhere else in his head. "I know this is important to you, but I've got to do this. It's not—just stay away from midtown, okay?"

Nick didn't understand. "What the hell does that have to do—"

"Promise me," Seth snapped, that hardened expression back on his face. He reached down and put his hand on top of Nick's, squeezing tightly. "Stay away. Because of the flooding."

"I promise," Nick said. "Because of the flooding."

"Thanks. I'll text you later, okay? Just . . . don't go to any nuclear power plants. That idea is ridiculous, and you'll most likely end up dead. Think of something else."

"Well, maybe if you'd found some freaking *meteors*, I wouldn't have to—"

And then the most extraordinary thing happened, something that caused all Nick's thoughts to come to a screeching halt.

Seth leaned down and kissed his cheek.

Nick felt the quick, hot pulse of breath against his skin, the scrape of lips and then—

He turned slowly to look up at Seth.

Seth, who looked horrified by what he'd just done. "I—uh— Holy crap, I've got to go."

Nick watched as Seth walked backwards, staring wide-eyed at Nick. He walked into a girl who told him to watch where he was going, and then into a bookshelf, knocking books onto the ground, much to the consternation of the librarian who looked like she was about to descend into an apoplectic fit.

Nick stared, dumbfounded, as Seth finally turned around and ran from the library. Nick couldn't be sure he'd ever seen Seth move that fast in his life.

He reached up and pressed a finger to where Seth's lips had been just a moment before.

"Huh," Nick said to no one in particular.

"I will see you *banned*," the librarian whisper-shouted.

Jazz and Gibby found Nick an hour later, staring forlornly at his laptop. The internet had never betrayed him like this before. He didn't know how to handle it. From not giving him blueprints to a nuclear power plant to finding out if friends kissed each other goodbye on the cheeks if they weren't French, it was useless.

Gibby ruffled his hair as she slumped gracefully into a chair next to Nick. "Where's Seth?"

"Animal shelter emergency," Nick mumbled, feeling his face grow warm.

"Animal shelter emergency?" Jazz asked, standing next to Nick, looking at his computer screen. Thankfully, he'd already closed the tab with the search *what are you supposed to do when your best friend kisses your cheek*. "What's that supposed to mean?"

"You look very pretty," Nick told her, because she deserved to hear it on a regular basis. She was wearing her cheerleader uniform, the Centennial Fighting Wombat grinning from where it was stitched on her chest. Also, he hoped it would prove to be a distraction so she wouldn't see the Seth-kissed-my-face expression he most likely wore.

"Thank you. Animal shelter?"

"Flooding, apparently."

"Flooding," Gibby repeated slowly. "Um, excuse me for a moment."

She stood and walked away quickly, pulling her phone from her back pocket.

Nick stared after her. "What is with everyone leaving in a dramatic fashion today?"

Jazz took the seat her girlfriend had vacated. "We're friends with a bunch of drama queens. What's that?" She pointed at his laptop.

"Generic blueprints for a nuclear power plant where I was supposed to get hit with radiation to give me superpowers."

Jazz sighed. "Drama queens. All of you."

"Hey!"

"Probably not safe."

"Now you sound like Seth."

"That's a nice thing to say. He's pretty smart."

"Yeah, except for when he ditches me. *Again.*"

Jazz frowned. "I'm sure he didn't want to. You know there's nowhere he'd rather be than with you."

"Then why isn't he here?"

She kicked his shin underneath the table. "Because the world doesn't revolve around you, idiot. Other things happen, even if we don't want them to."

Nick groaned as he reached down to rub his leg. "I deserved that."

"Probably."

"It's just . . . he's been weird lately."

"Weird how?"

Nick shook his head as he closed his laptop. There was nothing else he could do with it now. "He's always busy. He's distracted. I barely saw him over the summer, and even when I did, it was like he wasn't there. I don't know. I'm probably making it a bigger deal than it is. I don't know if you've noticed, but I tend to do that sometimes."

"No. Really?" She smiled at him, but it faded before too long. "Okay, maybe this summer was a little weird. It seemed to be you and me more than anyone else after Gibby left with her parents on their trip."

"Right? Not that I didn't *want* you to be there, or anything. You're perfect."

She laughed. "Thanks, Nicky. I know I'm not Seth or Gibby, but I like to think we got to be pretty good friends on our own, right?"

"Right," Nick said promptly, because it was true. Jazz wasn't just Gibby's girlfriend. Maybe that was how it'd started, but this past summer changed that for him. Jazz was funny and kind, and sometimes when she laughed, Nick thought it was one of the nicest sounds in the world. He was happy to have her, even if right now he was feeling sorry for himself.

Then she said, "Maybe he's scared." Nick didn't like the sound of that.

"Of what?" he asked, perplexed. Seth wasn't afraid of anything, not really. He was brave and awesome, and Nick couldn't think of a single thing that frightened him aside from snakes, but that was okay because snakes were terrible creatures that served no purpose.

"Things changing," Jazz said, picking up Nick's pencil from the table and twirling it deftly between her fingers. "It's going to be different soon. Everything will be."

"What will?"

"This." She shrugged. "Us. Gibby's going to graduate, and go to college, and then it's just going to be the three of us. Then *we're* going to graduate, and who knows what will happen then?"

"We're still going to be friends," Nick said with a frown. "Even if we end up going to different places, that's not going to change."

"It might," Jazz said, and that didn't sit well with Nick. "We could become different people. People don't always stay friends with the people they grow up with. In fact, most don't."

He took the pencil from her since she was starting to twirl it with anger. "Gibby loves you. You know that, right?"

Her smile was tight. "I know."

"Then you should trust her to know what's right. And on the off chance that your paths split, well. Maybe it doesn't have to be forever. Or if it does, it doesn't mean what you had mattered any less."

She shook her head. "I don't think people give you enough credit. You're smarter than you look."

"Thanks. I think. You too."

"Seth loves you."

Nick blushed. He couldn't help it. He could still feel the way Seth's nose had pressed near his ear. "Um," he managed to say. "I . . . know? He's my best friend. Of course he does."

"And you love him."

Nick nodded dumbly.

"You're aware of *that* at least."

Nick's face felt like it was on fire. "Am I missing something here?"

She opened her mouth—to say what, Nick had no idea—but she was interrupted when Gibby came back to the table. "What are you guys talking about?"

"Life," Jazz said airily. "And all that it entails."

"Sounds deep."

Jazz hummed. "You have no idea. Isn't that right, Nicky?"

"Right," Nick said, feeling twitchier than normal.

Jazz looked up at Gibby. "And where did you run off to?"

"Phone call," Gibby said easily. "Nothing important. We should—uh-oh."

"What uh-oh?" Jazz asked.

"Nick has his thinking face. And it's red. I don't think I've ever seen his red thinking face before."

"Uh-oh."

"Maybe I should go visit Seth at the animal shelter," Nick said, tapping his fingers against the table. "I mean, it's obviously important to him, right? Does it make me a bad friend that I never went there this summer? I should take an interest in *his* interests, right? I mean, that's what you're supposed to do when your best friend starts something new."

"No," Gibby blurted.

Nick and Jazz turned slowly to look at her. "Why not?"

"Because," Gibby said. "It's . . . uh. Probably super busy. With the . . . flooding thing. And, Nicky, aren't you allergic to cats? There's probably lots of cats."

Oh. Right. But still. "It's not *that* bad. I mean, yeah, I swell up and get blotchy and then almost die, but so what? If Seth likes it, then I should like it too, right?"

"Oh sure," Gibby said quickly. "Totally. But I don't think he'd want you to get sick because of him. That'd make him feel bad, and you know how Seth looks when he feels bad."

"My greatest weakness," Nick breathed. When Seth Gray felt bad about something, his eyes got really wide and his bottom lip trembled, and all Nick wanted to do was hug him close and protect him from everything.

"Exactly," Gibby said. "And we can't have him getting distracted from all those cats. Besides, he'll probably be done sooner than you think—"

Nick's phone beeped.

Then Jazz's.

Then Gibby's.

The librarian glared at them, but then her phone beeped too, and she frowned down at it.

Nick picked his phone up to see an alert across the screen.

EXTRAORDINARY ACTIVITY IN MIDTOWN. EXPECT DELAYS. AVOID AREA IF POSSIBLE.

"Whoa," Nick breathed. "Do you think it's Shadow Star?"

"I don't know," Gibby said. "But we should probably stay away since we were told to."

"Right," Nick said. "But what if we—"

"No."

"But we could—"

"No."

"Maybe just—"

"No."

Nick glared at Gibby. "You know, when I'm an Extraordinary, I'm going to be able to do whatever I want."

"And I tremble in fear at the very thought. But until that time comes, you're still squishy and fragile, and even though you sometimes act like it, you're not stupid enough to get in the middle of whatever's going on."

"I feel like there was a compliment buried under all that somewhere."

"Keep telling yourself that, Nicky. Now, why don't you explain to me in great detail Phase Two of your plan. I don't think I understood it the first time."

Jazz groaned.

"I'd be happy to," Nick said, sitting up. "Maybe you should take copious notes just to be safe."

* * *

Nick was almost home when he got a text from Dad, telling him he'd been called in to work early, and didn't know when he'd be back. Nick wondered if it had to do with the Extraordinaries, but his dad didn't respond when he asked.

The porch light was on, even though it was still daylight. Nick was about to put his key in the door when he got another alert. He pulled out his phone.

BREAKING NEWS: SHADOW STAR BATTLING PYRO STORM ABOVE THE STREETS OF NOVA CITY.

Nick stared at his phone, synapses misfiring.

It took him a moment to reboot, and then he nearly broke his key trying to get inside the house. The door banged against the wall as he threw it open, not even bothering to close it behind him. He ran to the living room, picking up the remote to the TV off the coffee table. He almost dropped it but managed to hit the power button. He flipped through the channels until he found the news.

And stared in wonder.

It was a live shot from the Action News chopper. A picture of Rebecca Firestone was in the corner, smiling wide and beautiful. Her voice was speaking over the sound of the helicopter, saying things like *I've never seen them like this before* and *They've been going at it for the better part of an hour now* and *Oh my god.*

But Nick barely heard her.

Because there they were.

Shadow Star and Pyro Storm.

It was quick and brutal, the camera barely able to keep up with their movements. They were on top of one of the skyscrapers in midtown. Nick thought it was one of the financial buildings. A sharp bloom of fire burst from Pyro Storm, rocketing toward Shadow Star. The hero managed to leap out of the way before he was burned to a crisp, climbing up the large antenna tower effortlessly. His shadow stretched out behind him, and as Nick watched, it reached out and grabbed Pyro Storm around the ankles, lifting him up and slamming him back onto the roof, cracking the cement underneath him.

It was vicious in ways Nick hadn't seen before.

Yes, Pyro Storm was a villain, and *yes,* he was the archnemesis of Shadow Star, but it was always . . . not like this. They fought, but it rarely came to an all-out brawl. Pyro Storm would come up with some ridiculous scheme, Shadow Star would swoop in and save the day, and they'd go their separate ways. Hell, there were people who were sure the two were in on it together, that it was done for nothing more than attention. Usually, no one got hurt, no matter how harebrained Pyro Storm's ideas got.

This was different. It looked like they were trying to hurt each other.

Or, rather, Pyro Storm was trying to hurt Shadow Star. All Shadow Star was doing was reacting. He was on the defensive.

Every time Pyro Storm lashed out, Shadow Star would move away quickly, knocking the villain off his feet again and again. Their mouths were moving like they were shouting at each other, but they were too far away to be heard.

Then Shadow Star turned his head toward the Action News chopper, and the camera zoomed in on his mask-covered face, his mouth the only thing visible.

He smiled.

Nick felt a chill race down his spine.

Pyro Storm brought his hands up and pointed them at Shadow Star. A swirl of fire grew in his hands. Shadow Star moved slowly. A ball of fire shot toward him, and a shadow rose up from the rooftop. It was shredded as the fire burst through it, but it caused the fireball to be deflected toward the helicopter. Rebecca Firestone shouted to *pull up pull up pull up* as Shadow Star tackled Pyro Storm. The ball of fire went underneath the helicopter, missing it by a few feet, trailing flame and smoke behind it.

Pyro Storm snarled and kicked his feet against Shadow Star's chest, knocking him dangerously close to the edge of the roof. Before Shadow Star could recover, Pyro Storm swung his arm out in a flat arc, a wave of fire roaring toward Shadow Star and—

Shadow Star fell off the other side of the building.

Nick dropped the remote.

"Oh no," Rebecca Firestone whispered.

"No," Nick said. "No, no, no. It's fine. He's *fine*."

Even Pyro Storm seemed stunned.

He walked slowly toward the edge of the building, his cape billowing around him. Any moment now, Nick knew with all his might that Shadow Star would reappear and everything would be fine. He hadn't fallen, because he was a hero and heroes never fell.

"Come on," Nick muttered. "Come on, come on, come *on*."

Pyro Storm peered over the edge of the building.

The camera shook harshly when Rebecca Firestone shouted and Shadow Star launched himself up and over the edge of the roof, feet going into Pyro Storm's face. Pyro Storm was knocked off his feet and Nick screamed, raising his hands above his head in triumph. Shadow Star landed on the roof, crouched, one hand flat on the ground, the other raised behind him.

Pyro Storm tried to get up, but Shadow Star was already moving, shadows crawling along the roof, wrapping themselves around Pyro Storm's legs and arms, holding him down. Shadow Star stood above him as Pyro Storm snarled at him. Shadow Star squatted next to him, and though it couldn't be heard what they were saying, Nick knew Shadow Star was most likely lecturing Pyro Storm on turning away from evil and using his powers for good. Pyro Storm was telling him that he would never do such a thing, that he was a *villain,* and would do *villain things.*

(Nick knew this because he'd written a similar scene in chapter 34 of *This Is Where We Scorch the Earth.* Fiction often imitated real life, after all.)

Then Shadow Star stood, waving his hand. The shadows holding Pyro Storm down dissipated. He held his hand out to help Pyro Storm to his feet, but the villain knocked it away. Shadow Star shook his head and took a step back as Pyro Storm pushed himself up.

They stood facing each other for a moment, before Pyro Storm rocketed away, cape trailing behind him, the air burning.

Shadow Star stared after him for a moment before he shook his head. He glanced back at the chopper, saluted the camera, then leapt from the roof and disappeared from sight.

Nick watched the screen, slack-jawed, even as Rebecca Firestone breathlessly said that she'd never seen such a fight, and though damage to property was minimal, it appeared that things were escalating. "I'll have to see if Shadow Star is willing to talk about this latest attack by Pyro Storm. If he is, you'll hear it here first. This is Rebecca Firestone, Action News."

9

Rebecca Firestone didn't speak with Shadow Star, even on the last broadcast at ten.

Dad had texted, saying everything was fine.

Seth didn't text at all.

By the time the front door opened early the next morning, Nick was already showered and dressed, standing in the kitchen, trying to figure out how he managed to burn toast when it was on the lowest setting. He hadn't been distracted, not really, so it must have been a faulty toaster.

Dad looked tired, his duty belt sagging around his waist, bags under his eyes. He yawned when he came into the kitchen, blinking blearily as he went to the coffee maker that was programmed to start brewing at four in the morning. He poured himself a cup of decaf—keeping it black, much to Nick's disgust—took a sip, and sighed.

Then he seemed to notice Nick.

He frowned.

Nick smiled.

Dad looked down at his watch, then back up at Nick. He saw the burnt toast on a plate, and the bowl of oatmeal with fruit already sitting on the table.

He said, "Hey."

"Hi," Nick said, smiling wider.

"What did you do?"

Nick scowled at him. "I didn't do anything."

Dad took another sip of liquid death. "You're up—and dressed—before I even got home. You made breakfast—"

"You're welcome, though the toast is burnt and the oatmeal is lumpy for reasons I don't want to discuss."

"—and I don't think this has ever happened before. Ever."

"Can't a son do something nice for his hardworking father without there being a hidden agenda?"

Dad waited.

"It's altruistic," Nick insisted.

Dad snorted. "Is that right?"

"*Yes*. The fact that you think I would do something nice for untoward reasons is frankly offensive. I will accept your apology when you're ready to give it."

"I'll keep that in mind," Dad said. "Burnt toast and lumpy oatmeal?"

Nick shrugged. "It could have been worse. It's probably best that we don't discuss what happened to the eggs I tried making first."

"Is that what that smell is?"

"Yeah. Apparently no matter how much Febreeze one sprays, that egg smell tends to stick around. Who knew? Sit! Take a load off!"

Dad did just that, sliding off his duty belt and placing it on the counter.

Nick grabbed a chair and dragged it next to his dad's. He sat, elbows on the table, and watched his father closely.

Dad looked like he was trying not to be amused but failed miserably.

He swirled the oatmeal. It wasn't as lumpy as it'd been moments before, much to Nick's relief. He watched as Dad took a bite. "Good?"

Dad nodded. "Good. Thanks, kid."

"You're welcome."

Nick waited, because it was the right thing to do.

"This about yesterday?"

"Absolutely not. I'm a teenager. Sometimes I'm late, and it can't be avoided."

"Uh-huh. See that it doesn't happen again."

Nick pushed the plate of toast toward his dad's hand.

Dad took a bite. It was mostly blackened, but it didn't seem like he had to choke it down, so Nick was pleased.

He waited until his dad swallowed before he said, "Now that you've had an opportunity to come home and relax, a question, if I may?"

"There it is."

"It's just a *question*."

"What happened to being altruistic?"

"There are strawberries in your oatmeal. That seems pretty selfless to me."

"Oh boy." Dad wiped his mouth with a napkin before leaning back in his chair. "Okay, hit me with it."

That was easier than Nick had expected. "There was an . . . event. In Nova City yesterday."

"Was there? Seems to me there were many events. Nova City is a pretty big place."

Aggravating, that was what he was. He was good, but Nick was better. "Absolutely. But I couldn't help but notice that you had to go in early yesterday afternoon, right around the time that this particular event was beginning to take place."

"Interesting."

"Quite. Now, if I were a betting man—"

"Oh, I wouldn't go that far. Betting *child*, maybe."

"—*betting man,* I would think those two things were related."

"Those seem to be some big odds."

"I'm a cop's kid," Nick reminded him. "I'm pretty sure I know how to make deductions that prove to be correct."

Dad smiled tiredly at him. "You are, aren't you? Okay, I'll play along. Let's say I was at a certain event. What do you want?"

"Five questions, and you have to answer every one truthfully."

"Three questions, and I'll decide which ones get an answer."

"*Four* questions, and if there's one you can't answer because of an open investigation, you can hint around it enough so I can figure it out on my own."

"No questions, and you leave for school now to ensure we don't have a repeat of yesterday."

Nick glared at him. "Are we really doing this again?"

"Funny, I was just thinking the same thing."

So. Aggravating. "Not funny."

Dad shrugged. "I'm your father. Trust me when I say I've got a sense of humor."

Nick threw his hands up. "*Fine.* Since apparently we live in Communist *China,* we'll do it your way."

"World Studies going well, then?"

Nick nodded. "I'm learning a lot. First test next week. All right, old man. You ready for this?"

"Hit me, kid."

Nick leaned forward eagerly. "Did you see him?"

Dad sipped his coffee before answering. He really was the worst. "I did."

"Did you *talk* to him?"

"I didn't. Last question."

Nick couldn't believe it was almost over already. "I'd like to renegotiate the terms of our agreement, if I may."

"You may not."

Such a hard-ass. "Okay, let me think."

"You've got thirty seconds."

Nick gaped at him. "But—you know I can't—why are you *like* this?"

"To make your life miserable. Twenty seconds."

"Okay, wait. Just wait. Let me—"

"Ten seconds."

"Time does *not* move that fast, you liar—"

"Three. Two. One."

"Why do you think they were fighting like that?" Nick blurted.

Dad blinked like he hadn't been expecting that question. "What?"

"It doesn't make sense," Nick said. "They've always been . . . not like that. It was like something happened, and they were taking it to another level. Sure, they've fought before, but they've never been in an all-out *brawl* like that. Why were they going after each other with such hatred?"

Dad rubbed his chin thoughtfully. "Your guess is as good as

mine. I don't know what goes on in the mind of an Extraordinary. On one hand, you've got your boyfriend doing what he can to—"

"He's not my *boyfriend,* oh my god, how can you *say* that—"

"—even if he can be a pain in the ass, and on the other hand, you've got that fire guy who just seems to like causing chaos for the hell of it. But the shadow fella and the fire guy have always been . . . what? Enemies?"

"Shadow fella and fire guy," Nick repeated. "It's like you're deliberately trying to hurt me. Really. Stab me in the heart, why don't you. It'd be easier."

"You know more about this kind of thing than I do," Dad said. "Don't you stalk—I mean, don't you *follow* everything they do? Obsessively? To the point I should probably be more concerned than I am?"

"A little," Nick admitted. "I've got a handle on it. I'll let you know if it gets to the point that might necessitate serving me a restraining order."

"I'm glad you know yourself that well."

"But, like I was saying, it has never been that bad before, right? I mean, Pyro Storm doesn't really try to hurt people like that. Mostly. Yeah, there was that one time when he accidentally lit that guy's hair on fire when he tried to take a picture with him, but Pyro Storm put it out quickly. And the guy was in denial about his combover, so actually, Pyro Storm was probably doing him a favor. Live bald and proud, man."

"Maybe something happened that changed things," Dad said quietly. "It doesn't take much to tip people over the edge. You lose something, Nicky, and you find yourself doing things you didn't think you were capable of."

Nick swallowed thickly. He knew what Dad was implying. He'd always been about protecting and serving, but then one of his witnesses had said the wrong thing at the wrong time and had gotten a broken nose because of it. "But that doesn't mean you still can't be a good person, right? Just because you did something wrong doesn't mean that's who you are. And even if you *keep* doing the wrong thing, you can still be saved. Maybe they just need someone to listen to them, to hear the storm in their heads."

Dad stared at him. Nick tried not to squirm. Then, "You know, if you didn't have this . . . thing for Shadow Star, I would almost think that you could be him."

It was bittersweet to hear, to know his dad thought he could be an Extraordinary even though he was the furthest thing from it. "That'd sure be some twist, huh? Wouldn't even see me coming."

"Right," Dad said slowly. "Do you know something, Nick? You can tell me if something's wrong. You know that. I know it was . . . rough, for a little while. But we've gotten better, haven't we? You can come to me with anything."

"I know." And Nick did. Mostly. "I don't know more than I already told you." He sighed. "I mean, I've only talked to Shadow Star that one time after he saved me from—" Nick felt the words dry up in his mouth. His skin buzzed. Shit. Shit, shit, *shit*—

Dad's eyes narrowed as he sat forward. "What? What do you mean he *saved* you?"

Nick winced. "Uh. I was . . . talking about my story? That I'm writing? In my head?"

Dad slammed a hand on the table, making it shake. Nick flinched when the spoon fell out of the bowl of oatmeal and clattered onto the table. "We talked about this. You told me you wouldn't lie to me. Not again."

"It's not like that, I swear! I didn't—"

"Did you, or did you not, have contact with Shadow Star?"

And oh, Dad was angry. "It's not a big deal," Nick managed to say, hating the way his eyes were already starting to burn. He'd never been able to control his emotions in the face of his father's anger. It was extremely rare to see Dad this pissed off, so much so that Nick could probably count the number of times it'd happened on one hand. And even then, this was only the second time it'd been directed toward him. The last time had been after the Owen debacle. He hated how easily he cracked right down the middle. "I swear, Dad. It wasn't—"

Dad closed his eyes, breathing heavily through his nose. "I'm going to give you this one chance. That's it. You better take it, Nick. Or you can expect a whole lotta changes around here that you won't like."

Nick's breath hitched in his chest as he struggled to maintain his composure. His voice broke when he said, "I didn't do anything wrong. I just—it was the first day of school. I was late coming home because I'd gotten detention—"

"You what?"

Crap. He hadn't meant to say that. He needed to power through. "And it was raining and Gibby was with me and the train was delayed. We were taking a shortcut, okay? That's all it was. And these guys came and tried to mug us, and Shadow Star kicked their asses, and that was it. I promise. That's all that happened."

Dad's eyes flashed open. "You were *mugged* and you didn't think to tell me?"

Nick gripped the edges of the table. "I didn't want you to worry."

"Really," Dad snapped. "Or did you not want me to find out about getting in trouble on your first day back?"

"That wasn't my fault either! Mr. Hanson was trying to stifle me!"

Dad stood, his chair scraping on the floor. "We *talked* about this. You need to start taking some responsibility, Nick. You can't keep trying to blame others for the things you do. How the hell are you going to grow up when you keep pulling this crap? Are you trying to make things harder for us?"

Nick blinked rapidly. "I'm not—"

Dad began to pace, shoulders stiff. "Because I asked you for this one thing. For this year to be *different*. For you to do everything you could to be the best possible person you could be. And all I'm seeing here is that it's more of the same."

"I'm sorry I'm such a disappointment to you," Nick said bitterly, wiping his eyes.

"Dammit, kid. First it was Owen, and I let it go. And then it's this—this *Shadow Star,* and this weird obsession you have with him. I just don't—why do you have to be this way? Why do you have to be the way you are?"

Nick knew the power of words. He knew that sometimes when they landed, they exploded with the force of a carelessly tossed grenade.

Nick heard what his father said. He heard every word. They exploded at his feet and shredded his skin. It'd turned so quickly. They'd been laughing only a few minutes before. He didn't know how he'd lost control of the conversation this fast.

He stood slowly, eyes wide and shocked. He stared at the table, unable to meet his father's gaze. He didn't want to see that look on his face anymore, anger mixed with disappointment, all directed at him. It hurt. Everything hurt.

"Crap," Dad whispered. Then, "Look. Kid. I didn't—I didn't mean it like that. I'm tired."

Nick nodded stiffly but didn't speak.

"I . . ." Dad sounded frustrated. "I just need you to do better. I just need you to *be* better. Can you do that? For me?"

Nick nodded again.

"Hey, Nick. Look at me. I'm—"

"I've got to go," Nick said hoarsely. "I'm going to be late if I don't leave now. And I'd hate to disappoint you again."

Dad sighed. "Come on, Nicky. Would you just—" He heard his father take a step toward him.

Nick took a step back.

"Okay," Dad said stiffly. "If that's—okay."

Nick turned and left.

He was on the train, surrounded by people and staring blankly ahead when his phone buzzed. Nick thought about ignoring it.

He pulled it out of his pocket.

A text from his dad.

He *really* thought about ignoring it.

But maybe it was an apology. Maybe it was Dad saying he was sorry, that he didn't mean it, that he was just fine with the way Nick was, that he didn't need him to be anything more.

He opened the message.

You forgot to take your pill this morning. Called the
school. Nurse will have your dose. See her before class.

And that was it.

Nick deleted the message before sliding the phone back in his
pocket.

The train car rocked gently beneath his feet.

He didn't wait for the others at Franklin Street. He didn't want
to see anyone. Not when his head was messed up. His skin felt
too tight, and it was like his nerves were electrified. His thoughts
jumped too quickly, and he couldn't focus. He tapped his fingers
against his hip as he walked.

He went directly to the nurse when he got to school.

She had his pill waiting for him.

She smiled as she handed it over with a tiny paper cup filled with
water.

Nick swallowed down, opening his mouth when she asked to
check.

"Have a good day," she said cheerfully.

Gibby and Jazz were at the lunch table when he walked into the
cafeteria. "Hey," Jazz said, looking up at him. "Missed you this
morning."

"Sorry," Nick said, keeping his voice even. "Was early and didn't
feel like sticking around."

Gibby rolled her eyes. "Maybe send us a text letting us know
next time. We were almost late, waiting for you."

"Didn't think. Sorry." He looked around. "Where's Seth? Or
Owen?"

"Seth texted this morning on our thread," Jazz said, tilting her
head at Nick. "Said he wasn't feeling well and was staying home

today. Don't know where Owen is. He'll show up when he feels like it, I'm sure."

"Sick?" Nick asked. "He was fine yesterday." When he'd kissed Nick on the cheek and then run away to save the animals from the flooding. Nick had almost forgotten about it with everything that had happened since then.

Gibby coughed. "Must have been those cats he had to save, or whatever. Ferals carry all kinds of weird crap."

"He's sick with a cat disease?" Jazz asked. "I wonder if he'll cough up a hairball."

That startled a laugh out of Nick. "Oh, man, that would be so gross. And awesome."

Gibby squeezed Jazz's hand. "I'm not sure that's quite how it works."

Jazz rolled her eyes. "You're the one who said he got sick because of feral cats."

"I know. And I accept any and all blame. I'm sure he'll be fine. Probably will be back by tomorrow."

Nick tugged at a hangnail on his finger. "I'll go see him after school. Make sure he's not dying."

Gibby hesitated. "You sure that's a good idea? He might be contagious."

"Eh. I eat a lot of oranges."

"I don't think I've ever seen you eat an orange in the entire time I've known you," Jazz said. "And speaking of, why aren't you eating?"

He'd stormed out of the house without grabbing his lunch because his dad wished he was someone different. "Forgot it. And I was supposed to remind Dad to add money to my lunch account, but I forgot."

"You can have some of mine," Jazz said. "I have chicken and avocado salad with lime and cilantro. There's also bread and olive oil."

"I've got cold pizza and an apple," Gibby said, peering into her own lunch bag. "Should be more than enough to go around."

Nick shrugged. "Not that hungry."

Jazz narrowed her eyes at him. "You will eat our food with us, Nicky. And you'll like it."

"All right, all right. Twist my arm, why don't ya." He grimaced. "On second thought, please don't do that. You're much stronger than I am."

"As long as we have an understanding," she said primly, spreading her cloth napkin in her lap.

Gibby handed him a piece of pizza. Jazz put chicken and avocado on top of it. It tasted disgusting, but it made him feel a little bit better. "Neither of you have heard from Owen?"

Jazz shook her head. "But that's not weird, right? I don't think I've ever gotten a text from him."

"Me either," Gibby said.

Nick frowned. "He texts me all the time."

Gibby rolled her eyes. "That's because he wants to suck your—"

"No need to be crude while we're eating," Jazz told her.

"Oh, I didn't know we were so civilized here at our metal lunch table surrounded by screaming teenagers. I *shan't* forget again, Your Majesty."

"I saw him yesterday," Nick said suddenly. "When I was late. His dad dropped him off."

Jazz's fork stopped halfway to her mouth. "You saw Simon Burke? Here?"

"Yeah. And it was weird too. They were arguing." Maybe not *that* weird. Nick had done just the same with his father that very morning. "I don't know. It looked intense. Whatever it was, Owen told me he was skipping the rest of the day. Guess he decided to do it today too."

Gibby snorted. "And he tried to make you go with him, didn't he?"

"Yeah, but I said no. I'm—it's not like that. Not anymore."

"Did Simon Burke see you?" Jazz asked.

Nick shook his head. "I don't think so. Why?"

"He's scary. At least that's what my dad says. He's ruthless. He'll do anything to get what he wants. I only met him once, but it was a long time ago. He didn't seem very nice to me."

"That's probably how one gets to be a super rich CEO," Gibby said. "You gotta be able to squash the little guy. Owen's pretty much on his way already, isn't he?"

"Hey," Nick said, feeling weirdly defensive. "Owen's not *that* bad." He paused, considering. "Okay, maybe he is, but he's not like his father. That guy gives me the creeps."

"Sure, Nicky. Whatever you say." She took a bite of pepperoni and olive. "How's Phase Two going?"

Phase Two was pretty much dead in the water, but he needed to keep the faith. "There aren't any meteor showers in the near future. And I think that most of the nuclear power plants near here are probably under armed guard."

"That's just unfair," Jazz said. "Don't they know all you want is a little radiation poisoning?"

Thank god for Jazz. "Right? It's not like I'd be hurting anyone."

"Except for yourself," Gibby said. "Like, what if instead of giving you powers, it made all your teeth fall out and your eyelids melt?"

"You wouldn't be able to blink," Jazz told him. "Or eat solid foods. And you'd probably grow tumors all over your body. I don't know if I could be seen in public with someone who had no teeth or eyelids and a lot of tumors due to self-inflicted radiation poisoning. I do have a reputation to maintain."

"Hate to break it to you," Gibby said, "but your reputation was pretty much shot when you decided to take up with the likes of us. We aren't exactly the top of the food chain. I don't even know if we're *on* the food chain."

"More like the flies that surround the predators at the top of the food chain," Nick said.

"I suppose," Jazz said. "But I think it's better to be real with you than fake with everyone else."

Nick gaped at her.

"What?" she asked him.

He shook his head slowly. "I just—huh."

"Is that a good *huh*?"

"Oh yeah. You're awesome. You sound like a fortune cookie."

She looked pleased. "Why, thank you. I like the way they taste."

Gibby grinned at her. "She's pretty great, right?" She glanced at Nick. "But it's probably for the best about the meteors and the power plants."

Well . . . yeah, but still. "What do you mean?"

She shrugged. "You saw the way Pyro Storm and Shadow Star were going after each other last night. Don't tell me you didn't. You turned your TV on as soon as you got home. And licked the screen."

Nick scowled at her. "What does that have to do with me?"

"It's dangerous," Gibby said gently. "The way they were fighting was just . . . brutal. How could you want to be a part of that?"

"It's not *about* that—"

"Of course it is. Maybe not all of it, but it's a big part. There's always going to be something bad with all the good. You can't be a hero without there being a villain."

"I think he can do it," Jazz said. "If anyone is capable of it, it's Nick. He'd probably end up being the best Extraordinary there was."

"*Thank* you, Jazz," Nick said, glaring at Gibby. "It's nice to know I have at least one person on my side."

Gibby shook her head. "Don't take this the wrong way, okay? But you're not exactly known for your follow-through."

Nick bristled. "What the hell is that supposed to mean?"

"He took it the wrong way," Jazz whispered to Gibby.

Gibby ignored her. "It means you get an idea in your head, and then run with it full tilt before getting distracted by something else entirely. It's not a bad thing. It's just part of who you are."

He knew she wasn't being mean. He knew she wasn't trying to hurt him. He *knew*. But Dad's voice was still ringing in his ears from their fight that morning, and it almost sounded like Gibby was echoing what he had said. And that wasn't fair. "I can do things," Nick snapped at her.

She held up her hands. "Whoa, I never said you couldn't. I'm just saying—"

"I can do anything I put my mind to."

"I know—"

"I don't like it when you tell me that I can't. I don't like it when people think I'm not capable of doing things. Because I *am*. I know I talk a lot, and I know my brain makes me do or say things that people don't always get, but that doesn't make the things I want any less important."

Jazz and Gibby both looked taken aback. "I'm . . . sorry?" Gibby said. "I didn't mean anything bad by it. It's—"

Jazz wasn't exactly subtle with the elbow she thrust into Gibby's side. "You okay, Nick? You seem a little off today. More growly than usual." She bared her teeth at Nick and made her hands into claws. "Grr."

Nick wished Seth were here. Even if he'd kissed Nick on the cheek and confused the hell out of him, Seth would know what to say to make things better. Sometimes, when Nick got so frustrated he didn't know how to form words, Seth would step in and speak for him and make things all right again. That was his superpower. The Nick Whisperer. Of all the days for Seth to be sick. "I'm fine," Nick said, mustering up a smile that stretched too thin. "I'm just tired."

Jazz frowned at him. "You need to take care of yourself."

"I'm trying." He looked at Gibby. And because he knew she wasn't the type to back down, she met his gaze. "I can do this," he told her. "You don't have to help me if you don't want to. And that's okay. But I can be more than I am. I can become something better. Something more."

She looked troubled. "Why do you have to be an Extraordinary to be better? Why can't you just be extraordinary with what you already have?"

Nick didn't want to hear it. Gibby didn't understand. "Let me have this, okay? I don't ask you for much, but I'm asking you for this."

She nodded, though she didn't look happy about it. "Sure, Nicky. Yeah. Of course. I mean, anything you want, you know? I've got your back."

"Good," he said. "Because Phrase Three is going to start soon, and I know it's going to work. It has to. I'm going to become something unlike anything Nova City has ever seen."

And if he proved everyone wrong in the process?

Well, that would be just fine.

He was walking to class when he pulled his phone out of his pocket. There were messages from Jazz and Gibby from that morning, asking where he was, if he was running late. There was a message from Seth in their group thread, saying he was sick. Jazz and Gibby had told him to feel better.

Dad hadn't texted again. That stung, but Nick pushed it away. He pulled up the text thread he had with Seth.

U sick?

The response came almost immediately. Yeah. Nothing bad. Just a cold. You okay? Gibby & Jazz said you didn't show this morning.

Fine. Just early. U sure its not feral cat disease?

What? What are you talking about? What cats?

The ones u went to help yesterday w the flooding. Nick almost added *after you kissed my cheek,* but didn't. One thing at a time.

No, Nick. It's not a feral cat disease.

Thank Jebus. U can't die.

I won't. No need to come over. I'll see you tomorrow.

Class. Later!

No need to come over? That was certainly an invitation if Nick had ever heard one.

10

Bob and Martha Gray lived in an old neighborhood along a row of lovingly maintained brownstones. Bob was the brother of Seth's father, and after Seth's parents passed, Bob and his wife, Martha, had taken in Seth and made a home for him. They'd never had kids of their own, but they had room in their house and hearts, and Seth was given a place to grieve and grow. Martha was a retired nurse, and Bob still worked as a super for an apartment building uptown, his life as a meter butler years behind him. Nick knew their home almost as well as he knew his own, though he hadn't been over in a long while.

Their street was lined with trees, the leaves turning from green to gold. The air was cool, and horns honked as soon as the lights changed. A cop car rolled by, but Nick ignored it. His dad still hadn't texted him.

He'd have to deal with that later.

Nick went up the steps to the Gray house and rang the doorbell. Martha had told him long ago that he could come in whenever he pleased, but he needed to make a good impression today.

They'd come to his mom's funeral. Bob had worn an ill-fitting suit—too small for his ever-expanding middle—and Martha had hugged him so hard, he felt his bones creak. She didn't tell him she was sorry, or that everything would get better. Nick would have screamed if she had—he'd heard it so many times already. Instead, as Seth stood at his side and held his hand, she'd whispered to him that if he ever needed an escape, to come to their house, and she would help him do whatever was needed.

He'd never forgotten that, even through the hazy fog that descended for months when Before had become After.

He heard the familiar chimes ring in the house and stepped back to wait. Bob was probably still at work, Seth up in his room, comforter pulled over his head and crinkled tissues on the floor by his bed.

He could see the outline of someone approaching through the glass on the door. He forced a smile on his face as the door opened.

Martha's eyes widened in shock when she saw him. It was brief, and he couldn't be sure it even happened, since she smiled brightly. "Nick! Well, isn't *this* a surprise. Whatever are you doing here? Shouldn't you be in class?"

"Hi, Mrs. Gray. I just came to see Seth, since he was sick. And it's three thirty. School got out almost an hour ago."

Her smile widened. "Of *course* it's three thirty and school is out already. Why, I must have lost track of time. Come in! Come *in*, dear child, and let me look at you. It's been far too long since I've seen your face."

He didn't even get a chance to respond before she'd grabbed him by the arm and pulled him into the house, shutting the door behind him. "Yes," she said, and she was speaking so loudly, it was almost like she was shouting. "It has been *forever* since *Nicholas Bell has been in this house.* And *right* at this very moment!"

Nick tilted his head at her. "Are you all right?"

"Fine, dear, just fine," she said loudly as she dragged him toward the kitchen. "Come! Come, even though it's been *months* since you've been here, *Nick,* you still have an affinity for my peanut butter cookies, don't you? I just made a fresh batch yesterday, and we should make sure you have at least six or seven before you *head upstairs* to see Seth, the poor boy."

"Uh, sure?" Nick said. "Also, you're a lot stronger than I expected you to be for someone your age. No offense."

"None taken," she said, looking back at him and smiling again. The wrinkles around her eyes deepened. "I used to have to lift patients at least three times your size. Built up some muscles. Speaking of, you're still as skinny as all get out. Maybe ten cookies before you go up and see *Seth.*"

Nick winced as she bellowed that last word.

The kitchen was as homey as he remembered it, small and tidy.

Martha and Bob had lived in the same brownstone since they'd married more than thirty years earlier. When Nick had asked why they didn't have any kids before Seth, Martha told him he shouldn't ask others that as it might be painful for some people, but in her case, life always seemed to get in the way. But then she'd said that maybe someone somewhere knew that Seth would need a home one day, and it was a good enough reason for her.

She shoved Nick down at the large table where he'd sat many times before, the vase of autumn flowers in the middle rattling but not tipping over. "There," she said. "Comfy? Good. Now, I know that one cannot have ten peanut butter cookies without having a glass of—"

A crash came from somewhere below.

Nick looked down at the floor. "Is there someone in the basement?"

Martha laughed a little wildly. "Of course not! Seth is ill upstairs, and Bob is at the apartment building fixing a sprung pipe."

"Uh, then what was that noise?"

"I didn't hear any—"

Another crash. This time the floor shook.

"Oh," Martha said. She turned toward the cookie jar shaped like a duck that she'd found in a flea market in 1978, or so she'd told Nick. Rather proudly too. "*That*. That is . . . the washing machine. Absolutely dreadful thing. It needs a new . . . filtering . . . valve. Yes, a new *filtering valve*. Bob is going to get right on that as soon as he gets home. In fact, after he's done with the leaking pipe at the apartment, he was going to go pick up—"

Footsteps ran up the basement stairs.

Then the basement door opened.

Then it slammed closed.

Then more footsteps up the stairs to the second floor.

Another door slammed shut upstairs.

Martha turned with a plate stacked high with peanut butter cookies. "Our house is haunted!" she said cheerfully. "It's just the oddest thing."

"Haunted," Nick said slowly as he picked up a cookie from the plate she'd set in front of him. "So . . . that was a ghost?"

She nodded, her white hair falling in her face as she went back to the fridge to pour a glass of milk. "Oh, yes. We did some research on it and everything. Apparently, this whole block used to be a tuberculosis . . . insane . . . asylum. Yes, *exactly*. People got tuberculosis and they went insane and then they *died*. Right where you're sitting. And now their spirits have awoken for reasons that don't need to be looked into, and here we are. Isn't that wonderful? Eat your cookie."

Nick stared at her.

She set a glass of milk in front of him and waited.

Finally, Nick breathed, "Whoa. A tuberculosis insane asylum and now there are *ghosts*? Why didn't Seth tell me about this? Don't you know what this means? My god, I'll have to look into it when I get home. We need to find out where they were buried so we can salt and burn their bones to put the spirits to rest. And if they're malevolent, we may need to hire a medium."

"Exactly," Martha said, patting his hand. "You do that. Have another cookie. In fact, I will insist you eat every single cookie on that plate before going upstairs."

"There's like, twenty cookies here."

"Then you best get started," she trilled. "And while you eat everything, you can tell me what you've been up to every day since I've seen you last. And be detailed. You know how I love details."

"That's . . . a lot of days. I haven't seen you since . . ."

"May twenty-second," Martha said. "After you and that boy broke up, and you came over here and cried, and I made you grilled cheese and tomato soup like when you were ten."

"I didn't *cry*," Nick mumbled through a mouthful of peanut butter cookie.

"Oh, I apologize," she said. "Your face must have been wet from the rain that wasn't falling at the time. Describe every day, Nicky. And I'll know if you missed one."

By the time Nick escaped and made his way upstairs, he was fuller than he'd been in a long time. He'd made it to July 2 and had eighteen cookies before Martha had suddenly cut him off and said he could go upstairs. If anything, it reaffirmed that he had a sharp memory and the capacity to eat a crapload of cookies. Both were good things to know about himself.

The old wooden stairs creaked under his Chucks, his hand sliding along the railing. The wall to his right was covered with framed photographs: Bob and Martha with big hair and parachute pants, Bob and Martha on vacation in front of a gigantic ball of yarn, Bob and Martha and little Seth at a park, snow falling all around them.

Nick was in some too, here and there. Nick and Seth in a blanket fort. Nick and Seth dressed like Jean Grey and Wolverine (Nick was *nine,* okay?) Nick and Seth standing on the pier, holding tufts of pink cotton candy almost as big as they were. Nick and Seth sitting in front of a TV, shoulder to shoulder, Nick's head tilted back in a laugh and Seth smiling quietly.

It was physical history of a good life, the wall cluttered with shared moments, some of which Nick had forgotten about.

As always, Nick stopped near the top of the stairs in front of one photograph in particular. The frame was old and worn, and the glass had a little crack in the right corner. The subjects were a little blurry and out of focus, but it reminded Nick of the one of him and Mom, standing near the lighthouse.

In it, Seth was four, and he was sitting on the shoulders of a thin, bespectacled man with a receding hairline. The man had his hands wrapped around Seth's ankles, and Seth's hands were thrown up in the air, curled into little fists. A woman stood next to the man, looking up at Seth, a smile on her face that Nick recognized on her son time and time again.

Nick had never met these two people. They'd been gone before the day on the swings. Seth had a few memories of them that he hoarded like a dragon does gold. Nick knew a couple of them, but not all. He didn't mind. He was aware that sometimes, things needed to be kept hidden in shadow because if they were brought out too much into the light, they would fade.

He wondered if Seth talked to them like Nick did with his mom.

He moved on.

There were three doors in the hallway at the top of the stairs. The door to the right led to the only bathroom in the house. The door to the left was Martha and Bob's bedroom, all old wood and frilly lace, much to Bob's consternation.

The last door—the one at the end of the hall—had a battered sign hanging off of it.

SETH'S ROOM

He knocked on the door.

"Come in!" a breathless voice said.

Nick frowned and shook his head before opening the door.

From the ceiling hung a replica model of a 1918 Yellow Curtiss JN-4 biplane. The propeller was broken, Nick's contribution to the entire project that had started out great, but then had caused him to be bored out of his mind. It wasn't that he didn't want to sit still for six hours and put together a model airplane. It was just that he was incapable of doing so. So, on hour three, he'd been so twitchy that he'd accidentally broken the propeller, the audible *snap* making him look down at his hands in horror. But Seth had shrugged, saying their plane would look as if it'd been in war now, which made it better.

Seth was good like that.

There were bookshelves filled with hundreds of books, most of which Nick had never touched and would never read. There was, however, a shelf toward the bottom that was lined with graphic novels and stacks of comic books Nick had given Seth. And Seth had read each and every one dutifully. Or, at least, he'd tried to read each and every one, but Nick had been so excited at the sight of a comic book in his best friend's hands that he'd sat right behind Seth peering over his shoulder, pointing out each panel, telling him all the backstory that Seth would have missed. He'd been worried, at first, that Seth wouldn't like them (and worse, that he'd think they were *stupid*), but that hadn't happened. He spent hours with Nick talking about heroes and villains, letting Nick babble at him about how *cool* Storm was, or how hardcore Venom could be.

It was different now, since Shadow Star and Pyro Storm appeared. They were comic books come to life, right in his city. Nick had known about Extraordinaries before, but they'd been the stuff of legends, in places far away from home. It wasn't until he'd seen with his own eyes Pyro Storm fly or Shadow Star crawl up the side of a building that it'd hit Nick just how astonishing they could be. After Guardian left for unknown reasons years earlier, the idea of Extraordinaries had been something the people of Nova City only saw from their television and computer screens. It was easy to think of them as almost fictional. It wasn't until Pyro Storm and Shadow Star had revealed themselves that people started to give a shit again about Extraordinaries.

When Nick became an Extraordinary and teamed up on and off the field with Shadow Star, maybe someone would write a comic book about him, filled with colorful panels of *POW* and *BLAM* and heroic deeds against the forces of evil.

He made a mental note to put together a pitch for Marvel and DC and Vertigo after he'd gotten his powers. He did have to expand his brand, after all. Comic books, TV shows, movies. He hoped they would hire someone with nice abs to play him. That seemed like it'd be the right thing to do, even if it would be embellishing a little.

Seth was lying in bed, propped up by two pillows. His comforter was pulled up to his chin, and he was staring at Nick with wide eyes. A trickle of sweat ran down his forehead.

"Hi!" he squeaked. He coughed. Then, in a much lower voice, said, "Hi."

"Hi," Nick said, closing the door behind him. "Are you dying?"

"Um. No?"

"That's good." Nick let his backpack fall to the floor. "Because Martha told me about the ghosts here, and it would totally suck if you died and became trapped like they did. I don't know how I'd feel about having to salt and burn your bones."

Seth squinted at him. "The . . . ghosts?"

"Yes, the ghosts." Nick frowned. "And speaking of, I can't believe you didn't tell me your house used to be a tuberculosis insane asylum and is haunted now. That seems like information one tells his best friend."

"Tuberculosis . . . insane . . . asylum?"

Seth's cold must have infected his brain. He sounded like he didn't know what Nick was talking about. "Right," Nick said slowly. "The tuberculosis insane asylum. Your aunt just told me all about it. Didn't you hear those footsteps running up the stairs and the door slamming?" Nick's eyes widened as he looked around. "Oh my god, are they here right now?"

"*Oh*," Seth said. "Right. The ghosts! Sorry. I thought you were talking about something else. This flu. Man, it is really making me woozy."

"I thought you had a cold."

Seth nodded furiously. "Right. A cold. That's exactly what I meant." He coughed roughly. "Oh man, such a bad cold. So sick. From the flooding. You should leave since I'm contagious, and I don't want you to catch it."

"I ate oranges," Nick told him, sitting on the edge of the bed. Seth pulled his feet away to make room.

"I don't think I've ever seen you eat an orange."

"Why is everyone saying that to me today?" Nick wondered aloud. "I do eat fruit, you know. Like, maybe not *all* the time, but I do."

"When was the last time you ate an orange?"

Nick didn't think he'd eaten an orange in at least three years. "This morning. So I'm chock full of vitamin C and therefore, immune to your affliction."

"Well, better to be safe than sorry," Seth said, pulling his covers up to his mouth. "You should probably go home, and then we can talk on the phone."

Nick shrugged. "I'm already here. If I'm going to be infected, it's happened by now."

Seth sighed.

"Are you okay? You're acting kinda weird."

"I'm fine," Seth said. "Just, you know. Medicine head, and all that." He coughed again.

Seth needed to take better care of himself. "Do you need me to bring you something? I was going to get you soup, but then I didn't have any money, so I didn't."

"Thought that counts, I suppose."

"Right? You're welcome."

"You're all heart, Nicky."

Nick opened his mouth to say something about how boring

today had been, or about how he'd fought with his dad, or maybe even about how Shadow Star and Pyro Storm had brawled all-out the night before. He could have said any number of things. But then his mouth was hijacked by a rebel part of his brain, and he said, "You kissed me on the cheek yesterday."

Seth's eyes widened above his blanket. "I . . . did?"

"Wow," Nick breathed. "I did *not* mean to bring that up. Honestly, I was going to try and work my way up to it in like five or six weeks."

"And yet there it is."

"Right? I'm braver than I give myself credit for." He grinned. "I'm going to make a good Extraordinary."

"It's weird how not weird it is that I can totally follow your line of thinking."

"You're fluent in Nick, I guess."

"Years of practice."

Nick felt like he was about to burst. "So the kissing! We should talk about the kissing!"

Seth winced. "I would really rather not, if it's all the same to you."

Nick patted his foot under the comforter. It felt like he was wearing boots, but it must have just been the blankets. Seth would never wear boots to bed. That would be ridiculous. "Too late. It's already out there."

"It's not that big of a deal."

That caused a strange twist in Nick's stomach that almost felt like disappointment. "Oh."

"I mean, friends do that all the time."

"They do?"

Seth shrugged. "I read they do."

"What? Where?"

Seth was sweating even more. "The internet."

"Where did you find that?" Nick demanded. "I tried to look it up, and all I could find were quizzes about what I'd be like in bed that I absolutely did not take!" He'd taken three of them. According to one, he was a modern woman in the streets, and a tigress in the sheets. He didn't know what to do with any of that. Tigers were cool and all, but he didn't think he had the posture to be a modern woman.

The comforter dropped a little. "Why were you looking that up?"

Nick blanched. "Um. For reasons completely unrelated to the topic at hand."

"Really?"

"Yes," Nick said, suddenly defensive. His skin felt warm, and he wondered if he'd already been infected. "You know I like to look things up. It's one of my things."

Seth was looking at him strangely. If Nick didn't know any better, he'd have thought Seth was almost . . . hopeful. "I just—I don't know. It felt like the right thing to do. I was going to face . . . all that flooding, and I didn't want to do it without saying good-bye."

"All that flooding," Nick repeated.

"Right."

"So you kissed me."

"On the *cheek*. You're acting like I stuck my tongue down your—"

"Whoa," Nick gasped. "I wasn't acting like that at *all*."

Seth paled. He must have been really sick. "I didn't mean it like that!"

Then a thought struck Nick that made him frown. "Do you go around kissing a lot of people?"

"What? No!"

"What about the secret girlfriend and/or boyfriend you have?"

Seth groaned. "I don't have a secret girlfriend and/or boyfriend. How many times do I have to tell you that?"

"Many more times," Nick said. "Because I don't believe you. I know I can be dumb about a lot of things, but you can't expect me to believe that you were at the animal shelter volunteering *all summer*."

Seth said, "I was. There was a shortage of volunteers, and I had to do my part!"

"For the animals."

"Exactly."

Nick was starting to get a little annoyed. "Why, though? I get that it's the right thing to do because cats and dogs are cool and all, but do they need you all the time? I mean, there was a flooding problem, and you were the one they called? It's like they own you." Then Nick was struck with another thought. "Do they own you? Is there some kind of secret ASPCA no-kill-shelter mafia that you belong to now? Have they bugged you? Are they *listening right now*?" He glared up at the biplane, sure it was the perfect place to hide a recording device.

"Oh my god. How the hell did you get from volunteering to the mafia?"

"It's best not to question such things," Nick said. "And I notice you didn't deny it. If we need to get you to a safe house, cough once. I don't actually have a safe house, but I have forty dollars in singles under my mattress, and that should be enough for one of those hotels downtown that rent by the hour."

"Nicky, there's no mafia."

"Maybe that's what they want you to—"

"Nick," Seth said through gritted teeth, and that shut Nick right up. Because Seth, tolerant and wonderful Seth, looked exasperated. Nick had seen it before, though never on Seth's face. He'd gotten it from teachers. He'd gotten it from other kids. He'd gotten it from random strangers. It was *the* look. Like Nick had spoken too much. Or had gone too far. Or had said something so stupid and crazy and *out there* that it was impossible to understand how such words could have come out of a normal, sane person. Yeah, Nick had gotten that look from many, many people in his life, but never from those he loved.

Until today.

Dad. Seth. The two people he counted on most.

He didn't know how to handle that. It hurt in ways he wasn't expecting. It wasn't like he could help it, and maybe that was part of the problem. Maybe he made too big a deal out of everything. And maybe, just maybe, Seth was getting tired of it.

"Um," Nick said, unsure of what to do. His hands were shaking, so he rubbed them on his jeans. "I didn't mean . . ."

Seth let out a sharp huff of air. "Whatever's going on in your head right now, you need to stop. It's not bad."

Which was exactly what someone would say when it *was* bad. "Maybe I should just go home." That sounded good. He could go home and shut himself in his room. He could do his homework and be a good son, and maybe when Seth was feeling better, they could forget all about this.

Nick shouldn't have eaten all those cookies.

"I don't *want* you to—" Seth sat up in the bed. As he did, the comforter sank lower to his chest. He was wearing a white undershirt, and for a moment, Nick was distracted by how strong his chest looked, how sharp his collarbones were, but then he saw the bruise on Seth's neck, a purple thing that almost looked like—

"Is that a hickey?" Nick asked, voice high-pitched.

Seth quickly brought his hand up to cover the bruise, but it was large, and the edges still peeked out beneath his fingers. Either someone had attached their really large mouth to Seth's neck, or he'd gotten hurt, somehow. "It's not a hickey."

"What happened? Are you okay? Does it hurt? Can I touch it?"

Seth flushed. "You can't touch—it's fine. It's nothing. Just . . . hurt myself. Down in the basement."

Nick nodded solemnly. "Because of the washing machine. Your aunt told me that it was on the fritz."

"Yes. Exactly. I was trying to fix the washing machine. The motor is broken."

"I thought she said it was the filtering valve?"

"Uh. That's what I meant. The filtering valve is broken."

"Oh."

Seth sighed again. "Nick, look. There isn't any no-kill-shelter mafia. There's no secret girlfriend and/or boyfriend." He paused for a moment, took a deep breath and said, "And I'm sorry I kissed you on the cheek. I shouldn't have done that. I know you don't—"

"It's okay," Nick said hastily, not wanting Seth to take it back *completely*. Right? Right. "It just . . . surprised me. You've never done that before."

Seth looked down at his hands. "Well, maybe I haven't had a reason to."

Nick felt like he was on fire. "And you do now?"

Seth shrugged. "There's . . . things. About me. Things I haven't told you. Not because I don't trust you, but because I wanted . . . I didn't know how you would see me. After."

"What things?"

"You wouldn't understand."

That almost sounded like an insult, but Nick kept the hurt from his face. "Why?"

Seth looked back up with a fierce expression. It was familiar, though Nick couldn't place why. "You've got this idea about what it means to be an Extraordinary. You think it's a gift that will solve everything. But it won't. You don't have any idea what it does to a person, and how much easier it'd be to let it all go. To just let the bad things happen. But you can't."

"I would never do that," Nick snapped. "When I become an Extraordinary, I'm gonna do good for everyone. I wouldn't ever want it to go away."

Seth laughed bitterly. "You say that now. Just wait until—"

"I know you never wanted it," Nick said, standing up from the bed. His head almost hit the biplane. "Not like I do. And that's okay. That's your choice. This is mine."

"Why? Why do you want this?"

Nick shook his head. "I've told you this before."

"Right. Because of Shadow Star. Because you think he's this person you've built up in your head. What if he's nothing like you think he is? What if all you're going to get is disappointment?"

"No," Nick said, taking a step back. "It's not—okay, it *was* like that. And maybe part of it still is. Because he's amazing and brave, and no one can tell me otherwise. Just because you can't do what he does, doesn't mean you get to talk crap about him."

"What changed? Why do you want to be one now?"

Nick's skin was itching. It felt like his brain was leaking out his ears. "For the people. To keep them safe. Shadow Star can't do it all on his own, right? He needs my help. If I can do that, if I can really help him, that'll help Nova City, and then it'll help my dad. And then maybe he won't hate the way I am now."

Seth looked shocked. "Nick, your dad doesn't hate you. He doesn't hate anything about you."

Nick's fingers were twitching. "Sure seemed like it this morning when he asked me why I had to be the way I was."

"Are you sure that's what he said? You have a tendency to . . . exaggerate things."

Nick really wanted to go home now. The walls were closing in, and his thoughts were jumbled and angry. "Great. I didn't know you felt that way." He scooped his backpack up from the floor. "I'll keep that in mind for the future."

But before he could turn toward the door, Seth tried to get out of the bed. He swung his legs out from underneath the comforter. Nick hadn't been wrong. Seth was wearing boots. And sweats that clung to his legs. And the undershirt that was tight against his chest and shoulders. Seth groaned, clutching a hand around his stomach, gritting his teeth.

Nick took a step back. This wasn't the Seth he knew. The Seth *he* knew was chubby and wore sweaters and bow ties and sometimes stuck his tongue out between his teeth when he was concentrating really hard. He was resilient and dependable and made Nick feel important.

This Seth looked strong, even though he also looked like he was hurting. The muscles in his arms bunched as he gripped his stomach, breathing through his nose. He looked like he hadn't exactly lost weight—except in his face—but more so that it'd been redistributed and possibly turned to muscle.

Nick didn't know what to do with that, especially since his brain seemed to have shorted out. "You're buff," he said stupidly. "Why are you buff?"

Seth chuckled through gritted teeth. "Hard work."

"Why didn't I notice?" Nick asked.

"Maybe because you don't always see things that are right in front of you."

That stung more than Nick thought it would. Because all he could hear in that was Dad asking him why he had to be the way he was. "That's not fair. You know how my head is—"

"Oh, I know," Seth said. "I know exactly how your head is. But it can't be an excuse, Nick. Not forever. You want to be an

Extraordinary? Fine. There's a bus filled with kids that's about to fall off a bridge. There's an apartment building ten miles away that's on fire and about to collapse filled with people who can't escape on their own. Who do you save?"

"I don't . . . that's not—"

Seth looked up at him, eyes blazing. "Who do you save, Nick? You want to help the city, right? That's what you said. You want to help the city. The people. Your dad. Who do you save?"

"I would help one," Nick said. "And Shadow Star would help the others. That way everyone is okay, and no one would get hurt. And maybe I'd even convince Pyro Storm to help put out the fire, because he can't be *all* bad—"

"Funny how that works," Seth muttered. He shook his head. "You have faith, Nick. That's good. But it's not going to be enough."

Nick bristled. "What the hell, man? All I wanted was to come over here and check on you—"

"Even though I told you to stay away—"

"—and now you've got bruises and muscles and you're wearing boots in bed—"

"It's my house. I can do what I want."

"—and you're trying to quiz me or something, and you're talking crap about Shadow Star who is the greatest Extraordinary alive. And maybe you don't want me to be like him. Or Pyro Storm. Maybe you're just jealous about—"

Seth's laugh was almost hysterical. "Jealous? About *Extraordinaries*? That's not even . . ." He tilted his head. "Huh. That actually makes a lot of sense."

Nick wasn't expecting that. "It does? I mean, of course it does. You're just jealous that . . . that, um. Okay, wait. Why are you jealous?"

Seth looked up at him again. That same strange glint was in his eyes. "I'm right here, you know? I have been. For a long time."

Nick was confused. "I know."

"And then there was Owen, and you—"

"Made a sexy but regrettable mistake," Nick admitted. "I blame teenage hormones and this thing he could do with his tongue." He grimaced. "That makes me sound terrible."

"And now you've got this stupid crush on Shadow Star."

"Don't," Nick snapped. "It's not stupid, okay? He saved me, and he knows who I am without me having to tell him, which means he might like me or something, and even if he doesn't, I can show him that I can be—"

"Who is he, Nick?"

That stopped Nick right in his tracks. "What?"

Seth stared at him intently. "Who is he? He's Shadow Star. But who is he behind his mask?"

"That doesn't matter to me."

"It might if you find out. It might change everything. What if it were me?"

Nicholas Bell did what was possibly the stupidest thing in a short, short life filled with many stupid things. He didn't mean to, of course. It was a knee-jerk reaction. He didn't think he could have stopped it even if he'd tried.

He laughed. He *laughed,* because the idea of Seth of all people being Shadow Star was so preposterous, he couldn't even fathom it.

Seth's expression hardened.

"I'm sorry," Nick gasped, trying to fight it down but failing quite spectacularly. "You're Seth. There's no way you could—I mean, that's dumb. Come on, man. Don't do that. You don't need to be him. You're fine the way you are. And besides, it's not like you would keep that a secret from me, right? I mean, if you were Shadow Star, you'd tell me. It's just . . . dumb."

Seth nodded tightly. "Right. Dumb. Of course. I don't know what I was thinking."

Nick flailed. The conversation had spun out of control. "Oh, hey. Wait. I didn't mean it like that. You're my favorite person in the whole world next to my dad. You know that, right? *You're* not dumb."

"Just the idea of me being an Extraordinary is."

Nick felt like he was on ice, and it was cracking beneath his feet. "I don't know what you're trying to say."

"I kissed your cheek."

Nick felt his face grow warm again. "I . . . yeah."

Seth looked away. "You should go."

Nick blinked. "Wait, what? What did I do? Are you mad at me?"

Seth smiled tightly. "I just want to be by myself. Sick, remember? Can't have you catching it."

"We still need to talk about me becoming—"

"Please. Just . . . go."

Since Nick was helpless when Seth said *please,* he turned and left. Before he closed the door, he looked over his shoulder. Seth sat on his bed, face in his hands.

He left, shutting the door.

B ob was waiting at the bottom of the stairs. He wore a pair of overalls stained with grease. He looked older than Nick remembered, the lines around his eyes and mouth deeper. His hair hung in white wisps around his face. Nick could hear Martha moving in the kitchen.

"Nicky," Bob said, his voice a deep rumble. "Everything okay?"

No, it really wasn't. He shook his head.

"Heard some raised voices."

Nick winced. "Sorry about that. Just a frank exchange of ideas."

"You boys okay?"

Nick didn't know if they were or not. He couldn't even be sure what they'd argued about. He just knew he was mad at pretty much everyone, mostly for nonsensical reasons. He wasn't sure if that included Seth. "I'm sorry to tell you that your nephew is a jerk." Okay, so maybe it did include Seth.

Bob barely reacted. "He's a teenager. That's to be expected."

"But I might be one too."

"A teenager or a jerk?"

Nick liked Bob a lot. "Both."

Bob nodded slowly. "Seems like things are changing."

"Tell me about it," Nick muttered, pulling on one of the straps to his backpack. "When did Seth get biceps?"

Bob chuckled. "Noticed that, did you? Growing up, I guess."

"That's not fair. He gets muscles, and I get a little mustache that makes me look like I should be wearing a trench coat and flashing people."

"That was . . . oddly specific."

Nick sighed. "I tend to do that."

"You'll come into yours," Bob said, patting him on the shoulder. "He's going through a lot right now. More than you could possibly know."

"Why won't he just tell me?" Nick asked, suddenly exhausted. "I'm his best friend. He can tell me anything. It's how we've always been."

"Can he?" Bob asked. "Maybe he needs to hear that from you."

Oof. That was pointed, but fair. "I try to be a good friend. But sometimes, other stuff comes up. I get stuck in my own head and forget what I should be doing instead of what I want to be doing."

"That's how life goes. Things happen. It's difficult. Sometimes, people drift apart. They get set upon different paths. Doesn't mean they care about each other any less."

Nick stared at him in horror. "That's not going to happen. I'm going to be with Seth forever."

Bob's lips twitched. "How . . . expected. And if he said the same to you?"

Nick blushed furiously. "I. Um. That would be. Neat?"

"Oh, so I guess the fact that he's in love with you would—"

"Robert Gray!" Martha said furiously, coming out of the kitchen, a dish towel in her hands. "You close those flapping lips of yours *right this second*."

Bob scowled at her. "Someone needs to say it. Aren't you tired of all the pining? You're lucky I didn't tell him about how Seth is—"

She slapped the dish towel over his mouth while glaring up at him.

He waggled his eyebrows at her.

They looked at Nick.

Nick, who was in the middle of a full system shutdown.

"Oh dear," Martha said as she pulled the dish towel away. "I think you've broken him."

Bob poked Nick on the cheek. "Imagine how he'd react if I told him the other thing."

"*Robert Gray.*"

His eyes were twinkling when he said, "Probably a good idea just to keep it at one thing at a time."

"Why, you old rascal. You're gonna get it, I promise."

"I should hope so," Bob said, kissing her cheek.

Three minutes later, Nick found himself standing on the porch of the Gray brownstone, a plate of cookies in his hand, the door closing behind him after Martha told him to come back as soon as he could.

It took him at least ten more minutes before he was able to somehow make his legs work again.

He didn't remember much about the walk home.

11

It's well known that regardless of what else they are, teenage boys are inherently stupid.

Oh, they *try* to act like they aren't; their egos don't allow for such magnanimity. They strut and preen like tiny little show dogs, carrying themselves with an undeserved sense of accomplishment. They can be rude and mostly daft, their lack of self- and spatial-awareness making it a slight wonder they've somehow managed to stay alive in order to puff out their body-spray-saturated chests and put copious amounts of product in their hair.

The *problem* with this is, sometimes, certain events can occur to break through this shield of teenage futility.

Nicholas Bell was a stupid teenage boy. He was partially aware of this fact, but still. He was absolutely convinced that he could become an Extraordinary, that he was destined for something more. Maybe he wasn't a tiny show dog, per se, but he did believe himself to be somewhat invincible.

That was, of course, until Bob Gray flapped his lips and told Nick something that altered the shape of the entire world.

"Oh my god," Nick said while in bed, staring up at the ceiling.

"Oh my god," Nick said, three hours later, still staring up at the ceiling.

His mother smiled at him like she always did.

In addition to being inherently stupid, most teenage boys tend to have an attention span that leaves a lot to be desired. Now, imagine if you will, an inherently stupid teenage boy who is afflicted with an attention deficit disorder of the most hyperactive variety regulated by something with the ridiculous name of Concentra. And, as luck would have it, this same teenage boy got maybe an hour or two of sleep before his alarm went off and he managed to trudge his way down the stairs like some amorphous blob.

Only to reach the kitchen and remember he was angry with his father.

"Crap," this teenage boy muttered when he saw his dad in the kitchen and the previous day's events burst through the fog.

Dad grunted in return.

Cereal sat on the counter next to an empty bowl and a carton of milk. This was almost enough to distract Nick since he was reminded from one of his late-night internet adventures that Canadians had bags of milk instead of cartons or jugs (something he would never understand), but then he remembered Dad asking why he had to be this way, and he forgot all about Canadian milk bags. Nick's lunch sat in a brown paper sack next to the milk.

He and Dad had fought before. They were two guys living together under one roof, so it was to be expected. However, even after the Great Romance of Nick and Owen when Nick wasn't doing so hot in school and his father had sat him down to have the talk where Things Were Going To Change, he'd never felt like . . . this. Like he was a burden.

Dad leaned against the counter, the newspaper in his hands, but Nick knew he wasn't reading it. He was waiting to see what kind of mood Nick was in.

Well, two could play at this game, because Nick was in a foul mood. But it wasn't the usual *I hate everything because all my feelings are real and valid* kind of foul mood that seemed to grace sixteen-year-old boys facing an identity crisis. No, *this* foul mood was tinged with *my best friend's uncle told me my best friend wants my junk and stuff* and also *I wish I had superpowers but it's not working out so well.*

It was unquestionably the worst kind of foul mood, and he was probably the only person in the world who felt this way. No one could ever understand.

The cereal was off-brand. It was called Cinnamon Bread-Shaped Chomps. Nick wondered if this was Dad's way of apologizing, because Nick wasn't allowed to eat Cinnamon Bread-Shaped Chomps, given how much sugar was in a couple of spoonfuls. He was suspicious, sure he'd open the box up and see raisins inside atop bran flakes as a final *screw you*.

Imagine his surprise when Cinnamon Bread-Shaped Chomps spilled into the bowl.

A tiny pill sat next to the spoon on the table too, so that pretty much made the cereal moot.

It was then that Nick had a terrible idea as he poured milk over the cereal, one that he was sure he'd probably end up regretting, but seemed like a good one in the here and now.

"I'm taking my pill," he announced grandly.

Dad looked over the paper, his expression bland.

Nick made sure his dad watched as he put it in his mouth.

He swallowed, Adam's apple bobbing up and down.

Dad went back to the paper.

Nick pulled the pill out from under his tongue. It was gritty in his fingers. He shoved it into his pocket. It left an acidic taste in his mouth, but it was soon nothing but a distant memory under cinnamon and something that was vaguely bread-shaped.

His dad wanted him to be someone different?

Fine.

He finished his breakfast.

He put the bowl in the sink. He put the milk in the fridge.

He picked up his backpack after placing his lunch inside and turned to leave the kitchen.

"Nick."

He stopped, convinced he'd been caught. His dad had used his supercop senses and had known the moment Nick tried to hide the pill. He'd take Nick to the precinct to interrogate him, and then Nick would be forced to spill what Bob had told him yesterday, and how confused that made him because if he was being honest, Seth had biceps apparently, but he was sort of fond of the way Seth had looked before, and if he was *really* thinking about it, he was maybe fond of the way Seth talked and breathed and existed in ways he hadn't really thought about, and he didn't want to seem shallow if he found out that he *might* have a crush on his best friend now. Because what would that say about him if Seth was all buff now with massive shoulders and then Nick decided he wanted to touch them? It shouldn't matter how a person looked, it was the inside that counted.

That was completely at odds with his destiny with Shadow Star, because they were obviously meant to be together, right? Nick wrote stories about him and had his autograph, and Shadow Star knew his name, so that had to mean something. Life would just be so much easier if Seth and Shadow Star were the same person, but that was ridiculous. Because Shadow Star was a superhero who saved the city from the forces of evil while Seth had to deal with feral cat emergencies which, to be fair, weren't any less important. They were just important on a different scale.

Add in the fact that Nick had to become an Extraordinary so he could help the big lug standing in front of him, even if he wasn't feeling exactly charitable at the moment.

"What?" he asked, wondering if this was the moment when everything would be okay again.

Dad stared at him for a beat, then sighed. "Have a good day at school."

Nick swallowed thickly and opened his mouth to say something, but turned around and walked out of the kitchen instead.

He was running a little behind by the time he reached the Franklin Street station. Jazz and Gibby were waiting for him on the bench near the stairs. Seth's train would be arriving in a few minutes, which meant Nick had a little bit of time to decide how to act. Seth hadn't texted to say he wasn't coming in to school today, so Nick expected him shortly.

"Hey, Nicky," Jazz said as he approached. She squinted up at him. "You okay? You look . . . sweaty."

"I'm fine," Nick said, though it came out in a squeak. He coughed and lowered his voice at least four octaves. "I'm fine." It sounded like he was snarling. "Um. Have you seen Seth?"

Gibby narrowed her eyes. "No. Why?"

"No reason. No reason at all." He laughed awkwardly. "I mean, why would there need to be a reason for anything at all ever?"

"Are you sure you're okay?" Jazz asked, sounding concerned. "You're really sweaty."

"It's not sweat. It's . . . raining."

"Strange," Gibby said. "There wasn't a cloud in the sky fifteen minutes ago."

"A flash flood," Nick said, glancing around the station. He didn't see Seth yet. "Just on my street. Freak thing. Probably will never happen again. So, listen. Here's the thing. Today is going to be weird, and you *can't say anything.*"

Jazz and Gibby exchanged a look and had one of their silent conversations that Nick would never understand. They looked back at him.

"Why is it going to be weird?" Gibby asked.

"Just . . . like. Okay. So. Um. Feelings. And I—there were ghosts. Tuberculosis insane asylum ghosts. And I had Cinnamon Bread-Shaped Chomps this morning for an apology, so I'm a little wired. And I'm still so mad. But. I don't know at who? I think it's at almost everyone. Like. Is that okay? *I* think it's okay. And then there's Phase Three. I don't know. It's just this whole thing."

"Wow," Jazz whispered. "That was . . . I don't know what that was."

"Why are you mad at us?" Gibby demanded.

Nick wasn't quite sure, so he told them as much.

They didn't seem appeased.

"You sound like you have a lot to work through," Jazz told him sagely.

Nick was relieved. "Right? It's just . . . I'm having all these *feelings*—"

"Hey, guys," Seth said from behind them.

Now, it should be said that Nick had never really had someone in love with him before. Yes, it would have to mean Bob was telling the truth, but since Nick never heard him lie about anything before, he didn't think Bob would have picked such a horrible time to start.

In terms of the love life of Nicholas Bell, his experience was rather short. He wasn't by any means an expert in *l'art d'amour.* So when faced with the fact that someone who he considered his best friend and who he was also fighting with apparently wanted to put his face on Nick's face, he discovered quite quickly just how awkward things could be.

It didn't help that Seth was standing there, looking like he did, wearing an oversized sweater vest over a collared shirt, chinos, loafers, and a goddamn polka-dotted *cravat* of all things. How dare he.

"Seth!" Nick cried, his voice much louder than he anticipated. "Buddy! Pal! Hey! Hi! How are you?"

Seth, for his part, took it in stride, though he did appear to be somewhat startled at the rather sweaty best friend practically shouting in his face. "I'm fine."

Nick nodded furiously to the point where he wondered if whiplash was possible. "Good. Good, good, good. That's . . . good. You feeling better? Like . . . just. Better?"

"I am," he said slowly. "Are you okay?"

"Never better!" Nick bellowed, wiping his forehead. His hand came away soaked. "I brought you something." He reached into his backpack and pulled out the present he'd stopped at a bodega for. It had made him miss his usual train. "It's Mexican candy! Skwinkles Salsagheti!"

"I can see that," Seth said, staring down at the plastic package Nick had practically shoved into his hands. "And you got me Skwinkles Salsagheti because . . ."

Because the bodega—like most bodegas—catered to the Hispanic community, and there wasn't anything with nougat in the entire store. The meltdown he'd had meant that he wasn't allowed to go back to that particular bodega. "It reminded me of you," Nick said, for lack of anything better.

"What's happening?" Jazz whispered to Gibby.

"I have no idea," Gibby whispered back. "I only like girls."

"O . . . kay," Seth said. "Thanks. I think."

Nick nodded so hard, he felt bones crack. That probably wasn't good. "Yep. Just looking out for my best bud. My bro. My brotato chip. My pot-broast. We're just Bromeo and Dudeliet." Nick actively forced his mouth shut before he could make things worse.

Seth stared at him strangely for a moment before shaking his head. "I—look. About how we left things yesterday—"

"Nope," Nick said, taking a step back. "Nope, nope, nope. Don't even worry about it. Enjoy your Skwinkles Salsagheti. ¡*Muy rapido!*"

And in a move he would most likely regret for the rest of his life, Nick turned and ran up the stairs and all the way to school, leaving his friends behind.

His day didn't get much better after that.

There was a pop quiz in AP History that he was pretty sure he boffed big-time.

When called on to explain a Byronic hero in English class, Nick managed to give a three-minute presentation on the mating habits of box turtles before the teacher mercifully put him out of his misery.

He was twitchier than normal, and even though he knew there was a mushed pill in his pocket, he didn't dare take it out, knowing he had to prove a point. Maybe proving a point during the middle of a life-altering romantic crisis was not the best time to try and quit cold turkey, but Nick was nothing if not spontaneous.

And, for one of the first times in his known life, he was actually dreading how quickly the day seemed to be moving. He stared in horror up at the clock as it approached lunchtime, knowing he'd once again be faced with Seth, and he wasn't sure how he felt about that. What if Seth had misunderstood the gift of Mexican candy and had thought it meant intent? Did Nick mean for it to have intent? If so, what did *that* mean? And why did Seth have to wear a freaking cravat today of all days? And when had cravats become some sort of weakness?

When the bell rang for lunch, Nick gave very serious consideration to applying for a passport, waiting the requisite four to six weeks for it to arrive, and then fleeing the country.

However, given that he was underage, it meant he would have to ask his father for help applying, and Dad was on his shit list, Cinnamon Bread-Shaped Chomps aside.

He walked slowly toward the lunchroom. He understood what it must feel like to be in a gulag.

Seth was already at the lunch table with Gibby and Jazz. Their heads were bowed together and they whispered furiously. Nick's curiosity pierced through the haze he'd been mired in since the day before. What could they be discussing so intently? It was a mystery that needed to be solved, and by god, Nick would *solve it*. Maybe they had come up with plans for a more secure Phase Three, and he could be an Extraordinary by this afternoon! Wouldn't that just make this weird day better? Of course it would.

But before he could take a step toward his friends, an arm fell on his shoulders, and he was pulled close to another body, a voice near his ears. "Hiya, Nicky. Why're you just standing here? Who're we staring at?"

Nick shivered at the hot breath on his neck. "Owen," he managed to say. "Glad you could show up and—holy god, what happened to your *face*?"

Nick pulled away to stare at Owen in disbelief. He was smiling that wicked smile, even though it had to hurt. It looked as if Owen had been punched right in the eye, the bruise dark, the skin puffy. Owen shrugged. "It's not too bad. You should see the other guy." He glanced over Nick's shoulder to their lunch table before looking back at Nick. "Aw, are you worried about little old me? Nicky, I'm touched. Really." He reached out and pinched Nick's cheek.

Nick knocked his hand away. "What happened?"

Owen rolled his eyes. "It's not a big deal. Just a bit of sparring. A lucky punch, that's all. I've had worse."

"Sparring," Nick repeated slowly.

"Yep. Gotta keep in shape, you know? I mean, how else could I get your attention?" His smile widened. "I know how you like the muscles."

Nick scowled at him. "I don't like anything about you."

"Now, now. We both know that's not true. You missed me. Admit it."

"I didn't even notice you were gone."

Owen laughed. "Someone got a backbone in the last couple of days. It'll do you good when you become an Extraordinary, I think."

Nick blinked. That sounded suspiciously close to a compliment. "Really?"

"Sure. That's still a thing, right? You still want to be an Extraordinary?"

"Yeah, it's still a thing. Other things have . . . happened, but it's not going to stop me."

Owen studied Nick so intently, Nick started squirming. Then, "It's good to see you're so adamant about it. Tell you what, Nicky. When you're ready to play with the big boys, you let me know. I might be able to help you."

Nick frowned. "Help me with what?"

Owen pinched his cheek again. "Is that a formal request?"

Nick shoved him away. "No. I don't need your help with anything. I can do it on my own."

"Sure, Nicky. Just remember that I offered, huh?"

And because Nick had a heart, messed up though it might be, he had to ask. "It was just . . . sparring, right? Not—" He hesitated, unsure if he was overstepping.

"Not what?"

"Not your dad?" Nick blurted before he could stop himself.

Owen looked taken aback, but he recovered quickly. And for a moment, the mask slipped again. "Nah. He wouldn't raise a hand to me. Never has. I promise, okay? It's not like that."

"If you say so."

"I do. Now, shall we go see why they're talking about us?"

"How do you know they're talking about us?"

Owen winked at him. "Because they're trying to act like they aren't."

Nick looked over at the table. Sure enough, Gibby was waving her hands at Jazz and Seth, whispering something that Nick couldn't hear. Both Seth and Jazz turned their heads to look at Nick and Owen.

"Great," Nick muttered.

"Eh," Owen said. "If people aren't talking about you, then you're doing something wrong."

If breakfast had been uncomfortable and the train station awkward, then lunch was absolutely excruciating.

It didn't help that Jazz was staring at him weirdly, or that

Gibby kept muttering under her breath about *idiot boys*. And Seth seemed barely able to meet Nick's gaze for more than a second or two before he'd look away, pulling at his polka-dotted cravat. Nick also wanted to pull on it.

And it absolutely did not help that Owen seemed to be more . . . hands-on than usual. He leaned into Nick, bumped his shoulder, laughed quietly as he whispered in Nick's ear. Seth scowled at Owen for almost the entirety of lunch, his forehead wrinkled, cheeks flushed.

"So," Nick said, trying desperately to make things normal again. "I've decided to move on to Phase Three."

"I assume that Phase Three is better than One or Two," Gibby said through a mouthful of what appeared to be peanut butter and strawberry jam.

"It is," Nick said, shoving Owen away after he flicked his ear. "It's the best phase. Everyone says so."

"Who is everyone?" Jazz asked.

Nick ignored her. He didn't have time for things like facts. "I plan on implementing Phase Three this Saturday, and I expect all of you to be there. This could potentially be one of the most significant experiences of my life, and I will need your support when I make the transition from normal to Extraordinary."

"How is this going to be any different than the other times?" Gibby asked.

"Because it *will*," Nick insisted. "The other phases were all child's play compared to this. Phase Three is the big one."

"What are you going to do?" Seth asked. Nick looked over at him, and then sighed inwardly when Seth turned away almost immediately.

"It's a surprise," Nick said. "Trust me, though. This time it'll work."

"Is it illegal?" Owen asked. "Because if it is, I am totally down."

Nick glared at him. "No, it's not illegal. My dad's a cop. I wouldn't do that."

"You were looking up plans to break into a nuclear power plant," Jazz reminded him.

"Right, but I didn't do it. It's one thing to think of doing something illegal, but it's another to actually do it."

"Your moral compass might need some fine-tuning," Gibby told him. "Just for the record."

Nick waved a hand dismissively at her. "Whatever. The point is that I've got the most perfect plan of all plans. You need to be there. Agreed?"

"Agreed," Jazz said, because she was amazing.

"Fine," Gibby said, sounding bored. She was slightly less amazing.

"Maybe," Owen said, because he was a jerk. "If nothing better comes up."

Nick turned to Seth, who was picking at a smashed sandwich. "Seth?"

Seth shrugged. "If you think it's right."

"Maybe try that with a little more enthusiasm."

Seth scowled a little harder. "Yeah, I'll be there."

"Good," Nick said brightly, clapping his hands. "Then let Phase Three commence!" Then, "Well, not right this second. Because we still have school. And it's not Saturday. So."

Nick!"

Nick turned to see Seth rushing toward him down the steps. He'd been waiting for his friends after the last bell before they headed for the train. Nick looked behind Seth to see if Gibby or Jazz were coming, but Seth was alone.

"Hey," he said. "Where is everyone?"

Seth stopped in front of him and rubbed the back of his neck. "Um. They're . . . not here."

"I can see that. Thank you for stating the obvious."

Seth sighed. "It's just us today."

"Oh. Okay. That's . . . great." It wasn't great. Or maybe it was the greatest. Nick was instantly covered in flop sweat. Was this like a date? Seth loved him, and Nick . . . felt some way toward him back, and it was just the two of them, and what if Seth wanted to go get something to eat? At a *restaurant*? Nick probably had four dollars in his wallet. And maybe, like, forty cents. Skwinkles Salsagheti had ended up costing more than he thought it would, but it was totally okay. Maybe they could get tacos or something. One taco. For the both of them. "We'll have to split it right down the middle," Nick said, slightly panicked.

"Split what?"

Nick forgot that Seth couldn't read his mind. "Nothing! Absolutely nothing at all. Gosh, it's certainly a nice day out today!"

"You okay?"

What a loaded question. "Yes?"

"Good," Seth said. "Come on."

Oh no. This was a date.

It wasn't a date.

It was just two bros walking side by side down the sidewalk. They'd done it a billion times before. Sure, they'd never done it after Seth's uncle had flapped his lips, but still. Two bros doing bro stuff.

"Just being bros," Nick said aloud.

Seth stared at him strangely. "You're acting weird."

Nick shrugged and looked away. "It's been a very weird forty-eight hours."

"Yeah? How come?"

Nick liked that. He liked that a lot. Because regardless of what else was going on between them, regardless of how uneven their footing, Seth gave a damn. He always had. "Had a fight with my dad."

"You told me. Sucks."

"Yeah. And I didn't take my pill this morning."

"I thought as much. You're a little more jittery than normal."

Nick sighed. "I dunno. I was mad, and he bought me Cinnamon Bread-Shaped Chomps because that's how he says sorry, and I ate it, but I still wasn't in a forgiving mood, so I didn't do anything about it."

"Is this about what he said?"

Nick looked away, unable to answer, Dad's voice still ringing in his head.

"Is that why . . ." Seth shook his head.

"Is that why what?"

Seth swallowed thickly. "Is that why yesterday you—I don't know. You were agitated. We didn't leave things okay."

"Maybe. I'm sorry I acted like a jerk. I'm glad you feel better."

"Yeah," Seth said, and actually looked up at Nick. "I'm feeling okay now." Then, "Did my uncle say something to you?"

A bright flare of panic roared through Nick, and he said, "Not really. I barely saw him."

"That's . . . that's good."

"Yeah. Oh, hey, look. Train's on time. Hurry up!"

He could barely ignore the stuttering *thumpthumpthump* of his heart.

It didn't help, later, when they were sitting side by side on the train, that Seth opened his backpack and pulled out the package of Skwinkles Salsagheti. "I thought maybe we could, you know. Share them."

This was totally maybe a date. Right?

Nick cleared his throat. "Uh. Sure. That would be—that's cool."

"Okay. I've never had these before."

"Me either."

"They look . . . edible?"

"They're probably sour," Nick said. "Mom spent time in Mexico when she was a kid. She said a lot of the candy is sour there."

"I didn't know that."

"Yeah. Grandma and Grandpa went there to help build houses or something. She was there for almost a year."

"That's why she was good at Spanish?"

Nick nodded, pleased Seth had remembered. "Yeah. She said the best way to learn a language is to be immersed in it. You don't have a choice otherwise."

"She was pretty great."

Her memory still hurt, but it had lost its sharp edges. "I think so too."

Seth handed him a strand of Salsagheti. "Supposed to be watermelon-flavored."

"You want me to go first?"

Seth smiled quietly at him. "Same time?"

"Okay." Nick tilted his head back, holding the candy dangling over his mouth. He glanced over, and Seth was doing the same. "Ready? One. Two. *Three.*"

Nick had been right. It was sour. Edible, but sour.

He tilted his head forward in time to see Seth's eyes bulging, his face screwed up in a grimace, a piece of Salsagheti hanging out of his mouth. "So good," Seth managed to say, though he sounded like he was dying.

"Oh my god," Nick said, laughing at him. "You hate it!"

"I don't hate it. I just wasn't expecting it to taste like *that*."

"Like what?"

Seth swallowed it down. "Like it murdered my mouth."

Nick bumped his shoulder. Seth bumped back.

Maybe it wasn't a date.

But it was still good.

Good, that is, until Seth didn't show on Saturday when they were supposed to meet. Neither did Owen, but Seth was the one Nick had been looking for. The past couple of days had been better, and Nick thought he and Seth were getting back to where they belonged. Nick's dad was still acting distant, and Nick had managed to avoid taking his pills for three days running, but things were mostly okay. He had a headache, but it wasn't as bad as it could have been. *Yes,* his toothpaste tube had exploded for absolutely no reason this morning, but that was not going to ruin what was probably going to be the most important day of his life.

"Maybe he's just behind schedule," Jazz said as Nick looked down at his phone for what felt like the hundredth time in the last ten minutes. "The trains don't run as often on the weekends. One of the lines could be delayed."

"Then why isn't he texting back?" Nick asked, brow furrowed.

"I don't know, Nicky."

"Whatever it is," Gibby said, "I'm sure he has a good reason. You know that, right? He's not blowing you off or anything."

"Like he did all summer?"

Gibby sighed. "It wasn't—he was busy, Nicky. We all get busy. You know that. It doesn't mean he wants to be with you any less. It happens, sometimes."

Nick knew he was being unreasonable. Gibby was right. It *did* happen, sometimes. It seemed to be happening more and more lately, but that was nothing in the face of all the years that Seth had been there for him. So *what* if this was one of the biggest moments of Nick's life and Seth had promised? No big deal.

"You've got your grumpy face," Jazz told him.

"It's not grumpy," he said grumpily.

"We can wait a little bit longer," Gibby said. "He could still show. In the meantime, why don't you tell us why we're at the river? I gotta tell you, Nick. This place reeks like death."

And it did. The Westfield River was disgusting. He'd had them meet him at one of the piers, but away from the ones that had all the tourists. In the distance, he could see a couple of old guys fishing off a dock who probably never actually caught anything, instead dropping their lines in the water and gabbing. The river was polluted to the point where anything actually caught would not be edible.

Which was exactly why Nick was here.

He climbed up onto a wooden post and faced the river, hands on his hips as he posed grandly, a gentle breeze blowing against his face carrying the scent of rancid farts and spoiled meat, but he ignored it, because this was his moment. This was *his* time to shine.

"Phase Three," he announced, sure that Gibby and Jazz had the same shivers down their spines as he did. How could they not? They were about to witness something (dare he say it) *extraordinary*.

There was silence from behind him.

He knew it was sinking in. He gave them a moment.

Still more silence.

He looked over his shoulder.

Gibby and Jazz were staring at him.

He stared back.

Jazz sneezed. "Excuse me," she said daintily.

Nick was not impressed. He glared at them both.

"Oh!" Gibby said. "I get it now." She cleared her throat. "Phase Three? Why, whatever could you be speaking of?"

"That was really good," Jazz told her.

"I know," Gibby said.

At least they were sort of trying. "I'm glad you asked!" He turned back toward the river, raising his voice so they wouldn't miss a word. "Today, you are going to witness something—"

A phone chimed behind him. Nick closed his eyes and breathed through his nose.

"My bad," Jazz said. "My dad. Gotta . . . text him back . . . and . . . done. Go ahead and continue with whatever you're doing."

Nick took another moment before he opened his eyes. No big deal. "Today, you are going to wit—"

Another phone beeped. "Wow," Gibby said. "Talk about some weird timing. That was me this time. Sorry. Sorry. I think it's a wrong number. They're asking if the 1997 Toyota Camry is still for sale."

"What's a 1997 Toyota Camry?" Jazz asked, sounding confused.

"Something you'll never understand," Gibby told her. "Gonna tell them it's a wrong number and . . . okay, we're good!"

Third time's the charm. "Today, you are going to witness something amazing." He waited a moment. No phone beeped. Good. He was about to blow some minds. "Phase Three is here, and I'm going to—"

Another phone chimed.

Nick whirled around, a snarl on his face.

Or, at least he *tried* to whirl around. Given that he was standing on a wooden pylon, there wasn't enough room to do much. And given that Nick—on a good day—was not exactly the most graceful of creatures, he started to fall backward into the river.

He was saved when Gibby grabbed him by the front of his coat and pulled him forward. He almost landed on top of her when he fell off the pylon, but somehow managed to land on his feet.

"You idiot," she muttered as she took a step back. "What the hell were you thinking?"

"Phones off!" he cried. "Everyone turn your phones off right this second! You kids these days with your texts and snaps and tweets! I will not be interrupted again."

"That was your phone this time," Jazz told him.

Nick blinked. "No, it wasn't." He reached into his pocket and pulled out his phone. "Oh. Would you look at that. It was. Ha ha ha. How weird."

Jazz's phone beeped.

And then Gibby's.

He thought about grabbing them and chucking them into the river, but figured he would get kicked in the testicles, so he decided against it.

He looked at his own phone again. An alert:

EXTRAORDINARY ACTIVITY. SHADOW STAR AND PYRO STORM ARE NEAR BURKE TOWER.

"Why?" he moaned. "Why does this have to be happening now?"

"I wonder why they're fighting again?" Jazz asked. "They seem to be at each other's throats more and more lately."

Gibby looked troubled. "I don't know. But someone's going to get hurt."

Nick made the hardest decision of his life. Instead of trying to find a livestream of what was going on with Shadow Star, he silenced his phone and put it back in his pocket. "It doesn't matter. At least not right this second. If Phase Three works like I think it will, then I'll be in a position to help Shadow Star take down Pyro Storm. And then we'll become friends, which will tentatively lead toward something more. There will be shy hesitation, but then one day, after saving Nova City from a madman who wants to turn the entire city to ice, there will be kissing and butt stuff and we'll live happily ever after."

Jazz and Gibby stared at him.

Nick shifted his weight from foot to foot.

"That was . . . detailed," Jazz finally said.

Gibby cocked her head. "Are you okay, Nicky?"

"I'm fine."

"You're twitchier than normal."

Oh yeah. That certainly seemed to be the case. His body was thrumming, and his thoughts were jumping more than usual. He told himself he was just filled with nervous energy, that today was exciting, and that it had nothing to do with being borderline desperate. This was going to work, and he knew it, which explained why he kept tapping his fingers against his thigh. It had absolutely nothing to do with the fact that he was three days past the last dose of Concentra. His head was pounding, but it was *fine*.

"I'm good," Nick told them quickly, wanting to get back on track. "You don't need to worry about me. Phase Three. Prepare to be amazed!"

"What is it?" Jazz asked. "And can it happen within the next five minutes? Because I have a fencing lesson this afternoon, and I want a scone beforehand."

"You and your pre-fencing scones," Gibby said fondly. "It's adorable."

It really was adorable, but Nick didn't want to get distracted again. He reached into his pocket and pulled out the thing that was going to ensure that today was the last day he'd be normal and boring. After this moment, he was going to be an Extraordinary, and everything would be awesome.

"Ta da!" he said rather frantically, opening his hand and showing Jazz and Gibby his secret weapon.

"Ooh," Jazz said. "Pretty."

Gibby squinted at the object that lay in his hand. "Why do you have drag queen jewelry? Are you going to be a drag queen? I mean, I'm all for however you want to express yourself, but Nick, I gotta say, I don't know if you've got the legs for it."

Nick didn't know whether to be offended or not. His legs weren't *that* bad. "It's not drag queen jewelry!"

"Are you sure? Because it's either from a drag queen, or you found a prop for a historically inaccurate big-budget movie about ancient Egyptians where all the characters are played by white people."

"What are you even—it's a *decoder* ring." He looked down at it. "I mean, yes, it's big and has a gaudy ruby set in what looks like an oversized sun that covers, like, three of my knuckles, but look at these *symbols* on the side!" He showed them the hieroglyphs carved into the band of the ring.

"That's not a ruby," Jazz told him, not unkindly.

"How do you know?"

She shrugged. "My mom has a lot of rubies. What you have there is a rhinestone."

"Ooh," Nick breathed. "A rhinestone. So it comes from the Rhine River that begins in the Swiss canton of Graubünden in the southeastern part of the Swiss Alps? Wow. I never thought it would be so international. That makes it even more special."

"What the hell?" Gibby said faintly. "You know about the Rhine but you don't know what a rhinestone is? I can't even with you right now. Nick, it's fake. A rhinestone is costume jewelry. You know, like drag queens wear."

Nick jerked his head up. "What? That's not—that can't be true! The seller on eBay said that it was a mystical and magical ring from the ancient lands that invoked feelings of power fit for royalty!"

Gibby snorted. "Royalty. So, like, drag queens."

"Would you lay off with the drag queens. It's not for drag queens!"

"Who sold it to you?"

Nick pulled his phone out again, ready to prove Gibby wrong. He pulled up his eBay account. "I'll show you. And I'll accept your apology when you're ready. And since I'm such a nice guy, I won't even make you grovel. And . . . okay. Hold on. Service here sucks. It's still loading. God, that smell is terrible. I can't believe I'm about to—*aha*. See. The seller is Veronica B. Dazzled, and her bio says she is known for her dramatic improv, death drops, and high kicks, spilling tea, and being the biggest star in Milwaukee. You can also see her perform her one-woman show, *The Queen and I,* on Wednesdays and Fridays at—oh goddammit, she's a drag queen."

"It's moments like these when I relish our friendship," Gibby said.

"Whatever," Nick said, putting his phone away. "That doesn't change a thing. For all we know, Veronica B. Dazzled could be some kind of drag queen witch or sorceress, and this ring is actually a magical decoder ring meant to find one person to wear it so the ring's power can fill the wearer and make them into an Extraordinary. And I am going to put it on right here, right now. Prepare yourselves!"

Jazz took a step back.

Gibby looked at her. "Really?"

"He's good at selling it. I almost believe him."

Gibby sighed. "I can't believe this is how I'm choosing to spend my weekend."

Nick held his hands over his head, the ring clutched in the left, his pointer finger extended on his right. "Please work," he whispered before he closed his eyes and slid the ring onto his finger.

He was not overwhelmed with power the moment he wore it.

He waited.

Nothing.

He opened one eye, looking at Gibby and Jazz. "Am I glowing?"

They shook their heads.

"Am I wearing some kind of costume now?"

They shook their heads again.

"Do I look different at all?"

"Well," Gibby said. "I suppose the ring suits you better than I thought it would. Maybe you could do the whole drag queen thing after all."

"I paid thirty-seven dollars for this! Plus shipping!"

"Well, according to this website I found," Jazz said, staring down at her phone, "maybe this will help. You'll need to answer a few questions."

"You found a website about how to make magical decoder rings work?" Nick demanded. "How? I spent *hours* trying to find one!"

She shrugged. "Maybe. First question: How would you define your sense of style?"

"Different and sexy!"

Gibby snorted. "Yeah, I don't know about that."

"What was the name of your first pet?" Jazz asked.

Nick didn't know what kind of archaic magic Jazz was conducting, but he was so on board. "I had a goldfish named Jerome. Does that count?"

"I bet it does," Jazz said, typing something into her phone. "What kind of makeup do you like?"

"Um. None?"

"Interesting. Last question. Are you fierce and fabulous or meek and mild?"

"I don't . . . know?"

"Meek and mild," Gibby told her.

"Meek and mild," Jazz muttered. "And . . . okay. That's it. Give it a second and it'll come up."

"A spell to make the ring work?" Nick asked hopefully.

She smiled as she looked up at him. "Here it is. Ready?"

He was *so* ready. "Hit me!"

"Charlamaine Monroe."

"Whoa," Nick breathed. "Is that . . . Latin? Or, like, ancient Greek?" He looked down at his ring. The stone caught the sunlight and flashed. He raised the ring high above his head and shouted, "*Charlamaine Monroe!*"

Nothing happened.

"That's your drag queen name," Jazz told him.

Nick lowered his hand slowly. "What?"

Gibby burst out laughing.

"It was a drag queen name generator," Jazz explained. "I figure if you're going to wear the ring, you at least needed to have a drag queen name. Charlamaine Monroe. I like it. It suits you." Her eyes widened. "And think about it! Your ship name with Shadow Star would be *ShadowMaine*."

Gibby doubled over, clutching her sides. It sounded like she was crying.

"I hate you guys so much," Nick muttered. "It's a good thing I have a part two of Phase Three."

And he immediately started stripping.

Gibby wiped her eyes as she stood upright. "Okay, I know I shouldn't have laughed, but you don't need to get naked. Please don't hurt me like that. The threat of your pasty, skinny-boy body is enough of a punishment."

Nick set down his jacket and shirt on the ground as he toed off his shoes. He unbuttoned his jeans and kicked them off. When he finished, he stood in nothing but boxers and—

"Your socks have ducks on them," Jazz said. "Why do your socks have ducks on them?"

"Because I *like* them," he snapped at her. "Now, Phase Three part two! I have the magical decoder ring, and I will now jump into the Westfield River. The sludge in the river will mesh with the ring and morph me into an Extraordinary. I will be able to control water and mud and . . . other river-related things, and the world will be in awe of Nicholas Bell, also known as the Extraordinary Charlamaine Monroe! That's right, Jazz. You thought you could trick me, but I am going to *own it*."

"Oh no," Jazz whispered.

"Now, wait a minute," Gibby said, taking a step forward. "Nick, you don't need to do this, okay? It was a joke, man. Please don't jump into the river. I'm pretty sure this is where they found that foot last year. Like, an entire human foot. Please don't jump into dismembered foot water—and oh my god, why did you bring *goggles*?"

Nick fit the goggles over his eyes. "Protection. Everyone knows you should wear goggles when you go swimming. It helps your eyes."

"Nick, seriously," Gibby said, sounding alarmed. "Let's figure out something else, okay? Or, hey! Maybe we should go find a TV somewhere to see if Pyro Storm and Shadow Star are still fighting or whatever. Wouldn't that be cool? Maybe they've hit each other so hard, their costumes are torn and you can see skin!"

That was almost enough to derail him. "Foul temptress," he hissed at her. "I know what you're trying to do, but it won't work! I've thought this through."

"See, that's the thing. I don't know if you have. This is dumb, Nick. You *know* it is."

The funny thing was, he *did* know that. Everything about this was stupid. But he couldn't find a way to tell them how desperate he was, that he was out of ideas and that he had nothing left. He couldn't tell them about his father's words ringing in his ears over and over again: *Why do you have to be the way you are?* Pity. That was what he'd get from them. Pity. He didn't want it. He wanted to be different.

"Nick," Jazz said. "If you jump in that water, you won't be allowed to stand next to me for at least a week. That's how long it'll take for the smell to go away."

"Small price to pay for what I'll get in return," Nick said, and he turned away from them.

Gibby tried one last time. "Nicky, no."

"Nicky, *yes,*" he crowed, and took off toward the edge of the pier. The wood creaked underneath his feet, and the rancid air whipped by his face. He clutched his hands into fists, feeling the ring that had cost thirty-seven dollars plus shipping sent to him by a drag queen from Milwaukee named Veronica B. Dazzled. And as he reached the end of the pier and jumped as far as he could into the Westfield River, Nicholas Bell just *knew* it was going to work.

12

I t didn't work.

He sat on the sidewalk near the pier, water and something black and foul dripping off him, hands handcuffed behind his back, two cops standing in front of him, arms crossed. Their patrol car was behind them, the light bar flashing red and blue.

"Okay," the cop on the left said. "Let's go through this one more time. You jumped into the river because . . ."

Nick sighed. "Because I wanted to go swimming. That's not illegal. I'm a citizen of Nova City. I know my rights!"

The cop on the right snorted. "You broke at least three city ordinances, kid. There's a reason you can't go swimming here."

"Well, then there should be a sign that says that!"

"Like the one right over there?" Left Cop said, pointing to a large sign about five feet away that showed a black stick figure jumping into black triangles with a big red X going right through the middle.

"That could mean anything," Nick muttered. "For all I know, that means don't jump onto shark fins."

"And the words right underneath that say something about absolutely no swimming?" Right Cop asked.

Nick shivered. He was cold and smelled like ass. "I have ADHD. Sometimes, it's hard for me to focus. Are you holding me responsible for my disability? Because I'll have you know, that's just cruel."

Left Cop snorted. "Mr. Bell, I highly doubt it affects your reading comprehension."

"Yeah," Nick said. "That was low, even for me. There are people out there with worse disabilities, and also people who actually can't read. I feel bad now. You know what? I've learned my lesson and humbly ask that we forget all about it. How about you let me out of the cuffs and I'll promise to never do anything like this again? My friends can hold me to that promise." He nodded toward Jazz and Gibby who stood next to the cop car. Jazz waved at him. He tried to wave back, but since his hands were still handcuffed, he could only jerk his elbow a little bit. "How about it, guys? Everything good?"

"What do you think?" Right Cop asked Left Cop.

"It could work," Left Cop said. "But then, we've already radioed dispatch. And I haven't arrested anyone today. You know how I get when I haven't arrested someone in a while."

"There is that," Right Cop said. "And also, Aaron Bell would probably be upset that we let his son go when we were told in no uncertain terms releasing him wasn't going to happen."

Nick panicked. "You know my *dad*? I mean, I have no idea who Aaron Bell is. He sounds devious. You should ignore him."

"Says the guy who jumped into the Westfield River wearing nothing but his underwear and a ring for drag queens."

"It's not for drag queens!"

Right Cop rolled his eyes. "My son performs at a bar in midtown as Ivy Chantal. He's got the same ring, kid."

"How's he doing with that?" Left Cop asked.

"Great," Right Cop said. "Makes good money for school with his performances. Helps out his old man quite a bit. Books are expensive these days."

"That's wonderful," Left Cop said. "I had a blast when we went last time. We'll have to do it again. Mr. Bell, by order of your father, you are under arrest. You have the right to remain silent. Anything you say can and will be used—"

"Record this," Nick bellowed at Jazz and Gibby. "Record this so I can use this in a lawsuit I'm going to file against my dad and the city for police brutality! I will have—"

"—my vengeance," Nick's tinny little voice said from the phone sitting on the table in the interrogation room. "I will have my vengeance!"

The video cut off.

"Gibby didn't need to forward the video to you," Nick muttered, laying on his arms on the table. "That was rude."

Cap snorted and pulled his phone back in front of him. "I hope your friendship survives."

"And the dust mask you're wearing is a little overkill, don't you think?"

Cap adjusted the strap around his head. His mustache stuck out oddly from the sides of the mask. "You smell terrible."

Nick buried his head in his arms, the blanket he was wrapped in slipping off his shoulders. "Today is the worst."

"Eh. You're alive, aren't you? Mostly naked and stinking up my interrogation room, but alive. At least for now."

"Because of the potential diseases I might get?"

Cap shrugged. "Or because of your father."

Nick groaned. He was afraid of that.

"You have to admit, Nick. This was pretty stupid. Even for you."

"I admit nothing." Then, "Is he mad?"

"Oh, sure."

"Great."

"He's also relieved that you're okay."

Nick could work with that.

"But mostly mad."

Or maybe he should stage a jailbreak and flee the city. "I'm grounded, aren't I?"

"I suspect so." Cap sobered, and Nick knew he was in for it. "You could have gotten hurt, Nick. Or worse. At the very least, you took away police resources from someone that might have needed help. Those guys aren't in my precinct, but they still took the time to bring you here."

Nick's stomach twisted slickly. "I didn't think of it that way. I'm sorry, Cap. I wasn't trying to hurt anyone. It was . . . stupid, I guess."

"You're lucky they know your dad. You could be sitting in a cell on Sixth right now. Not the best place to be."

Nick's face heated with shame. His head hurt, and his thoughts were racing. He was exhausted, and his skin was thrumming. "It won't happen again."

"See that it doesn't," Cap said, though he sounded amused.

"Am I going to be charged with anything?"

"Nah," Cap said. "I figure the way you smell probably is enough punishment, don't you?"

"For sure. Maybe you can tell Dad that too. See what he thinks."

Cap laughed. "Sorry, kid. I think I'll leave that between the two of you." He stood, grunting as his knees popped. "Sit tight. We'll get you home soon." He went to the door, but before he opened it, he looked over his shoulder back at his prisoner. "He loves you, you know?"

Nick didn't raise his head. He blinked rapidly against his arm. "He asked me why I had to be the way I am."

"We say things we don't mean, Nick. All the time. I know it can be hard after everything you've both been through. But he loves you more than you could ever know. And you need to remember that, okay? He may yell a little, but it's a cop's worst nightmare to hear the name of their loved one coming in over the radio. You scared him. So you let him yell, you let him ground you, and while you do that, remember that he loves you, and he's so relieved you're safe."

Nick didn't speak as Cap left, closing the door behind him.

Ten minutes later, the door opened again. Nick raised his head to see Dad standing in the doorway in his uniform. The look on his face didn't bode well for Nick.

"Get up," Dad said, and Nick moved quickly. The cheap flip-flops he'd been given after he'd arrived at the precinct slapped against the floor. Dad's nose wrinkled as Nick got closer, making Nick feel more miserable. Dad didn't move out of the doorway, so Nick stopped in front of him, averting his gaze. He bounced slightly on his knees. He couldn't help it. He should have taken the Concentra.

"You're grounded," Dad said, and Nick winced at the anger in his voice. "You'll go to school during the week, and then you'll come right home and do your homework. No friends. No internet unless it's for school. On the weekends, you'll have a list of chores to keep you busy. There's no timeline for this. It'll go on for as long as I think is necessary. Do you understand me?"

Nick nodded but didn't speak. Nothing he could say could fix this.

"I'm keeping your phone too. You won't need it—"

And *there* it was. *There* was the panic that had been simmering at an increasing level ever since he managed to pull himself from the Westfield River to the sound of approaching sirens, the fishermen on the dock farther down the way still staring at him. *There* was the panic that he'd tried his best to swallow down.

It should have been nothing. Nick had made a stupid mistake, sure. He'd made *many* stupid mistakes. He should have taken the pills when they'd been given to him. He shouldn't have jumped into the river. He shouldn't have spent thirty-seven dollars plus shipping on a ring from a drag queen.

And he should have been someone who his dad could be proud of. That way, Dad wouldn't have had to ask why Nick was the way he was, as if he hadn't been trying his damnedest to become someone different, to become someone better. Someone Extraordinary.

Maybe if Nick had been an Extraordinary to begin with, none of this would have happened. But he wasn't, and here they were.

Dad was trying to take his phone away, and Nick *couldn't breathe.*

"Hey, hey, hey," he heard his dad say through the storm in his head. "Nicky, breathe. Come on—holy *shit,* the smell—breathe, kiddo. Just breathe with me, okay? I need you to listen to me. Listen to the sound of my voice." Nick felt a big hand press against his chest, familiar and safe and warm, and he latched onto it as best he could, struggling to fill his lungs. "In, Nicky. In with me. Breathe in, one. Two. Three. Hold it. Hold it. And out. One. Two. Three. There you go. That's better. Again. In."

Nick breathed. It hurt, and his heart felt like it was rattling around in his chest and throat, but he breathed. The storm began to clear, leaving the ache right behind his eyes.

Dad stood in front of him looking concerned, hand still pressed against Nick's chest. Nick knew his dad loved him, and oh, did he love him fiercely in return. When Before became After, when he went from two parents to only having one, he'd become almost obsessive about keeping his dad safe and healthy and whole. Losing one had almost destroyed him. Losing another would finish the job.

"What brought that on?" Dad asked. Even though Nick stunk to high heaven, Dad was still close.

"Phone," Nick croaked out.

Dad frowned. "What about your—" Nick saw the moment it hit him. "Ah, kiddo. I'm sorry. I didn't think." He sighed. "I shouldn't have said that."

"It's okay," Nick said, trying to smile but failing spectacularly. "Just . . . don't take it. Please." Because it would be the only way Nick would know if something happened to his dad while he was at work. He couldn't deal with the thought of that lifeline being taken away from him. "I know I messed up, but please don't do that."

"I won't." Then Dad grew stern again. "But that's all you get it for. I'm going to call the service provider and restrict your data usage. I'm serious about this, Nick."

"Okay."

"Dammit, kid." Dad shook his head, and Nick could see he wasn't angry anymore. Only disappointed, and that stung even more. "What the hell were you thinking?"

Nick didn't have an answer to that. He never really could explain why he thought some things were good ideas. "I don't know."

"You're going home. I'm going to have someone drive you there, and you will *stay* there. God help you if I find out otherwise, you understand me? I don't have time to do it myself. Your stupid Pyro Star and Shadow Whatever are making more work for everyone."

"Pyro Storm and Shadow Star," Nick corrected automatically. Then, "What happened now?"

"Oh, no. Absolutely not. You don't get to know anything. Grounded, Nick. Remember?"

Nick scowled at him. "I'll find out from the television when I get home."

Dad narrowed his eyes. "No TV."

Nick gasped. "How am I supposed to stay informed? Do you really want your only son to not know what's going on in the world? Current events are important to the shaping of my young mind!"

"I'm sure you'll find some way to deal," Dad said. "And while you're sitting in silence without any electronic devices to distract you, perhaps you can use that time to come up with an idea or two about the changes that need to be made. Because the talk we're going to have won't be a good one if you don't give me something."

It was apt how he smelled, given the shit he was in.

The unfortunate assignment of taking Nick home was given to a rookie. He looked resigned at the outset, but when he got a good whiff of Nick, the resignation morphed into outright horror. Cap just grinned and slapped him on the back, saying something about having to start somewhere.

"You don't give him any grief," Dad warned as he handed Nick a plastic bag filled with his clothes, wallet, and phone. "If I hear you said anything but *yes, sir* or *no, sir*, you can bet that this grounding you've found yourself in will extend well into your thirties."

"You can't ground me into my thirties!"

"Watch me. Shape up, Nick, or you'll find out what it's like to be thirty-two and explaining to your friends that you can't go out because your dad grounded you and you have to get home before curfew."

Nick thought this could potentially be considered child abuse, but since he didn't want to risk being thirty-two and not being able to get online, he kept it to himself. Instead, he said, "Whatever. You suck. Everything sucks. My life is so hard. No one understands me."

"And I feel just terrible about it. Get home, get cleaned up, and do your homework. I'll be following up with the school next week to check in and see how you're doing. Anything I should know about beforehand?"

Nick grimaced. "Um. No? If you hear anything about the mating habits of box turtles, know that it didn't start out that way, and I have no idea how I got there."

Dad looked toward the ceiling for reasons Nick didn't quite understand. "Box turtles."

"And also, maybe give consideration for leniency if anything is said about an AP History pop quiz, emphasis on the word *pop,* as in it popped out of nowhere. Which is unfair."

"Nick," Dad warned.

"Gotta go, bye! Bye, Dad! Goodbye! Officer Rookie, move. Move right now. Oh my god, why are you still *sitting* there? Stop making that face at me, I don't smell that bad. Okay, maybe I do, but seriously. Cap told you to move, so *move.*"

Apparently, Officer Rookie didn't like being pushed out of the precinct, but Nick figured he needed the experience.

O fficer Rookie refused to let him sit in the front seat, instead relegating him to the back like a common criminal. And since it was the second time in the space of a few hours that Nick had ridden in the back of a cop car, he wasn't in a very good mood. Add in the fact that he was grounded for what would most likely amount to the rest of his life *and* that apparently his nose was starting to work again and he could smell himself even though all the windows were rolled down—Nick wasn't having a very good day.

It didn't help that when he got his phone again, there were texts from Jazz (DON'T BECOME A SNITCH IN JAIL BECAUSE SNITCHES GET STITCHES) and Gibby (u need to bathe in tomato juice u idiot), but nothing from Seth. Nothing from Owen either, but Nick found he didn't care too much about that.

Seth, however, was another story entirely. Nick didn't know if he should be furious or worried that Seth hadn't responded. Unless Seth had gotten sick again, Nick didn't understand why he couldn't have at least had the courtesy to answer Nick's many texts, each more irritated than the last. After all, they'd shared Skwinkles Salsagheti on a sort of not-date, and Nick thought that'd meant something. The past couple of days had been . . . nice? Sure, Nick didn't really know how he felt about the whole idea of him and Seth being . . . him and Seth, but it had to mean *something* when Nick's heart fluttered a little when Seth had shown up to school the next day after the not-date wearing a bow tie with little unicorns on it. He'd stared at Seth for so long that Seth had blushed and asked if everything was okay. Nick had nodded, unsure of how to say anything that didn't end with *Why are you so amazing all the time?*

Because Nick was destined to be Shadow Star's boyfriend, right? After all, Shadow Star had known his name without Nick giving it to him and had said he was cute. Yeah, he'd been repeating what Gibby had told him in order to take the picture after Nick had accidentally kissed the side of his head, but still. It was *something*.

Nick sighed dramatically and slumped in the back seat. "My love life is in shambles, Officer Rookie."

"I told you, my name is Chris. You can call me that, or Officer Morton."

Nick snorted. Amateur. Who did he think he was dealing with? "Okay, Officer Rookie. Whatever you say. Anyway, my love life is in shambles."

"I can't believe I went to the academy for this," Officer Rookie muttered. "To be a chauffeur to a smelly child. I don't get paid enough to deal with this."

"Police officers are woefully underpaid," Nick agreed. "Especially for the line of work they're in. It's dangerous on a daily basis, and they should be compensated."

"Thanks." He sounded surprised. "That's nice of you—"

"As I was saying, my love life is in shambles. Everything sucks." He turned to stare forlornly out the window. "I'm having feelings, Officer Rookie, and I don't know what to do with them."

"We should probably not talk at all," Officer Rookie said. "Make things easier for every—"

"On one hand," Nick said, "there's my best friend. He's awesome and funny and wonderful, and sometimes, when he concentrates really hard, he scrunches up his forehead, and I think there's a chance I might want to put my face on his face, even if he doesn't show up when he's supposed to."

"Do you understand what *not talk at all* means? Because I was serious when I said—"

"And on the other hand, there's Shadow Star. The Extraordinary who owns my heart because he's brave and selfless and can climb walls and defeat bad guys. And he saved me once, and even though I didn't tell him, he knew my full name and said I was cute."

Nick frowned. "Well, sort of. He was coerced into saying it by a baby butch, but I totally believed him because he wouldn't lie about things like that."

Officer Rookie sounded like he was going through his own existential crisis. "You'll be an officer of the law, they said. You'll help people, they said. You'll get a *Taser*, they said, even if they also said you couldn't use it whenever you wanted."

Nick barely heard a single word from Officer Rookie. "And it's not like I want to have to make a choice like this, you know? I mean, yes, it can be said that I've known Seth for practically my whole life whereas Shadow Star and I have only spoken once, for like, five minutes, but those five minutes were so . . . *electric*. There was something there, and it was awesome." He sighed dreamily as he looked out the window again. "But on the flip side, Seth got weirdly muscular when I wasn't looking. It's like puberty hit him late, or whatever. Not that it matters. I thought he was perfect the way he was before. I mean, he wears ascots, Officer Rookie. If you saw him wearing one, you'd probably want to kiss him too." Nick turned to glare at Officer Rookie. "Except he's only sixteen, and you're, like, thirty. That's disgusting and illegal. Get that thought out of your head right now."

"I'm not *thirty*," Office Rookie said. "I'm twenty-four."

What the f—? "That's still illegal! Why are you arguing with me on this? You stay away from Seth!"

"I'm not trying to—you know what? No. I'm not going to get involved."

"Damn right, you're not. That's creepy, Officer Rookie."

Officer Rookie sighed dramatically as the heavy traffic slowed to a stop. "If I give you some advice, can we finish the rest of this ride in silence?"

"I have ADHD. I don't do many things in silence."

Officer Rookie muttered something under his breath. It didn't sound complimentary. Rude. "Shadow Star is cool and all, okay? I get it. He's an Extraordinary, and some of the things he can do are nuts. But he's always going to put the needs of Nova City first. For whatever reason, he thinks it's his job. And you won't be able to compete with that."

"But—"

"And you have your best friend, who sounds like a really great guy. Maybe he's busier than he's been before, but it sounds like you really care for him. And you know him well. Why would you still be vacillating between the two? The answer is obvious."

"Huh. I've never thought of it that way before." Nick narrowed his eyes. "What's your play here, Officer Rookie? You trying to convince me one way or the other so you can go for the one I didn't choose? So if you're not trying to get with a teenager, you've got some kind of superhero kink and you—"

A streak of light appeared from above, meteor-bright and harsh.

Nick *knew* that light.

He heard shouts coming from outside the car, and he leaned his head out the open window.

There, high above the streets of Nova City, were Shadow Star and Pyro Storm.

Nick squeaked when a bright bloom of fire burst from Pyro Storm, hurtling directly toward Shadow Star. Shadow Star managed to leap off the roof of an apartment building, narrowly avoiding getting caught in the flames.

"Dammit," Officer Rookie whispered. He picked up the receiver to the radio and barked something into it. He threw it back down, twisting to look at Nick. "You *stay here,* do you get me? I swear to god, if you get out of this car, I will find you, and I will mace you."

"That's police intimidation—oh, you're already gone."

Officer Rookie slammed the door to the cruiser, shouting at people to get back into their cars. Traffic was gridlocked, so it wasn't as if they could actually go anywhere, but Nick knew it was safer in the vehicles than out.

Officer Rookie took off down the street, leaving a mostly naked, rancid boy in the back seat of his police cruiser.

All in all, it had been a very weird day.

And, it must be said, Nick did try to listen to Officer Rookie. He really did. He heard Cap's voice in his head, telling him Dad loved him. He remembered the exhausted look on Dad's face at the sight of him in the interrogation room.

The *problem* with all of that was Nicholas Bell happened to look up in time to see Pyro Storm lay a devastating kick right to Shadow Star's head, knocking him off the side of the building and into a darkened alley.

"No!" Nick shouted as Shadow Star fell. He couldn't see where he'd landed, but Pyro Storm disappeared into the same alley.

Nick made a choice.

He threw off the blanket and climbed out the window of the cruiser.

He managed to land on his feet on the sidewalk. No one seemed to pay him much mind, too busy hurrying away in case the battle between the Extraordinaries escalated into something more violent. Nick was well aware he was in public in only his underwear and flip-flops, but he didn't have time to think about how his lack of any sort of muscle definition was on complete display for any pervert who wanted to ogle him. He darted into the alley, jumping over a manhole cover spouting steam. He landed in something wet, and he made a strangled noise but refused to look down to see exactly what it was. He was better off not knowing.

The sky above was overcast, and the lack of light made the shadows in the long alley darker. Nick looked from side to side as he moved, trying to find where Shadow Star had landed. If he was injured, he'd need someone to protect him from Pyro Storm. Maybe Pyro Storm would get one whiff of Nick and run in the opposite direction. Nick never wanted his superpower to be smelling bad, but if it worked, he might have to reconsider. Stink Man, ship name ShadowStink. It needed fine-tuning.

The sounds of the street faded behind him as he made his way down the alley, the buildings looming around him, the shadows stretching farther as he passed an overflowing dumpster. Laundry hung from a line in a window above him, flapping in the breeze. A cat ran in front of Nick, disappearing into a pile of old boxes sitting against the building.

He turned his head to follow it and while distracted, bumped into something hot.

Something *scalding*.

It was about this time that Nick thought maybe he should have listened to Officer Rookie and stayed in the cruiser.

Because he'd run into Pyro Storm. His back, to be more specific. His cape, which had a stylized flame right in the center, flapped against Nick's bare legs.

"Um," Nick managed to say.

Pyro Storm turned slowly to look at him. His bloodred mask covered most of his face, leaving only his mouth exposed. The eyeholes of the mask were covered in a white material that kept Nick from seeing what his eyes looked like.

Pyro Storm said, "Why are you only in your underwear?" He raised his hands like he was reaching for Nick, and no, not today, *asshole.*

"Take *this!*" Nick bellowed somewhat heroically.

Then he punched Pyro Storm in the side of the head.

While his father always said to avoid fighting if at all possible, he still taught Nick how to defend himself. Thankfully, the only thing he'd ever had to hit in his life was the punching bag at the gym they'd gone to in the magical time known as Before.

But Nick had not forgotten what he'd been taught, and while the punch wouldn't go down as the best punch in history, it was still pretty good. He brought his arm back, fist curled, and then let it fly.

And learned rather quickly that Pyro Storm had a hard head. Either that, or his mask was made of the densest material known to man. The pain was immediate and fierce, his hand quickly going numb. Nick hissed between his teeth as he pulled his arm back, shaking it out as he winced.

"Did you *punch* me?" Pyro Storm growled. "Why would you do that?" His voice was modulated much like Shadow Star's was, making it deeper than it probably was in real life.

"Because you're a villain," Nick said, holding his hand to his chest. "And you hurt Shadow Star, who I think I have feelings for, even though it's recently become complicated due to other factors."

"Oh my god," Pyro Storm said, rubbing the side of his head. "So you punch me? Who does that?"

Nick blinked. "Well. I guess . . . I do?"

Pyro Storm sighed. "Did you hurt your hand?"

Nick squinted at him. "A little? But why do you care? Shouldn't you be kidnapping me and tying me to the top of a bridge or something while you gloat over your plans to take over Nova City?"

"You're so dumb," Pyro Storm muttered. "Let me see your—" His mouth twisted as he reared back. "What is that *smell*?"

Nick. It was all Nick. "I have no idea," he said. "Probably this dank alleyway. I think I stepped in something back there that used to be alive, so."

Nick tried to scrabble backward when Pyro Storm reached out again to grab his hand, but he didn't get very far. Pyro Storm wore thick gloves, but Nick could still feel the heat emanating from him. He lifted Nick's hand close to his face, and the white lenses over his eyes flashed brightly, like he was *scanning* Nick's hand. He pressed against Nick's knuckles, causing him to hiss. "It's not broken," Pyro Storm finally said. "You split the skin a little, but it's fine. Put some ice on it when you get home to keep it from swelling."

Nick jerked his hand away. "So, you're not going to kidnap me and hold me for ransom in order to have leverage for your dastardly deeds?"

"What? Why would I do that? Look. Nick. It's not what you think, okay? I'm not—"

"I never told you my name." Nick could barely breathe as he took another step back.

"Yeah, you did," Pyro Storm said. "Right before you punched me in the head."

Nick stared at him. "I really don't think that happened."

"Who are you going to believe? Me? Or you, who's standing in an alley wearing . . . is that . . . do you have lions on your underwear?"

Nick tried to cover himself as best he could, wondering what it said about his life that he was in an alley with the evil villain Pyro Storm, who was staring at his junk. Probably nothing good. "It's been a lion kind of day!"

"What does that even mean?"

Nick wasn't quite sure. "It made sense when I woke up this morning."

"Look, Nick, go home, okay? You can't be here. Not for this." Pyro Storm turned to walk away.

"You can't hurt him!" Nick said shrilly. "You can't hurt Shadow Star!"

Pyro Storm stopped, shoulders slumping. "I'm not trying to hurt anyone."

Lies, nothing but *lies,* and that pissed Nick off. "Uh, yeah. You are. You always do! You always try and enact some reprehensible scheme in order to create chaos and unrest, and every time, you're stopped by the hero of Nova City. Just because you're his archnemesis, doesn't mean you get to hurt him all the time. Why can't you be good? Wouldn't it be so much easier if you guys were friends? That way, you both could be heroes and go after people like bank robbers or pimps or drug dealers or stockbrokers who commit fraud."

Pyro Storm looked over his shoulder back at Nick. "You've got me all figured out, haven't you? I'm the bad guy, and only Shadow Star is good."

Nick blinked. "Um. Yes?"

"What if you're wrong?"

And in a burst of fire, Pyro Storm flew up and out of the alley.

Nick stared after him until the trail of smoke disappeared.

For a moment, he thought he saw something moving in the shadows.

But when he looked closer, he didn't see a thing.

"What took you so long?" Nick asked when Officer Rookie got back into the cruiser. "I've been sitting here just like you said. For *hours.* I didn't even consider leaving out the window at any point at all."

Officer Rookie shook his head. "It was forty-five minutes at most. And thank you for not— How in god's name did you get dirtier?"

Nick shrugged. "Some guy ran by and threw something grimy through the open window. It was very traumatic. I'd like to go home, where I will stay and not get into any trouble ever again. You've really opened my eyes, Officer Rookie, in ways that even my father couldn't do. You should be proud for helping me avoid a life of crime."

Officer Rookie frowned. "Really?"

Oh, poor Rook. He'd never survive in this line of work. "Oh yes. Consider me your first success story."

Officer Rookie rubbed his jaw. "Wow. I feel good now. Thank you. I needed to hear that. Shadow Star and Pyro Storm got away, and I was feeling pretty down."

"Great!" Nick said brightly. "It's what I'm here for."

Officer Rookie whistled the rest of the way to Nick's house.

13

He was surprised the next morning when he opened the door to find Owen Burke standing on his front steps.

Owen grinned at him. "Hey, Nicky."

"Hi?" He looked behind Owen, but he seemed to be alone. "What are you doing here?"

Owen shrugged and pushed his way past Nick into the house. "Do I need a reason to come visit a very dear friend of mine?"

Nick closed the door slowly. "That's . . . not how I would describe our relationship."

Owen shrugged off his jacket, hanging it on a hook near the door. He wore a green V-neck shirt that showed off his chest. Nick refused to look at it. "And how would you describe our relationship?"

It was too early for deep questions. "Begrudging," Nick said. "What do you want?"

"Oh, Nicky. I came to apologize for missing out on yesterday." He walked farther into the house, hand trailing along the wall. "Jazz told me what happened."

Of course she did. "Traitor," Nick muttered as he followed Owen. "That still doesn't explain why you need to be here on a Sunday morning. You could have waited until school tomorrow."

"It felt important," Owen told him. "I forgot how . . . quaint your house is. It's charming."

"Wow. That wasn't condescending at all."

Owen flashed another smile at Nick as they went into the kitchen. "It wasn't meant to be. I like it here. I always have. Remember that one time we made out against the refrigerator? That was fun." He picked up a piece of bacon leftover from breakfast and bit into it.

"Yay," Nick said flatly. "I love it when we reminisce."

"You do?"

"No. You can't be here. You're going to get me in more trouble than I'm already in. My dad's asleep upstairs, and I'm not allowed to have anyone over. Or text on my phone. Or do much of anything, aside from sitting on my bed and contemplating how miserable my life is."

Owen clicked his tongue. "Grounded?"

Bingo. "Indefinitely."

"Sucks. But I suppose that's what happens when you jump into a river while trying to become an Extraordinary."

"Don't remind me," Nick mumbled as he started clearing the dishes from the table. "In hindsight, it wasn't one of my better ideas."

"Could have used a little work," Owen agreed. "But your heart is in the right place." He paused in front of the counter, looking down at a sheet of paper Dad had left there. "What's this?"

Nick groaned. "Would you stop being nosy? In fact, you should probably leave. I still have a headache from all the fumes from yesterday. I'm tired and cranky. I want to go back to bed and feel sorry for myself."

"*The Punishment of Nicholas Bell,*" Owen read from the paper. "Yikes. This doesn't sound good."

It wasn't. Dad still thought he was funny, even when he was doling out a life sentence. "Let's just say that breakfast this morning was not one of the better meals I've had. It didn't help that I failed a history quiz. Did you know that teachers respond to emails over the weekend? *I* didn't know that. Don't they have lives outside of school? They really need to stop caring so much about the futures of their students."

"This is pretty extensive," Owen murmured. "No TV, no internet. Phone for emergencies only. Two hours of homework every night. A list of chores. *Paint the baseboards.* What the hell is a baseboard?"

"The bane of my existence," Nick said, grabbing *The Punishment of Nicholas Bell* away from Owen. "It's busywork to keep me out of trouble."

"That's not necessarily a bad thing."

Nick scowled at him as he folded the paper and shoved it in his pocket. "Oh, gee. Thanks. I'm so glad you're in agreement with my father. Maybe you should consider working on your relationship with your own before you—ugh. I'm sorry. That was a messed-up thing to say."

Owen shrugged, though Nick didn't miss the way the skin tightened around his eyes. "You're not wrong. At least your dad cares."

Nick didn't like the fact that he was feeling sorry for Owen Burke so early on a Sunday morning. Not after the day he'd had yesterday. "I guess. Though I think he cares a little too much."

"He's your dad. He's supposed to."

Nick rolled his eyes as he went to grab the last of the dishes. "I'll keep that in mind. Look, this has been—"

Owen tapped his fingers on the counter. "Heard from Seth?"

That made Nick pause. "What? Why?"

"Gibby said Seth didn't show up yesterday either."

Another traitor. "Yeah." He dumped the bowls into the sink. "I need new friends."

"Aw, Nicky. Don't make that face at me. I feel real bad about it. Honest."

"No, you don't. He texted me last night. Said something came up, and he'd explain later."

"Wow," Owen said, sounding rather gleeful. "That seems to be happening a lot lately. I wonder why that is?"

"I don't know," Nick admitted, as he flipped on the faucet and picked up a bowl. "It's . . . complicated, I guess. Or so he says."

"Are you two still ridiculously in love?"

Nick dropped the bowl into the sink. It clattered loudly. He froze, waiting to hear movement from upstairs. Nothing came. He turned off the faucet before whirling around, glaring at Owen. "What the hell are you talking about?"

Owen snorted. "Like I need to tell you."

"Try."

"Seth's always had a crush on you," Owen said, hoisting himself up onto the counter like he belonged there. "Everyone can see it."

Self-awareness, or the complete lack thereof, was a bitch of a thing. "They can? I didn't see anything!"

"That's because you're adorably clueless about most things." Owen grinned at him. "I think it's cute."

"How long has he had a crush on me?" Nick demanded. "And why didn't you tell me?"

Owen laughed, flashing those perfect teeth. "Because I had a crush on you too. Why would I tell you about it, when I wanted you for myself?"

Nick grimaced. "Dude, that's gross. You're gross."

"Eh. I never claimed to be a saint. And it's been going on forever. Maybe you don't see the way he looks at you, but the rest of us do. And it's not exactly one way, you know. When we were dating, it was always *Seth did this* or *Seth said that*. Honestly, it got really annoying after the first few days."

"We were together for three months." Sort of. *Together* was a bit of a misnomer.

"I know," Owen said. "Imagine how I felt by the end." He batted his eyes. "Why, I even began to doubt my worth."

"Oh, that's crap. You're the most conceited person I know."

Owen pressed a hand against his chest. "That hurt. Right here. And it did upset me, I think. Everything was Seth, Seth, Seth. Always has been."

"This is a little life changing for me," Nick said, feeling numb. "Do I need to apologize? I don't know if I need to apologize."

Owen waved him away. "Nah, I got over it a long time ago."

"Still. I'm sorry."

"You could make it up to me, you know."

Nick didn't like the sound of that. "How?"

Owen waggled his eyebrows. "For old time's sake?"

Yeah, no. "Never again. Consider it an extended lapse in judgment, and one that won't happen again."

"You wound me."

"I don't know if that's possible." Though Nick didn't know if he believed that anymore. He hadn't realized Owen was actually capable of being hurt. Sure, he was human, but he'd always been so cool and aloof and— "You broke up with me."

"I did," Owen said, sounding bored. "Thought it was best. Right thing to do, and all that. I'm a nice guy."

"You're really not. Mostly."

"Mostly. I'll take it. So, you're in love, or whatever. That's great, man."

"I don't—it's not—ugh." He scrubbed a hand over his face. "I don't know what I'm doing. Everything is so weird right now. I didn't sleep very good last night. Not after what Pyro Storm told me about—"

"Pyro Storm?" Owen said, and Nick looked up in time to see Owen's eyes narrow. "You talked with Pyro Storm?"

Nick nodded. "It was . . . I don't know what it was. I thought he was supposed to be this bad guy, but he—"

Owen hopped off the counter. He was frowning. "Nick, what the hell are you doing? Pyro Storm is *dangerous*. You could have been hurt."

"I know that. But that's the thing." Nick began to pace back and forth. "He and Shadow Star were fighting yesterday, right? And it was all *ka-bam* and *ka-pow,* and then I was standing in this alleyway in my underwear—"

"Wait, *what?*"

"—and then Pyro Storm was there, and then I punched him on the side of the head, and he held my hand to make sure I was okay, and it was so strange. Like, if he was supposed to be a villain, why didn't he toast me right then and there? And then there's the *other* thing. He knew my name like Shadow Star did. Why do they both know my name? Am I some kind of Extraordinary catnip and they all want in on my bidness?" Nick stopped pacing, thinking hard. "I shouldn't be having those images in my head. I mean, how would that even work, all three of us? There'd be so many *fingers*—"

"I thought you were all about Shadow Star," Owen said stiffly. "I mean, he was there first and all, right?"

"That's just it," Nick said. "I don't think he was. I need to show you something. Come up to my room."

"You don't need to tell me twice. Should I take off my shirt now, or . . . ?"

"Oh my god. Keep all your clothes on, or I'm going to shove you down the stairs."

Owen held his hands up in defeat. "So violent. Have you always been like this? If so, I'm lucky I escaped with my life."

Nick ignored him, heading for the stairs, knowing Owen would follow. He reached the top and paused outside his dad's door, listening. He held a finger to his lips for Owen to keep his mouth shut. There was a moment of silence, then a loud snore came from the other side of the door. Nick sighed in relief before continuing to his room.

He waited until Owen followed him in before closing the door quietly. He went to his bed and lifted the mattress, reaching under to find the sheets of paper he'd shoved underneath the night before.

"We're going to look at your porn?" Owen asked. "Gotta admit, Nicky, I don't know if you and I have the same tastes, exactly. Guys in spandex really aren't my thing."

Nick groaned as he pulled the papers out and let the mattress fall back down. "It's not porn. It's stuff I printed out last night before Dad locked me out of the internet when he got home."

"He was serious about the no internet thing?" Owen asked, eyes wide. "How are you going to survive?"

"I don't know. He said when *he* was a kid, they actually had to go to the library to look things up. I can't believe a time existed when things were so archaic. Can you imagine actually having to use a physical map for directions? If I had to do that, I'd probably get lost and die. It's ludicrous. You should see some of the pictures of him from the eighties. I'm shocked humanity survived the decade given its propensity for mullets." Nick spread the papers on his bed. "Okay, so look. It's here, right? Two years ago, after . . . well. After. It's . . ." He swallowed thickly, surprised at how hard it hit him.

He felt a hand on his shoulder. "It's okay, Nicky. Take your time."

He shrugged the hand away, shaking his head. Focus. Focus. "I'm fine." He cleared his throat and tried again. "So, two years ago, we get reports of a new Extraordinary in Nova City. There hadn't been one in years, since Guardian disappeared. There were sightings of moving darkness, and crooks getting held down by their shadows until the police arrived. It's only a couple of weeks after that when Rebecca Firestone picks up the story and becomes the so-called official voice of the Extraordinary known as Shadow Star."

"You really don't like her, do you?"

Nick scoffed. "I'm absolutely convinced she's got some kind of blackmail on Shadow Star, and he's forced to cooperate with her, even though he knows she's evil and will probably try and steal his soul."

"She's not *that* bad. I mean, she's hot. She's got that going for her at least."

Nick ignored him, only because his hand still hurt from punching Pyro Storm yesterday, and he didn't want to injure himself further. "A few months later, Shadow Star and Pyro Storm have their first skirmish." Nick shuffled the pages until he found the one he was looking for. "Rebecca Firestone reported on it before anyone else and said there was a new Extraordinary in Nova City. That he was causing destruction and mayhem and impeding Shadow Star's work."

Owen sounded like he was choking. "Did you print out a screenshot of a YouTube video of the report?"

Of course that was what he'd zero in on. "I was in a hurry. I wasn't thinking. It's—stop laughing, Owen, I swear to god. So after, the *Nova City Gazette* picks up the story, publishing on the front page that Shadow Star has a new enemy. And everyone runs with it. Later, Shadow Star gives Rebecca Firestone an interview, saying he's doing everything he can to stop Pyro Storm from taking over the city. He was here first, and he wants to keep us all safe."

"Okay," Owen said slowly. "So . . . what. You think Pyro Storm isn't actually evil?"

Nick hesitated. "I mean, he has to be, right? He's done all these illegal things, and Shadow Star has always stopped him. And there's been all those other times that they've fought when Pyro Storm tried to take over this city. But it's not about that. Look." Nick handed Owen another printout.

"*High-Rise Fire Put out by Mysterious Means,*" Owen read dutifully. "I remember this. It was a four-alarm fire, right? It spread quicker than anyone expected it to."

"Right," Nick said excitedly. "And people were trapped, with no way to get to them on, like, thirty different floors. Except for some reason, the fire went out *by itself*. No one could explain how it happened. Or why."

"And you think it was Pyro Storm."

Damn right. "What else could it be? The one Extraordinary who can manipulate fire and suddenly, a raging inferno goes out by itself? Come on."

Owen's brow furrowed. "I don't know, Nicky, but let's say you're right. Let's say he did put out the fire. On the other hand, what if he started it too?"

Nick shook his head. "That's the thing. He didn't. It was faulty wiring on multiple levels. It turns out the electrical contractors cut major corners. An investigation by the city showed it wasn't the first time either. They found instances of malfeasance in twelve other construction projects. Multiple lawsuits came out of it. The contracting firm closed, and people are in jail because of what they did."

"That doesn't mean he didn't have anything to do with it," Owen pointed out.

"So, he coincidentally picked a building where obvious blame could be placed on something else?"

"Or he knew that it could be," Owen said. "Look, Nick. I get what you're saying. Maybe Pyro Storm did put out that fire. But that doesn't mean he's good."

Nick frowned. "I'm not trying to say he is. I'm trying to show you he was here first. The fire happened three weeks before the first reported sightings of Shadow Star. And there are other fires that go back further, months even, when the fire was put out in a way that can't be explained."

Owen shrugged. "Okay. Let's say you're right. So what?"

Nick gaped at him. "So *what*? How can you say—"

"What's the point?" Owen asked, waving a hand at the papers on Nick's bed. "What are you trying to prove? So what if Pyro Storm was here first. Why does it matter?"

Nick looked down at the bed, his thoughts a storm. "I don't . . . know."

"I get it, Nick. I really do. I mean, you fixate, you know? That's part of who you are. You get attached to things, and it's like you get these blinders on. It's endearing. Mostly."

Endearing. He'd been called that before, but it'd never sounded good. "Thanks."

"I'm not trying to be a jerk," Owen said gently. "Just telling it like it is. I want to know why it matters so much to you. So Pyro Storm was here first. Or maybe Shadow Star was. Or maybe they both got here at the same time. Any way you look at it, it doesn't change how things are now, right? Did you ever stop to think what would happen if they were both villains?"

Nick shook his head furiously. "That's not how these things work. There is a hero, and then there's his opposite. It's how it's always been."

"Life isn't a comic book, Nick. There isn't always good and evil."

"I know that, but it's—"

"Who would your opposite be?"

Nick blinked. "What?"

Owen cocked his head. "You want to be an Extraordinary, right? That's the whole point of your little game."

What a dick. "It's not a game—"

"Let's say you succeed. Who would your opposite be? It'd have to be someone really terrible, wouldn't it? Because you're so good."

Nick laughed nervously. He'd never really considered that before. It made sense. If he was going to be a hero, he'd need someone as an antagonistic foil. A yang to his yin. "I'm not that good. Ask my dad."

Owen reached out and squeezed Nick's hand before pulling away again. "Maybe he doesn't understand."

"What do you mean?"

Owen shrugged. "You. How your mind works. How you see things. I think most people don't get it. I mean, here you are, working your ass off trying to be something more, and what's it getting you?"

Alarm bells blared in Nick's head. "Oh, hey. No. It's not that bad, I guess. He's—"

Owen snorted. "You're essentially a prisoner in your own house."

"Well . . . yeah. That's kind of what being grounded means."

"But aren't you old enough and smart enough to make your own decisions?"

Oh boy. "I'm sixteen years old. I jumped into a dirty river wearing a ring I bought on the internet from a drag queen. That's empirical evidence that I shouldn't be trusted with pretty much anything."

Owen's smile was dazzling. "Misguided, then. But your heart was in the right place. You wanted to become something more than what you are. I understand that, Nick. I do. Probably better than anyone. Dear ol' Dad straps a gun to his waist and a badge to his chest and goes to work every day knowing there's a chance he might not come home. And that's scary. So you, in all your wisdom, try to make yourself into something better so you can protect him."

Nick thought the floor was swaying beneath his feet. No one else had gotten that. Why did it have to be Owen of all people? "How did you know?"

"Because I know you, Nick. We're cut from the same cloth. Two sides of the same coin. It's like a dance, you and me."

Nick sat on the edge of his bed before his legs gave out.

Owen stood only a few feet away. "I know it started as something else. Your little crush on Shadow Star is cute. But you've got a depth to you I don't think people see."

"And you can?"

Owen laughed. "Eh. People underestimate me, and that's to their detriment. They see a spoiled rich kid who does whatever he wants without thinking of the consequences."

"Uh. You *are* a spoiled rich kid who does whatever he wants without thinking of the consequences. No offense," he added hastily.

"Maybe. But that's only part of who I am. You see, Nick, when people underestimate you, they tend to write you off. They don't see what else is there, underneath the surface. You know me. I'm not *just* that."

Owen had a point. Sure, he was a dick and he absolutely was a spoiled rich kid, but he was funny and smart, and sometimes, he could even be kind. Yeah, it was usually after he'd done something harsh and almost cruel, but Nick was no saint himself. "Your father?"

Owen winced but covered it up quickly. "It's complicated. My parents aren't like yours. My dad isn't like yours. He doesn't need protecting. He's got an entire security team for that. But that doesn't mean I love him any less. I would do anything for him, if only for him to see me as someone capable. As someone worthy."

"You are," Nick said honestly. "You're pretty okay."

"Oof. Thank you for the ringing endorsement. Truly. You set my heart aflutter."

"I'm being serious." Potentially.

Owen watched him for a moment. Then, "Okay."

"Okay?"

"Yeah, okay. Geez. Don't be such a sap, Bell. You've got a reputation to maintain. Sort of."

Nick's head hurt. He was exhausted, but he pushed through it. "I want to do something important. It was . . . okay. Before. And then it became After, and it wasn't okay anymore. And I'm *trying*. I really am. And maybe it started off as wanting to get Shadow Star to notice me—"

"Not a bad thing. You're an obsessive superfan. Like the K-pop fandoms that go to concerts and throw their underwear onstage."

"—but it turned into something else. And I can do this. I know I can. I just need to figure out how. I don't want to be the weird kid anymore. I don't want my mouth to say things before my brain even starts to think. I don't want to take medication in order to be able to focus. I just . . . want to do that on my own. I want to be seen." Nick swallowed thickly. "I want to matter."

Owen nodded slowly. "It's like the Extraordinaries. Shadow Star and Pyro Storm. People see them as good and evil. As black and white. But who are they behind the mask? Why did they become the people they are? Why is Shadow Star the hero? Why is Pyro Storm the villain? Don't you want to find out?"

Yes. Yes, he did. "That's what I've been trying to—"

Owen waved his hand dismissively. "Oh, I know. You've been trying. It's endearing."

That word again. "That's one way to put it," Nick muttered.

"What if . . ." Owen shook his head. "Nah. That's probably not a good idea."

Hook, line, and sinker. "What?"

Owen smiled tightly. "I get it. Sometimes, I get dumb ideas in my head too. I thought of something, but it probably wouldn't work. Best we don't think about it."

"What is it?" Nick demanded. "Tell me!"

Owen looked dubious. "I mean, it's dangerous. And it'd be a lot of hard work. We couldn't tell anyone about it."

Nick felt like he was about to explode. "What do you know?"

Owen glanced at the door, like he was making sure it was still shut and no one was listening in. "What if I told you there was a way to become an Extraordinary, and all you had to do was take a chance?"

Goose bumps prickled along Nick's arms, the hairs standing on their ends as if electrified. "What are you talking about?"

"I probably shouldn't be saying anything," Owen said gravely. "But I don't know who else to tell."

"You can tell me," Nick said. "I can keep a secret."

"You can, can't you? That's one thing I've always liked about you." Owen sat next to Nick on the bed. Their knees bumped together. There was a beat of silence, and Nick thought he was going to crawl out of his skin. Then, "I overheard my father talking in his office at the house."

That . . . wasn't what Nick had been expecting. Simon Burke? What the hell did he have to do with Extraorinaries? "About what?"

Owen lowered his voice until it was barely above a whisper. "Something big. Something top secret. Something that he doesn't want anyone to know about. Burke Pharmaceuticals. The top three floors are research and development. Scientists working on the next big thing to make you sane. Or skinny. Or prettier. Or smarter. To make clean water. To increase crop yield. Burke Pharmaceuticals is in the business of making the world a better place because the future is now."

"Everyone knows that," Nick said. "It's their slogan on all the commercials."

"Right. It's the public face. But what if I were to tell you there was another floor in Burke Tower? One that's only known to a select few? Deep underneath the streets of Nova City."

Nick's heart stuttered. "What do they do there?"

"Oh, it's still research and development, but nothing that's shown in public offerings. It's all very hush-hush, but I'm underestimated, even by him. He didn't expect me to hear. He didn't expect me to care. His door was wide open, and I heard everything."

"Heard what?"

Owen looked down at his hands. "Can I trust you with this, Nicky?"

He had to play it cool. Suave. "You know you can. I mean, we're friends, right?"

Owen smiled quietly. "Yeah. I guess we are." He took a deep breath and let it out slowly. "My father has figured out a way to make people Extraordinaries."

And Nick . . . Nick didn't know what to do with that. He burst out laughing, only stopping when Owen didn't join in. It was ridiculous, right? Of course it was. There was no way to— "What the hell are you talking about?"

"It's a pill. One tiny little pill. And, depending upon what kind you take, you could turn into smoke. Or summon storms from nothing." He looked back up at Nick. "One pill, and you could *fly*."

Stunned, Nick couldn't even make the smallest of sounds.

"I think it's meant for military application," Owen continued as if he hadn't just blown Nick's mind. "To make soldiers faster. Better. Stronger. At least that's how it started. But could you imagine what would happen if *you* took it? Nick, you could be the Extraordinary you always wanted to be. There's a catch, of course, because it doesn't last forever, and you'd have to *keep* taking the pills in order for your powers to work. But you're used to that, aren't you? You already take pills. It'd be easy, Nicky. Except . . ."

Nick managed to find his voice, though it was hoarse. "Except what?"

Owen looked regretful. "Except I'm not supposed to know about it. No one is. And it's on a secure floor in Burke Tower. I mean, even if I could steal my father's keycard without him knowing and find some way to bypass security, it would still be dangerous. I couldn't do it on my own."

Nick blanched at that. "I don't—"

"Is that your mom?"

Nick followed Owen's gaze, mind reeling. The photograph on the nightstand. "Yeah. That's . . . her. Look, Owen, I don't know if—"

"She's pretty. I've never seen a picture of her before. That must have been rough."

Nick turned his head away. "It was."

He felt Owen's hand on top of his again. "I don't know what you went through, then. I don't know if anyone will. It's . . . different. But I know what it feels like to lose people, Nick. And to never want that to happen again. You lie awake at night and think if only you'd been there. If only you had the power to do something to prevent it from happening. Or, at the very least, to keep something like it from happening again. To you. To others. I know what it's like to want to never be scared again. To be able to *do* something about it. And I could do that for you, if you'd let me."

Nick stood abruptly. Owen's hand fell back onto the bed. Suddenly, Nick didn't know what he was doing, or how he'd let it get this far. He didn't want Owen in his room or in his house. It felt too big, too much. "I can't do that."

Owen looked surprised. "What?"

Nick shook his head. "Look, I know you're trying to help. Thank you. Maybe this whole thing was stupid. Me, trying to become an Extraordinary. It's ridiculous, okay? I know that. Even if I wanted it to work, it was never going to."

"But this could—"

"Owen, you're talking about committing a crime against your dad. Which could lead to us getting arrested by *my* dad. Do you know how much trouble we could get into? How disappointed he would be in me? I can't do that to him. I won't. He's already got enough going on, and I don't want to make things worse."

Owen bristled, his brow furrowing. "But it wouldn't matter by then, would it? Because you would already be something more than you are now. He would have no choice but to see you for what you really are. Not some disordered kid who can't keep his thoughts straight for a single second without—"

"That's not fair," Nick snapped at him.

Owen winced. "You're right. I'm sorry. That was uncalled-for."

"I did stupid crap and look where it's gotten me. My dad's pissed at me, I still have river mud in my ears, my best friend is acting weird, and I don't know what to do about it. Shadow Star and Pyro Storm *both* know who I am, and I don't know why. School has just started, and I'm already messing up. I can't, okay?"

Owen stood stiffly. "I get it, Nicky. You want to keep on being the way you are—"

"No," Nick retorted. "I don't. I want to be someone my dad can be proud of."

"Then why?"

"Because maybe I should try to do it on my own."

Owen nodded. "Admirable. Foolish, probably. And slightly stupid. But admirable." He winked at Nick, that wicked smile back on his face. "Don't tell anyone what I've told you, okay? Our little secret."

"I won't," Nick promised. "But you shouldn't try to do anything either. I don't want to see anything happen to you."

"Aw, Nicky," Owen said, reaching up and patting Nick on the cheek. "It's sweet how much you care. If you change your mind, you know where to find me."

"I won't," Nick said firmly. "You should probably go. I can't get into any more trouble."

"Sure, Nick. I mean, if you want. Or, there's an empty bed right here that we could roll around on—"

Nick shoved him toward his bedroom door.

14

On Monday morning, Nick stood in front of his father and swallowed his pill. It wouldn't give him superpowers, but it would stop the storm in his head. That had to count for something.

"Toast and eggs on the table," Dad told him. He looked tired, the bags under his eyes almost purple. "I want you home after school. I mean it, Nick."

"Yeah," he whispered. "Okay."

You look like crap," Gibby told him at the train station.

"Thanks."

"That bad?" Jazz asked.

Nick shrugged.

"Nah," Owen said, coming up from behind him, putting his arm around Nick's shoulders. "Nicky here just needs some lovin'. Don't you, Nicky?"

Nick rolled his eyes. "Not from you."

"You wound me, sir."

Nick shoved Owen away.

"Hey," a voice said from behind him.

Nick turned. Seth stood there, backpack slung over his shoulder. His green tie was in a Windsor knot today. It looked nice. Nick was extremely annoyed.

"You look like crap too," Gibby said.

And he did. Seth was pale, his curly hair messed up more than usual. His chinos were wrinkled, and he had a scuff on his loafers.

"I think we've all got a case of the Mondays," Jazz said, standing up from the bench. "It'll get better."

"Can I talk to you?" Seth asked Nick.

Nick shrugged. "Later. I can't be late for first period. I'm grounded."

Seth frowned. "I want to tell you—"

"Later, Seth." And he turned toward the stairs that led to Franklin Street.

Owen fell into step beside him. Nick didn't turn to see if the others were following.

And since Mr. Bell seems to find my lesson so illuminating, perhaps he would like to explain Euler's formula, and what it produces for sine, cosine, and tangent?"

Nick snapped his head forward, finding Mr. Hanson glowering down at him in front of his desk. Other students were staring at him. Some were whispering behind their hands, glancing back at him, smiling mean little smiles. "Sorry," he muttered. "I wasn't trying—"

"That's certainly an apt statement," Mr. Hanson said, already glowering at Nick. "You weren't trying. Maybe, in the future, consider trying at all, Mr. Bell. I would hate to email your father as he requested when there were signs of . . . apathy."

The whispers got louder.

Nick sank lower in his seat.

All right?" Jazz asked as Nick slumped onto the lunch table, laying his head on his arms.

"No," he said, voice muffled. "I think I want to die."

"Yeah," Gibby said, reaching over and rubbing the back of his head. "That's not dramatic at all."

"I'm being serious."

"I know," Gibby said. "That's what makes it so sad."

Before Nick could reply with what would most likely be a half-hearted retort, someone put their bag next to his head and took a seat beside him. He sat up to see Seth staring down at him. "Oh look, everyone. Seth is here. He didn't disappear again with no explanation whatsoever."

"Don't be a jerk," Gibby admonished when Seth flinched.

Jazz glanced back and forth between them. "He probably has a perfectly reasonable explanation for why he wasn't there to see you take off your clothes and jump into a river."

"Wearing drag queen jewelry," Gibby said.

"Wearing drag queen jewelry," Jazz agreed. "I have the video if you want to see it. Would you like that, Seth? Would you like to see the video of Nick in his underwear?"

Seth blushed and shuffled his feet. Nick was almost overcome with the desire to reach out and hold his hand, but since he was mad at Seth, he couldn't do that. He had to stick to his guns.

"I don't know what you're talking about," Seth muttered.

"Uh-huh," Jazz said. "Of course not. Why would anyone say exactly what they were thinking? That's just madness."

Seth's face reddened further. "I, uh. I brought you something."

Nick forgot about his anger for a moment. He liked presents. "You did?"

Seth shrugged. "It's not much."

"Give it to me," Nick demanded. "Whatever it is, I must have it now so I can decide if it's enough to forgive you for being a terrible best friend."

Seth muttered something under his breath and reached down into his backpack. He pulled out brightly colored plastic and shoved it at Nick. "Here."

Skwinkles Salsagheti.

Nick stared at it.

"It's mango-flavored," Seth said quietly.

It might have been the nicest thing anyone had ever given him. "Thanks. I'm still mad at you, but . . . thanks."

"I know. I'll explain though, okay? I promise. Give me a few days. I'll tell you."

"Tell me what?" Nick asked as he looked up at Seth.

"Everything," Seth said.

"Everything?" Gibby said, breathless. "Seth, are you sure that's—"

"Everything," Seth said firmly, not looking away from Nick.

"Okay," Nick said slowly. He cocked his head. "Is it bad?"

"I don't . . . think so?"

"Is it a secret girlfriend and/or boyfriend?"

"No, Nick. It's not."

"Am I going to be perfectly satisfied with this explanation?"

"I have absolutely no idea."

"Huh," Nick said. "Now I'm intrigued. Well played, Seth. Well played."

Seth looked relieved.

Gibby looked worried.

Jazz looked confused.

"Who died?" Owen asked, appearing out of nowhere as he always did. He sat next to Gibby, reaching over and stealing a limp piece of pizza.

Nick ignored him, moving his backpack out of the way so Seth could sit.

If their hands brushed together under the table more than once, well.

No one knew but them.

His AP History pop quiz was handed back to him, facedown.

That was never a good sign.

He lifted up the corner.

D+

The plus sign felt really unnecessary.

The house was empty when he got home.

He took a selfie in the living room and sent it to his dad.

Good, came the reply. Do your homework. Pasta in the fridge. See you in the morning.

I'm trying," he told his mother's smiling face. Cars honked on the street below. He pulled the comforter up and over his shoulder. "I'm trying to be who he wants me to be."

She didn't say anything in return. She never did.

* * *

On Tuesday morning, he took his pill in front of his father.

There was cereal sitting on the counter.

Off brand, of course.

Leprachaun Marshmallow Ornaments.

His dad was trying.

So Nick did too.

He pulled his chair over to sit right next to him. They read the newspaper together while spooning marshmallows into their mouths. They didn't talk much, but it seemed like a start.

It was okay. It was going to be okay.

You look better today," Jazz told him in the train station.

Nick shrugged. "Slept more."

"That's it?" Gibby asked, eyes narrowed. "Nothing else happened?"

"What else could there be?"

"You and Owen seemed rather chummy yesterday."

"Chummy," Nick repeated.

"Hey," Seth said, coming up from behind them. He was wearing a bow tie with koala bears on it. Nick wanted to put him in his pocket and keep him forever.

"Hi," Nick said, blushing and looking down at his beat-up Chucks.

"Hello," Seth said, rubbing the back of his neck.

"Aw," Jazz cooed.

"Oh my god," Gibby muttered. "This is excruciating to watch."

Owen wasn't at lunch.

Nick thought about asking after him, but then Seth appeared, and he blushed again.

He also thought about trying to hold Seth's hand under the table.

He couldn't work up the courage.

Seth pressed his foot against Nick's.

Nick thought he might burst into flames.

* * *

He took another selfie when he got home. This time, he scrunched up his face and stuck out his tongue.

Cute, Dad wrote back. Though I'm probably the only one who thinks so.

Rude.

Do your homework, kid. There's a casserole in the fridge from Cap's wife.

Is it edible?

No. Make a sandwich instead.

He finished his homework early.

He thought about writing more of his fanfiction.

For the first time in a long time, he found himself not caring about it at all.

Would he turn into one of those evil people that abandoned their stories and offered no resolution even though people wanted nothing more?

God, he hoped not.

It was raining when he woke up Wednesday morning. The sky was dark through the window in his room. The clouds looked heavy.

The house was quiet.

He blinked up at the ceiling before turning his head to look at the clock on his desk.

His alarm was about to go off.

Why was the house silent?

He should have heard his dad moving down in the kitchen.

He grabbed his phone.

There was a text from his dad from a few hours before. It said something had come up, and he'd be working late. Eat breakfast. Go to the nurse at school for your pill. I'll text you when I get home.

"I'm an eighties latchkey kid," Nick muttered to no one. "Probably messed up for life because of it."

Thunder rumbled as he ate a banana-and-peanut-butter sandwich. He wondered if it was going to rain all day.

He locked the door behind him when he left the house, fumbling with his umbrella.

Gibby and Jazz were waiting for him on the bench in the train station.

"Did you hear?" Jazz asked as soon as he approached.

He frowned. "Hear what?"

"Shadow Star and Pyro Storm! Apparently, something big went down last night, but no one knows what. Like, hardcore. Explosions and destruction and everything."

Nick looked at his phone, only to remember he didn't have internet access. He groaned. "I'm grounded. I can't look up anything. It's practically medieval."

"Here," Jazz said, holding out her phone.

Gibby snatched it away before he could take it, saying, "We're going to be late." Jazz looked confused as Gibby handed her phone back.

Nick glared at her. "Seth's not even here. We can't leave him."

Gibby sighed. "He's not coming in today. He texted me this morning. Sick again."

That . . . didn't make sense. "He was fine yesterday. And he didn't text me about it." Nick pulled out his phone to make sure, but the last text had been from the night before, when Seth had written nite xx. Nick had stared at it for a long time, smiling wider than he had in a long time.

"I don't know, Nicky," Gibby told him. "I just know he's not coming in today."

"Is it bad?" he asked, texting Seth to ask if he was really sick.

"What?"

He shoved his phone back in his pocket. "Whatever went on with Shadow Star and Pyro Storm. Dad didn't come home this morning. Said he had to work late."

Jazz hesitated. "Well, no one died. Or, that's what they're saying. All I know is that it was near Burke Tower."

Nick sighed irritably. "We can ask Owen at lunch."

Owen wasn't at lunch.

Seth hadn't texted back.

Neither had Dad.

Nick ate part of Jazz's salad until he realized there was pineapple in it. He'd never been so offended in his life.

Later, Nick would look back and remember it was still raining when his phone started buzzing in his pocket. There was another rumble of thunder when he realized it wasn't an incoming text as the vibration continued.

It was a phone call.

His blood ran cold as he pulled the phone out of his pocket, glancing down at the screen.

CAP

Nick's breath hitched. He couldn't move.

The vibration stopped.

ONE MISSED CALL, the screen read.

Maybe it was a mistake.

Maybe Cap had meant to call someone else.

He had almost convinced himself of it when the screen lit up again.

Cap was calling.

He stood. His chair scraped against the floor.

Everyone turned to stare at him.

"Nick?" Mrs. Auster asked. "Are you okay?"

He didn't answer.

He headed for the door, phone clutched in his hand, ignoring his name being called, the other students whispering.

The hallway was almost empty. A janitor was at the other end, wiping the windows.

He connected the phone call and brought it up to his ear. He tried to speak, but all that came out was the smallest of noises.

"Nicky?" Cap asked.

Nick nodded, and then immediately felt ridiculous. "Yeah?" he managed to say.

"I need you to listen to me, okay? Listen to my words. Don't speak until I finish, okay?"

No. No, no, no.

"He's okay. I need you to hear that, above all else. He's okay. He's . . . he's in the hospital, Nick, and I'm not gonna lie. It's gonna look bad. These things often do. But he's gonna get the best help, the best doctors. I'll make sure of it. And I promise you, he's going to be okay. I'm sending a patrol car to get you right now. I want you to wait for them in the office. They'll bring you to me, and we'll deal with this together. Do you understand?"

No. No, he didn't. He didn't understand any of this. It was getting hard to breathe, and at some point, he'd squeezed his eyes shut tight as if that would keep all of this away.

"Nick," Cap said sharply. "Tell me you understand."

"Yeah," he croaked out. "I understand. Office. Patrol car. Will take me to you and—" He couldn't finish the rest.

"I want you to hang up and go there now. I'm going to call them next, okay? They'll be expecting you. Move, Nicky. Get to me."

Nick moved.

A lady from the office met him halfway.

The principal was waiting in the front office. He put an arm around Nick's shoulders, leading him toward another office. He sat him down in a comfortable chair. He spoke, but Nick barely heard him. He nodded where he thought he should.

A small paper cup was placed in his hand.

Someone tried to take his phone.

He jerked it away.

The water spilled.

Nick tried to apologize, but he couldn't get the words out.

He was told it didn't matter.

Someone brought his backpack.

Nick said thank you.

It felt like hours before a cop showed up.

Officer Rookie.

Nick tried to be brave.

Officer Rookie hugged him.

Nick cried.

Officer Rookie promised not to tell anyone.

He didn't have to sit in the back of the patrol car this time.

"You don't smell as bad," Officer Rookie told him.

Nick nodded.

Officer Rookie sighed and closed the passenger door. He rounded the front of the cruiser.

Nick looked down at his phone.

Maybe . . .

He highlighted a name.

Connected the call.

It rang once.

Then:

"You've reached Seth's voicemail. I'm probably busy. And nobody calls anyone anymore unless it's an emergency. Send a text. Unless it's an emergency."

"I need you," Nick said simply.

Officer Rookie got into the driver's seat as Nick hung up the phone. "All right?"

Nick shook his head.

"Yeah. Stupid question. Sorry, Nick."

Officer Rookie was good.

He was really good.

No matter what Nick asked, he refused to answer any question about what happened. All he would say was that Nick's dad was going to be fine, *he's going to be fine, Nick, I promise.*

"Cap told you what to say, didn't he?"

Officer Rookie shrugged. "Told me you'd be persistent." He glanced at Nick. "He's right, though. Your dad is going to be okay. Kid like you? All the more reason to get better as quickly as he can. I doubt he'd want to leave you on your own for long. Probably end up burning the house down."

Nick choked on a laugh, though his eyes were wet. "He's pretty much the only thing standing between me and total annihilation."

Officer Rookie chuckled. "I haven't been around long, Nick. Still on probation. You know how it is."

"I know, Officer Rookie."

"But your dad. He . . . I don't know everything that happened. Before. People talk, but I don't listen. You know? Not my thing."

"Yeah," Nick said, staring out the window.

"All I care about is that I trust your dad to have my back anytime. Okay? No matter what. He's a good man."

Nick nodded, leaning his head against the cool glass. It was still raining.

"I don't know him all that well, but I do know him enough to say he's proud of you. I know you've been through some crap. The both of you. And I get it, probably better than you might think. But you can always tell how proud he is of you. Talks about you all the time."

Nick balled his hands into fists in his lap.

"Thought you should know he thinks the world of you. You're a good kid, Nick. Even if you did smell like my grandad's cow pasture the first time I met you."

"Please, Officer Rookie," Nick muttered. "I kind of already have a boyfriend. And we talked about this. I'm only sixteen. It's illegal."

Officer Rookie sighed.

But when they reached an intersection that was backed up for almost an entire city block, he switched on the lights and siren and drove on the sidewalk, so Nick thought he wasn't that bad.

Cap was waiting for him just inside the automatic doors of the hospital. Officer Rookie told him he'd go park and see him in a bit. Nick barely managed to shut the passenger door behind him before he took off toward the entrance.

Cap smiled, though it didn't reach his eyes. "Is he okay?" Nick demanded, out of breath.

Cap nodded. "He will be. Everyone's optimistic. Got his bell rung. Knocked him out. Couple of broken ribs." He hesitated. Then, "One punctured his lung, and it collapsed, but you *know* that's something they can fix, Nick. Right? You know that?"

Oh, sure. Nick knew that. Nick knew all sorts of things when it came to injuries. Product of being a cop's kid. In the mystical time known as Before, Dad would regale him with stories of grotesque injuries he'd seen on the job, much to Mom's dismay. Traffic accidents, a guy who'd been wearing flip-flops when he'd had to lay down his motorcycle to avoid a collision and lost a bunch of his toes, a guy getting three of his teeth literally punched down his throat.

Then Before had become After, and it . . . well. Nothing had been the same After, but Dad didn't talk as much about his job anymore. Not when he'd had to tell Nick that it'd been quick for her, that she hadn't suffered, that she was there one moment then gone the next. Nick had struggled to understand the horror of it all, but he'd gotten there. Eventually.

So yeah. He knew what Cap meant, all right.

"He looks bad," Cap said quietly. "That's what you're gonna think when you see him. It looks worse than it actually is. It's the bruising, okay? The swelling. He's got a breathing tube helping him out for now, but it's only because of the lung. It'll be out before you know it. When he wakes up, he's going to be cranky, I can tell you that much. Busted some ribs myself years back. Hurts like a son of a bitch, and there's not a whole lot you can do about it. It'll heal. You still have to breathe, right?"

Nick nodded, unable to speak around the lump in his throat.

Cap dropped a heavy hand on his shoulder, squeezing tightly. "He's strong, Nick. So strong. And he's got a lot to fight for. He's not going anywhere. I can promise you that."

Nick wanted to shove Cap's hand away, because no one could promise that. No one could say they would stay forever. Maybe Cap didn't understand, and it wasn't his fault, but Nick couldn't help but feel irrationally furious. *She* hadn't made any promises, but Nick knew she'd have fought as hard as she could to stay with them. Yes, it'd been fast, it'd been over quick, she hadn't *suffered,* but even though she hadn't made a promise out loud, it shouldn't have needed to be said.

"What happened?" Nick whispered.

"We can talk about that later, Nicky. You don't need to—"

"Please."

Cap sighed. "It was the Extraordinaries. I don't know—something happened. I've never seen them like this. Shadow Star. Pyro Storm. We don't know what set them off, but they were going after each other in ways they hadn't before. There was a condemned apartment building. Down near Sixth and Torrance. Big transient population. It's not the best place, Nick. And that building should have been torn down a long time ago, but it's been delayed for years. Bureaucratic nonsense."

Dad had been brave, Cap told him. He wouldn't expect anything less from one of his officers. They'd been inside the apartment building, trying to get the homeless people to safety, the sounds of the Extraordinaries attacking each other echoing through the streets. His dad had been one of the last people in the apartment building, checking to make sure they'd gotten everyone out. He'd found a woman huddling in a corner, bent over what looked like a pile of dirty rags.

It turned out to be a baby.

She'd been terrified, unable to move. Until Dad picked up her baby. Then she came to life, snatching the child out of his arms. He'd pulled them toward the front of the building.

They'd almost made it out to the street when the Extraordinaries slammed through the roof, seven stories above them. They'd crashed through floor after floor, the building groaning dangerously.

The explosion, when it came, was fierce and bright. There was a flash of light, then fire bloomed from the inside, the remaining windows shattering in the shockwave. Shadow Star was knocked through the front of the building and out onto the street, landing on top of a cruiser.

As the building began to burn, Pyro Storm burst out of the flames, going after Shadow Star.

The building collapsed behind him.

Dad had managed to get the woman and her baby out the front, shoving them through the entrance. The woman had been knocked off her feet, curling her body around her child as she hit the ground.

Nick's dad hadn't been so lucky. A beam had collapsed on top of him.

Dad was brave. But so were his brothers and sisters on the force.

They'd rushed forward and managed to pull him out in time. He'd been unconscious, and his breath had rattled dangerously in his chest, but he was alive. And remarkably, the explosion must have burned the fire out. All that remained were hot, glowing embers in the charred wood and brickwork.

No one else was hurt. The woman had a few scrapes, and the baby had a scratch on their cheek, but that was all. It could have been much, much worse.

"And that's what you need to focus on," Cap told him. "That's what you need to remember. He's a hero, Nick. He was doing his job. He saved those people. And yes, he was hurt, but he's alive. Tough guy with a hard head. They gotta keep an eye on it, make sure his brain just got a little rattled and nothing more, but it's going to be okay. *He's* going to be okay."

"Did you get them?" Nick asked, hands shaking. "Did you get Pyro Storm?"

Cap shook his head. "They were gone." He hesitated. "I don't want you to leap to any conclusions. We don't know what exactly happened. We don't know if it was—"

"It was him," Nick snapped. "It was Pyro Storm. He did this, okay? He's the bad guy. Shadow Star was trying to stop him. He was trying to save Nova City. If he'd known my dad was still in there, he would have done everything he could to help."

Cap smiled tightly. "Okay, Nick. Sure. I understand. But let's not worry about that right now. Let's get you up to see your dad. I know he's going to want to hear the sound of your voice."

It was too much for Nick to handle. As soon as the elevator doors closed, he collapsed against Cap, splintering off into pieces. Cap wrapped an arm around his shoulder, whispering that it would be all right.

They got off on the fifth floor, Nick wiping his eyes. He didn't want anyone to see that he'd been crying. But what he saw threatened to set him off all over again.

Cops lined the hallway, men and women in rows standing against either wall. Some looked exhausted, faces streaked with dust and grime, their heads tilted back against the wall, eyes closed.

They were all in uniform, service caps clutched in their hands in front of them.

When they saw Nick, they all snapped to attention, squaring their shoulders.

Cap kept his arm around Nick's shoulders, leading him down the hallway. Every officer nodded in turn at Nick as he passed them by. Nick acknowledged each of them. Some he recognized. Some he didn't. Officer Rookie had somehow made it up before Nick and Cap did, and he offered a small smile to Nick before schooling his face again.

Toward the end of the row of officers was a group of men standing in plainclothes, badges hanging around their necks.

Detectives.

His father's former coworkers.

These were the people who had fought for Aaron Bell when Before had become After, and his dad had lashed out against someone he shouldn't have. They were the ones that had argued with Internal Affairs and the higher-ups, telling them in no uncertain terms that Detective Bell shouldn't be dismissed, that he was an unmatched asset to the Nova City Police Department, and to lose him would mean losing someone who bled blue.

In the end, he'd been demoted, but Nick had never forgotten. Dad had tried to shield him from the majority of it, but Nick had known more than he probably should have.

They clapped him on the back as he walked by, telling him it was fine, it was going to be fine. *You'll see, Aaron's gonna pull through, Nicky, he's going to pull through and be back on the job before you know it.*

They reached an open doorway.

Cap stopped him before he could see inside.

"Remember," he told Nick. "It always looks worse than it actually is."

It looked bad.

That couldn't be denied.

It looked so bad that the floor tilted beneath Nick's feet. Gut-punched and heartsore, it took him a moment to figure out how to make his legs work again.

There were two nurses in the room, and they smiled at him before turning back to the man on the bed.

Machines beeped and whirred, and Nick found himself distracted by the beat of his father's heart, a spike of green that rose and fell. It was steady.

There was tape over his father's eyes, keeping his eyelids shut.

There was a strap around his neck, attached to a breathing tube, holding it in place.

There were bandages wrapped around his right arm, where he'd been burned.

But it was the bruising that was the worst of all.

It looked as if every inch of visible skin was covered in deep bruises, blue and red and violet. His chest rose and fell, and there was a white clip attached to the tip of one of his fingers, but even his knuckles were purple, as if all parts of him had been crushed.

"You must be Nick," one of the nurses said, sounding inordinately cheerful.

Nick nodded, unable to take his eyes off his dad.

"I'm Becky. I'll be your father's nurse today. This is Renee. She's going to be helping me out. You need anything, all you need to do is ask us, okay?"

"Or one of the officers outside," Renee said, shaking her head. "I'm pretty sure they'd do anything you wanted too."

"Your dad's doctor will be in here in a little bit to talk to you," Becky said, changing out an empty IV bag for a full one. "He'll be able to answer any questions you have. You can come over here if you want. I know your dad will want to hear your voice."

But Nick couldn't move.

All he could do was watch the heartbeat.

"Nick?" Cap asked.

He turned and ran.

Gibby and Jazz found him.

He didn't know how long he'd been curled under a table in the empty room he'd found on the second floor. It looked as if it'd been used for storage. Chairs were stacked on top of one another. Cleaning supplies sat on shelves against the wall. It smelled like bleach.

The door opened, light and noise filtering in from the hallway.

He heard a sigh above him. "In here."

He blinked as two sets of legs appeared in front of him.

He turned his head.

Jazz and Gibby crouched down.

"Hey," Jazz said, smoothing out her skirt.

"Hi," he said back.

"Everyone's looking for you," Gibby said. "You'd think all those cops would be better at it than they are."

"How did you find me?" Nick asked, looking at the underside of the table.

"Small dark room. It's where I'd go too. It's the tenth one we checked."

"They were looking on the roof," Jazz said. "It's like they don't even know you. Can I come under the table with you?"

Nick shrugged. "The floor is kind of dirty."

Jazz snorted. "Like I care."

Nick pushed himself closer to the wall to make room for Jazz. She crawled underneath the table, cursing quietly as she hit her head. She lay down beside him, taking his hand in hers and squeezing gently. Nick's lip trembled, and he looked away.

Gibby reached back and closed the door behind her before she sat down, bringing her legs up to her chest and wrapping her arms around them.

Jazz spoke first. "I think someone drew a penis on the underside of this table."

Nick choked. "It's a stain."

"What? No, it's not. That's definitely a penis. Okay, maybe it's water, but it looks like a dong."

"What does that say about you that you see penises?" Gibby asked her. "It doesn't look like—okay, that's a penis."

"I wonder if it's like one of those inkblot tests," Jazz said. "What does it mean that I see a penis?"

Nick shook his head. "Probably a sign of the onset of a debilitating mental illness. Hooray."

"I don't know how I feel about that."

"It's okay," Gibby said. "I'll still love you anyway."

"Even if I see penises where there are none?"

"Even then."

"Oh my god," Nick groaned. "You should leave if you're going to be adorably weird. I'm vulnerable right now, and I don't know if I can take it."

"Nah," Jazz said easily. "I think I'll stay right where I am, if that's okay with you."

It was very okay with Nick, though he didn't say it out loud. "I just . . . needed to hide."

Gibby hummed. "Don't blame you. It's tough."

"It was the heartbeat."

Jazz squeezed his hand again. "What about it?"

Nick's eyes felt like they were filled with sand. "The beeping. And the line. It was a lot. It scared me. Because it was him, but it didn't look like him."

"Looks a little beat up, right?"

Nick shrugged. "A lot beat up." He swallowed thickly, trying to stay in control. "I didn't mean to leave."

"I don't think anyone's mad at you for that," Gibby said. "And if they are, they'll have to get through Jazz and me first."

"I can beat up men twice my size," Jazz said. "I got your back. And your front."

Nick closed his eyes. He didn't want to know the answer, but he had to ask. "Seth?"

It was Gibby who answered. "He's . . . I don't know, Nick. I know he wants to be here."

"But he's not."

Gibby hesitated. "No. He's not."

Nick opened his eyes. "Where is he?"

Gibby shrugged and looked down. She picked at the frayed hem of her jeans. "It's . . . there are things going on, Nick. Things that I can't explain."

"Why?"

"It's not my place. You need to hear it from him."

Nick chuckled bitterly. "Don't see how that's going to happen. He's not here, after all."

"He wants—"

"Maybe I don't care what he wants. My *dad* is in the hospital, and he can't even take the time to answer the phone? I tried to call him, and you know what happened? It rang three times before it went to voicemail. If his phone was off, it would have rung once. If his phone was on and he missed the call, it would have rung six times. But it rang *three*. Which means he saw who was calling and then sent it to voicemail."

Gibby winced. "You can't know that."

"Do you know where he is?"

Gibby didn't answer.

Jazz looked at her. "Do you?"

Gibby sighed. "Look, it's not my place to tell. I made a promise that—"

Nick sat up. Of course, he hit his head on the table. "Motherfu—*ow*. Why is this table so *hard*?"

"It does have a penis on it," Jazz said helpfully. "Maybe it likes that kind of thing."

Nick glared down at her. "You're not funny."

"Excuse you. I'm hysterical."

"She really is," Gibby said. She sighed as Nick and Jazz looked at her again. "I . . . crap." Her shoulders slumped. "It's not what you think. Believe me when I say that Seth would want nothing more than to be here, okay?"

"Then where is he?" Nick asked. "Why can't he even pick up the phone when my dad is in the hospital because of Pyro Storm?"

Gibby lifted her head sharply. "That's not true."

"It is," Nick said fiercely. "Cap told me what happened. Shadow Star and Pyro Storm were fighting and crashed into a building. And then it exploded, and there was fire everywhere. Pyro Storm was trying to kill Shadow Star, and he didn't give a damn who else he hurt in the process. He's the bad guy. The villain. He did this. It's always been him."

"No," Gibby said, shaking her head. "Nick, that's not—you know what? I don't care anymore. I'm tired of all of this." She stared at him for a moment. She took a deep breath and let it out slowly. Then, "Nick, there's something I have to tell you. It's about—"

The door opened.

Light spilled in.

Officer Rookie sighed. "*There* you are. Dammit, Nick. As soon as we can look back on all of this and laugh, I'm going to handcuff you and put you in the back seat again."

"Wow," Jazz said. "Isn't that illegal? Nick is underage. You shouldn't be flirting with a sixteen-year-old. You're, like, thirty."

Nick sniffled. "That's what *I* said. But apparently Officer Rookie finds me irresistible. I mean, I don't blame him. I'm pretty cute."

Officer Rookie rolled his eyes. "Whatever gets your rocks off."

"Ew," Gibby, Jazz, and Nick said.

"You probably shouldn't be talking about that with minors," Jazz told him.

"You'll go to jail," Gibby said.

"Be nice to Officer Rookie," Nick said.

"*Thank* you, Nick—"

"I mean, it's not his fault he has a crush on me."

"Who has a crush on you?" Cap asked, appearing in the doorway.

Officer Rookie looked as if he were about to die. "No one, sir! It's absolutely nothing!"

Cap narrowed his eyes suspiciously. "Hmm."

"It's fine, Cap," Nick said.

"Is it? Why don't you let me be the judge of that? Officer Morton, I'll handle this from here. Make yourself useful elsewhere."

Officer Rookie nodded and fled.

"Strange guy," Cap said, staring after him.

"He's all right," Nick said, crawling over Jazz to get out from underneath the table. "He'll make a good cop."

"Yeah? Seal of approval?"

Nick nodded. "Little wet behind the ears, but he has to start somewhere."

Cap rubbed his chin thoughtfully. "Good to know." He glanced at Nick. "We okay?"

Nick shrugged and looked down at his shoes.

"Sounds about right."

"Sorry. I shouldn't have run away."

"Sometimes we have to run away in order to clear our heads and put ourselves together as best we can. The important thing is that we return stronger than when we left."

It's easier to stand together than it is to struggle apart.

"I don't know if I'm strong enough," Nick admitted.

"I think you are," Cap said.

"Me too," Gibby said while she helped her girlfriend up.

"The strongest," Jazz agreed. "And even if you're not, you've got us."

Nick loved them very much.

* * *

Mary Caplan came and fussed over Nick. She was a no-nonsense Black woman who told him in no uncertain terms that he would be staying with them when he tried to tell her he'd be fine on his own. "Don't even try and come at me with that bull," she told him. "I won't hear of it. You will stay with us, and I'm going to feed you like you wouldn't believe. You're far too skinny. I made meatloaf and pot roast and bought sixteen frozen pizzas before I came here. You'll eat all of it, and you will like it."

"This is going to be great," Cap whispered to him.

"Oh, don't believe any of that is for *you*, Rodney Caplan," Mary said, mouth a thin line. "You get kale."

"But—"

She glared at him.

Cap sighed. "Yes, ma'am."

She leaned forward and kissed her husband on the cheek.

Cap smiled adoringly at her.

Nick didn't understand old people.

Jazz and Gibby went with Mary to the Bell home to pack Nick a bag. As weirded out as he was by the idea of them digging around his underwear drawer, he wanted to stay with his dad as long as he could.

Becky smiled at him when he returned, gesturing toward a chair set up next to the bed. "Doctor Chaudry will come talk to you in a minute. Your dad is in good hands."

Nick sat in the chair. "Is he—is he hurting right now?"

Becky shook her head. "It looks worse than it is, trust me. He's probably going to be in some pain when he wakes up, but that's what morphine is for. We'll get him stoned, and you can record him for blackmail later."

Nick liked the way Becky thought.

Doctor Chaudry gave him the breakdown. Two broken ribs, punctured lung. Superficial burns on his arm. Contusions. Abrasions.

"It's the head injury we're watching the most," he told him.

"There's some swelling, but it should go down. The breathing tube is for his lung. If there's repeated pneumothorax, we'll need to consider surgery, but we'll have to wait and see."

"When will he wake up?" Nick asked, fidgeting in his chair.

Doctor Chaudry smiled at him. "Soon, Nick. Probably within a couple of days. He's healthy and strong. He'll have to take it easy for a while, but I think he's going to be fine."

He was finally left alone as night began to fall, the rain slacking off to a miserable drizzle. The officers had shifts to get to, or they needed to go home to their families. Officer Rookie volunteered to stay with Nick, but Nick shook his head. Before he left, Officer Rookie wrote down his phone number on a piece of paper, telling Nick to call if he needed anything.

"Why, Officer Rookie, you sly dog. Way to slip me your number while I'm in a vulnerable place—"

Nick was almost offended at how fast Officer Rookie fled the room.

Turning back to his father, he hesitated before reaching out and touching the back of Dad's hand. His skin was warm, and Nick struggled to swallow past the lump in his throat.

"Hey," he managed to say. "Um. Becky told me that it was okay to talk to you. That you probably wouldn't hear me, but she thinks it helps. She's—uh. She's your nurse. She seems really nice, I guess. So. That's good."

Nick looked at his hand atop his father's. He was paler than his dad. He'd never noticed that before.

"I'm—" He coughed and cleared his throat. "I'm proud of you. I'm sorry if I don't tell you that enough. I am. I don't . . . I don't know why we don't say that to each other more. I know I screw up sometimes. And that's my fault. I don't mean to be this way. Not always. I know it's rough. Without her. I don't even know how we got this far. But we did. And we're going to go further. I need you. I don't want to do this on my own. You're my dad." A tear trickled down his cheek, but he didn't wipe it away. "I'm grounded, remember? So it'd be pretty great of you to wake up now so I don't do anything I'm not supposed to."

His dad's chest rose and fell as the machines beeped and hissed.

Nick lay his head down on the side of the bed near their joined hands.

He stayed that way for a long time.

15

Nick lay in bed that night, fuller than he'd ever been in his life, though he hadn't had much of an appetite when he'd sat down at the Caplan table. Mary hadn't taken no for an answer, and Nick ate what was probably an entire cow's worth of meatloaf.

The bed was soft, and the room warm, but the sheets were slightly scratchy, and the shadows crawled in weird shapes on the walls. He could never sleep well in unfamiliar places, and with the added stress of everything that had happened, he didn't think he was going to nod off any time soon. Oh, he was exhausted, but it was to the point of being too tired to actually sleep. It didn't help that his brain was in overdrive without any sign of slowing.

And to make matters worse, he'd tried to call Seth again, only to have it ring once before going to voicemail. His phone was turned off. Nick thought about calling his aunt or uncle to find out what the hell was going on, but in the end, decided against it. Martha had left a voicemail while he'd been sitting with his father, telling him she loved him, and to call her if he needed anything. They would be by in the next couple of days, she said. And then, weirdly, she ended the message by saying, "I know things may seem a certain way. But there's a reason for everything, Nicky. I need you to remember that. We love you, and we'll see you soon."

He saved the voicemail.

There were texts from Gibby and Jazz while they were at his house, telling him his room smelled like *boy*, and that they were absolutely not impressed with how many pairs of tube socks he owned. Jazz also said his bed was comfortable, but when Gibby tried to kiss her while she was sitting on it, she pushed her away, because she wouldn't do that to Nick. Also, Gibby had just eaten a cold piece of pizza from Nick's fridge, and her breath smelled like onions and olives, and it was disgusting.

He smiled at the messages before locking the phone and setting it on the small nightstand.

He punched the pillow a few times, trying to find a comfortable position to lie in so he could attempt sleep. He pulled the comforter up to his shoulder, lying back down and facing the window, the light from the streetlamps soft through the second-story window.

And then—

There.

Someone stood on the roof of the house across the street.

He fell out of bed with a squawk, cursing as he pulled himself back up toward the window.

The figure was gone.

It was near eleven when he sat up in the bed, rubbing a hand over his face. His head was buzzing. He hadn't taken a Concentra since the morning before. He'd have to ask Mary or Cap about it. Dad had them locked away at home, but there were the emergency doses at school they could get. He wasn't going to school for the rest of the week, but maybe someone could get it for him.

He reached over and grabbed the remote to the small TV sitting on top of the bureau of drawers against the wall. It was probably older than Nick, but Mary assured him it worked fine. He didn't have the heart to tell her he was grounded and couldn't watch TV.

Maybe he could find some stupid infomercial or a DIY channel that could help bore him to sleep.

He hit the power button.

The screen came to life.

A voice filled the room as a graphic flew across the screen. "Local. Breaking. Weather. Sports. This is . . . Action News with Steve Davis."

Steve Davis appeared on-screen behind a desk, smiling widely. Nick had never noticed how his teeth were so big. Or so white. "Good evening," Steve Davis intoned. "We are continuing to follow the story from earlier today where a building collapsed on the 1600 block of Sixth Avenue. In what can only be described as chaos, the skies above Nova City were alight with an ongoing event between the Extraordinaries known as Shadow Star and Pyro Storm. The all-out fight began late last night and went well into the early hours of the morning, during which Shadow Star and Pyro Storm showed each other no mercy. Though no deaths have been reported, the battle between the Extraordinaries did spill into the streets of Nova City, eventually leading to the destruction of a condemned apartment building. As the building collapsed, an officer of the Nova City Police Department was injured."

Nick's breath lodged in his throat as his dad's picture appeared on the screen. He was against a blue background, in uniform. "A police spokesperson has confirmed that Aaron Bell, an officer with NCPD for twenty years, was injured while rescuing a member of the transient population."

Steven Davis smiled wider. "If that name is familiar, it's because Officer Bell was involved in an altercation two years ago in which he assaulted a witness in a high-profile case. A detective at the time, Officer Bell did not face charges, but did receive a demotion. The witness filed a lawsuit against Aaron Bell and Nova City, which was settled out of court."

Nick wanted to punch Steve Davis's perfect teeth down his throat.

"The spokesperson also said that Officer Bell, while in the intensive care unit, is expected to make a full recovery. Nova City General released a statement, saying Officer Bell is listed in fair condition, though they declined to comment further."

His dad's picture disappeared as the camera centered back on Steve Davis. "And now, in an Action News exclusive, we go to Rebecca Firestone."

The screen switched to a rainswept street corner that Nick vaguely recognized. Rebecca Firestone smiled beatifically. She held an umbrella in one hand and a microphone in the other. "Thank you, Steve. The events of the past twenty-four hours have shown an escalation in the violence between Extraordinaries. In their short yet complex history, Shadow Star and Pyro Storm have been adversarial, but have always managed to keep the ferocity to a minimum. That changed today."

Rebecca Firestone disappeared when an aerial shot replaced her. It showed a cloud of smoke and dust rising from a collapsed building, debris spilling out onto the street. "This was the scene earlier today when an apartment building collapsed in a fight between Shadow Star and Pyro Storm. Officials say the building was condemned due to structural integrity issues and was scheduled to be demolished last year. However, due to ongoing lawsuits from former tenants and a legal quagmire concerning the replacement of the building, the demolition was postponed indefinitely. In the interim, the Haversford Apartments became a haven for the transient population of Nova City. The city attempted to dissuade people from entering by boarding up the building and placing a fence around it, but Action News has learned that in the last year alone, the fence had to be repaired forty-seven times. A spokesperson for the housing development issued a statement in conjunction with the mayor's office, stating that while every attempt was made to keep people from entering the building, they, and I quote, 'can't be there twenty-four-seven to enforce this.'"

Rebecca Firestone appeared again, eyes sparkling. "And here to explain today's events is Shadow Star himself."

Nick almost fell off the bed as the camera shot pulled back.

There, standing in the inky darkness next to Rebecca Firestone, was Shadow Star.

He was in full costume, the lenses over his eyes slightly narrowed. He stood with his arms clasped behind his back. His broad shoulders were squared, and he looked calm and confident. His costume glittered under the lights from the camera. It took a moment for Nick to realize why his stance looked familiar. The cops, in the hallway. They'd stood the same way.

For the first time since he became aware of Shadow Star's existence, Nicholas Bell felt . . . nothing.

Wait.

That was a lie.

He felt *something,* but it wasn't like it'd been before. Even days ago, the very sight of Shadow Star would have sent him into a fit of teenage hormones, most likely ending with flop sweats and a partial erection. His eyes would be wide, and he'd be breathing heavily through his mouth, taking in every single inch of Shadow Star that he could.

It wasn't like that now.

Now, Nick felt . . . He didn't know how he felt. While there was a trace of that obsessive attraction still clinging to the back of his mind, it'd been replaced by something different. His palms were sweaty, his stomach twisted slickly.

It didn't help that Shadow Star was *smiling* at Rebecca Firestone, smiling as if Aaron Bell didn't lay unconscious in a hospital, a tube shoved down his throat. As if Nick wasn't in a strange house in a strange bed because he had nowhere else to go. As if Nick hadn't just had what was probably the second worst day of his life. Fiery disappointment bled through his rib cage, lodging firmly in his chest.

"Thank you, Rebecca," Shadow Star said, voice modulated to a deep pitch. "It's nice to see you again."

Rebecca's smile widened. "We appreciate you speaking with us in what I'm sure is a busy time for you."

Shadow Star shrugged. "It's always busy in Nova City. Crime never sleeps."

Nick barely avoided rolling his eyes.

Rebecca chuckled. "I bet it doesn't. Can you tell the viewers what happened today?"

Shadow Star looked directly at the camera. "Of course. Early this morning, the villain known as Pyro Storm attempted to gain access to Burke Tower. It's not the first time he's tried it, but he's become more aggressive in his tactics."

"Why is he trying to get into Burke Tower?"

"I don't know, Rebecca," Shadow Star said. "I haven't discovered that yet. But it doesn't matter. What Pyro Storm was trying to do is against the law, and he must be stopped. And since I'm the only one capable of such a thing, I did what I had to in order to ensure the safety of those inside Burke Tower."

"Burke Tower," Rebecca Firestone told the viewers, "is of course where Burke Pharmaceuticals is located. We asked the contractor who runs security for Burke Tower for a statement, but have yet to receive a response." She turned back to Shadow Star. "In the past, you've been able to keep the skirmishes between you and Pyro Storm to a minimum. What's changed?"

"I don't know," Shadow Star said, and he sounded frustrated. Nick almost felt sorry for him. "Something's changed. He's becoming unstable. I urge the good people of Nova City to stay as far away from him as possible. He's dangerous. A threat to our way of life. I'm going to do everything I can to stop him and to keep the city safe."

"You're so brave," Rebecca Firestone said, putting her hand on his arm.

"Holy shit," Nick muttered. "You're embarrassing yourself. Turn it down, Firestone. Have some dignity."

"It's not a matter of bravery," Shadow Star replied. "It's about doing what's right."

Rebecca Firestone frowned as if she hadn't expected that answer. She recovered quickly. "An NCPD officer was injured in the line of duty today in direct correlation with the battle between you and Pyro Storm. Is there anything you'd like to say to the family of Officer Bell?"

Nick held his breath.

Shadow Star turned away from Rebecca and looked at the camera again. "Yes, there is. If they're watching, I would like Officer Bell's family to know I will do everything I can to make sure justice is served. I hope I can be strong enough to make sure something like this doesn't happen to anyone again."

"What a lovely thing to—"

"There's more."

"Oh. Sorry. Go right ahead."

Nick felt as if Shadow Star were staring directly at him. "I promise you. I won't stop until Pyro Storm has paid for his crimes. He won't get away with this. I meant what I said in the alley when our picture was taken."

Rebecca Firestone blinked. "What? What picture? What alley?"

Shadow Star cocked his head, as if hearing something in the distance. "The city needs me," he growled. "I must heed her call."

There was a swirling burst of light that cast shadows all around. By the time the glare faded, Shadow Star was gone.

Rebecca Firestone looked flustered, as if she had a lady boner on camera and didn't know how to deal with it. Nick could understand that completely. "Well, you heard it here first. Shadow Star has promised he will take out the menace known as Pyro Storm. A fitting end to what will surely be a day to remember. Back to you, Steve."

"Thanks, Rebecca. That was certainly illuminating. He seems to be the hero that Nova City needs. In other news, do squirrels have feelings? One expert's answer may surprise you. Stay tuned."

Nick grabbed the remote and turned the television off.

The room fell into darkness.

I meant what I said in the alley when our picture was taken.

Had he meant . . . ?

It'd been raining.

Nick had accidentally probably on purpose kissed the side of his head.

Then—

There we go. Shadow Star, you don't need to smile because you're brooding and deep or whatever.

Exactly. I breathe the shadows of the dark, and—

Everyone say I think Nick is super cute!

I think Nick is super cute.

"What the hell?" Nick whispered. "He couldn't have—"

Right?

But what if?

Did it even matter? Weren't there more important things to focus on?

He picked up his phone. The screen lit up. He stared down at it.

He was on the cusp of something big. Something great. He didn't want it, but he didn't know if he had a choice.

He called the one person who could help him. The one person who could make it all okay.

It rang once. Twice. Three times.

A voice spoke.

"You've reached Seth's voicemail. I'm probably busy. And nobody calls anyone anymore unless it's an emergency. Send a text like a normal person. Unless it's an emergency."

He didn't leave a message.

He remembered the way his father looked in the hospital, bruised and beaten.

He remembered being told that Before had become After.

Maybe it had all been leading to this.

Here. Now. This moment.

This was his origin story.

He found another name on his phone.

Highlighted it.

And yes, he hesitated, for the briefest of moments. The brave often do.

But in the end, he did the only thing he could.

It rang once. Twice. Three—

"Nicky," a voice said, sounding smug. "Isn't it a little late for you?"

He took a deep breath and said, "Owen. I'm ready now. How do we do it?"

16

Nick sat by his father's hospital bed, holding his hand.

People came and went.

They smiled at him softly, sympathy clear on their faces.

He hated it.

Dad looked the same.

There were no changes.

He hated that too.

You were going to tell me something yesterday," Nick said suddenly. Gibby looked up at him warily from across the table in the hospital cafeteria. If Nick closed his eyes, he could almost pretend they were at school having lunch. Seth would be by his side, Gibby and Jazz across from him. Owen would be stealing food, grinning wickedly.

"What?" Gibby asked. She looked over at Jazz, who shrugged. They'd brought Nick his homework after school, but Nick didn't care about that.

"Yesterday. In that supply closet. Before Officer Rookie came in. You said that you were tired of all of this. That there was something you had to tell me. What was it?"

Gibby looked away. "I don't remember."

"You don't?"

"It doesn't matter, Nicky. Wasn't important."

Nick didn't believe her.

* * *

There was a knock at the door, startling Nick from watching his father's heartbeat on the monitor.

"Come in," Nick said hoarsely. He reached up and wiped his eyes. It was probably Becky coming to tell him who the night nurse would be. She said it'd be someone new, but that she'd introduce them at the shift change. They didn't care if he was crying. They probably saw it a lot.

But it wasn't a nurse. It was Martha Gray.

Nick stood, suddenly embarrassed. He didn't know why. "Hi. Um. I didn't know you were coming."

Martha smiled respectfully, purse clutched in front of her. "I hope you don't mind. Is it okay that I'm here? I can come back later, if you want."

Nick shook his head. "No, it's okay." Then, with his heart thudding faster, he looked behind her, wondering if Seth had come too. If he had, maybe things would be different. Maybe he wouldn't have to go through with what he'd planned.

He wasn't there.

Martha's smile faded. She looked grief-stricken. "Only me, I'm afraid."

It hurt. A lot. "Yeah," Nick said. "Sure. That's fine. I mean, it's just my dad, right?"

Martha took a step forward. "Nick, you have to believe me when I say he wants to be here. Probably more than anything in the world."

"Then why isn't he here?"

"Sometimes, there are things bigger than our wishes or desires." She closed the door behind her. Nick looked away as she walked around to the other side of the bed. She blinked rapidly as she set her purse on the windowsill. She turned and stared down at his father before she reached out and took his hand in hers. She reached up and brushed a lock of hair from his forehead. "How is he?"

"The same."

"When will he wake up?"

"No one knows. Tomorrow. The next day. Someday."

She hummed a little under her breath. "I wanted you to come stay with us, but I was told you were at the chief's home."

Nick slumped down in his chair. "Yeah."

"Safest place you could probably be."

"I suppose."

She pulled the blanket covering his dad a little higher. "Bob wanted to be here. But there was an emergency at the building he manages. Something having to do with a potential gas leak. He wanted me to tell you he loves you, and he'll be here as soon as he can get away. Funny thing, gas leaks. Ignite a single spark, and it could lead to disaster. Tell me. Did they find out the cause of the explosion yet?"

"It was Pyro Storm," Nick said, voice hard.

"Is that so?"

"Yes."

"You seem sure."

Nick shrugged. "It's the only explanation."

"Can I tell you a story?"

Nick loved Martha. He did. But he wasn't in the mood for this. Not now. "Visitor hours are almost—"

"A boy came to live with us once. We didn't expect it. We weren't ready for it. Especially not one who had lost so much. We were grieving ourselves, and then suddenly we had a child with nowhere else to go."

Nick closed his eyes.

"He'd been hurt," Martha said. "In the accident. His parents had died, and he had lived, but his heart was broken, and he was covered in bandages. They called it a mechanical failure. Something wrong with the train. I don't remember specifics. Bob's better at these things. Many people died. But this boy, this sweet, little boy somehow managed to survive. He was found buried under scorched metal, his mother and father lying on top of him. When I saw him for the first time, it was in a room almost like this one. His eyes were closed, and I thought he was having a nightmare. So, I did the only thing I could—I held his hand and told him that everything was going to be all right. That even though his heart was breaking, we would keep him safe."

Nick shuddered, trying to keep from curling in on himself.

"He shouldn't have survived. He was our little miracle. Stronger than people gave him credit for. And he lived. He was sad, of course. And he had terrible nightmares. He would wake screaming in the dark, calling out for his mother and father, trying to get to them. Trying to save them. He never could before we would wake him, and we had to witness his heart break all over again each time he woke."

"Why are you telling me this?" Nick asked through gritted teeth.

She acted as if he hadn't spoken at all. "Bob and I didn't know how to be parents. We did the best we could. I worried it wouldn't be enough. That *we* wouldn't be enough. Oh, we loved him immensely. We gave him everything we thought he could ever want. Love is such a weapon in the face of darkness, if you only know how to wield it."

Nick felt a tear track down his cheek.

"He was always quiet. Always watching. He barely talked. Until one day, he came home from school, babbling a mile a minute about a boy who came onto the swings with him, even though neither of them could actually swing. He said this boy was smart and kind and nice, and that his father was a police officer. He announced quite loudly this boy was named Nicholas Bell, and that they were going to be best friends forever. It was the most I'd ever heard him speak at one time since he'd come to live with us. I didn't know who this Nicholas Bell was, but I thought it was possible he was the godsend we'd been waiting for."

Nick sniffled as he shook his head. "I'm not worth—"

"You *are*," Martha snapped, and Nick opened his eyes. She was staring at him, her own eyes shining. "I know you have trouble believing it, but you are. I know how you see Seth, Nick. I've spent years watching you both. You think the sun rises and sets with him. That all the stars in the sky appear because of him. But what you fail to see, *always,* is that he thinks the same of you."

"Then why isn't he here?" Nick growled, standing from the chair. He started to pace back and forth. "If what you're saying is true, then where the hell is he? This is my d-d-*dad*."

Above the bed, the light sizzled and went out.

They both looked up. The bulbs were dark.

"Huh," Martha said. "Would you look at that?"

Nick rubbed the side of his head. He was getting another headache. Mary Caplan was supposed to bring him one of his pills. He'd forgotten to take it this afternoon.

"We were at home when the call came," Martha said, still staring up at the burned-out light. "It was Gibby's parents on the other end."

Nick was confused. "They called you about my dad? But—"

"About your mother, Nick."

Nick went cold. "What?"

"They called us. They told us what happened to her. I thought Seth was going to tear the world apart to get to you. Do you remember?"

Nick hesitated, but then shook his head. "Everything from back then is a fog. I remember being with Dad, and then Seth was there. I don't remember what time it was. Or where we were."

"That's to be expected. Trauma can alter the mind. Make it . . . change. It can rob you of your memories. He was there, Nick, as quickly as he could be. And he saw what it did to you. He understood what you were going through, maybe better than anyone else. He didn't remember his own loss but knew what it had done to him. And he made a promise to you. He told you he would do everything he could to make sure nothing like that ever happened again."

"I don't understand," Nick said helplessly.

"He wants to be here," Martha repeated. "More than anything. But things are different now. And it's hurting him more than you could ever know. I know that's a cold comfort, but you need to hear it."

Nick hung his head.

He heard her moving around the side of the bed, and he didn't try to fight it when she took him in her arms. He sagged against her, laying his head on her shoulder. She rubbed his back, whispering quietly in his ear. "It was that day on the swings that changed everything for him. Since then, what he's done has been about you. I know you can't always see it, Nick. But sometimes, there are things greater than us. Things we must do to keep those we love safe. And he loves you. He *loves you*."

She held him as he broke again.

She left a short time later, after having leaned over the bed and kissed his dad on the forehead. She stood at the door, purse in hand. She squeezed his shoulder and said she would see him soon.

She was about to leave when she stopped. "Nick?"

"Yeah?" he asked. He was exhausted.

"This will get better. All of this. I promise."

He didn't know what to say, so he said nothing at all.

She smiled tightly. And then she was gone.

It was almost time for him to leave.

Mary Caplan was waiting for him.

He held his father's hand.

He said, "I'm going to make sure nothing like this ever happens to you again."

He heard the beep of his father's heartbeat as he turned and walked away.

Not hungry?" Mary asked while he picked at the plate she'd placed in front of him.

He shrugged. "Just tired, I guess. Probably will make it an early night."

"I have an appointment in the morning. It shouldn't take too long. You can either wait until I get done or take the train to the hospital. Either way is fine."

"Don't worry about me," he said. "I'll take the train. Where's Cap?"

She sighed. "Where else? Working. Always working. This business with the Extraordinaries, it . . . changes you."

That was the idea, but he didn't say it aloud. "I'm sure it'll be over soon."

She frowned. "What makes you say that?"

Nick pushed his plate away. "I think I'm ready for bed."

He was almost out of the kitchen when she said his name. "Your pill. You forgot to take your pill."

He swallowed it dry.

It tasted bitter going down.

But his headache went away almost immediately.

Funny, that.

Fic: This Is Where We Scorch the Earth
Author: ShadowStar744
Chapter 69 of ? (SORRY GUYS)
268,130 words
Pairing: Shadow Star/Original Male Character
Rated: PG-13 (Rating might go up, but I don't know if I would be good at it, ugh)
Tags: True Love, Pining, Gentle Shadow Star, Violence, Happy Ending, First Kiss, Maybe Some Smut if I Can Talk Myself into It, But Who Knows

NOT A CHAPTER

Hey, guys. I know this probably isn't the update you expected. I'm sorry. Unfortunately, I have bad news. Some big things have changed in my life, things I didn't expect. It's put me in a place where I have to make a choice about what kind of future I want to have. What's expected of me. Who I need to become. How I can help those who need it most.

I won't be updating the story for a while. Maybe a long while. I don't see Extraordinaries the same way. They used to be these mythical beings, capable of feats that boggled the mind. But now I know they're capable of hurting others. And that's something I never expected. Something I never thought would be possible.

I know this doesn't make much sense, and I apologize for that. This isn't some kind of code for me saying I'm going to hurt myself, so please don't think that. Far from it, in fact. I'm going do everything I can to make sure that those I love don't get hurt ever again.

I am going to do something extraordinary.

Thank you for making me feel special.

I'll talk to you soon.

ShadowStar744

He waited until he heard Mary Caplan go to bed. He pressed his ear against the bedroom door. It was quiet. He shouldered his backpack before opening the door slowly, peeking his head out into the darkened hallway. The house settled around him. No light came from underneath Cap and Mary's bedroom door.

He wore only socks as he tiptoed down the hallway, carrying his shoes just to be safe. He managed to avoid the step that Mary said always squeaked. He pulled open the front door as quietly as he could, locking it behind him with the key Cap had given him. He dropped his Chucks to the ground, shoving his feet inside.

And then he disappeared into the night.

What are you wearing?" Owen asked as he squinted at Nick when he approached. Owen was leaning against the doorway of a closed cell phone store.

Nick looked down. He had on black jeans and a black hoodie. The hood was pulled up over his head. "My breaking-and-entering costume."

"Your shoes are purple."

Nick frowned. "Yeah, Gibby brought these instead of my black ones. I didn't have time to go back and get them. My bad. Do you think it's going to give us away? I'm wearing black socks, so I can take them off if I need to."

Owen sighed. "You look ridiculous."

"Oh yeah? Well, you look . . . okay. You look like you always do. Why aren't you wearing a costume?"

Owen grinned. "Don't need one. Come on. Let's get this over with." He took Nick by the elbow and started tugging him down the block.

Burke Tower was lit up like a beacon in the night, propelling them forward.

How's your dad?" Owen asked as they approached the building.

"Fine," Nick muttered, dodging a group of late-night tourists gazing up at the skyscrapers around them. "He's going to wake up soon, and then he'll get to go home."

"Yeah? That's good. Sorry I haven't stopped by."

"It doesn't matter. The room's not very big. Not anything you could have done."

"Still. Hospitals creep me out. I was in them a lot as a kid, and I don't ever go back to them if I don't have to."

Nick stopped walking.

Owen glanced back at him. "What?"

"I didn't know you'd been in the hospital."

Owen rolled his eyes. "Because I never told you. It's not that big of a deal. You coming or what?"

Nick followed him. "Why did you have to go to the hospital?"

"Maybe it was because I was crazy," Owen said, waggling his eyebrows. "Kept me wrapped up in a straitjacket and everything."

Nick shoved him. "The only thing that's ever been straight about you."

Owen laughed. "Funny guy. I forget that sometimes. I don't know why it surprises me."

"Thanks? I think."

"It wasn't anything major," Owen said, his breath clouding behind him in a warm stream. "Saw things that weren't there."

Nick blinked. "Like hallucinations?"

"Sort of. They thought there was something wrong with my eyes, at first. And then with my brain."

"What was it?"

Owen looked up, the light from his father's building covering his skin. "Never figured it out. I got on medication, and it went away." He turned his head and winked at Nick. "I was one of the lucky ones, I guess."

A memory rose through the storm in Nick's head, bright as a shooting star.

And my medicine? I need it.

Not right now. You've had enough for the time being. Go. You've already made me late enough as it is.

"That's . . ." He didn't know how to finish. He decided on, "Weird."

Owen staggered dramatically. "Ouch, Nicky. And here I thought we were getting closer again. Why would you insult me on a date?"

Nick was scandalized. "We're not on a *date*. Why would you say that?"

"I asked you out, and you said yes."

"You told me we were going to break into your dad's work and steal pills to make me into an Extraordinary!"

"Well, yeah. Pretty great date idea, right?"

Nick punched Owen in the arm. "Dude, not cool. You know I'm—you know Seth and me are—we're *something*, okay?"

Owen made a face. "Like I could forget that. How is dear old Seth, anyway?"

"He's fine," Nick muttered. "I think."

"You don't know for sure?"

"I haven't talked to him in a little while."

"Why?"

Nick threw up his hands. "I don't know! He's busy, or whatever. Can we not talk about that right now? We have other things to focus on. And this is not a date."

"He hasn't even been by to see your father?" Owen sounded offended on Nick's behalf. "What a dick move."

"You haven't either," Nick reminded him.

"I told you I don't like—"

"Hospitals, yeah. But when he was a kid, he was in the hospital too. Maybe it's the same for him."

Owen's eyes narrowed. "Is that right? Why?"

"He was in—you really don't know this?"

"No."

"He was on a train with his parents. It crashed. They died. He didn't."

Owen groaned. "Of course that's what happened. This could absolutely not be any more cliché."

"What the hell are you talking about?"

Owen waved his hand dismissively. "It doesn't matter. We're here. Follow my lead."

"What? What do you mean follow your lead? Owen, what are you doing? Owen!"

Apparently, following Owen's lead meant marching right through the front doors of Burke Tower. It was late, and the doors were locked, but that didn't stop Owen from pulling out a keycard and pressing it against a black box fixed to the outside of the building. A light flashed green, and there was an audible click before one of the glass doors swung open.

Owen walked in.

Nick hesitated.

Then followed.

The floor was shiny and looked expensive. Nick was sure that it hadn't been designed with purple Chucks in mind.

There was a large fountain in the center of the room, water cascading down a thin sheet of glass. Nick watched as the glass lit up, and Simon Burke's face appeared in the water. "Welcome to Burke Pharmaceuticals," he said in a booming voice. "The future begins now."

"He paid someone six figures to come up with that slogan," Owen said.

Nick couldn't comprehend that kind of money. "Seems like he overpaid."

Owen snorted. "Try telling him that."

A row of metal detectors stood in the middle of the lobby, darkened. A security guard sat behind a wooden desk on a raised dais. He barely looked older than they did. He arched an eyebrow as they approached. "Mr. Burke," he said. "You're here late." He sat up in his chair, blushing slightly.

"You know how it is, Brett," Owen said easily. "Dad forgets something in his office, and I have to be the dutiful son and pick it up for him."

"No rest for the wicked."

Owen grinned as he leaned forward, elbows on the desk. "You calling me wicked, Brett?"

Brett looked flustered. "That's not—I'm not trying to—" He looked over Owen's shoulder at Nick. "Who's your friend?"

Owen glanced back at him. "Oh, Nicky? He's here to keep me company."

"That's it?"

"That's it."

Brett scratched the back of his head. "I don't know if I can let him in with you, Mr. Burke. I don't think your dad would be too happy about that."

Owen reached out and straightened Brett's tie. "Maybe it could be our little secret."

Brett sighed. "Don't do anything that's going to get me fired."

"I wouldn't *dream* of it. Not seeing your face would be a travesty of epic proportions."

"Uh, sure," Brett said, visibly sweating. "Yeah. Hey, I was thinking. Maybe we could go out for—"

"Can you buzz us in?" Owen asked sweetly.

Brett nodded jerkily, but reached forward and hit a button on the desk. "Just make sure you swipe the card in case anyone asks."

"Thanks, Brett," Owen said. He looked back at Nick again. "Ready?"

Nick nodded, unsure of what the hell was going on. It didn't stop him from following Owen through a metal gate next to the desk. The gate snapped closed behind them.

Nick figured they'd head toward the bank of elevators, so he was surprised when Owen veered to the left, heading down a long hallway with vaulted ceilings, and dark, wooden doors lining either side. The walls were covered with black screens, a stylized BP spinning lazily in the middle. Through floor-to-ceiling windows, Nick saw a man moving in what looked like a conference room, bopping his head as the tile buffer whirred loudly across the floor.

Now that he was here, Nick wasn't sure this was the best idea.

He thought about finding a way to get out of it, to convince Owen they needed to think this through, but every time he opened his mouth to say just that, he saw his father, unconscious in his hospital bed, the machines beeping and hissing around him, the line of his heartbeat bouncing.

"All right?" Owen asked, glancing back at him.

No. "Yeah."

They turned left, and then right, and then right again, and Nick wasn't sure he could find his own way out. Burke Tower was a labyrinth. He didn't know how anyone found their way around here.

"It's bigger than it looks," Nick told Owen. "This whole place."

A strange look crossed Owen's face. "It's all about layers, Nick. My family tends to have a certain . . . flair for the dramatics. My grandfather built this place from the ground up. And when he died, my father continued his work." He chuckled bitterly. "And one day, it will all be mine, and I'll wear the crown, heavy though it is."

Nick shrugged awkwardly. Owen's carefully placed mask seemed to be slipping again, and it made him uncomfortable. "You don't have to do anything you don't want to do."

"My family isn't like yours. There are certain expectations. Any choice I would've had in this life was taken from me the moment I was born."

"That . . . sucks." Dumb, but he didn't know what else to say. Vulnerable Owen wasn't something Nick knew how to deal with.

Owen laughed. "Oh, Nicky. Such a way with words."

"You're making a choice here, right?"

"What do you mean?"

Nick shrugged. "Being here. Doing . . . what we're doing. You chose to tell me about it. You chose to bring me here."

Owen shook his head. "This isn't about choice, Nick. This was inevitable."

"I don't understand."

"I know. There's a lot of things you don't understand."

Nick felt a drop of sweat slide down the back of his neck. "What about you?"

"What about me?"

"You're going to do this too, aren't you? Become an Extraordinary? I don't know if I want to do this by myself."

"Getting cold feet?"

"No. I just—why would you want to be normal when you can be something more?"

Nick didn't like the glint in Owen's eyes. "Exactly what I've always thought. This is going to be good, Nick. You'll see. We're here."

They stopped in front of ornate double doors. There was a black box next to the doors, similar to the one on the outside of Burke Tower. But instead of using the same card, Owen pulled a different one out of his pocket. He swiped it through the thin slot. It beeped . . . and a little light turned red.

Owen frowned.

He swiped it again.

A beep. A red light.

"Huh," Owen said.

"What's wrong?"

"Card's not working. My father must have had the doors recoded. Can never be too careful these days. Keep an eye out."

"Maybe we should—"

"It'll only take a second, Nick."

Nick turned and looked down the hallway. It was empty.

"I like you, Nick," Owen said. "I always have. I know—I know things were weird between us for a little while. And I know I haven't been as good a friend as I could be, but there's a reason for that."

Nick looked back over his shoulder. Owen hunched over the black box. Nick couldn't see what he was doing to it, but he could see Owen's arms moving. "Because you're a stuck-up jerk?"

"A little. But I don't suppose it matters now, does it? You've got Seth."

"I don't know about that," Nick muttered. "He's . . . Something's going on with him, and I don't know what."

"Life," Owen said airily. "We're teenagers. Everything is unnecessarily complicated. We're told we have to be a certain way, even if we know it's wrong. We're not taken seriously. Our ideas are cast aside as though they're without merit. Sometimes, we need to act out so that people pay attention to us. So that people know we mean what we say. That we're capable. That we shouldn't be dismissed."

Nick didn't know what he was talking about. "I thought putting a cricket into a microwave was going to make me into a superhero. I'm pretty sure I shouldn't be allowed to have ideas of my own anymore."

Owen shook his head. "Maybe it wasn't the most well thought-out plan, but your heart was in the right place. You made a decision to become something greater than what you were."

"Because I had a crush on an Extraordinary. It's stupid, if you think about it."

"But it's not just because of that anymore, is it?"

"I . . . No. It's not. But I don't think—"

Nick saw a flash of light out of the corner of his eyes. He whirled around in time to see one of the doors swing open. "How did you do that?"

Owen grinned, sharp. "I have my ways. Come on. We're almost there."

Nick looked back over his shoulder.

The hallway was still empty.

He turned toward the door . . .

. . . and went inside.

The office was extravagant, more than anything Nick had seen so far. Three of the four walls were lined with floor-to-ceiling bookcases, the shelves filled with tomes bound in bright colors. A ladder sat attached to a rail system that wrapped around the front of the bookshelves.

The fourth wall was a gigantic screen, the same BP symbol spinning in the middle.

A large wooden desk sat in front of the screen. There were three separate computer monitors on the desk, but Owen ignored them.

"I thought you said it was in the basement," Nick said.

"It is."

"Then why are we—"

"Watch."

Nick took a step back when Owen touched the spines of three different books in quick succession, each one lighting up under his fingertips. There was a deep, concussive sound, and then part of the bookshelf moved backward before sliding out of sight, revealing an elevator.

"Whoa," Nick breathed. He hadn't known until that exact moment that a bookcase hiding a secret entrance was one of his kinks. It definitely was now.

"Pretty cool, right?" Owen asked. "Like I said. Dramatic." He pressed a panel near the elevator doors. They opened.

Nick hesitated.

Owen saw it. "What is it?"

"Why are you doing this?"

Owen looked surprised. "I told you before. I want to help you—"

Nick shook his head. "You don't help anyone but yourself."

"Yikes."

Nick winced. "I didn't mean it like that."

"Yeah, you did. But that's fair." Owen sighed. "Think of this as me trying to better myself. Being selfless, even."

"Owen."

"Okay, maybe not *selfless,* but you get the idea. Can't a guy help a friend out?"

"What's in it for you?" Nick asked suspiciously.

"I get to say I know a kick-ass Extraordinary." Owen took a step back toward the elevator. "We're going to change the world, Nick. Of course I'd want to be a part of that. Don't you? Think about it. If you were given the power to make sure your dad would never be hurt again, wouldn't you take it? Why would you want to go through the experience of losing a parent all over again? You couldn't save your mother but—"

"Don't," Nick growled. "Don't bring her into this."

Owen held up his hands. "Sorry. I didn't—that wasn't what I meant. I'm just saying that this will keep those you love safe. And isn't that the most important thing of all?"

Nick was moving before he even realized it. He shoved past Owen and walked into the elevator. He turned around, arched an eyebrow, and said, "You coming?"

Owen smiled, eyes alight with mischief.

They didn't speak as the elevator descended. It was a longer trip than Nick expected it to be, lasting almost a full minute. There were no numbers counting up or down inside the elevator, only a single green button that Owen had pressed. Nick tried to clear his head, taking deep, even breaths. He was so close, *so close* to having what he'd wanted for the longest time. He couldn't back out now.

The elevator slowed to a halt.

The doors slid open.

In front of them was a wide-open space, sectioned off by walls of glass. Tiny lights lined the floor, illuminating the walkway that stretched in front of them, much longer than Nick expected it to be.

"Okay," Owen said. "This is it. The overhead lights will stay off. There aren't any security cameras down here. They wanted to keep it off the main security grid. Anything recorded is done closed circuit. But it's better to be safe than sorry. Always remember to keep to the shadows."

And that . . . that gave Nick pause. "What?"

Owen glanced back at him as he stepped out of the elevator. "Stay low and quiet, Nick. It's . . . what? Why are you looking at me like that?"

Nick shook his head slowly. "Uh. Nothing. Never mind. Déjà vu, I guess."

"That's the strangest feeling, isn't it? Like you've been here before. Or it's precognition. I think my father has a pill for that too, to be honest. Maybe that's the one you'd like to take?"

Nick blanched. "That's . . . I can't—"

"Let's go."

Nick followed.

Owen led them toward the other side of the room, ignoring the walls of glass on either side of them. Inside, large machines sat silent.

There were microscopes and computers and what Nick thought was an oversized centrifuge, though he couldn't see inside it.

They stopped in front of a sheet of glass.

"There," Owen said. "There it is."

Nick stepped forward.

There were seven different tubes on the inside.

In each of the tubes, hung suspended in midair, was a pill.

Green.

Yellow

Violet.

Blue.

Orange.

Black.

White.

"That's it?" Nick whispered.

"That's it," Owen said somewhere near Nick's ear. "Tiny things, aren't they? Though they'll surely pack a wallop."

"What . . . what do they do?"

"Green is super strength, capable of turning you into a human wrecking ball. Yellow is the power of flight. Violet is the ability to summon storms. Blue can make you become a conductor of electricity. Orange is fire. Black is smoke. Or maybe shadow. I'd stay away from that one if I were you. I'm told it's . . . intense. I wouldn't want that for you. Perhaps the blue. Or the green."

Shadow. "And the white?"

Owen shook his head regretfully. "The white one is off-limits. Even for you, Nicky. It's the most unstable. It's telekinesis. The power to move things with your mind. We can't touch that one. According to my father's tests, the last person who was given the white pill lost their mind. It's not quite there yet. One day. This isn't even all of them, just the ones currently being tested."

Everything felt too big, too wild. Unreal. "Oh," he said dumbly.

Owen put a hand on his shoulder. "So. Which one will it be?"

"I don't know," Nick admitted. "It's . . . a lot." A choice, finally, here at last, if Owen was to be believed, and Nick didn't know why he'd lie. Not about this. Owen could be an asshole, but Nick didn't think he'd try and pull something over on Nick, not when he was hurting. "You said I'd have to keep taking them in order to stay an Extraordinary?"

Owen nodded gravely. "Yes, but let's not worry about that yet. Choose one, Nick, and see how it goes. If you don't like it, you can try another. And another. I'll make sure of it. One pill to make everything go away, to protect all those you love the most. My father thinks . . . well. In addition to the military applications, he thinks these things should only be for the people who can afford them. The elite, willing to part with their riches in order to have the upper hand on those beneath them. It's ridiculous, isn't it? They should be for everyone. Anyone who wants to fight back against those who would take from them." He sighed, a long whispery sound that crawled along Nick's skin, leaving gooseflesh prickling in its wake. "Someone like you wouldn't even be given a chance. And how is that fair? After all, it's *your* father who suffered."

It's easier to stand together than it is to struggle apart. Dad had taught him that. It'd been close, hadn't it? Dad had been so close to dying, and where would Nick be then?

Alone. He'd be alone.

Still, he hesitated. "Are they addictive?" They had to be. If they gave the power Owen claimed, then why would anyone want to stop?

Owen laughed, but there was a harder edge to it. "*Addictive* isn't quite the right word for it. I don't mean to rush you, but we're running out of time. You need to decide, Nicky."

Nick pressed a hand against the glass encasing the tubes, staring at the pills. "Aren't you going to do this too?"

"This is for you," Owen said. "Don't worry about me."

Green. Yellow. Violet. Blue. Orange. Black. White.

Nick's mind raced.

He thought of the way the machines beeped around his father, his skin mottled with bruises. He thought of his mother smiling near a lighthouse, forever frozen in a moment in time. Anything. He would do anything to keep his people safe.

Including this, even if it was temporary. Being a temporary hero was better than being nothing at all.

"I think . . . I think I'll—"

"That's enough," another voice said from behind them.

They whirled around.

There, standing near the elevator, was Pyro Storm. Nick froze at the sight of him.

Owen chuckled. "Well, well, well. Isn't this a surprise?"

"Is it?" Pyro Storm asked. "Because I think this is exactly what you wanted."

"Oh? How do you figure that?"

Pyro Storm glanced at Nick. "Because you think you're forcing my hand."

Owen took a step forward. "Someone had to. You can't hide behind the mask forever."

"And you can?"

Owen spread his hands. "I'm not the one wearing a mask here, am I? That would be you."

"Um," Nick said in a thin voice. "I have no idea what's going on right now, but I think I'd like to leave."

They ignored him. "I do it because I have to," Pyro Storm said, teeth bared. "So I can keep the ones I love from harm."

Nick blinked at that. Pyro Storm was a villain. Why would he be worried about people getting hurt? He'd hurt Nick's dad. He'd—

"See," Owen said, voice filled with contempt, "that's always been your problem. You're so sanctimonious. And where has it gotten you? You've been vilified for everything you've done. You're Public Enemy Number One. Nothing you've done has changed that."

Pyro Storm took a step forward. "Only because you've done everything you can to get in my way. You've spun these lies in order to elevate yourself. I allowed it because I didn't know what else to do. But now you've brought Nick into this, and I won't play your games anymore."

"You *allowed* it?" Owen asked incredulously. "You didn't allow *anything*. The world sees you for what you really are. You're the villain in this story. The archnemesis. I have become the hero this city needs, and not even you can stop me. Soon, I'll hold it all in the palm of my hand." He glanced back at Nick. "And maybe I'll get myself a sidekick. Nick will do just fine, won't he?"

"Leave him out of this," Pyro Storm snapped. "He's done nothing wrong. He doesn't deserve you messing with him."

"Messing with him?" Owen said, laughing. "Oh, that's rich coming from you. Why don't you tell him so he can see who's messing with who?"

Pyro Storm's mouth twisted into a snarl. "I'm not—"

"Oh, Seth," Owen said. "Aren't you tired of lying by now?"

Nick was sure he'd misheard. *Sure* that Owen hadn't said what Nick thought he had.

Because it wasn't right. It couldn't be right. It had to be a mistake.

"What?" he heard himself ask.

"Oops," Owen said gleefully. "My bad. Didn't mean for that to slip out."

Pyro Storm hung his head.

Like he was defeated. Like he was—

No. *Not* like he was defeated.

He reached up and grasped the sides of his head.

And slid the helmet off.

Nick knew that hair, didn't he? Of course he did. He'd sometimes thought about what it'd be like running his hands through the curls.

Seth Gray looked up, looking wary, almost frightened.

"No," Nick said, taking a step back. "That's not—you can't be . . ."

"I wanted to tell you," Seth said, voice cracking. "So many times. And I tried. I swear I tried. I could never get it out. It's—"

"Aw," Owen said. "This is so sweet. Isn't this sweet, Nicky? Our dear, lovely Seth is Pyro Storm." His smile faded. "But that would mean—*oh*. That would mean he's the villain of Nova City, wouldn't it? That would mean he was the one who hurt your *father.*"

Seth's eyes widened. "No! I didn't. I swear, Nick. It was barely a spark. The smallest of flames. I could control it. I always had control. It wasn't—and it . . . it . . ." He shook his head slowly as his face hardened. "You goddamn bastard. You were very specific, weren't you? Getting me to that building. Normally, you're all over the place. I wondered why you stayed in one place that whole time.

I didn't see it, then. You planned it. Like you planned all of this. Nick. Here. Knowing I would follow because I would follow him anywhere." He squared his shoulders, and Nick felt a chill run down his spine. "I know, Owen. I know what you are. These pills. You aren't like me. I have this . . . this thing inside me. It's always been there. But you . . . you take these pills in order to do what you do."

Owen's eyes narrowed to slits. "You think you're better than me? You think that because you're a freak that I can't be like you? You're wrong. My father gave me a gift in order to protect what mattered most."

"He *experimented* on you," Seth said, taking a step toward them, cautious and slow. "He changed you. He made you into what you are. It's not fair, Owen. He should never have done what he did to you. You were just a kid. We're *still* kids. But you can be better than him. You can rise above what he did to you. You can say no. You're not some junkie. Whatever else you are, I can see the good in you."

"Junkie," Owen repeated slowly. "*Junkie.* That's what you think I am?"

Seth shook his head. "That's not what I meant. You—"

"I'm so sorry, Nick," Owen said, and he sounded truly regretful, "that it came to this. I know it's tough, finding out your best friend has been the bad guy all along. Imagine my surprise when I found out. Hell, I could barely stand it. Sitting across from him in the cafeteria every day, knowing who he was. All I ever wanted to protect this city. Protect our friends. Protect *you.* And fortunately for all of us, I found myself in a position to do just that."

He reached into his pocket. When he pulled his hand back out, he was clutching shiny black pills, at least half a dozen. He bounced them in his hand as he grinned. "My own private stash. Dad didn't know I'd pocketed them. Let's see how much of a junkie I am."

"No," Seth whispered as Owen brought his hand toward his own mouth. He shoved the pills inside, throat working as he swallowed them dry. "Nick, you need to *run.*"

Before Nick could even process what was happening, Owen raised his arms, loose sleeves sliding down. On his wrists were a set of thick metal bracelets. There was a bright flash of light that made Nick cry out and cover his face. He heard Seth scream his name as he stumbled backward, hitting the wall of glass behind him. By the time his vision began to clear as he lowered his hands, Seth was struggling in midair, his own shadow wrapped around him, holding him in place. Licks of fire burned from him, but they couldn't dispel the shadows.

"There," Owen breathed. "That's better. Man, they work fast the more you take. I have to remember that. Holy shit, the *rush*."

"Stop," Seth gasped as his own shadow tightened around him. "You have to stop."

"Always remember to keep to the shadows," Owen Burke said. "Catchy, isn't it? Rebecca Firestone came up with it. She has her uses, inept as she is. Good for public relations, but not much else. Nick. If you're going to take a pill, now is the time."

"Nick, don't," Seth managed to say, still trying to free himself from his own shadow. "It's not—it's not right. It's him. *He's* the villain. He always has been. You need to get out of here. Run. Please. Just *run*."

Nick was frozen in place, his world crumbling down around him. "You're Shadow Star?"

Owen laughed as Seth began to choke. "Yeah. Sorry about that. Secret identity, you know? Though, I'm touched at the crush you have on me. It was weird how I was almost jealous of myself when we dated. Broke up with you because dear ol' Dad thought you were a liability and threatened to cut off my supply, but that's in the past. I won't be manipulated by him anymore. Do it, Nick. Do it before Seth finds a way to break free and burn us all. I need you, Nick. I need you to help me keep this city safe. Keep your *father* safe."

"He did this," Seth croaked. "He's the bad guy, Nicky. Not me. I swear. It's Shadow Star. It's always been Shadow Star."

"That's not very nice," Owen said, frowning. "I've worked hard to cultivate this image. Me, the brooding savior of the city. You, the villain every hero needs. You should be *thanking* me." Owen curled his hands into fists, and the shadow hands around Seth's throat squeezed tighter. Seth's eyes were starting to bulge as his legs kicked uselessly. "Nick. This is your last chance. Take a pill. Become the Extraordinary you were always meant to be."

Then Nicholas Bell said, "Put him down."

Owen faltered, fists opening slightly. Seth took in a great, gasping breath.

Nick took a step toward Owen. "I said, put him *down*."

Owen narrowed his eyes. "What? Nicky, it's me. I'm Shadow Star. Your hero, remember? I'm everything you wanted."

Nick swallowed thickly. His head was pounding. "I know. And he's Pyro Storm. But he's still my friend, same as you. Put him down. Please. We can talk about this, okay? I don't care which one of you is the bad guy here. I don't want anyone else to get hurt."

Owen's expression softened. "That's . . . so *like* you." He tilted his head back and laughed. "God. You're pathetic. What the hell is wrong with you?"

Nick was taken aback. "Hey! You don't have to be so frigging rude—"

"I'm offering you everything you've ever wanted. I am giving you the chance to be an Extraordinary. And the only thing you're focused on is that we're all *friends*? No wonder you've never been able to do anything. You've got no spine. And to think I was going to let you be my sidekick. I had such big plans for you, Nick." He scoffed as he shook his head. "Well, that's months of work down the drain. Oh well. You win some, you lose some. Time for plan B." He turned back to Seth. "Pyro Storm, it's been fun, but I'm bored with you now. I think I'm ready to move on to bigger and better things." He snapped his hands closed again, and Seth began to choke.

Nick's head felt like it was splitting apart as he took a step forward. The ground tilted beneath his feet as a gray wave of pain rolled over him.

Seth's face was white as his eyes started rolling back in his head.

Owen grinned wickedly.

Nick brought his hands up to the sides of his head as another lance of exquisite pain pierced through him.

He did the only thing he could.

He screamed.

The air rippled around him, and the glass walls shattered as if struck by an unseen force. Owen was knocked off his feet, landing roughly on the ground. Seth flew back against the wall near the elevator, slumping down, chin resting against his chest, unmoving.

Glass fell, shards breaking apart as they hit the floor. The lights showered sparks. The centrifuge whirred erratically before it flew against the wall.

Somewhere deep inside Burke Tower, an alarm began to shriek.

Nick didn't know what had happened. He'd never seen Pyro Storm or Shadow Star do anything like that before. But his vision was clearer, the ache in his head receding marginally. He looked over his shoulder.

The colored pills hadn't been affected. They still hung suspended.

He could do it. Right now. If he wanted to. He could take one of them. Or all of them.

He could be an Extraordinary.

Instead, Nick turned back around. He moved past Owen, who groaned but made no move to get up. He'd worry about him later.

Seth lifted his head as he approached. Blood trickled down his cheek. It looked as if he'd been cut. He smiled weakly as Nick knelt beside him. "Hey, Nicky."

"Shut up," Nick snapped at him, hands trembling. "I'm so angry with you."

Seth flinched. "Yeah. I figured you might be."

"You hurt my dad."

"It wasn't—it wasn't me. I was trying to—" He paused, shaking his head. "We don't have time. We have to get Owen out of here before he wakes up . . . What? I don't—would you listen to me?"

Nick scowled. "What? I *am* listening to you—"

"I'm not talking to you." Seth turned his head so Nick could see his right ear. Inside, there appeared to be an earpiece of some kind. "I'm talking to my aunt."

"Your *aunt* knows? How long has she— Oh my god, your house isn't haunted. She is such a liar. She distracted me with cookies and lies! It was you all along!"

"She says she's sorry about that. She'll make you a new batch to make it up to you."

"Oh. Well. That's nice of her. She doesn't have to—*Wait a minute*."

"Didn't work," Seth muttered. Then, "Ugh, fine. That's—don't yell at me, Gibby!"

"*Gibby* knows too?" Nick cried. "Is everyone in my life a vile betrayer?"

"That wasn't my idea," Seth said with a glare. "She figured it out on her own. Followed me one day and wouldn't take no for an answer. Nosey little—now she's yelling at me again."

"Does Jazz know?"

"No." Seth sat back against the wall, using it to push himself up. Nick held on to his arm, the material under his hands warm to the touch. "She's not part of this."

"Oh, but *Gibby* is. *I'm* supposed to be your best friend. I gave you Skwinkles Salsagheti. We went on a date." He frowned. "I think? I'm still kind of fuzzy on the details, but it could have been!"

Seth rolled his eyes as he huffed out a breath. "Consider it retribution for every single time you've mentioned Shadow Star's name with that dreamy look on your face."

"That doesn't *even* begin to compare—"

"You wrote *fanfiction* about him and—"

"How was *I* to know that—"

"And I gave you Skwinkles Salsagheti *back,* so don't talk to me about—"

Nick was furious. "You're a goddamn Extraordinary. Do you know what that makes me? That makes me the clueless comedic relief! I never wanted to be the clueless comedic relief! I'm supposed to be the hero!" He grabbed Seth's head, turning it to the side so he could have access to the earpiece. "And, Gibby, you're in so much trouble. Martha, you too. You're going to rue the day you tried to pull a fast one on me. Do you hear me? *Rue.*"

Seth shoved him away. Nick would have gone sprawling had Seth not grabbed his arm at the last moment, pulling him back upright as if Nick weighed nothing at all. "Oh, right," he said weakly. "I forgot you were all buff and crap now."

"Buff and crap," Seth muttered. "That's just great."

"I liked you the way you were before." And for some reason, this thought struck Nick harder than almost everything else. He took a step back. "You lied to me. All this time. It's been years. Shadow Star and Pyro Storm, you've kept this from me. I talked about Shadow Star incessantly. And you let me. Did you laugh behind my back? Both of you?"

Seth's eyes widened. "No. Nick, it was never like that. I swear to you. I never—"

Nick didn't believe him. "It's like I don't even know who you are. And even if I thought I did, you're still . . . Pyro Storm. You were always the villain."

Seth looked tormented. "I'm still me, Nicky. I swear. This is a mask. It's *nothing*. It's only the smallest part of me. I never wanted—I just needed to keep you—"

"Safe?" Nick retorted. "I'm sick of people telling me that. I'm not fragile. I can handle myself. I distracted Owen long enough to get you to explode all the glass, didn't I?"

Seth shook his head. "I didn't—Nick, we'll talk about this later, okay? I need to get you out of here."

"Oh, we'll talk about this later, all right, Seth Gray. You're in so much trouble. It's going to take the rest of our lives for me to be able to forgive you. I hope you're prepared for some epic groveling. I wrote a two-hundred-thousand-word masturbatory ode to *Owen* of all people. Do you know how that makes me feel? Unclean is how it makes me feel!"

"Oh, *god*," Owen moaned behind them. "Spare me, please. I really don't want to have to listen to you two fawn all over each other. It's really harshing my buzz. Though, Seth, you should probably remember that I taught Nicky here everything he knows. No matter what happens, I had him first."

Nick glowered at him. "*First?* Listen here, you motherf—"

Nick was spun dizzyingly around as Seth shoved him toward the elevator, putting himself between them. "Go," he said over his shoulder. "Now. Get out of here."

Nick glared at him. "I don't know if you're in any position to tell me what to do right now."

Owen bared bloody teeth in a silent snarl as he pushed himself up off the ground. "Let him stay. See what happens when you witness the full extent of my power."

Nick and Seth turned their heads slowly to gape at Owen.

"What?" Owen asked.

"Dude," Nick said, aghast. "Seriously. The full extent of your *power*? What's next? With great power comes great responsibility? Kiss my damn ass, you dumb—"

"Maybe don't try to rile up the supervillain," Seth muttered.

"Do you say stupid things like he does?" Nick demanded. "Because if you do, I don't think I can be seen in public with you. God, what the hell was I thinking? Both of you suck. Extraordinaries are the worst. My new dream is to become a dentist with my own private practice in Idaho. People with superpowers are terrible."

"Hey!"

Owen pulled himself to his full height, tilting his head side to side as he stretched his neck. He reached up and wiped away the blood from his lips before he spat on the ground. Shadows gathered at his feet, roiling like liquid tentacles. They crawled up his legs, and for a moment, Nick thought they were going to swallow him whole. Instead, left in their wake was Shadow Star's *costume,* rising until it covered his shoulders. If Nick wasn't so pissed off, he'd think it was badass. "It's all out in the open now, Seth. Everything. He sees you for what you truly are. Even I can see the doubt in his eyes. No matter what happens next, he will always remember how you lied to him. How you couldn't even keep his father safe."

"Maybe," Seth said quietly. "Maybe he'll never want to speak to me again. Maybe everything I ever wanted is gone now. That's on me. But that doesn't mean I won't fight for him until my last breath."

Owen snorted. "Who says romance is dead? I'm tired of this back and forth. I've been waiting for this moment for years, to see that exact look on his face. And now that I have, it's time for Shadow Star to rise and put an end to the villain Pyro Storm. The people of Nova City will love me for protecting them. And one day, Nick will see the error of his ways, and we'll move on without you. You'll be nothing but a bad dream."

Nick made a face. "That's probably not going to happen. Owen, I don't know if you know this, but pretty much everything is terrible right now. Like, I feel super betrayed. And why would we move on without Seth? What's going to happen to him?"

"He thinks he's going to kill me," Seth said.

"Bingo!" Owen said, smiling wildly.

Nick took a step back. "But . . . you can't *kill* people. That's not what Extraordinaries do. That's murder!"

"He's so naïve," Owen said to Seth. "It would be amusing if it weren't so depressing."

Seth looked back at Nick again, eyes glittering in the low light. "I need you to listen to me, Nicky. Can you do that?"

"No," Nick said, shaking his head. "You're not—no one's going to *die*. That's not how this works. That's not how it's supposed to be."

"I'll do everything I can, okay? But you have to get out of here. I need you to be safe."

"Seth," Nick said, and his voice cracked right down the middle.

Seth's smile trembled. "It'll be okay."

"Bored now," Owen said, and shadows scurried across the floor.

Seth reached back and shoved Nick toward the elevator. Nick felt a sharp blast of heat as he stumbled backward, a bright bloom of fire bursting in front of him. He stared in awe as the air burned, dispelling the shadows in the light.

"*Run!*" Seth shouted.

"But—"

"Go, Nick! Please *go!*"

Nick ran.

He was halfway across the room when he saw movement out of the corner of his eye. He glanced over in time to see a shadow racing along the wall next to him. It was amorphous until it stretched out from the wall, *reaching* for Nick. He could see the outline of what looked like *claws,* and let out a strangled gasp as he ducked right as it swiped at him. It missed him by inches. Owen shouted furiously, but Nick didn't look back.

He hit the panel next to the elevator so hard, he thought he broke it.

It lit up under his hand.

* 309 *

The doors slid open.

He lurched through, slamming his palm on the panel inside the elevator. He turned in time to see—

"Oh my god," he breathed.

Seth was suspended in midair, arms outstretched, fire leaking from his hands and burning around him. His cape swirled behind him, flaming sparks cascading.

He looked over his shoulder directly at Nick.

He smiled.

And then he exploded.

Nick was knocked back by the concussive blast of air that made it through the elevator doors before they closed. His head hit the wall behind him, and he groaned, covering his face as a wall of fire roared toward—

The doors closed.

The elevator car shook.

But then began to ascend.

He was running down the hallway following exit signs when he heard shouts coming from somewhere ahead of him, flashlight beams bouncing along the floor. He found an unlocked door and managed to get inside a small office before whoever it was rounded the corner. He didn't close the door all the way, peering through the crack. A group of security guards ran by, guns drawn.

The alarms blared overhead.

Once he was sure the security guards were gone, Nick opened the door and stepped back out into the hallway. He'd only managed to take a few steps before a hand grabbed his hoodie and jerked him around.

He was face-to-face with Brett.

"You," Brett said, eyes wide. "What the hell is going on?"

"Shadow Star," Nick spat. "Pyro Storm. They're fighting somewhere in the building."

"Where's Owen? Why isn't he with you?"

"We got separated trying to get out of here. I don't know where he is!"

Brett shook him. "Did you have anything to do with this?"

"No, man! I'm a kid. I didn't do *anything*. I just wanna leave!"

"Fine," Brett spat. "But if you see Owen, you tell him I'm not going to get fired over this. I swear, if his dad finds out that I—"

The ground shook beneath their feet. Brett's grip on Nick fell away as he stumbled back. "What the hell was that?"

Nick didn't know, but he didn't think it was a good idea to stay and find out. "I'm gonna go, if that's all right with you."

But Brett had already turned away from him.

Nick ran again.

He heard Brett shout something after him, but it was lost to the pounding in his head.

He jumped over the turnstile, almost tripping and falling flat on his face. He managed to stay upright, and hit the door they'd come in, praying it wasn't locked.

It wasn't.

Cold air washed over him as he took in a gasping breath.

The sounds of sirens filled the air.

He could see the swirl of red and blue reflecting off the buildings around him.

He hid behind a bus stop near Burke Tower.

The cop cars flew by, lights flashing, sirens wailing.

"They after you?" a voice asked, making Nick jump and scream.

He turned around to see a man sitting in a doorway, his shopping cart next to him filled with cans and socks. He'd never been more relieved to see something so normal after what had just happened.

"No," Nick said, voice shaky. "Not me."

"It's okay if they are; I won't tell. Unless there's a reward. Then I'd tell. There a reward?"

"It's not about—"

"Would you look at that?" the man whispered, eyes wide.

Nick looked back at Burke Tower.

The windows were reflecting orange and red.

But it wasn't coming from outside.

It was coming from within.

Fire.

It rose higher and higher, like it was hurtling through each floor of Burke Tower.

Nick tilted his head back as it reached the top, and there was an explosion as it burst through the roof, a trail of flames rocketing into the air. It shot across the night sky and disappeared into the sky.

"Probably aliens," the homeless man said. "Took me in '78, but I cut out the implant so they can't find me! And now I have all the socks I could ever want!"

"Have a nice night," Nick muttered, pulling the hood over his head.

He hurried away, leaving the man cackling in the doorway behind him.

17

He went to the only place he felt safe.

He kept out of sight, taking the stairs rather than the elevator. He wasn't supposed to be at the hospital, and if he got caught, he'd probably be in more trouble than he already was. He was still wearing all black (except, of course, for his purple Chucks—Gibby was useless), but that wouldn't help him. Not here. It'd probably bring more attention to him than anything else.

He'd made it up three floors when he heard a door open somewhere above him. He panicked, looking for somewhere to hide in the stairwell. There was nowhere for him to go. He held his breath, the footsteps echoing on the stairs as whoever it was came down.

Another door opened, and the footsteps disappeared.

He sighed in relief.

The fifth floor was mostly silent. There was a man sitting at the nurse's station, but he had his back to Nick. A woman moved down the hall, staring at a clipboard, but she turned and went in the opposite direction.

Nick crouched as low as he could as he passed by the nurse's station. If someone saw him now, they'd probably call the police before anything else. He looked absurd, back pressed against the desk, inching forward as quietly as he could, hood pulled up over his head.

Somehow, by the grace of a god that smiled down at the idiocy of teenage boys, he made it past the nurse's station undetected. He hurried down the hall toward—

"Nick?"

Crap. He'd been so close.

He turned around.

Becky stood behind him, head tilted to the side.

He waved. "Hey. How are you? You look . . . nice."

The man from the nurse's station stuck his head over the desk and looked at them. "Everything all right?"

Becky waved him away. "Yeah, this is Mr. Bell's son, Nick. Apparently, he doesn't understand the concept of visiting hours. It's okay."

"I understand *visiting hours*," Nick said, scowling. "I chose to ignore them. And what're you doing here so late? I thought you worked during the day."

"Working a double to cover for someone else. Nice shoes."

"Oh. Thanks. The color's called eggplant. They seemed like a good idea when I bought them, but now I'm not so sure."

The nurse at the station sat back down in his chair.

Nick gave very serious consideration to whirling around and running as fast as he could when Becky approached, but it'd been a long night, and he was resigned to his fate. "Please don't send me away. I just . . ." He couldn't finish, the words drying on his tongue.

She reached up and pulled his hood back, letting it fall. She frowned. "You look exhausted."

Understatement, that, if he looked anything like he felt. "It's been a very weird night. I couldn't sleep. And I needed to see him." He tried not to be embarrassed as his voice wavered.

Becky sighed. "Tell you what. Why don't you go on in. Make yourself feel better."

Nick nodded, not trusting himself to speak. That sounded good.

She put a hand on his shoulder, squeezing gently. "Go. I was in there a few minutes ago. I need to make a phone call."

His eyes snapped up to hers.

She smiled at him as she dropped her hand. "You know someone has to be missing you. Or they will be when they wake up and you're not there. It's only fair, Nick."

Yeah. It was. Mary Caplan would probably panic in the morning. And then she'd call Cap, and it'd turn into this whole *thing* where Nick would probably be fitted with an ankle bracelet that would track him wherever he went. Cap wouldn't be happy, especially since he was probably dealing with the fallout at Burke Tower right at that very moment.

"Okay," he said. "Since I'm magnanimous, I will agree to this condition."

"How nice of you. Thank you for your generosity."

He narrowed his eyes. "We're in a hospital, Nurse Becky. This is no place for sarcasm."

She rolled her eyes. "Kid, trust me when I say a hospital is the perfect place for sarcasm. And I'd consider moving my butt if I were you, before I change my mind."

Nick moved his butt.

Everything was the same. The machines still beeped and hissed. His father's eyes were still taped shut, the tube still down his throat.

Nick closed the door behind him. He was going to pull a chair next to the bed, but he was tired and heartsore. His eyes felt like they were filled with sand, and there were shards in his chest that poked him as he breathed.

He moved to the other side of the bed.

Carefully, he climbed onto it, not wanting to jostle his dad. He toed off his Chucks as he sat, letting them fall to the floor. He turned around, stretching his legs out. His knees bumped into his dad's thigh, and he apologized even though his dad couldn't hear him. As soon as the words left his mouth, he wished he could take them back.

He realized, then, how stupid he must look. It was the middle of the night, and here he was, climbing into bed with his dad like he was little and had just woken up from a scary dream. His eyes started to burn as he lifted his dad's arm and lay near his shoulder. He brought the arm down across him, holding on to his hand tightly.

Dad didn't wake up.

"Please don't leave me," Nick whispered. He closed his eyes.

He woke to the sound of voices.

A weak, gray light filtered through the window as he cracked open his eyes.

"—and he hasn't moved at all, even when I put a blanket on him. I think he needed some reassurance. It's tough having a parent in the hospital."

Someone sighed. "I know. I really should have seen this coming. I appreciate you calling me."

"I tried Mr. Caplan first, but got a voicemail. I didn't leave a message in case I got ahold of you. Didn't want to worry anyone unnecessarily."

"Probably for the best. I don't know when Rodney will have a chance to check his phone, given what's going on with the Extraordinaries."

"I saw the alerts on my phone, but it's been a busy night and I haven't had a chance to follow up. Is it bad?"

"I don't know. They're at it again. A nuisance, if you ask me."

"I can't imagine what it takes to— Looks like someone's awake."

He turned his head.

Becky stood in the doorway, Mary Caplan next to her, hand clutching the strap of her purse tightly.

"Sorry," he mumbled.

Mary shook her head. "I'll let it slide this time, Nick. Just keep me in the loop, okay? I would have come with you myself if this is what you needed."

Properly chastened, he mumbled, "Okay."

"Why don't you take Mrs. Caplan to get a cup of coffee," Becky said cheerfully. "I need to empty your dad's catheter bag, and I'm pretty sure you don't need to be here for that."

"Why would you *say* that? There are things I don't need to know. What the hell, Becky." Then, because he couldn't not, he added, "Is there a lot?"

She laughed at him.

So weird.

There were a few people blinking sleepily in the hospital cafeteria. Mary made Nick sit at a table in the corner, before saying she'd be right back.

Nick pulled his phone from his pocket.

He had missed calls and texts.

Gibby had tried to call him three times. Martha twice. Bob once. There were voicemails, but he ignored those for the moment.

Gibby had texted him, demanding he pick up the phone or she was going to kick his ass.

Martha's said she wanted to talk to him.

Bob wrote that he'd be there when Nick was ready.

There was one from Jazz, wondering why Gibby wanted to know if Nick was with her, and since he wasn't, where Nick could possibly be?

Nothing from Seth or Owen.

Mary returned, placing a banana, a muffin, and a bottle of juice in front of him. "You'll eat all of it. And drink all of the juice."

"I'm not hungry."

"I received a phone call three hours ago. The only time a phone rings in the middle of the night is to deliver bad news. For all I knew, something had happened to Rodney while he was on duty. So, imagine my surprise when the hospital told me the boy I was responsible for had shown up on his own. You will do as I say, and you will like it."

"But I—"

"Less talking, more banana."

Nick picked up the banana. "You're very good at the guilt-trip thing."

She sniffed. "I prefer to think of it as knowing what's best."

"Oh. Well. You're very good at that, then."

"Thank you." She sipped her coffee, watching him peel the banana. He made a show of taking a big bite and chewing obnoxiously. She wasn't impressed. "This is hurting you more than me, just so you know."

He slumped in his seat. "Sorry."

"So you've already said. I appreciate it, but we're going to move on from it now."

"Okay."

"I'm not mad."

"Okay."

"Eat the muffin."

He did.

She waited until he was halfway through it when she said, "Rodney was shot once."

Nick looked up at her. He tried to swallow without chewing and ended up choking. He coughed, spraying crumbs on the table.

Mary cocked her head. "Delightful."

He glared at her, opening the juice bottle and taking a drink to help clear his throat. "You did that on purpose."

"And you'll never prove it. Though, I suppose if you're going to choke on food, at least you're in a good place to do it."

"I didn't know that about Cap."

She shrugged, taking another drink of coffee. "It was a long time ago. Back when he was a beat cop. Two years on the job, and he got a call for a domestic disturbance. Scary thing, those, though I suppose all calls that come in have a chance of being dangerous. He arrived, and the man didn't want to leave. The woman had a restraining order against him, and there were warrants out for his arrest. He also had a gun and shot Rodney in the arm." She set the cup on the table, holding it between her hands. "In the grand scheme of things, it was nothing life-threatening. But imagine getting a call saying that someone you love has been hurt in the line of duty."

"I don't have to imagine that."

She shook her head. "Of course you don't. I panicked, only hearing the words *Rodney's been shot* over and over again in my head. By the time I got to the hospital, I created this entire world in my head, one where Rodney was dying, or already dead. I was going to have to put on a brave face when I arrived, I knew, but I cried almost the whole way on the train. So even though I knew he was gone, I dried my eyes and strode in, ready to face what was to come. But instead of losing him, I was brought to one of the rooms. Rodney was spouting off at the doctor, saying it was just a flesh wound, and he would absolutely *not* be admitted, that it was wrapped, and he was ready to go. He looked relieved when he saw me, saying I would vouch for him."

Nick winced. "Not the best move."

Mary laughed. "No. Not the best move. There was an officer waiting in the hall, and I told him he'd probably need to arrest me right then and there, because I was about to commit assault. I was . . . so angry. It wasn't rational. Or fair, really. But that's the price, I think, for loving a hero. We're a lighthouse, Nick. A beacon to help them find their way home."

Nick could barely breathe.

"They're brave," Mary said. "But we are too. Because while they're out there, saving the world, we're the ones they come home to. And it may not always be fair, and there are times when you know they're in harm's way, but they'll always fight like the dickens to get back where they belong." She reached over and put her hand on top of Nick's. "Rodney does that for me. And I know your dad does the same for you. After everything you've both been through, he's going to do everything he can to see your face."

Nick believed her.

And he wondered if there was someone else fighting for him too.

Mary's phone rang a little later. "That'll be Rodney," she said, looking at the screen. "What do you say we keep your adventure last night between us?"

If she only knew the half of it. "That sounds all right with me."

"I thought as much. Give me a moment, okay? I expect the juice to be gone by the time I get back. Mind me now, Nick."

"Yes, ma'am."

"Hello, love," she said as she answered the phone. "Busy night?" She stood from the table and walked away to an empty corner of the cafeteria. Nick heard her laugh at something Cap must have said in response.

Nick wanted to lay his head on the table and shut his eyes for a little bit, but he didn't know if that was the best idea. He needed to make it through the day, and he'd sleep easier tonight. He didn't know what day it was. Thursday? Friday? Regardless, he wasn't going to school. They'd see how things went over the weekend, but it wasn't the most important thing. Sure, Dad would probably have a fit when he woke up and found out that Nick had skipped more than a few days, but Nick would deal with it then. Gladly, even. Hell, if Dad wanted to ground him for longer, that was fine.

He rubbed a hand over his face. He had to get his priorities in order.

His dad was a few floors above him, resting as comfortably as he could.

That was number one.

After that was Seth. And Owen.

It was disturbing, all that he hadn't noticed. The way they sniped at each other, veiled threats that made little sense at the time without context. Now, though? Now he could see them for what they were.

He was troubled by just how much had been said right in front of him. What had Seth told him?

It's lonely. That's the one thing you don't expect. How lonely it is. Because you can't tell anyone about it. You can't tell your family because they wouldn't understand. You can't tell your friends because they could become targets, and you don't want them to get hurt. So you keep on going by yourself, hoping one day it will get better, and the only thing that's in your head is why you started to begin with. Why you put on that stupid costume in the first place. The promise you made to yourself. And some days, that's almost not enough.

It had been a confession, and Nick had brushed it away. He'd been so focused on his own desire to be something *more* that he hadn't heard what Seth was trying to tell him. Maybe he wouldn't have been able to understand exactly what Seth was saying, but he hadn't even tried.

His response had been to tell Seth they needed to write fanfiction together.

"Crap," Nick muttered. "Crap, crap, crap. I'm a terrible best friend. And apparently the comedic relief and/or young adult love interest, but I'll have to deal with that part later."

"What was that?" Mary asked, coming back to the table.

Nick groaned. "I hate dawning realizations. They're so . . ."

"Accurate?"

"*Yes*," he said fiercely. "And it's so blatantly obvious what I should've—"

The doors to the cafeteria slammed open. A harried nurse burst in, turning her head wildly from side to side. Nick recognized her. She'd been with Becky when he'd arrived at the hospital. Renee.

Her gaze fixed on Nick.

She started jogging toward them.

No. No, no, nonono—

"Hey," she said, sounding breathless. "Nick. I'm so glad I found you. Becky told me you'd be here."

Nick stood, skin thrumming. "Is it my dad?" he choked out. "Is he okay?"

She smiled. "He's awake."

Nick wasn't allowed in the room for a long time. He paced back and forth in the waiting area, ranting and raving about his rights, telling Mary he was going to call the police and have everyone in the hospital arrested for barring him from his father. Mary smiled sagely and reminded him that the last time he'd interacted with the police, he'd been nearly naked and handcuffed.

Which, of course, set Nick off all over again about his rights. He decided loudly that he was going to consider filing a lawsuit, then immediately apologized, saying he would never do that because Cap might be out of a job.

Mary snorted. "I don't think you'd have to worry about that. In fact, go ahead. I can't wait to see what comes out during discovery."

They had to make sure Dad was breathing okay, and if his brains were scrambled or not. Those weren't the technical terms used, but Nick was pretty sure that was what they'd meant. He wondered if his dad would have amnesia and would even remember having a son. Nick decided that life wasn't a telenovela, and he should consider being optimistic.

The problem with trying for optimism, especially when one is a teenager, is that it's rather difficult to do in a hospital when one is not allowed to go *into the room*. Renee had told him that if Dad was doing well, they'd try to remove the tube from his throat. Nick had asked if it would be like pulling out Excalibur, only with more saliva and a potential for vomit. It was *then* she'd told him he couldn't go in right away, and he figured he was being discriminated against.

It took close to two hours before Renee came back for him. By that time, he'd damn near worn a groove in the carpet. His head had started to hurt worse, but Mary had brought his medication with her, and he'd been able to catch it before it went too far. Weirdly, a generic painting had fallen off the wall during hour one, making everyone jump. Five minutes later, the TV hanging in the corner had gone on the fritz, refusing to turn back on to the home renovation show that had been playing.

But Nick forgot about all of it when he saw Renee.

He stopped, hands shaking.

She beckoned him with a finger.

Somehow, he got his legs to work, wobbly though they were.

Mary followed him and took his hand when they approached Renee.

"The doctor will come in and fill in the blanks for you a little later, but it looks all right for now. We need to continue to monitor for potential pneumothorax. And he's going to be sore for a little while, in his chest and throat. It's best if you don't let him talk too much for the next few days, though with the way he was demanding you be let into the room, I don't know how successful that'll be. Maybe help him keep it to a minimum?"

Nick blinked, sure he'd misheard. "Me? He wanted me? He remembers who I am? He doesn't have amnesia?"

"Oh, boy. No, Nick. He doesn't have amnesia. His memory is a little spotty about what happened, but that's it." She shook her head. "He told us if we didn't let you in the room in the next five minutes, he was calling for his chief to arrest us all."

Nick gaped at her. "Then why are we standing here? Do you *want* to go to jail? Because my dad will make you!"

"They're obviously related," Renee told Mary.

"You don't know the half of it. Nick, why don't you go ahead. I'll follow in a moment. I should call Rodney back. Let him know the good news."

Nick barely heard her. He grabbed Renee by the arm and was tugging her toward the elevators, asking her if Dad could go home today (no), if he was allowed to eat a cheeseburger if Nick brought him one (no), and if he still had a catheter bag attached to him (yes—which, so gross).

He held her arm almost the entire way, only letting go as they approached the open door to his dad's room. Nick heard a hoarse voice rasping something he couldn't make out. Becky responded. "He's on his way, Mr. Bell. If you try and get up again, I will restrain you to the bed, so help me god. Stop talking."

There was a grunted response, but it was all Nick needed to hear. He stumbled into the room right as his dad turned his head toward him.

Nick thought himself a little brave. Sometimes, he could be smart. He didn't always make the best decisions. He tried to be a good person. He didn't always succeed, even though he tried his best.

But it had been a strange last few days, and once upon a time, Before had changed to After in the blink of an eye.

He knew how close it had come again.

So when Nicholas Bell burst into tears, there was absolutely nothing he could do to stop it.

He was tired and still a little unsure if this wasn't some dream.

So yes, he cried as his father held out a hand toward him.

Nick went. Of course he did.

And when a strong arm wrapped around his neck, pulling him close, he collapsed.

"It's okay, Nicky," his father whispered into his hair. "I've got you. It's okay."

It lasted far longer than Nick would care to admit. Just when he thought he'd gotten a hold on it, off he'd go all over again, Dad rubbing a hand on his back. He tried to apologize for the tears and snot he'd gotten on Dad's hospital gown, but the words were incoherent as he sobbed.

Eventually, he subsided into weak hiccups, face hot and swollen as he pulled away to wipe at his eyes.

Dad was pale as he watched Nick reach for a Kleenex next to the bed to blow his nose. At some point, Becky and Renee had left them alone. Nick was relieved they hadn't witnessed him breaking. He'd have to thank them later.

"Sorry," Nick muttered, throwing one Kleenex away before grabbing another.

"Don't worry about it," Dad said, each word sounding scraped and raw.

"You're not supposed to talk."

Dad frowned. "I'll damn well do as I please, so don't you—"

"I will call the doctor in here right now, don't think I won't—"

"I am the parent here, not you—" But then Dad grimaced like he was in pain, and Nick was sure he was about to relapse into a coma and would forget him right now, the amnesia rolling over him like a gigantic wave, and Nick would be a stranger—

"Breathe, kid," Dad said. "Chest hurts. Busted ribs. That's all it is."

"You can't forget me!" Nick said wildly. "You have to fight the amnesia." He reached out and took Dad's face in his hands, squeezing gingerly. "I'm your son. *Nick*. Say it. *Nnnnnnniiiiick*."

Dad rolled his eyes. "Like I could ever forget you."

That made Nick's heart stumble in his chest. He thought he was going to cry again, but since he'd done it twice in as many days, he decided it was probably best if he tried to be a man for a little while. Then he thought that was sexist, so he allowed another tear to spill onto his cheek. Nick was—and always would be—invested in dismantling the patriarchy. Tumblr had taught him that.

"I am pretty hard to forget," he managed to say.

"How are you?"

"If I tell you, will you stop talking? For all we know, you're ruining your vocal cords right now and they'll be damaged beyond repair. You sound like you've smoked fifty packs a day for twenty years."

Dad opened his mouth to argue but sighed instead. He nodded.

And because Nick believed in rewarding good behavior, he said, "Thank you. That's very good of you. And to answer your question, I'm terrible. My dad decided to let a building fall on top of him, and I might have feelings for my best friend, even though he's a liar and a fat mouth, and I think I once made out with someone who turned out to be the biggest douche, and it appears that three quarters of my friends have been lying to me about some pretty big things." He paused, considering. Then, "Also, I haven't taken a shower since . . . yesterday morning? Or maybe the day before. I don't know what day it is. But my pits are pretty rank, and I've been wearing the same underwear for a length of time that's definitely unsanitary."

Dad stared at him.

Nick said, "So, how are you?"

Dad started to answer.

Nick glared at him.

Dad closed his mouth.

Nick loved him very much.

A doctor came in later, speaking in medical terms that Nick couldn't Google because he was technically still grounded and the internet on his phone was blocked. They thought Nick's dad was going to be fine, but they were still going to run some more tests to make sure. Dad tried to argue, especially when he found out he wasn't going to be going home for a few days, but eventually agreed to start with a CT scan and go from there. He only agreed after Nick had threatened to leave him there and make Dad a ward of the state, but still. Nick would take grudging victories any day of the week.

The doctor said the best thing was rest, and that he should sleep. Nick panicked briefly, sure that was a terrible idea, because people with concussions *weren't* supposed to sleep. The doctor, oblivious to who Nick actually was, said rather sardonically that maybe Nick should allow him to be a doctor and make decisions when it came to the care of his patient.

Dad whispered hoarsely that it probably wasn't the best thing to say.

Nick was well aware of his lack of a medical degree. But he had read many, many fics about people getting head injuries and not being allowed to sleep, and he trusted them far more than he did this stranger who seemed to consider Nick a nuisance more than anything else. Becky—who had apparently been on her way home after working nearly twenty-four hours—managed to stop Nick mid-rant (in which he was threatening to have the doctor's license revoked, the *hack*) and she reminded him that doctors, while not exactly the most empathetic of individuals, tended to know what they were talking about.

Nick was of the mind that Becky had betrayed the Hippocratic oath.

She told him that was only for doctors, but that she wanted nothing but the best for him and his dad.

Nick got a little weepy again.

Becky hugged him.

Nick told her to go home, and she looked like she'd been hit by a truck.

Dad was asleep by the time he'd turned back around, a small smile on his face.

He was sitting with Mary in the waiting room when Cap arrived, looking a little worse for wear. Dad was getting his scans done. He'd been grumpy about being woken up, and that made Nick feel better. Especially when, with a scowl on his face, he'd reassured Nick he remembered who his son was.

Cap kissed his wife, then said, "Stand up, Nick."

Nick did. Cap was the chief, after all.

Cap hugged him.

Nick hugged him back.

"Told you, didn't I?" Cap said quietly. "Hardheaded, your dad. Wouldn't let this take him away. He's got too much waiting for him back at home."

"You better give him desk duty for the foreseeable future," Nick mumbled as Cap finally let him go.

"You got it, Nicky. Why are you out here?"

"Aaron's getting scanned," Mary said as Cap slumped into the chair next to her. He was in uniform, and he pulled his hat off his head, setting it in his lap. His mustache fluttered as he huffed out a breath. "Should be back shortly."

"Good, good. Going to have some words, he and I."

"Can I watch?" Nick asked.

"Sure."

"Rodney."

"Maybe not, Nick."

Mary patted Nick on the hand when he muttered threats under his breath.

"The woman?" Cap asked.

"Seems to be okay," Mary said, taking her husband's hand in hers. "Baby's fine too."

Nick didn't know what they were talking about. "What woman? Whose baby?"

Cap grunted. "The one your dad rescued before he got himself hurt. She's here too."

And Nick . . . didn't know what to think about that. He knew she wasn't to blame for what happened. She'd been looking for a place to stay. She hadn't asked to be trapped in the middle of a battle between Extraordinaries who—

Extraordinaries who Nick now knew the identities of.

His mouth went dry.

It'd be easy, wouldn't it? To tell Cap everything he knew. What he'd seen. What he'd done. All it would take would be opening his mouth and spilling everything and letting Cap handle it.

"Long day?" Mary asked, apparently unaware of the existential crisis happening right next to her.

"And night," Cap muttered. "Those damn Extraordinaries. They're getting worse. I don't know what happened, but they caused a lot of damage to Burke Tower. Someone was after something, but I have no idea what. Simon Burke isn't pleased."

Nick wondered if it were possible to disappear into the floor. He tapped his foot against it. Solid as always.

Mary scoffed. "Simon Burke will get over it. It's not as if he doesn't have more money than god."

Cap scrubbed a hand over his face. "That's what *I* said, but it didn't go over very well. Apparently, some of the work they do is very hush-hush. I'm convinced he's creating monsters in a laboratory somewhere for the government. Doesn't help that his kid is missing and—" Cap sat up abruptly, eyes narrowing as he looked at Nick.

Nick looked for the exits. There were two. He could probably make it before Cap caught up with him. He was wily. Cap liked red meat and cigars. It'd be no contest.

"Don't you know Owen Burke?"

"Like, biblically?" Nick asked, debating whether or not he would be considered a bad son for abandoning his father.

"What? No. I could have sworn that Aaron said you were friends." Cap frowned.

Nick's hands were very clammy. "Did he?"

"Yes," Cap said slowly. "Apparently, he was in Burke Tower last night. Had a friend with him."

"Huh," Nick said. "How strange. Well. I wouldn't know anything about that. I was at your house, safely tucked in bed like I was supposed to be."

Mary coughed, the traitor.

"Except for when I snuck out and came to the hospital," Nick amended. Later, he would have to remind Mary how it had been *her* idea not to tell Cap about that.

Cap wasn't pleased. "You snuck out and did *what*?"

"He was worried about Aaron," Mary said, and Nick forgave her a little. "Aaron's nurse called me and told me where Nick was."

"That right?" Cap said, still staring at Nick. "Is that all that happened, Nick?"

"Yes, sir."

"And you wouldn't happen to know where Owen is, would you?"

Probably locked in battle with Pyro Storm, who happened to be the guy that Nick gave Skwinkles Salsagheti to. And since that would probably not go over very well, Nick said, "No, sir." Because he knew the minds of cops made them suspicious about everything, he added, "I hope he's okay. You really don't know where he is?"

Nick was saved from saying anything more by the arrival of a cheerleader and a baby butch. Even though he was furious with one of them, he'd never been happier to see them in his life.

"Hey, Nicky," Jazz said, smiling sweetly. Nick could have kissed her. But he wouldn't, given that her girlfriend was standing right next to her, actively avoiding looking at Nick. "We tried to call but got your voicemail. Hope it's okay we're here."

Nick jumped up. "Oh, *sure*. You have no idea how happy I am to see you. In fact, let's go somewhere else so I can tell you exactly how happy I am."

"Don't go too far," Mary told him. "We don't know how long your dad will stay awake by the time he gets back."

Nick nodded, smiling tightly as he grabbed Jazz and Gibby by the hands, pulling them down the hall. He could feel Cap's gaze boring into his back, but he couldn't do anything about that now. If he were lucky, maybe Cap would be gone by the time he got back. Or, at the very least, distracted by Dad.

"Your dad's awake?" Jazz asked, squeezing his hand. "Nick, that's so great! Why didn't you say anything?"

"Phone's dead," Nick said through gritted teeth. "It's been a long day. Hasn't it, *Gibby*?"

Gibby said, "Yeah, that's putting it mildly."

Nick led them down the stairs to the second floor and back to the room where he hid when he'd first arrived at the hospital. The table with the penis drawn underneath it was still there, and Nick pulled Gibby and Jazz inside before shutting the door behind them.

"Is this our official hospital hangout spot?" Jazz asked. "I like that we have that."

"Where's Seth?" Nick demanded.

Jazz looked confused. "I don't . . . know? He wasn't in school again today." She looked between Nick and Gibby. "Why? What's going on?"

Gibby stared down at the floor.

That pissed Nick off. "Well? Care to explain?"

Gibby looked up. Her darkened eyes were bloodshot, like she hadn't gotten much sleep. Which, given that she'd been in Seth's ear the night before, made sense. "Look, Nick. If we could . . . wait. Okay?" She jerked her head toward Jazz. "Now might not be the right time."

She had a point. Jazz was oblivious to everything, and it was probably best to keep her that way. It didn't stop him from glaring daggers at Gibby.

"What's going on?" Jazz asked. "Why are you guys staring at each other like that?"

"It's nothing," Nick growled. "Just a frank exchange of ideas and questioning certain choices that were made."

"Maybe certain choices were made by people other than me," Gibby snapped. "Choices that I didn't agree with but had to respect anyway."

Nick scoffed. "Oh, I'm sure you fought so hard against those choices."

"I did! I told them you should know!"

"You could have told me!"

"It wasn't my secret to tell!"

"Maybe if you'd grown some *balls,* you could have—"

"Oh, you want to talk about balls, Nick? How about actually having some when it comes to Seth and—"

"Are you guys talking about how Seth and Owen are Pyro Storm and Shadow Star?" Jazz asked.

"Yes," Nick and Gibby snapped at the same time. It took a moment for it to sink in what she'd said. They both turned to gape at her.

Jazz nodded. "It makes sense now. Carry on."

Nick and Gibby breathed as one as Jazz smoothed out her cheerleader uniform like she hadn't just stunned them completely.

Nick recovered first. "How the hell did you know?"

Jazz rolled her eyes. "I figured it out a long time ago. I thought it was something we didn't talk about. I mean, come on. It was obvious."

Nick was incredulous. "It *was?*"

Jazz shrugged. "Every time there was a big fight between Shadow Star and Pyro Storm, Owen and Seth would be absent or late the next day. Or they'd show up with weird bruises. And then you dated Owen, who was most likely doing it to get a rise out of Seth, and not just because Seth already had feelings for you. It probably didn't help that Seth started being Pyro Storm shortly after your mom passed away, and then Owen tried to make it all about him by turning into Shadow Star. I mean, I get it. I would be upset too if I tried to do something to keep my friends and the city safe, and then this other Extraordinary comes out of nowhere and takes all the credit and then manages to infiltrate our friend group." Jazz's brow furrowed. "And then Rebecca Firestone gets involved and gives all the press to Owen and makes him look like the hero, even though it was really Seth doing most of the work."

Nick's mind was blown. "Holy crap."

"I want to make out with you so hard right now," Gibby said rather aggressively.

Jazz looked pleased with herself. "Did I really figure it out before either of you? Wow. I'm wonderful."

"This is literally the stupidest day of my life," Nick lamented to no one in particular.

"Oh, I don't know," Jazz said. "Remember when you jumped into the river wearing—"

"*Yes*, Jazz. I remember that because it only happened a few days ago! Can we please get back to the fact that *everyone* knew Owen and Seth were Extraordinaries before I did? I'm the one who stalked them! And how is it that I—oh my god, would you *stop* sticking your tongue down her throat! I'm young and queer and in a fragile place right now. I don't need to see that!"

Gibby pulled off of Jazz's lips with a wet smack that would most likely haunt Nick's dreams for the rest of his days. "She's amazing."

Nick rolled his eyes. "Yes, fine, Jazz, you're beautiful and smart, and I'm so annoyed that you figured it out before me."

"It's okay, Nicky," Jazz said, pulling out a compact from her backpack. She puckered her lips in her reflection, fixing her smudged lipstick. "Not all of us are capable of seeing what's clearly right in front of us."

"I feel like you're insulting me."

She pursed her lips as she folded the compact and stowed it away. "I wouldn't dream of it. But now that we're all in the know, what are we going to do about it?"

Gibby nodded. "We should—"

"Do nothing," Nick said.

Jazz blinked. "What's that now?"

"We should do nothing," Nick repeated. "It has nothing to do with us."

"Seth's our friend," Gibby said. "And he's more than that to you, whether you realize it or not. He needs us, Nick."

"Oh, does he? Funny. Because if he needed us, he would have told us the truth a long time ago."

"That's not fair—"

Nick groaned into his hands. "Fair? You want to talk about fair? My dad—the *only* parent I have left—was put in the hospital because of what they did. He somehow got in the middle of a fight he wouldn't have been involved in had they not been trying to kill each other. He got hurt because of them. He could've died."

"That wasn't Seth's fault," Gibby said weakly. "He was trying to do everything he could to stop Owen before people got hurt."

Nick shook his head as he dropped his hands. "Obviously he didn't do enough. If—" He swallowed thickly. "If it'd been worse, what then? What if . . . what if my dad had died? Would you still say he did everything he could? He sat across from Owen. Almost *daily*. Seth knew who Owen was, and yet he did nothing to stop it. That's not what heroes do. And Seth is no hero. He's a coward. And don't even get me started on Owen. He's . . . there're *pills* and . . ."

Gibby took a step toward him, hands balled into fists at her sides. "Seth only did this *because* of you! Everything he is, an Extraordinary, Pyro Storm, is *because* of you!"

Nick's knees felt wobbly. "What the hell are you talking about? He didn't—"

"Your mom died," Gibby spat. "And it sucked, Nick. For us because we didn't know how to help you, but more for you and your dad, okay? Both of you were so lost in your grief, and it tore at all of us. And Seth made a choice. You forget, I think, that the same

* 332 *

thing happened to him. Before, he was only Seth Gray, and there was nothing he could do to stop it. But After, he promised himself he would do everything he could to make sure you never had to go through that again. He always . . . since he was little." She sighed. "It was the train accident, Nick. It changed him into something else or activated something already in him. But he always felt guilty about it. That he was given a gift at such a high cost. He never wanted anything to do with it. Not until after your mom died. He saw what it did to you. He loved you so much that he put on a mask to keep Nova City safe. To keep your father safe. To keep *you* safe."

Nick ground his teeth together. "Which means he lied. All this time, he lied to me. He kept this from me. Kept all of it—"

Gibby's head snapped up. Her eyes were blazing. "Maybe if you weren't so self-centered, you could've figured it out on your own. Like I did. Like Jazz did. Jazz finds out, and she protects his secret. I find out and do all I can to help him. And what do you do when you find out? You bitch and moan about what it does to *you*."

"That's not fair! My dad is—"

"Your dad got hurt, and that's awful. But that wasn't Seth's fault. It was Owen's. It was a trap for Seth. Don't you get that? Owen was trying to kill Seth, Nick. Your dad was collateral damage."

"I don't care. It's on both of them."

Gibby looked away. "I can't believe . . ." She shook her head. "Whatever. You do what you want, Nick. You always do. I'm going to go help my friend because he needs me."

She turned and pushed the door open. It fell shut behind her.

"Huh," Jazz said, staring at the door. "That didn't go like I thought it would."

"Of course it didn't," Nick groused. "That's what happens when people lie to each other."

"Huh," Jazz said again. Then, "Are you going to yell at me now? If you are, I'd like to know in advance so I can cry to make you feel better."

Nick deflated. "No. I want to go back to my dad and forget all of this."

"That's going to be hard to do. Forgetting. Seems pointless."

"I can do it."

Jazz sighed. "I think you believe that. Can I tell you something?"

"Are you going to apologize?"

"I didn't do anything wrong."

"You . . . you knew about—ugh." Damn her for being right.

"That's what I thought. I worry a lot about what happens when Gibby leaves. You know. Graduates. While we stay here."

Nick struggled to keep his annoyance down. "I think there's bigger issues we need to—"

"I thought she'd go to college. Maybe move on to bigger and better things. Leave us all behind. Leave *me* behind. We'd break up, and maybe we'd stay friends who talked to each other every now and then, or maybe we wouldn't. I mean, it's not exactly realistic that you meet the love of your life when you're sixteen, right? And besides, we're young. People think we don't know what we're talking about. That our feelings aren't valid. I thought about it a lot. All the time, really. It hurt. But you know what I realized?"

"No, but you're going to tell me anyway."

She laughed. "I am. I realized that it's okay to have doubts. That I'm a person, and I have a right to feel the way I do, and so does she. If something happens down the road, it won't make anything I'm feeling now any less important. I care about her a great deal. It boils down to trust, I think. And faith. I lost my way a little bit. I forgot to believe in her and myself. So I told her about it. And you know what she said to me?"

Nick shook his head.

"She said that I was stupid. That she loved me, and that even if something happened in the future, it would never change this exact moment." Jazz smiled. "It's good to talk about how you're feeling. But it's even better to fight for the things you believe in. I'm fighting for her because I know she's fighting for me. Who's fighting for you, Nicky?"

Nick couldn't speak.

Jazz leaned over and kissed his cheek. "Sometimes, the people we want to protect the most might not understand why we do the things we do. But that doesn't mean they love us any less. Only you can decide where your faith lies. We're glad your dad's okay.

Call us if you need anything. Day or night. We'll always come running."

She left him standing next to the penis table.

Mary and Cap were gone by the time he went back to the fifth floor. A woman at the nurse's station said they went to grab a bite to eat and would bring him something when they returned.

His dad was back in his room, but he wasn't alone.

There was a woman sitting in a chair next to the bed, cradling a child in one arm, her other hand grasping one of Dad's.

Nick hesitated in the doorway. They didn't know he was there. He thought about speaking up, but then he heard the quiet sob coming from the woman.

"It's okay," Dad whispered, squeezing her hand. "It's okay."

"You save us," the woman said, her accent thick. "You save me. Aleksey." She muttered something in a language Nick didn't recognize. Then, "Why? Why you help?"

"Because it was the right thing to do," Dad said gruffly.

"Not everyone helps," the woman said, pulling her hand away as the baby started to fuss. "You did."

Dad shook his head. "Lady, it was my job—"

"Guardian," she insisted. "Guardian angel."

Dad flinched. Nick didn't know why, but Dad recovered quickly. "Can you do me a favor?"

She nodded. "Anything. Anything for you."

"I'm going to ask the hospital to help you. I don't want to see you back out on the streets, okay? There are shelters that can help women in your position. People who will take care of you and your kid until you can get on your feet. This is a chance for you."

"They take Aleksey from me?"

"Are you a good mother?"

"I try."

"Then I don't think they will. But you have to let them help you. Can you do that for me?"

"Yes. For guardian, I do."

Nick felt a tap on his shoulder. He looked behind him. A nurse he didn't recognize smiled at him, motioning that she needed to get by. He stepped aside. "Okay, Edyta. Mr. Bell needs his rest, just like you and Aleksey. Let's get you back to your room, okay?"

The woman rose slowly, but not before she leaned forward and kissed the back of Dad's hand. The nurse put an arm on her shoulders and led her from the room. The woman's face was tear-streaked, but her eyes were bright, and she cooed down at her baby. She didn't see Nick at all.

He watched as they walked down the hall before they rounded a corner.

He turned back to the room.

His dad was watching him, a small smile on his face. He looked tired.

"Got yourself a fan," Nick said quietly as he walked into the room, sitting in the chair by the bed. "Seems like she has stars in her eyes."

Dad snorted. "She's had it rough. Not used to being treated like a person. Hopefully that changes."

"How's your brain?"

"Mostly intact. Maybe only a little scrambled."

Nick nodded and looked away. He blinked rapidly.

"Hey, hey. Kid, come on. Nicky. Look at me."

Nick couldn't. At least not until he heard Dad trying to lift himself up out of the bed. He stood quickly, the chair scraping the floor behind him. Dad was grimacing, a trickle of sweat on his forehead. Nick scowled at him, carefully pressing on his shoulders. "Don't make me call the nurse in here. And I'll tell Cap when he gets back."

Dad glared at him. "You wouldn't dare."

"Try me."

Once he was sure Dad wasn't going to try and get up again, Nick started to turn back toward the chair. He was stopped by fingers circling his wrist and holding on tightly. His gaze followed the hand to a bandaged arm up to his father's face. Dad was frowning. "I'm going to be all right, kid."

Nick gave a little shrug. He didn't know how to put into words how relieved that made him, or how scared he'd been, and still was.

"We need to talk, Nicky. About some of the stuff you said. About some of the things I said."

"You're not supposed to be talking at all," Nick said hoarsely. "Remember?"

"I know. Just . . . let me get this out, and then I promise I'll shut up."

"Unlikely."

"Nick."

"Yeah, yeah."

Dad squeezed his wrist. "I said some things I shouldn't have. Things I can't take back, but wish I could more than anything. You didn't deserve that. I'm sorry."

"It's okay. I know I'm—"

"No, it's not okay." He started coughing. Nick was alarmed until Dad motioned to a cup with a straw sitting on a small table next to the bed. Nick grabbed it, and Dad sucked down the water. He coughed twice more before subsiding. "Shit, that hurt."

"Then maybe you *shouldn't talk*—"

"I love you," Dad said fiercely. "More than anything in this world. And I'm so damn proud of you and the man you've become. After everything we've been through, you had every right to curl up and let go. But you pushed yourself, and you pushed me. We survived, Nicky. I know some days it doesn't feel like it, but we have. And we're getting better. We're still going to make mistakes. I know I will. But as long as you remember there is nothing I wouldn't do for you, we're going to be okay."

Nick could barely breathe. "I thought . . . when you said that—when you asked me why I had to be this way . . . that you . . ."

Dad squeezed his eyes shut. "I know. I never should have said that. It wasn't fair to you."

Nick shuddered. "But you were right."

Dad shook his head. "No. Never. Never that."

"I was trying to be something I couldn't, trying to change myself to make—"

Dad opened his eyes. "I don't want you to change. All I ever want is for you to be healthy and whole and talk a mile a minute because your voice makes me happy—"

"I was trying to make myself an Extraordinary," Nick blurted before he could stop himself.

An inscrutable look crossed Dad's face, there and gone before Nick could begin to parse through it. "What?"

"This. All this . . . stupid crap. I was trying—I don't know. It started out for all the wrong reasons, and by the time I figured out how to do it for the *right* reasons, it still didn't work. And then I—"

"When was the last time you took your pill?"

That stopped Nick cold. "What?"

"Your pill, Nick. When was the last time you took your medication?"

Why the hell did *that* matter? "Uh. Earlier today. Mary brought it for me. Why?"

Dad relaxed slightly. "Just making sure. You're talking a little fast. Your head okay?"

"Yeah. It's fine. I'm not—"

"Why, Nick? Why would you think you needed to be an Extraordinary?"

Nick was getting whiplash at the changes in conversation. "It started out dumb. For reasons that don't make sense now, when I think about it. But it changed because of you. I wanted to do what I could to keep you safe." He shook his head. "I was too late. You're already here."

"I don't need you to protect me, Nicky. I'm the parent here. It's my job to do that for you."

"Why can't we do it for each other?"

Dad sighed. "Because you shouldn't have to worry about things like that. All I wanted you to focus on was growing up and finding your path. I don't need you to be an Extraordinary, Nicky. Not when you're already extraordinary to me."

Nick tried his best to hold back. But it was damn near impossible, and he burst out laughing. "Oh my god. That was terrible. You're such a dork."

Dad frowned. "It wasn't terrible. It was heartfelt. Why are you— would you stop laughing? I'm being serious here!"

"I know. That's what makes it hysterical. We were having a moment and you had to go and ruin it—"

"You're grounded for the rest of your natural life."

"Maybe I would feel more intimidated if you didn't look like you were going to cry with every breath you took."

"Broken ribs *hurt*, you little jerk."

"Why are you still talking?"

"Because you need to know that I love you just the way you are."

Nick's laughter faded. "I know, Dad."

"Good. Now that's done, on to the next. Seems like you've finally figured out that Seth wants to kiss you."

"*What?* Dad, no!"

"Dad, *yes*. Is it reciprocated?"

Nick thought about pressing the call button and demanding the nurse sedate his dad for the rest of the evening. "Why are we talking about this? Go back to the sappy stuff! I don't want *you* to be an Extraordinary, because you're already ex—"

"You should invite him over for dinner when I get home. It'll be you, me, Seth, and my gun."

Everything was terrible. "You can't threaten him! I'm not some debutante in the 1950s who needs their honor protected."

"Watch me threaten him. Do you remember what I showed you with the banana? You have to squeeze the base and roll the condom down slowly to make sure—"

"Why are you *like* this?"

"I'm not going to kill him," Dad said seriously. "I'm gonna threaten him a little. Make sure he knows that he doesn't get to stick anything in you without explicit consent."

Nick gaped at him. "What makes you think I'm going to be the one to have something stuck in me? Maybe I'm going to be the one doing the sticking!" He wished desperately he could take that back as soon as it left his mouth.

Dad looked Nick up and down before snorting. "Yeah, okay, Nicky. Keep telling yourself that."

"Ack! Nurse! *Nurse*. My father is losing his mind! Someone help me make him stop—"

They could hear footsteps running down the hall.

"Sorry," he called out. "I . . . didn't mean it?"

"Great," Dad said with a frown. "Now you're getting us both in trouble."

But no one came into the room. A nurse ran by the open door without looking in. And then another nurse ran by. And then another.

Nick didn't know what was happening. Dad let him go as Nick went to the doorway. A group of people had gathered in the waiting room down the corridor, staring at a TV mounted on the wall.

Another nurse rushed down the hallway, a harried look on her face.

"What's going on?" Nick asked her.

"Extraordinaries," she said, sounding breathless as she passed him by. "They're fighting. Midtown. It sounds bad. People are going to get hurt."

Nick's blood turned to ice as he turned quickly back into the room, heading for the TV in the corner.

"What happened?" Dad asked, wincing as he pressed a button on the bed to raise him up to a sitting position.

Nick didn't answer him. He picked up the remote off the table and turned the TV on. He flipped through the channels until he found what he was looking for.

He took a slow step backward.

"—and I've never seen anything like this," Rebecca Firestone said, and for the first time since Nick had heard her voice, she actually sounded *scared*. "They are ruthlessly attacking each other. It's like they're trying to kill each other. I can't believe this is— *Oh my god!*"

It looked like the end of the world.

The camera shot was shaky, Rebecca Firestone's voice almost drowned out by the winds whipping around the helicopter.

But it was clear enough.

Nick could see Burke Tower far in the background, silhouetted against the setting sun, the cloudy sky streaked pink and orange, the clouds alight. There were blurry movements, almost too fast for the camera to follow, bursts of bright fire and dark shadows.

They slowed briefly, Pyro Storm hovering high above the streets of Nova City, cape flapping around him, arms ablaze. Shadow Star was perched high on an antenna tower, hanging off of it with one arm, shadows gathering below him.

The chopper was too far away to pick up any conversation, but it was obvious they were shouting at each other, mouths twisting in fury.

"Our beloved hero, Shadow Star, is doing his best to hold back the villain known as Pyro Storm," Rebecca Firestone shouted. "Whatever evil scheme he has planned will be thwarted by the bravery of the savior in shadows. We won't be— What is he *doing*?"

The antenna tower began to list to the right, the shadows crawling along the roof twisting the metal. Struts and supports bent until they broke with an audible screech. Shadow Star backflipped off of the tower, landing in a crouch on the roof. He rose slowly, raising his arms. Lights burst from the bracelets on his wrists, making the shadows multiply. They took shape until they were corporeal, lifting the tower off the roof of the building.

And then Shadow Star hurled it at Pyro Storm.

"No," Nick whispered.

Instead of trying to get out of the way, Pyro Storm flew toward it. Right before he collided with the tower, he spun quickly, cape swirling around him as he soared through the tower, managing to avoid the metal struts. He'd almost made it to the other side when he was clipped in the shoulder by what looked like the corner of a satellite dish. He was knocked off course, a trail of blood falling behind him.

The antenna tower fell toward the busy streets below.

"I can't believe I'm seeing this!" Rebecca Firestone said, voice shrill. "Shadow Star just tried to stop Pyro Storm, but the villain managed to dodge his attack! And because of that, it's falling! Pyro Storm is going to cause so many people to get hurt! You saw it here first! This is all on Pyro Storm!"

Nick *really* hated Rebecca Firestone.

But before he could curse her name like she so deserved, Pyro Storm righted himself and turned away from Shadow Star. The antenna tower hurtled toward the ground. People below were screaming, running along the sidewalks, pushing each other viciously as they tried to flee. The growing shadow loomed large.

A bright flash of fire burst as Pyro Storm rocketed toward the tower. But instead of trying to knock it out of the way, he flew *by* it, landing on the street below so hard, the asphalt cracked beneath his feet. People huddled around him, hands over their heads as the tower crashed into the side of a building, causing it to spin wildly, glass shattering, mortar splitting and raining down after it.

The camera managed to focus right on Pyro Storm as he raised his hands over his head.

And then he exploded.

Or, at least that was what it looked like. A wave of fire roared and the screen whited out. Cries of horror came from up and down the halls of the hospital. Nick's dad grunted behind him.

But Nick stood still.

He waited.

He heard Rebecca Firestone screaming, the blades of the helicopter roaring in the background.

"Come on," Nick muttered. "Come on. Come *on.*"

The white light began to fade.

Rebecca Firestone's voice cut off.

Nick's blood rushed in his ears.

He wasn't sure what he was seeing at first. It looked as if the street was ablaze, fire rippling as it licked the sides of the buildings around it. For a moment, Nick thought Pyro Storm—*Seth*—had exploded, taking everyone with him.

But then he saw it for what it truly was.

The antenna tower hadn't landed on the street.

It was suspended *above* the street, having landed on a wave of fire in the shape of a dome. Nick watched as it broke in half, sliding almost lazily down each side of the dome, leaving ripples in the blaze as if it were the surface of a lake. The two halves landed on the street on either side of the dome before they tilted and fell against the sides of buildings. They didn't move after that.

The dome of fire dissipated.

In its center stood Pyro Storm, hand still raised above his head, chest heaving.

Around him were dozens of people, huddled on the ground. They were clinging to one another, clinging to *him*, holding on to his legs. Blood trickled down his arm from where he'd been hit by the tower.

Rebecca Firestone sounded strangled. "And Pyro Storm just . . . saved them. He could have let them die, but instead he . . . saved them?"

The people on the street rose slowly, looking around. When they saw the towers leaning against the buildings, they cheered, hugging one another and jumping up and down.

"Okay," Rebecca Firestone said. "It's not *that* great. He did *one thing*. Think about all the other times he tried to—"

Another voice came on-screen. "Uh, Rebecca? It's Steve Davis here, back at the Action News desk. Can you please tell us what you're seeing?"

"*Yes.* What I'm seeing is that Shadow Star tried to save the day, but he instead made an honest mistake, and there are people dancing in the streets because they weren't crushed. Some woman is trying to get Pyro Storm to hold her baby so she can take a picture! Doesn't she know that Pyro Storm most likely *eats* babies and—"

Her voice was cut off.

Steve Davis appeared on screen in a little box in the corner, looking uncomfortable. "It looks as if we're having technical difficulties with the audio. We still have a live video feed, but Rebecca Firestone won't be able to report on what she's—okay. Ah—hold on a moment. It looks like something's happening."

The camera panned away from where people were clapping Pyro Storm on the back, a second baby being thrust into his arms. The shot rose up until it focused on Shadow Star who stood at the edge of the roof, staring at the scene below.

He was surrounded by shadows.

It wasn't like anything Nick had seen before.

The shadows looked alive, like they were roiling. They reached out around him, shaped like tentacles, twisting along the side of the building.

And he looked furious.

Brick cracked. Windows broke. Below, people started screaming as debris rained down around them.

The camera jerked back toward the ground. The citizens of Nova City were running once again.

Pyro Storm was looking up at Shadow Star, a frown on his face.

Then everything went to hell. The screen seemed to *shake* as the camera spun, and there was a flash of Rebecca Firestone screaming silently, the pilot yelling as he clutched the cyclic-pitch lever, the tail boom and rotor crumpling as a large shadow wrapped around it and *yanked* and—

The screen went dark.

Steve Davis was pale. "I—we seem to have lost the feed." He looked beyond the camera into the studio, eyes wide. "I don't know if we—ah. I don't know if we'll get it back. There's—hold on." He reached up and touched his earpiece. His hand trembled. "Okay. I'm—ah. I'm being told that it appears the helicopter went down. We're trying to confirm if—yes. Yes, it appears the Action News Chopper has crashed, and . . . Shadow Star was the cause." He swallowed thickly. "I don't know if—we're going to take a quick commercial break. When we return, we'll continue with the live report of the mayhem in midtown today. Stay with us."

Nick turned off the TV.

He set down the remote.

He turned toward his Dad, who watched him with an unreadable expression. "If someone who loved you lied to you, kept things from you, hurt you, but they needed your help, would you do it?"

Dad's facade broke, and he looked stricken. "I—" He coughed, clearing his throat. "I would. Because I can never turn my back on someone who needs me. If I was lied to, if I was kept in the dark and my heart was breaking, I would still do everything I could. Sometimes, we lie to the ones we love most to keep them safe."

Nick nodded tightly. "I don't have time to explain, but I have to go."

Dad's eyes widened. "Wait, no, Nick, what are you talking about? Go *where*?"

Nick tried to smile. It trembled on his face before it collapsed. "You said that you didn't need me to be an Extraordinary because

I already *was* extraordinary. There's someone who needs to hear the same from me. If something happens and I don't get to say it, I'll regret it for the rest of my life." He backed toward the doorway.

Dad's eyes narrowed as he struggled to sit back up. "Nick, don't. Don't you do this. You stay *right* where you are."

Nick's eyes were wet, but he couldn't do anything about that now. "I love you. And I'm so happy you're my dad."

He turned and ran, his father shouting after him.

18

By the time he rang the doorbell, it was dark outside. It'd taken him nearly an hour to get here, even though the streets were as empty as he'd ever seen them. Those people who *had* been out were rushing, their gazes turned toward the sky as if they expected fire to rain down on them.

Nick heard the chimes echo in the house.

He waited.

Nothing.

He rang the doorbell again. And again. And again. And—

The door flew open. "One time is *enough*. I can't move as fast as I— *Nick?*"

Bob Gray looked shocked to find who stood on his porch.

"Hello," Nick said, mustering up all the courage he had. "I'd like to see Pyro Storm's secret lair. Please and thank you."

It was . . . disappointing.

Nick knew there were more important things to focus on right now, seeing as how his best friend who he might be in love with was fighting to the death with his ex-boyfriend, but he couldn't help it. He was finally standing in the lair of an Extraordinary, and it was *boring*.

There was exercise equipment scattered around the basement of the Gray home. A punching bag hanging from the ceiling. A chin-up bar on the doorway to the stairs.

There were scorch marks on the wall. On the ceiling. On the floor.

In the corner lay a discarded glove that looked like it was part of Pyro Storm's costume.

And the washer and dryer.

"Wow," Nick said. "This is probably the biggest letdown of my life." He winced, glancing at Bob. "Sorry."

Bob snorted. "Oh, this isn't everything." He walked over to a wall and pressed his hand against a panel. It lit up around his hand and a door Nick hadn't noticed slid open. "Ta-da."

"Oh my god," Nick whispered, unable to believe it was finally happening. The door would open, and they'd have to slide down a pole into underground caverns where—

"Hi, Nick," Martha said, sitting behind a desk in a small room. There was a computer monitor in front of her. Gibby sat beside her. Jazz stood next to Gibby.

And that was it.

That was it.

"Dammit," Nick muttered. "Worst superhero secret lair reveal ever."

Bob cuffed the back of his head. "I built that sliding door myself. Mind your manners, son. It took me six months."

"Good to see you, Nicky," Jazz said, reaching out to squeeze his hand as he came around the desk. "I knew you'd come. Gibby didn't. She said you were going to be a little dick about it."

"I didn't say that," Gibby said.

"Thanks, Gibby." Nick knew she'd have his back when all was said and done.

"I thought you were going to be a *whiny* little dick about it. There's a difference."

Fair play. "Ugh. Fine."

She eyed him warily. "You still mad at me?"

Nick shrugged. "Maybe. But if I am, I'll get over it. You're my friend."

Gibby looked relieved. "Awesome."

"But if you keep anything like this from me again, I'm gonna kick you in the junk."

"Duly noted," she said dryly.

"O-*kay*," Nick said, clapping his hands once. "Team Pyro Storm, assemble!"

They stared at him.

He frowned. "That's . . . that's not what you guys call your-selves?"

Martha shook her head.

"You guys don't have a name at all, do you?"

Bob scratched the back of his neck.

God, he was dealing with a bunch of amateurs. "Well, then, this is awkward. And unsatisfactory. In fact, ever since I got over the initial shock of the whole *my-best-friend-is-an-Extraordinary* thing, it's been one disappointment after another."

"You thought there'd be a secret lair, didn't you?" Gibby asked.

Nick sighed. "Is it too much to ask?"

"You didn't know about this room," Martha pointed out.

"Which has a pocket door," Bob said. "I could show you how it opens again if you missed it the first time."

"And there's a computer and everything," Jazz said.

Nick squinted at the monitor on the desk. "What is that? What does that say? Systemax? What the hell is a Systemax? That doesn't even sound like a real brand!"

"I got it at a garage sale," Martha said. "Paid twenty dollars for it."

Nick put his face in his hands and groaned. "Worst superhero backup team *ever*." He dropped his hands. "Okay. You know what? I can work with this. We can worry about upgrading everything later."

"On it," Jazz said. She smiled when they all looked at her. "My parents are rich. They have more money than they know what to do with. Upgrades, we can do. They'll consider it a philanthropic tax write-off even if we don't tell them what it's for."

"Awesome," Nick breathed. "And then we can talk new costumes for—"

"I sewed Seth's Pyro Storm costume myself," Martha said. "It's flame retardant and breathes really well. I got the material from the fabric store and a military surplus shop."

Nick groaned. "Why are you continuing to punch my dreams? Do you enjoy seeing me like this?"

"A little," Bob admitted. "It's nice to see you finally pulled your head out of your—"

"Robert," Martha said. "Honestly."

Nick didn't mind. He deserved it. In fact, it was probably time to man up for real. "I'm going to date your nephew so hard," Nick told them. "We need to help him so I can tell him that. Also, I like his hair and the way he smells and how he makes me laugh. And he needs to wear bow ties forever because there is nothing in the world more adorable than Seth Gray in a bow tie."

There. He felt better.

Jazz burst out laughing.

Gibby sat back in her chair, sighing as she stared up at the ceiling.

Martha and Bob were smiling.

"What?" Nick asked, confused. "What did I do?"

"Seth heard you," Gibby said. "So. Good job on that one."

"He what now?" Nick said, a sinking feeling in his stomach.

"Uh. Hi, Nicky," Seth said, his voice crackling from a speaker next to the monitor.

Nick stared down at it in horror. He opened his mouth to try and say something to salvage the situation, but all that came out was, "Eep."

"Oh man," Gibby said. "Seth, if only you could see the look on his face. You know what? I can make that happen." She pulled out her phone and snapped a photo. She hooked it up to the computer and tapped a few keys. "There. I uploaded it to your lenses."

Seth coughed. "Um. Thank you. That's . . . that's a good face."

"He can *see* that?" Nick managed to ask.

Gibby shrugged. "His mask is basically a computer. We can load things like maps and queer boys who're stunned for hysterical reasons to an interface."

"That's so cool," Nick said weakly. "And also so embarrassing. I'd be fine if we never brought up this moment again."

Gibby snorted. "We all know that's not going to happen."

"How's your dad?" Seth asked.

They all looked at Nick. "Um. Good? He's awake. And really annoyed he has to stay in the hospital."

"That's good, Nicky," Seth said. Then, "Hey, I need to . . . I'm sorry. For everything. I wish I'd done things differently. I never meant to hurt you. And I didn't hurt your dad, okay? Not on purpose."

"I know," Nick said quietly. "We'll figure it out. Where are you?"

"Looking for Owen." His voice hardened. "I don't know what he's trying to do, but he's dangerous. He's hopped up on those damn pills. They've made him too strong. More people would have been killed if I hadn't—"

"What do you mean *more*?" Nick asked, feeling cold. "I thought you stopped the antenna tower."

"He did," Martha said, as Bob put a hand on her shoulder. "But there was nothing he could do about the helicopter."

"It crashed into the side of a building," Jazz told him sadly. "They don't think anyone survived."

"Shit," Nick breathed. "He said—I think she was working with him, somehow. Rebecca Firestone. Building him up. Discrediting Pyro Storm. She made Shadow Star the hero and turned Seth into the villain. But why would he turn on her like that? It doesn't make sense."

"He's lashing out," Seth said. "I don't even think he has a plan. At least not anymore."

"What was his plan to begin with?"

No one answered.

"Uh, guys? Maybe fill me in here?"

Gibby sighed. "We think his plan was you."

Nick laughed.

No one else did.

Nick stopped laughing. "Oh, crap. You're serious."

"He took you to Burke Tower," Seth said. "To his father's laboratory. Why?"

Nick pressed his hands flat against the desk. "I asked him to. He said that his dad had found a way to turn someone Extraordinary. I refused at first, but then—" He shook his head. "Stuff happened. And I thought I didn't have a choice. So I asked him. And he did. This is my fault. All of this."

"No, son," Bob said. "It's not. He manipulated you. You were vulnerable, and he took advantage of that."

"I let myself be played," Nick said bitterly. "Regardless of what he did, I allowed it to happen. I should have seen it for what it was."

"You aren't responsible for what he's done," Martha told him.

"If anything, it's on us. We knew who he was, and so did Seth. We thought we could help him. That we could get through to him somehow, make him listen to reason. And at first, he wasn't *bad*. Seth could handle him himself." Her smile wobbled. "And then he started in with you, and things . . . stopped for a little while."

"It was a game," Seth said. "He was taunting me, I think. Or at least that was part of it. He had you, and then he didn't, and then he tried to pull you back in again. He was trying to use you against me."

Nick groaned. "This sucks. Not only am I the comedic relief/ love interest, I'm also the *clueless* comedic relief/love interest who is a pawn in a game I didn't even realize was being played. God, my life is so cliché."

"But why would he want Nick to be an Extraordinary?" Jazz asked. "Why take him to Burke Tower at all? If his plan was to change Nick, why not just bring a pill to him?"

"Would you have taken a pill Owen pulled out of his pocket?" Nick retorted. "It wouldn't have been the same. He knew I wouldn't trust it coming directly from him. But from a secret basement in Burke Tower? I'm a sucker for secret basements." He looked around the room. "Which is why this one is such a disappointment."

"And he saw how much Nick wanted it," Gibby said. "Especially when it started out being about Shadow Star." She grinned. "Remember the mugging in the alley?"

Nick winced. "Not my proudest moment."

"He would have made Nick an Extraordinary," Seth said, sounding grumpy. "At least temporarily. Give him a taste of power, get him hooked. And then he'd tell Nicky who he was. Who *I* was. He would've turned Nick against me. Convinced him that I was the villain all this time, that I needed to be stopped. He knew I'd follow you to Burke Tower. That whole scene was staged. Just like the apartment building."

"I wouldn't have done that," Nick snapped. "It wouldn't have worked." Suddenly unsure, he added, "Right?"

Except it almost had. If Pyro Storm hadn't shown up when he did, wouldn't Nick have done *exactly* what Owen wanted him to do? Taken a pill. Become something else. Who knew what would have happened then?

"It doesn't matter," Seth said. "Not anymore. You trust me?"

"Yes," Nick said immediately. Because of course he did.

"And you know Owen is the bad guy."

"Yeah."

"Which means he has to be stopped."

Nick blanched. "Are you—are you going to kill him?"

"No," Bob said sharply. "We don't kill people. Ever. We have to find a way to subdue him. He needs help, Nick. More than anything. We've waited this long because we were so scared Seth would be unmasked alongside him. But now we need to take that chance. If it happens, we'll deal with it then, as a family. The world needs to know who Shadow Star is and what he's capable of. He can't hide."

"How?" Nick asked.

Silence again.

"Seriously? You guys don't have a plan? *Any* plan? You have a Systemax computer in a basement of a row house and *no plan*?"

"Sometimes we have muffins when Seth gets back," Gibby said. "They're pretty good. Martha makes them."

Nick threw his hands in the air. "Useless. All of you. You're lucky I know everything there is to know about being an Extraordinary. I'm pretty much an expert. I write fanfiction, after all. Thank god you have me."

"Fanfiction?" Bob asked, brow furrowed. "What is . . . that?"

"I don't have time to answer your ridiculous questions right now," Nick told him. "I have a city to save. Move, Martha. I need the computer."

Martha glared at him.

"Oh, crap. Sorry. Move, please? Ma'am? Please?"

Martha rose from the chair. "Just because a villain is trying to take over Nova City doesn't mean we forget our manners."

Nick took her place, pulling the keyboard toward him. Next to it sat a small mic on a stand. The computer screen already showed a map of Nova City, a blinking light somewhere near Burke Tower. "Is that Seth?"

"Yeah," Bob said. "Tracker. Figured it'd be best in case something happened. He's been staying in the one place we thought Owen would come back to."

"Good," Nick muttered. "Okay, so in the outline of my real-person fanfiction, *This Is Where We Scorch the Earth*, there was going to be a point where I—I mean *Nate Belen*—was going to help—"

"Oh my god," Gibby mumbled. "We're doomed."

"—*was going to help* Shadow Star defeat Pyro Storm before they lived happily ever after."

"What is he talking about?" Bob asked Martha.

"I have absolutely no idea," she replied. "I think it's a Myspace thing."

"What's Myspace?"

"It's like Ask Jeeves."

Nick felt like he was dying a little inside, but he pushed on. "Part of the plot would have eventually led to Pyro Storm capturing Shadow Star, and I—*Nate* would have needed to come save him."

"I can't believe you made Seth beta read this," Jazz said. "In hindsight, that was a terrible decision."

"In hindsight, *many decisions are bad*," Nick said through gritted teeth. "But we don't dwell on them because they help us to grow as people and learn from our mistakes."

"Huh. So, *you* must have done a lot of growing lately—"

"Gibby!"

"Right. Shutting up now."

If they survived whatever came next, Nick was going to need to look into getting new people for their superhero backup team. The current roster was severely lacking. "As I was saying, Pyro Storm was going to capture Shadow Star, and Nate would have come in to save the day. But seeing as how everything I've ever known is a lie, we don't need to worry about the whole saving thing and focus on the part where we capture Shadow Star instead."

"He's never going to let that go, is he?" Bob asked Martha.

"Probably not," Martha said. "Teenage boys need to compensate for their shortcomings somehow."

"What was the plan?" Seth asked, voice crackling through the speakers. Nick watched as the dot on the screen moved slowly around Burke Tower. The fact that his best friend and potential future boyfriend was *flying* was not lost on Nick. He was going to have to ask later if he could ride on his back as Seth flew around. He was owed this. Big-time. He decided to put it aside for now because he was sitting near Seth's aunt and uncle, and he didn't want them knowing he was thinking about riding their nephew.

"Just to be clear," Nick said, "I haven't written it yet. But I did have it in an outline which had bullet points. Everyone knows that a good outline has bullet points, so I think we'll be fine."

"Dooooomed," Gibby moaned.

"I believe in you, Nicky," Seth said, and Nick thought back to the chubby boy on the swings, chocolate pudding on his chin. "If you think it'll work, we have to try."

"You need to burn away the shadows," Nick said into the mic. "That's his superpower. He can manipulate any shadow. You need to burn so brightly that all he sees is light. At least long enough until the pills wear off. Do we know how long it takes?"

"Too long," Seth said. "We have to stop him now."

"The bracelets," Gibby said thoughtfully. "The ones on his wrists. They have LED beams. Get rid of those and he won't be able to make new shadows. At the very least, it'll slow him down."

Bob leaned toward the speaker. "That level of power has gotta be strong, Seth. Stronger than anything you've ever done before. You need to keep it out of the city if you can. Can't let people get hurt."

Seth laughed, though it sounded strained. "Like when we first started?"

"You got it, son," Bob said. "Just like when we first started. But you're not like that anymore. You have control now. I don't need to worry about getting my eyebrows burned off these days."

It boggled Nick's mind, this history that he'd grown up alongside but had never known about. He had so many questions, but he'd save them for later.

"And what then?" Jazz asked. "If Seth's able to get him in a place where he can stop him, what happens next?" She looked troubled. "You said we won't kill him, and that's good. But what happens to him?"

Nick thought quickly. "That's not up to us, is it? If he's done all these things, if he's hurt people before, then he needs to answer for it. We'll turn him over to the police. Cap and my dad will know what to do."

"Do you think his dad knows?" Gibby asked. "I mean, if Simon Burke knows how to make Extraordinaries, don't you think he'd know about one living under his own roof?"

Nick's stomach sank to his feet. "Seth didn't tell you?"

"Little busy," Seth muttered. "Haven't had time."

Well, shit. "Burke knows," Nick said as he closed his eyes, thinking about Owen telling him how he'd been in the hospital because he'd seen things. Darkness. Shadows. He'd been given *medicine* to make it stop, but what if that had been a lie? "He's the one who made Owen who he is."

Jazz squinted at him. "What are you talking about?"

Nick opened his eyes, shaking his head. "Something Owen told me. He said he was sick when he was younger. Got put on medication. He was all but *telling* me he was Shadow Star, and I didn't see it. I was so focused on—I wasn't thinking. But all of this seems to go back to Burke Tower, right? What if Owen is trying to get revenge against his father for what he did to him? Burke Pharmaceuticals. For every experiment, for every creation, there have to be tests. On subjects."

"Simon Burke experimented on his own son?" Martha asked, hands clutched against her chest.

"He did. To be his own personal guard dog." Everything was falling into place, pieces of a puzzle coming together to form a terrible picture. "All those attacks on Burke Tower. His father used him to protect what was hidden inside, to keep the secrets safe. But it doesn't matter, at least not right now. We need to focus on stopping Owen first. All the rest we'll deal with later."

"We have to find him before we can stop him," Gibby said, leaning over Nick's shoulder to look at the screen. "Anything, Seth?"

"No," Seth said. "Nothing. It's like he's disappeared."

"Or he's waiting for the perfect moment to strike," Jazz said.

They all turned slowly to look at her.

"What?" she asked. "It's what *I* would do if I were a supervillain."

"And I thank god every day you're not," Gibby said, kissing her cheek. "Always remember to use your powers for good."

Jazz rolled her eyes. "Like I could ever be evil. I'm too cute to be a bad guy."

Maybe the current roster for their superhero backup team was actually perfect.

It was dark when Nick stepped out of the Gray house onto the street. The streetlamps were lit along the sidewalk, casting shadows on the cement. The air had a bite to it, and Nick pulled his jacket tighter around him as he took his phone from his pocket.

He'd turned it off after he'd left the hospital, knowing his dad would be calling. It was a dick move, but he had to do what was necessary in order to help Seth stop Owen. And knowing his dad, he probably would have had Nick's phone traced to find out where he was. Nick knew all about cell tower pings.

Sure enough, as soon as he'd turned the phone on, a notification came up telling him he had seven voicemails. He ignored them, looking for a number on his phone.

It only rang twice before a breathless voice picked up. "Nick? Is that you?"

"Hey, Cap," Nick said, looking up at the dark sky. There was too much light pollution to see even the brightest of stars.

"Oh, don't you *Hey, Cap* me. Do you have any idea how worried your dad is? They had to sedate him when he tried to leave the hospital!"

Nick's throat clicked as he swallowed. "Yeah, sorry about that. But I had to. Things are happening, Cap."

"Where are you? I'm going to send a patrol car to come get you."

"Can't do that. Not yet. And I'm keeping this short, so don't try and ping me."

"I'm going to arrest you," Cap growled. "And throw you in jail *myself*. Do you hear me? In fact, I'm going to reinstate chain gangs. Hard labor. That's all you're gonna get."

"That's a clear overreach of your position, and you should be ashamed of— Stop trying to distract me!"

"Tell me where you are, Nick."

"Listen, okay? I'm asking you to listen. There's going to be—"

A voice spoke behind him. "Hey, Nicky."

Nick whirled around. There was no one there.

"Nick?" Cap asked.

Nick's grip tightened on the phone. "Hold on. There's—"

A streetlamp blew out, glass shattering.

Nick took a step back.

Another streetlamp exploded.

And another.

And another.

"Oh no," Nick breathed. "Cap! You have to help Pyro Storm, you hear me? You have to help—"

The phone was ripped from his hand by a tentacle of shadows. Nick watched as his phone was twisted and crushed. The shadow relaxed its grip, and pieces of Nick's phone clattered on the sidewalk.

"Owen?" Nick breathed.

"My name," he said as he stepped out of the dark, "is *Shadow Star.*"

Nick was only able to make it a few feet before the shadows surrounded him.

Everything went black.

19

Nicholas Bell awoke, bound on the top of one of the spires on McManus Bridge.

Shadows wrapped around his legs and torso, holding him in place high above the Westfield River.

Birds flew by him, only a few feet away.

Nick discovered he had an extreme fear of heights. The timing could have been a bit better for such a realization, but supervillains apparently didn't give two shits about that.

"Oh my god," he said, struggling not to gag. Then, the anger of an artist whose work was plagiarized set in, and any fear of dying a terrible death by falling to the street below was shoved to the background. "Are you serious? You're using my fanfiction *against* me? That's a crappy thing to do, even for you. I didn't even know you'd read it, much less decided to steal it. Come up with your own ideas, you dick!"

"What can I say? I'm your biggest fan."

Nick looked down, regretting the move almost instantly. The cars on the bridge below looked so tiny, and all that was between him and an impression of a wannabe Jackson Pollock all over the pavement was a supervillain who read Nick's online self-insert real-person fanfiction and was now incorporating it into his diabolical schemes.

All in all, Nick wasn't having the best day. If he survived this, he was going to need to post a warning for his followers to be aware of who could be reading their fics, lest they be used for nefarious purposes.

And it certainly didn't help that Shadow Star—*Owen*—was standing on a metal platform in full costume about ten feet below him, smiling wildly. He wiggled his gloved fingers up at Nick as the lenses over his eyes flashed. His other hand was wrapped tightly around a person next to him on the platform.

"Rebecca Firestone," Nick gasped. "I thought you died in the helicopter crash!"

"That was just my cameraman and the pilot," she said. "Shadow Star saved me." She smiled dreamily at Owen. "Like he always does."

Nick made a face. "Oh my god, ew. Dude, you're, like, *forty*. Your lady boner for Shadow Star is both disgusting and problematic. Also, illegal."

She glared up at him. "I'm thirty-four."

Nick rolled his eyes. "Shadow Star is a seventeen-year-old high school student named Owen Burke. Also, I've made out with him, so suck it."

Rebecca Firestone snapped her head toward Shadow Star. "You *what*?"

Shadow Star shrugged. "Yeah. We did make out. It was pretty good."

"Pretty good," Nick growled, outraged. "I was *awesome*—"

"You're only seventeen?" Rebecca Firestone said, sounding like she was starting to panic. "But . . . that . . . I've had *thoughts* about—"

"Gross," Nick muttered. "Old people are so weird."

Rebecca Firestone got over her horror rather quickly. She began to try and beat Shadow Star over the head with her hands. Nick never thought he'd be in a position to cheer loudly for Rebecca Firestone about *anything*, much less punching Shadow Star in the face. But here he was, screaming down at her to *scratch his freaking eyes out* and *kick him in the balls*. She looked like she was about to do exactly that, but then the lights on Shadow Star's wrists lit up, making Nick turn his head. Out of the corner of his eye, he saw shadows slither around Rebecca Firestone, lifting her off the platform. One of her shoes slipped off and fell toward the ground below. Nick couldn't see where it landed.

Rebecca Firestone kicked and screamed as she was raised eye-level with Nick, her back pressed against a spire across from him.

The shadows tightened around her, holding her in place. She banged her head back against the spire, demanding that Shadow Star let her go this instant, and did he know all the things she'd done for him? She was a celebrated and an award-winning *journalist*, and she would not be treated this way!

"Yeah!" Nick crowed, getting caught up in the high stakes of televised investigative journalism. "You better let us go, or else!"

Rebecca Firestone glared at him. "I don't care what he does to *you*. I'm only talking about myself."

Nick gaped at her. "And to think I was just *stanning* you after hating everything about your existence ever since I first saw you! Guess what? I'm once again anti–Rebecca Firestone! You're the worst." Nick paused, considering. "Well, almost the worst. Shadow Star is pretty much winning *that* contest right now. But you're a close second. Congratulations."

Shadow Star rose between them, standing on a shifting pedestal of shadows. "Now, now. No need to fight over me. There's more than enough of me to go around."

Nick struggled against the shadows, trying to break free, but it was useless. And to top it all off, he was starting to get a headache. He wasn't having a very good night. Or life. "What do you want with me?"

"Oh, Nick. It's not *you* I want."

"What? Then why am I here?"

Owen laughed. "You know why."

"I have no idea what you're talking about."

"I think you do. Everyone knows to whom your heart belongs. And since I have captured you with my diabolical scheme, we both know who will come to your rescue. He *always* does."

Nick blinked. "Leave him alone or I'll—wait a minute. Are you quoting my *fanfiction*? Are you serious right now?"

Owen tilted his head back and cackled maniacally. It was a good evil laugh, much to Nick's dismay.

Rebecca Firestone didn't seem to find it funny. Neither did Nick, but he wasn't going to feel any kind of kinship with her again. He'd learned his lesson.

"No," Owen said. "Oh, no. You're supposed to say your line, Nicky. He doesn't care about you, even though we both know it's a lie. And then *I'll* tell you how wrong you are, how wrong you've always been. Because I would know. I've seen the expression on his face when you weren't looking, when you were giving me those big ol' *gosh golly gee* eyes of yours. Oh, Nicky. He was hurting. And yet, he still managed to hold himself back. He let you go, even though everything he's done has been for you." Owen sighed. "It was really quite precious. He saw the devastation left behind after your mother died. He told himself he was going to make the world a better place for you. It was . . . sweet. Misguided, but sweet. Especially when I knew I could do it better. After all, all it takes to become famous is a little flash, some good PR, and voila! Instant love and adoration." He turned and reached out, patting Rebecca Firestone on the cheek.

"You saved me," she snarled. "That scaffolding would have crushed me if you hadn't stopped it."

"Oh," Owen said. "You mean the scaffolding that I threw to begin with?"

Rebecca Firestone paled. "You didn't."

"I did," he said gleefully. "And you took the bait. Even I was surprised how easy it was. All I had to do was smile at you, and you did everything I wanted."

"Wow," Nick said smugly. "Look how easy you are. You should feel totally embarrassed right now."

"And *you*, Nick," Shadow Star said, whirling back around.

"Nope," he said. "Nope, nope, nope. We don't need to talk about me. Let me have that sick burn I got on Rebecca Firestone, and that'll be that. Also, maybe let me go? And turn yourself in."

"You are just like her."

Nick was going to straight up murder him. Screw what the Grays said about no killing. Owen was *dead*. "You take that back!"

"All I had to do was smile in your direction, and you were mine." Owen grinned at him. "Our dear, precious Pyro Storm didn't see me one day when I followed him home. Imagine my surprise when I found out he was a kid like me. A sweet, innocent boy who had such an obvious crush on this loud, annoying guy—it was *painful* to watch. But then I swooped in and took that from him. You didn't even notice. So what does that make you, Nick?"

Before Nick could respond, Rebecca Firestone said, "Owen Burke."

Owen turned again. "What was that?"

"Owen Burke," she repeated slowly. "That's . . . that's what he said your name was. Owen Burke . . . as in *Simon* Burke. You're . . . you're Simon Burke's son."

"I am," Owen said, taking a step toward her. The shadows underneath him shifted with every step he took, keeping him from falling. "You might even say that all of this is *because* of him."

"Shit," Nick moaned. "I hate being right. Also, a villain with daddy issues? Come on, Owen. Try being original for once. First, you steal my fanfiction, and now you're trying to be like every comic book baddie ever written? And don't even get me started how you're essentially ripping off Spider-Man by being a discount Harry Osborn. What the hell. Have some self-respect."

He barely saw Owen move before a gloved hand was wrapped around his throat, squeezing tightly. Nick choked, trying to kick his legs out against Owen, but the shadows held him down tight. Pain lanced through his head as Owen bared his teeth, snarling. "This isn't a game, Nicky. You still think we're playing, but we're not. You talk and talk and *talk* and never say anything at all. It's one of the things that pisses me off the most about you. God, it's no wonder your mother died. I wouldn't be surprised if she stepped in front of that bullet to get away from you."

A red sheen fell over Nick's eyes. Anger like he'd never felt boiled in his chest. His head was pounding, and all he wanted to do was lash out, to tear and punch and kick until Owen was nothing but a bloody mess of broken teeth and crushed bone.

"Good," Owen breathed. "Good, Nick. There it is. I could see it, you know. Even though no one else could. You have this darkness in you. Oh, you haven't had a chance to explore it, you haven't been able to harness it any way that mattered, but it's there, waiting to be let out. We're the same, Nicky. Even if you can't see it now, we're the same. The things we'd do to protect those we care about. If you had a chance to go back, to be there in that bank, what would you do?"

"Screw you," Nick spat.

Owen shook his head. "Such a brave face. You don't need to do that with me. I know you, Nick. Better than everyone. Because I *am* you. We're covered in shadows, you and me. It's easy to give into it when you want it badly enough. I know what you would've done for her. You would have stopped them by any means necessary. Even if it meant blood on your hands." His grip tightened. "Be gay. Do crimes."

He wasn't wrong, but Nick wasn't going to give him the satisfaction. "I am *nothing* like you."

"Aren't you?" Owen asked, his face inches from Nick's, his breath hot against Nick's cheeks. "Because I seem to remember you saying you would do anything to protect those you love. We're not like Pyro Storm, Nick. You're not like Seth. You and me, we have to fight tooth and nail just to be on his level. How is that fair? He won the genetic lottery, and the rest of us are supposed to *accept it*? Why should he get to have powers the rest of us don't? I may hate my father, but he still gave me the tools to become what I am. He didn't know how far I could take it. He will, though. Everyone will."

"Pyro Storm is coming for me," Nick snapped, spittle spraying from his mouth and landing on Owen's mask. It glistened in the light. "And he's gonna kick your ass."

Owen let go of this throat, reaching up to ruffle Nick's hair as he gasped in a deep breath. He gagged, eyes watering.

"It's kind of irritating how much he cares about you," Owen said. "Seriously, watching the two of you fumble around each other was embarrassing."

"Hey!"

"But it doesn't matter," Owen said, squaring his shoulders. "Because today is the day that I bring about the end of Pyro Storm. You're right. He'll come for you. And it'll be the last thing he ever does."

"Would you *stop quoting my fan—*"

"What about me?" Rebecca Firestone asked, and Nick again was unimpressed by her. She always tried to make it about herself. It was really an unattractive quality to have.

"You'll tell my story," Owen said, rising higher. In the distance,

Nick thought he could hear the sounds of approaching sirens. "This city will love me. You'll make sure of it."

"And if I don't?"

Owen shrugged. "I'll kill you and find someone else."

"I'm on board, then," she said quickly. "I'm thinking we try to go national. A sit-down interview. We need to meet the *real* Shadow Star. The boy—the *man* behind the mask."

"What about your scruples?" Nick demanded. "Your moral integrity? You're a *reporter*. You're supposed to be unbiased!"

She snorted. "Kid, I don't know what in the hell is going on, but I don't want to die. I would also like a Pulitzer."

"I will never watch Action News again! You hear me? Never!"

"Is he always this loud?" she asked Owen.

"Yes. Always. And filled with outrage over the weirdest things. This one time, I—"

But whatever example Owen was about to give was cut off as he exploded.

Not *literally*, but Nick didn't know that, at least not right away. One moment he was standing on a pillar of shadows above them, and the next, there was a bright burst of fire engulfing him. Nick shouted in terror, turning his face away from the immense heat that rolled over his skin. He felt the shadows binding him begin to loosen, and he slipped a little down the spire, shirt riding up on his back and pressing against cold metal. He heard Rebecca Firestone cry out across from him, and he managed to open his eyes in time to see her sliding down her own spire, feet dangling into nothing. Her other shoe fell off, a sharp wind blowing it out into the river.

Nick looked down and saw a dozen police cars screeching to a halt, their lights spinning. He was dizzy at the sight of them so far away. He couldn't even make out the sound of the doors flying open.

He lifted his head toward the sky.

Owen had been knocked off his shadow pedestal and was clinging to the top of Nick's spire, costume smoking, embers smoldering on his shoulder. He looked out, face twisted in fury.

Nick followed his gaze.

There, high above Nova City, cape billowing around him, was Pyro Storm.

"Quite the entrance," Owen said. "I'm impressed." He brushed off the embers on his shoulder. They winked out as they fell.

"This is over," Pyro Storm said, and Nick shivered at the steel in his voice. "I should've stopped you a long time ago. Everything you've done in the last few days, the people that were hurt, that *died*—that's all on me. I'll never forgive myself for that. But you shouldn't have touched Aaron Bell. And you shouldn't have touched Nick. Those weren't your first mistakes, but they're going to be your last."

Owen laughed wildly. "Always comes back to Nick, doesn't it? You talk about justice and saving people, but it was always about him. It's sad." He looked down at Nick. "Isn't it sad, Nicky? Almost as sad as your pathetic little crush on an Extraordinary who was right in front of you all this time."

Nick ground his teeth together. He thought the spire behind him started shaking, but he hoped it was just his imagination. It was the last thing he needed at the moment. "You're a dick, Owen. Had I known it was you, I never would have liked anything about Shadow Star."

"You weren't saying that last spring. In fact, I distinctly remember hearing *Owen, please more. Owen, right there, yeah*."

"What do you think is gonna happen here?" Pyro Storm asked him. "You know this is the end."

"I don't think it is," Owen said, holding onto the spire with one hand as he reached toward Pyro Storm. "You see, you need me as much as I need you. A hero is only as good as his villain. Think about it. You're nothing without me. And I do enjoy this dance we do." He smiled cruelly. "No matter where you go or what you do, I'll be there right behind you."

"Let Nick go," Pyro Storm ordered.

Owen shrugged. "Okay."

Two things happened at once.

The shadows holding Nick against the spire disappeared—

and,

Owen launched himself at Pyro Storm.

The latter concerned Nick almost as much as the former.

It was a strange split second, hanging suspended in midair

hundreds of feet above the McManus Bridge. He heard Seth shouting his name before Owen hit him directly in the chest, wrapping inky-black shadows around him, and they both fell away.

Nick didn't have time to make noise before he started to fall. One moment he was against the spire, and the next he started to plummet.

He'd always heard that in the seconds before one's death, life tended to flash before one's eyes. Nick could unequivocally say that was a freaking lie. His breath was caught in his throat, and he wanted to scream, to do *something* to let everyone within hearing distance know he did *not* want to become a smudge on the pavement below. A bright lance of pain—glassy and harsh—shot through his head, and even as he fell, he was knocked *forward*, right at Rebecca Firestone.

And since Nick absolutely did not want to die, he reached out for her even though she was shaking her head furiously and screaming at him to *back off*. Luckily for him, he didn't give a crap what Rebecca Firestone wanted. He wrapped a hand around her ankle, stopping his descent before he could pick up speed.

She grunted above him. "Let me go!"

"No!" he shrieked up at her. "I'd really rather not if that's okay with you!"

"You're going to break my leg!"

"Oh no! How terrible for you! I'm going to break my *everything* if I let—are you trying to kick your leg? Stop it!"

But she didn't. He felt the muscles in her leg tense as she jerked her foot. His fingers dug into her skin, the tendons in her ankle bunching under his grip. Nick swung precariously out into nothing, and—"Why is your ankle sweaty? Who has sweaty ankles! Oh my god, I'm going to—"

He slipped.

And landed on the metal platform less than a foot below him.

"Huh," Nick said, looking down at his feet. He bounced up and down, testing its weight. It held. "I didn't expect that. Awesome."

Then he immediately threw up over the side of the bridge. He couldn't even find the strength to be embarrassed about it.

He stood up, wiping his mouth with the back of his hand. "Ugh. I should not have eaten all that hospital Jell-O."

"Get me down!"

Nick looked up.

Rebecca Firestone struggled against the spire, the shadow bands still wrapped around her, holding her in place. Above, at the highest part of the bridge, Shadow Star and Pyro Storm were battling it out. Nick cheered when Owen was hit with a ball of fire, only to wince when a long shadow tentacle lashed out, striking Seth in the chest, sending him spiraling into a metal support beam.

"Kid, you gotta help me out!"

Nick glared up at her. "You tried to kill me!"

"Well, *yeah,* but it didn't work, right?"

"That's probably not the best argument that you—"

An amplified voice roared below him. "Nick? Nick! Can you hear me?"

Nick peered over the edge of the platform. It couldn't be—"Dad?"

Sure enough, standing next to one of the patrol cars, was his father, megaphone pressed against his lips. He was still in his hospital gown, but he wore a NCPD jacket. Cap stood next to him, staring up toward Nick. "There's a service ladder!" his dad said, voice blaring. "Off to your right! Start climbing down. I'm going to meet you half—" Cap said something that Dad didn't like, and they argued back and forth. Nick wanted to remind them that they didn't exactly have a lot of time but there was no way he'd be heard.

Cap finally grabbed the megaphone from Dad's hands. "Nick, get to the ladder! We're going to send someone up after you who's not an idiot with broken ribs. Move, kid!"

Nick looked around, trying to find the ladder they were talking about. The platform he was standing on was long and skinny, surrounded by metal struts. If he walked along it, he'd have to maneuver around the struts, but it'd be doable. And there, at the other end of the platform, was a metal ladder, leading down to another platform.

He took a step toward it.

Then, "Please."

He closed his eyes.

"You can't leave me up here," Rebecca Firestone said, voice quavering. "I don't want to die."

"Nick!" His dad had gotten hold of the megaphone again. "You need to move *now*! We'll help the woman."

A loud crash exploded above, and Nick's eyes snapped open as the bridge groaned. Nick stumbled toward the edge of the platform, managing to grab one of the struts before he could tumble over the side. He looked up in time to see Owen throw Seth into one of the spires. The spire broke with a metallic groan. It fell, bouncing off the struts, orange sparks shooting out with each impact. The cops below shouted as they ran. Nick saw Cap grab his dad and pull him out of the way as the spire fell onto one of the cruisers. The windows shattered and the car crumpled. Dad struggled against Cap, trying to get to the nearest ladder.

Nick knew what he had to do. He didn't like it. But even though he wasn't an Extraordinary, he sure as hell could act like one.

He turned away from the ladder and back toward Rebecca Firestone.

She struggled against the shadows around her, gasping as she stared up at the battle happening above them. Nick reached up and grabbed one of her legs, and she screamed as she looked down at him.

"Stop kicking," he snapped at her. "I'm trying to help you."

"Get me down!"

"I will if you stop yelling!"

"Don't shout at me! Do you have any idea who I am?"

"Oh my god," Nick muttered. "I hate you so much." He tried pulling on her leg, but the shadows held. He thought about trying to climb the spire, but he couldn't find anything to hold on to that wasn't a body part, and he did *not* want to climb Rebecca Firestone. If only there was a way to get rid of the shadows, he could—wait! Holy crap. That was it.

He reached into his pocket for his phone.

Only to remember how it'd been crushed when Owen had taken him. For all he knew, it was still on the sidewalk in front of the Gray house.

He looked up at Rebecca Firestone. "Do you have your phone?"

"What? Why do you need my phone? Get your own! I can't upgrade for another seven months—"

"You are the *worst* person to rescue. I'm not trying to take it. I want the flashlight on it."

"Why?"

Nick gave very serious consideration to turning around and leaving her right there. "For the shadows! It'll—"

Thumpthumpthumpthump.

Nick turned slowly.

A helicopter approached the bridge. Nick could see an Action News logo on the tail. Someone was hanging out the side, a camera pointed in their direction. "How many helicopters do you guys have? That seems excessive."

"Oh thank god," Rebecca Firestone said. "They'll rescue me."

"Lady, you're hanging from the top of a bridge. There's no way they can land. You need to get your phone. It's the only way I can get you—oh no."

A spotlight on the front of the helicopter burst to life.

It hit Nick first, blinding him. He raised his hands to shield his eyes.

It rose toward Rebecca Firestone. The effect was instantaneous. The shadows holding her in place disappeared. She fell, landing hard on the platform. She bounced . . . and rolled off the side.

Nick was already running, bathed in the spotlight and barely able to see. He fell to his knees and reached for her just as she slid off the edge of the platform. His hand hit her arm, and he wrapped his fingers around her wrist. Nick was jerked forward onto his stomach, the metal cold against his skin where his shirt had ridden up. He grimaced against the strain in his shoulder. "Stop . . . *moving*," he ground out.

Rebecca Firestone gasped, pulling on Nick's arm, legs flailing into nothing. The roar of the helicopter thundered in Nick's ears. People screamed below them. Nick didn't pay attention to any of it. All that mattered was his arm being torn out of its socket.

He tried to push himself up, but only succeeded in sliding closer to the edge of the platform. He looked through the metal grate to see Rebecca Firestone staring up at him, eyes bulging, mouth wide and slack.

God, his head hurt.

He gritted his teeth together and tried to rise again. The platform shuddered underneath him. He managed to get to his knees. Just when he thought it'd be enough, Rebecca Firestone's grip on his wrist slipped.

She began to fall again.

He caught her by the hand.

A slick wave of pain crashed over him as something popped wetly in his shoulder. Nick screamed, pitching forward.

The weight was suddenly lifted as Rebecca Firestone flew up in front of him, knocking him back. He landed on the platform, blinking up at the dark sky.

"Nick? Nick!"

A hand touched the side of his face.

Someone bent over him. A mask covered their face.

"Nick!"

"Hey," Nick whispered.

Seth breathed a sigh of relief. "Hey." He reached down to help Nick up. Nick cried out as fingers closed over his injured arm. "Sorry. Nicky, I'm sorry. You're hurt. It's—"

"It's fine," Nick grunted. He used his good arm to push himself up into a sitting position.

A metallic creak came from behind them, and Nick turned his head in time to see Rebecca Firestone disappearing down the ladder. "You're welcome!" Nick shouted after her. "Don't worry about us. We're totally fine!"

He turned back as Seth crouched in front of him, cape dragging along the platform. The light from the helicopter covered his face in shadows. Seth reached up and touched Nick's cheek with a gloved hand. "God, Nick. I thought—I thought you fell." He leaned forward and pressed his forehead against Nick's. "Don't ever scare me like that again."

Nick didn't know if what he was feeling right then was love, but he thought it was close. He loved Seth, yes; he had loved him almost from the moment he'd met him. But this was bigger, grander, and he needed Seth to understand. Nick (always and forever being Nick) blurted, "You make my heart so full, I think I'll die."

Seth jerked his head back, inhaling sharply. "What did you say?"

"I—"

Seth kissed him.

It was hotter than he expected. Literally. Seth's lips were so warm, it felt like he was burning from the inside out. And it was also slightly awkward, Seth's mask digging into Nick's skin. But Nick couldn't bring himself to care. He was too busy having his mind blown by the fact that he was being kissed by his best friend, and it felt like coming home.

It was probably the most ridiculous moment of his life. And, perhaps, the most wonderful.

Seth's hand came up to cup his cheek as the kiss deepened. He felt the swipe of Seth's tongue against his bottom lip before Seth broke the kiss, pressing his forehead against Nick's again.

"Wow," Nick breathed. "Even though my arm hurts like you wouldn't believe, *wow*."

And oh, how Seth smiled. "Yeah. Wow."

"It's about damn time. It only took me getting kidnapped by my villainous ex-boyfriend for you to—"

Seth groaned. "Moment ruined. Way to go, Nicky."

"I'm just *saying*—"

"You don't have to say *anything*. We're having our first kiss, and you're talking about your ex!"

"Who *kidnapped* me. I'm allowed to state the obvious. Do you know how traumatizing today has been for me?"

But Nick never got to hear what Seth's response would have been.

Because one moment, they were together, finally together, and it was everything Nick thought it would be.

And in the next, the platform broke away from the bridge, the struts crumpling around them as a black shadow wrapped around Seth, pulling him off into nothing.

Nick didn't have time to react, because he was falling.

It was here, then, at the end, that Nick's life flashed before his eyes.

There was a chubby boy sitting on the swings by himself, and Nick wanted nothing more than to be his friend forever.

A girl named Gibby laughed at a joke he made, and he felt like he could do anything.

Jazz was crying on his shoulder, having fought with her girlfriend. Nick wrapped an arm around her, holding her close, his face in her hair.

Owen smiled wickedly as he reached across the table, stealing a carrot.

They walked up the stairs from the Franklin Street station, all of them bumping shoulders and laughing.

Cap grinned at him, mustache drooping.

Martha Gray kissed his forehead as she shooed him up the stairs.

Bob Gray clapped him on the back while he flipped burgers on the grill.

And there was the *ocean,* and she was there, laying her head on his shoulder. She was telling him that she loved him, and she smiled like the sun, and he was *happy,* dear god, he was *happy* because he was with her.

He touched her smile in the frame on his nightstand.

He had his first kiss.

Then he had the only first kiss that mattered.

And there was a man, a big man, a strong man, who lifted Nick up on his shoulders, saying how proud he was of Nick, that he was brave and kind. He said he wished Nick didn't have to be the way he was, *why do you have to be this way?* He was asking Nick if he'd taken his pill. He was sitting on the edge of his bed, head slumped, and he was *crying,* his whole body shaking, a frilly pink scarf clutched in his hands, and Nick knew he was trying to be quiet, trying not to let anyone hear him, but Nick couldn't leave him alone. He sat next to him on the bed, taking his dad's hand in his, and they stayed there for the longest time. There was Cinnamon Bread-Shaped Chomps, because that was how they apologized to each other. There was the buzzing of his phone in the middle of a school day and the beeping of his father's heart from a machine next to his bed.

But everything faded away with the sound of Dad's voice.

I don't need you to be an Extraordinary, Nicky. Not when you're already extraordinary to me.

He'd lived a good life.

He'd made his mother smile. He'd made his father proud. He'd kissed the boy of his dreams. And he did it all without being an Extraordinary. In the end, maybe that was his superpower.

Deep in his head, the ache bit down like it was alive, its teeth sharp. He was being torn apart. He didn't like it. With the last of his strength, he pushed it away.

And for the first time in his life, it just . . . went.

There was a sharp *crack* around him, and everything stopped.

He opened his eyes. He stood on the bridge.

The cruisers were in front of him, lights spinning, a line of officers staring at him with matching expressions of awe.

Well, not *exactly* at him.

Above him.

Nick lifted his head.

The pieces of the bridge that had collapsed around him hung suspended in the air, swirling in a lazy circle.

"Huh," Nick said, squinting up at the pieces of the metal floating over him. "That's . . . I don't know what that is."

"Nick!"

He looked ahead.

Dad was there. Cap was trying to hold him back, but it was a losing battle.

Nick started to run toward him.

Dad broke free of Cap and stumbled forward, arm going around his stomach, a grimace on his face. Nick's Chucks slapped against the pavement and he was almost there when his dad's eyes widened. *"Nick!"* he screamed.

Nick looked up. The debris that had been floating in the air was starting to vibrate. Nick felt his heart hammer in his chest when the first piece fell, slamming onto the roadway, cracking the asphalt.

The rest of it came raining down around him. Nick raised his arms over his head as if it would be enough to protect him from thousands of pounds of steel. He zigzagged as a strut slammed into the road, bouncing off toward the guardrails, making the road shake under his feet.

He didn't stop moving until he felt his dad's hands on his

shoulders, telling him it was all right, that everything would be all right, that he was safe now, that he was safe, and by god, he was going to be grounded for the rest of his life, what the hell was he *thinking*?

Nick laughed, blinking away the burn in his eyes, chin resting on Dad's shoulder. "Okay," he managed to say. "I'm okay with that." His arm was hurting where it was pressed against his dad, but he didn't care. They were all right. They were—

Then:

The cops around them shouted in warning.

Nick whirled around.

Shadow Star stood on the bridge where Nick had landed. His costume had been burned away on his right shoulder and left leg. He was breathing heavily, head bowed, blood dripping from his mouth. Behind him, cops pulled their guns, pointing them at Shadow Star, shouting at him to *stand down, now!* They hid behind their cruisers, some near the trunks, others behind open doors.

Their light bars were lit up, red and blue spinning.

Much like the lights on the cruisers behind Nick.

The spotlight from the helicopter was directly on him while it hovered overhead.

The shadows danced around the debris in the roadway.

Shadow Star lifted his head and looked directly at Nick. He grinned wickedly. His teeth were bloodied. Part of his helmet had broken off, and a single eye was visible. It was wide and crazed. "Well," he said, panting. "This has certainly been exciting."

"I am ordering you to stand down," Cap barked into the megaphone.

Owen shook his head. "Already taken it this far, haven't I?"

Dad tried to drag Nick back toward the line of officers, but Nick pulled away. "Nick, *no*. We gotta go."

Nick looked over his shoulder, smiling tightly. "Dad, I know— it's Owen. I can get through to him."

Dad frowned. "Owen." Then, "Owen *Burke*? Nick, what the hell?"

Nick turned back toward Owen. He raised his voice and said, "It's over, Owen. No one else needs to get hurt."

"Nova City is *mine*. I won't let anyone take it from me."

Nick groaned. "Man, that shtick gets old real fast. You have to know how ridiculous you sound. Legit, man. Take the high road."

"Maybe don't piss him off more," Dad growled behind Nick.

Owen's mouth twisted into a snarl. "I'm the hero. I've always been the hero. Just because none of you can see it doesn't mean you can take it away from me. I'll show you. I'll show you *all*."

He raised his hands. The shadows rose around him, taking shape, becoming corporeal again.

The police on the other edge of the bridge took aim. Without turning, Nick knew the cops behind him were doing the same.

They would slaughter one another.

Dad grabbed his good arm, trying to pull him to safety.

"*No*," Nick snapped, trying to get free. "Dad, you don't understand, he's—"

Seth Gray landed between Nick and Owen.

His cape hung in tatters over his shoulders. His costume was shredded on his back, revealing bloodied skin. Somehow, he'd lost one of his boots, and his foot was bare. That hit Nick hard—for reasons he didn't understand.

Seth took a limping step toward Owen. "You won't hurt them. I won't let you, Shadow Star."

The shadows swirled around Owen. "You think you can stop me? There will always be darkness, no matter what you do. You can't stop it. Not now. It's too late. I'm going to show you what I'm truly capable of."

Seth took another step forward as the shadows grabbed support beams and lifted them off the ground, wielding them like oversized weapons. Cap was barking into the megaphone, telling both Extraordinaries to *stand down,* and the cops were getting restless, barrels tracking every movement Owen and Seth made.

This wasn't going to end well for anyone.

There will always be darkness.

This is how we burn the world.

You need to burn away the shadows.

Nick's eyes widened. "That's it."

He looked up at the helicopter. The spotlight still shone.

He looked over his shoulder. The cruisers were all pointed toward them.

Same on the other side.

He spun on his heels. "Dad, you have to get all the lights on. Spotlights. Headlights. All of them."

Dad's brow furrowed. "What are you talking about? We're getting you out of here *now*."

Nick shook his head. "I know what I'm doing. I need you to trust me. Please. Tell Cap. All the lights. Everything you've got."

Dad looked like he was going to argue, but instead, shook his head. "Don't do anything stupid."

Nick grinned at him. "Come on. Who do you think you're talking to?"

Dad gave him one last look before turning back toward Cap, hospital gown billowing around him. Nick was going to give him so much crap for not putting on pants if they survived this somehow.

Owen and Seth were advancing on each other. The shadows moved like some Lovecraftian nightmare. Nick almost froze at the sight of them, but there was no time to be afraid. It was time to be extraordinary. He had a city to save.

He ran to Seth's side. Seth opened his mouth, undoubtedly to tell Nick to get back, but Nick cut him off. "I know what to do. We stick to the plan. We burn away the shadows until there's nothing left."

"You're too late!" Owen shouted at them. "There's nothing you can do to stop me!"

"Holy hell," Nick muttered. "How on earth did you not punch him in the throat on a daily basis?"

"Restraint," Seth said with a scowl. "Anytime now, Nicky."

"You got enough juice left?"

"What are you talking about?"

"You're Pyro Storm," Nick said. "It's time for you to live up to your name. We're going to burn away the shadows. I need you to become the freaking *sun*. The cops are going to do the rest."

Seth nodded. "Stand back. It's time to finish this."

"Whoa," Nick breathed. "That gave me chills, dude. I'm going to climb you like a tree later—"

"Nick."

"Right. Standing back."

He moved behind Seth. He lay his forehead on the back of Seth's neck, warmed by the unnatural heat emanating from him. Seth raised his arms.

"Do it," Nick whispered.

The air around them lit up brightly. Fire blossomed from his hands, growing exponentially until it was a tsunami on either side of the bridge. Seth grunted as he pushed his hands forward, wave rushing along the guardrails, the top of which almost scraped the struts above.

Nick had never seen anything so beautiful before.

The sides of the bridge were blocked off by a wall of flames.

The shadows grew larger. Owen laughed. "It won't be enough! It's over. You've lost."

"Oh my god," Nick muttered. "He never shuts up." Then, turning his head back toward his father, he shouted, *Now!*"

Cap barked an order.

Headlights and spotlights burst into life on either side of the bridge.

They hit the shadows, destroying them instantly.

Owen cried out as the debris rained down around him.

Seth barreled forward, moving quicker than Nick could follow. He managed to avoid the metal beams falling around him as he pulled his fist back. Fire swirled around it.

Owen was distracted, bracelets lighting up, but the light mixed with the fire and the lights from the patrol cars. He shouted in frustration when he couldn't find any shadows.

He didn't see Seth coming.

Seth grabbed him by the wrists, fire leaking from his palms. The bracelets glowed, molten hot as Owen screamed in pain. The bracelets broke, falling to the ground where they hissed against the pavement.

"You shouldn't have touched Nicky," Seth growled. He punched Owen in the jaw, fire exploding in bright arcs. Owen's mask burned away as he flew back. He smashed into a support beam embedded in the roadway, striking it headfirst.

He slid down the beam, landing on the pavement. He didn't move.

The walls of fire died down around them, leaving the guardrails a fiery red.

Seth moved slowly until he stood in front of Owen. He crouched down in front of him. He paused for a moment, before he stood again, looking at Nick over his shoulder. "It's done."

Nick swallowed thickly. "Is he dead?"

Seth shook his head.

Nick ignored his dad's shouts coming from behind him. He walked until he stood beside Seth, looking down at Owen Burke. Shadow Star's mask was gone. He had scorch marks on his cheek. Part of his hair had been burned away. Owen took a shallow breath. And then another. And then another.

"You gotta get out of here," Nick muttered. "Before they try and arrest you."

"I'm not leaving you."

Nick absolutely did not swoon. "We can't let them know who you are. Nova City needs you to be its hero. And you can't do that if your secret identity is revealed. That's how it works. Go."

"Nicky, you can't—"

Nick kissed him.

It was brief, but he poured everything he could into it.

Seth looked slightly dazed as Nick pulled away. "I'm going to do that to you a lot, just so you know."

Seth reached up and touched his lips. "I'm okay with that."

"Go. I'll call you later."

Seth nodded as he stepped back. He didn't take his eyes off Nick as he rose slowly into the sky. Then, there was a great burst of fire and he rocketed off into the night.

Cops suddenly surrounded Nick, shouting things he couldn't quite make out. He felt a hand on his good shoulder. He turned to see his dad at his side, watching the fire Pyro Storm left behind. "Did you know I can tell the future?"

"I wasn't aware that was part of your dad powers, no."

"Well, I can. You want me to tell you what your future entails?"

Nick sighed.

Dad ignored him. "I'm seeing a very long, very involved conversation about many, many things. The least of which is why my son kissed an Extraordinary who saved us, even though he's supposed to be the bad guy."

Nick groaned. "Wow. That unfortunately sounds scarily accurate."

"And should we even mention how a certain best friend would feel about all of this?"

Nick needed to protect Seth's secret. He could do this. He could *do* this. "Um, well. You see. It's. Uh. Not. Like that?"

Dad shook his head. "You tell Seth that even though he can light things on fire, I'm still going to threaten the hell out of him with my gun when he comes over for dinner."

Nick gaped up at him. "That's not—I don't—what are you—"

"Secret's safe with me," Dad said. A strange look crossed over his face, but it was gone before Nick could figure out what it meant. "And now for a new prediction." He saw someone and said, "There you are. Take Nick to the ambulance. Shoulder looks like it's dislocated. Don't make me tell you twice. You can mace him if he resists."

Officer Rookie appeared out of nowhere. "Got it."

"What?" Nick said, outraged. "You can't—Officer Rookie, let me go! Dad! How *dare* you! I just saved the entire *city* and—Officer Rookie, how do you feel about bribes? Good, I hope. I have seven dollars with your name on it. Sidebar—you know how in movies when someone has to have their shoulder shoved back in place, they scream because it's supposed to hurt? That's not real, right? It's not going to hurt when it happens to me, right? Why are you laughing? Officer Rookie? Officer Rookie!"

EPILOGUE

"—and for that, Nova City has my most sincere apologies. Being a parent is . . . difficult. Being a parent of an Extraordinary is uncharted territory. I don't know what made my son do the things he did. He is loved. He had everything he could ever ask for. My wife and I are shocked that it has come to this. It might sound trite to say we never saw this coming, but it's the truth. But I still accept full responsibility for Owen Burke, because I am his father. And I know certain allegations have been made about my role in my son's descent into darkness, but I refute them completely and fully. I want nothing but the best for my child, and others like him. It was for this reason I opened Burke Tower to investigators, who found no evidence of wrongdoing.

"That being said, I am announcing a new initiative from Burke Pharmaceuticals. In addition to pledging funds to cover the costs of the damage my son was responsible for, we will begin a new study into what makes these Extraordinaries the way they are. Shadow Star and Pyro Storm are far from the only Extraordinaries in the world. I vow to help them in any way I can. An advisory board has been put in place to manage the dispersal of the funds with the utmost transparency. And I will gather the greatest team of scientists this world has ever seen in order to study the consequences of the Extraordinaries and help us understand our superpowered brethren. In his first inaugural address, Franklin Roosevelt said that the only thing we have to fear is fear itself. People tend to fear what they don't understand. Which is why we must know everything we can in order to prevent such occurrences from ever happening again.

"My son will be getting the best treatment possible in hopes that he can be rehabilitated. I am asking that Pyro Storm turn himself in to do the same. My wife and I request privacy at this time while we face this brave new world."

Reporters shouted questions.

Cameras flashed.

Simon Burke smiled and wrapped his arm around his wife, leading her away.

"And that was the scene today in front of Burke Tower," Rebecca Firestone said, staring into the camera. "A week after the events that saw the deaths of two Action News members and, as of this broadcast, an unknown total amount of damage, we still have more questions than answers. Owen Burke, the son of Simon Burke, has been revealed as the man behind the mask of the Extraordinary known as Shadow Star. Sources tell me he is in protective custody, pending charges to be filed against him. There has never been a situation quite like this before, and the NCPD is working with the attorney general's office in order to decide how best to proceed.

"In addition, there has been no sighting of Pyro Storm—the vigilante who is reportedly being hailed by some as the hero of Nova City—since the battle at McManus Bridge. His identity, at least for now, remains a secret. However, there is at least *one* person to whom his identity is potentially known. Nicholas Bell, the son of NCPD officer Aaron Bell, is a central figure to the ongoing mystery. Nicholas, who is a minor, was seen by numerous witnesses kissing Pyro Storm before he disappeared. Our Action News team was in a helicopter above the battle and recorded the footage of when he practically *mauled* the Extraordinary after Shadow Star had been subdued. We didn't have a live feed at the time, and our recordings were quickly subpoenaed as part of the ongoing investigation. We have submitted a Freedom of Information Act request in order to have copies of the footage returned to us. Attorneys for Action News tell me that they expect a response within the next few months.

"Our attempts to reach Nicholas Bell through his father have been unsuccessful. It does beg the question of what the NCPD knows about Shadow Star and Pyro Storm and their relationship with Nicholas Bell. Burke was a student at Centennial High School alongside Bell. The Nova City school district put out a statement, saying they are fully cooperating with authorities, but they do not comment on individual students due to privacy laws. However, we have been able to independently verify that Nicholas Bell is also known through his online moniker, ShadowStar744, and has written what can only be described as a lengthy manifesto thinly disguised as fanfiction. What did Bell know about Shadow Star and his plans for the city? We will bring you updates on the matter once further details are revealed.

"Only time will tell if we will discover who Pyro Storm is, and what will become of him, and other Extraordinaries like him. I'm Rebecca Firestone, Action News. Back to you, Steve."

Nicholas Bell found out having your shoulder shoved back into place hurt like the burning of a thousand suns filled with molten glass. He absolutely was not a fan.

He was in the hospital for two days. It would have been longer, except he was fortunate enough to share a room with his father, and if there was one thing the Bell men did not like, it was being cooped up in one place for long.

"Becky!" Nick whined. "Can we please go home?"

"Becky!" Dad barked. "Get the doctor in here *now* before I walk out of here again and take my son with me. And this time, I won't come back!"

Becky sighed and muttered something under her breath about how men were such babies.

They were discharged a couple of hours later.

Nick switched off the television, not wanting to see Steve Davis and his smug grin. Dad was in the kitchen, fixing dinner. Nick could hear him moving around, pots and pans clanging together. Nick grimaced, fiddling with the sling on his arm. He had to wear it for at least four more weeks, and already he hated everything about it. Sure, it was a badge of honor, a symbol for how he'd pretty much saved the entire city from complete and total annihilation at the hands of his supervillain ex-boyfriend, but he was done with it. It wasn't even something cool like a cast that could be signed.

His phone buzzed in his lap. Hey.

He grinned. Hey urself.

Saw Firestone's report. She unmasked u.

I HATE HER SO MUCH. MANIFESTO?!?!

Right???? Wtf

Nick shook his head. WTF indeed. She sucks (ʊ^ʊ)

It'll be ok. U ready 2 go back 2 school 2morrow?

Ugh. Don't remind me.

Homework 2 catch up on. Lots & lots of homework.

I hate u.

No u don't.

He really, really didn't. In fact: I miss u.

I know. Me 2. But it's for the best. Aunt and Uncle want me 2 lay low.

Probably a good idea. I'll still see u tomorrow, right?

Bright & early.

Kk. Gotta go. Dinner. Text you after?

Yes please. <3

Nick smiled quietly, feeling his face grow hot.

He sent back: <3

Mashed potatoes. Gravy. Hot, buttery rolls. Pot roast. Not a green vegetable in sight.

Nick was immediately suspicious. "All right. What did you do?"

Dad rolled his eyes, motioning for Nick to sit at the table. "I made dinner."

"Yeah, except you made all my favorite things. The only time you do that is when you feel guilty about something, or are getting ready to get all up in my business."

"Can't I do something nice for my son on the night before he goes back to school?"

Nick narrowed his eyes as he sat. "I'm on to you, old man. I see *everything*. You should—oh my *god*." He shoved more mashed potatoes in his mouth. "Dis us so *gooood*."

Dad sighed. "I can see that, even though I don't want to. Close your mouth while you chew, kid." He pulled out his own chair across from Nick, grimacing slightly as he sat. His ribs were still hurting him, though he'd stopped taking the pain medication days before. He hadn't let Nick take his after getting released from the hospital, reminding Nick that the opioid crisis was a very real problem and he'd be damned if he was going to let Nick sink into addiction.

Nick hadn't argued in the face of that logic, even if it was a bit overblown. And besides, he hadn't liked being high in the hospital, even though it'd numbed the pain. According to Nurse Becky, he'd spent a good three hours describing to anyone who would listen the shape of Seth's butt, and why it should be considered a national treasure. It wasn't one of his finest moments, even if it was the truth.

Dad sliced up a piece of pot roast before sliding it onto Nick's plate. Nick grinned at him through a mouthful of bread and gravy.

Dad didn't seem very impressed.

Nick swallowed before asking, "You have to go in tonight?"

Dad shook his head. "No. Tomorrow morning."

Nick blinked. "What? But you work nights."

Dad set down his fork, fixing his gaze on Nick. "There's been a change. I'll be working days from now on."

Huh. That was unexpected. "Why?"

"Maybe because I'm tired of spending so much time away from my son. Before long, you're going to be going off to college, and I want as much time with you as I can get. Cap allowed me to switch to days."

Nick was absurdly touched. But since his dad wasn't a fan of too much emotion, he only said, "Oh. That's good."

"Yeah," Dad said gruffly.

Screw it. They'd earned this. "I would like that. A lot."

Dad smiled quietly. "Yeah?"

"Yeah. I mean, it'd be nice, you know? Having you around."

"I thought so too. And as a bonus, it means that you and your boyfriend won't have a lot of time to rub against each other before I get home."

Nick choked on pot roast.

Dad took a sip of his water.

After he'd managed not to die, he spat, "Oh my god, why would you say that?"

"Kid, I was a teenage boy once."

"Yeah, when mastodons roamed the earth."

Dad snorted. "Keep telling yourself that, Nicky."

"We don't—we're not *rubbing* on each other. God! I haven't even seen him since . . ."

"Since he lit the bridge on fire and then punched Owen Burke in the face?"

Nick slumped in his chair. "So, we're going to talk about this now, are we? I *knew* this dinner was a bribe. You're not subtle, Officer Bell. At all."

"I'm allowed to be worried, kid. Comes with the whole being-a-dad gig."

Nick sighed. "I know. And while I appreciate your intrusive concern, you don't have to worry about me. *Or* Seth. He's not going to hurt me."

"I know that, Nick. Seth Gray would rather cut off his own arm than see any harm come to you. It's not him that I'm worried about."

Nick was confused. "Then what's the problem?"

"He's an Extraordinary. A powerful one at that. And no matter what he does, it's going to attract attention."

"That's not his fault. He's not trying—"

Dad held up his hand. "I'm not saying it is. But there are going to be people who won't like what he is. He's always going to have a target on his back. Which means the same thing could happen to you."

Nick didn't feel very hungry anymore. "So I shouldn't be his boyfriend? Or what about just his friend? Are you telling me I need to cut him out of my life altogether?"

"Of course not, Nicky. I would never ask that of you. And even if I did, what are the chances you would listen to me?"

"I would try," Nick admitted. "I'd probably be really pissed off at you for a long time, but then I'd see him in one of his sweater vest combos and decide he's worth it."

Dad stared at him.

Nick shrugged. "What? I can't help it if I think it's adorable. I mean, he's got this one bow tie that makes me want to—not finish that sentence, because you're my father, and I'm a virgin."

"Good to know," Dad said dryly. "Let's keep it that way for a while, shall we?"

That was okay with Nick. He wasn't in any rush, even if he was filled with certain inclinations that pointed toward his virginity being destroyed quite spectacularly. "Deal."

"I just . . ." Dad looked down at the table. "I need you to be careful, Nick. That's all I want, okay? You're old enough to make your own decisions, but that also means you need to think of the consequences. I can't have anything happen to you." He took a deep breath and let it out slowly. "Which is why I've accepted an offer."

Nick . . . didn't know what to do with that. "From who?"

"Cap."

"What kind of offer?"

"To head a new division with the NCPD."

So far so good. He hoped. "Doing what?"

"I'll be in charge of investigating the activities of Extraordinaries. Monitoring them. Helping them. Stopping those that need to be stopped."

Nick went cold. "You're going after Seth?"

Dad's eyes widened. "No, Nick. *No*. It's not like that. It's . . . think of it as checks and balances. I'll be working *with* Seth, if he decides to continue with being Pyro Storm. He's—I've gone back. Through the files. He was always trying to help. It was—"

"Owen," Nick said bitterly. "It was Owen that was causing all the trouble. He tried to take credit for everything. And we all fell for it." He shook his head. "But it wasn't all his fault. His dad hurt him. Made him do things. And Simon Burke is getting away with it."

"But you figured it out," Dad said lightly. "You saw the truth. And I have to believe it wasn't always that way for Owen. That had someone been there to guide him, he could have ended up differently. I don't want that to happen to anyone else. And it'll be my job to make sure it doesn't. Simon Burke won't get away with this. Not for long. I promise."

It was a cold comfort, but Nick let it go. "You'll be doing this by yourself?"

Dad shook his head. "No. I'll have officers under me. I've already asked Cap to give me Officer Rookie. He agreed, though we haven't told the rook yet."

"Oh man, I bet he hates that you call him that."

"I blame it all on you. He understands."

Nick chewed the inside of his cheek. "You'll have to talk to Seth," he said finally. "I don't know what he wants to do. He's . . . This took a lot out of him."

"I know. And I already did."

"What? When?"

"Thursday."

Nick could barely contain his outrage. "You said you had a doctor's appointment. You *liar*."

"I did. It didn't take very long. I went to the Gray house after."

Of all the deceitful— "You could have taken me. Maybe I would've liked to go too."

"I know. But I needed them to see I was doing this on my own.

It's not every day you tell a teenager and his guardians you're aware he can create fire out of nothing, and you want to help."

Okay. Now Nick was impressed. "Whoa. Badass."

"Language."

"It *is*."

Dad looked pleased. "It was, wasn't it?"

"What happened?"

"His voice got really high-pitched, and he squeaked a lot."

"Yeah," Nick said dreamily. "He's just the best."

"Oh boy. Not gonna touch that one." Dad shook his head. "They listened to me. I told them I would keep Seth's secret, as long as he doesn't do anything to force my hand. He asked if he could think about it. He didn't know if he wanted to be Pyro Storm anymore."

"I can't believe he didn't tell me any of this," Nick muttered.

"I asked him not to. I wanted you to hear it from me. It's . . . important, Nicky." His smile faded. "This work. What it would mean. The people we could help. And I'm not going to lie, it scares the hell out of me to think of you getting in harm's way because of who Seth is." His hands curled into fists. "I've—*we've* already lost a lot. I can't lose anyone anymore. I know I can't keep you from Seth, and I don't want to. But at least this will put me in a position to make sure you're never taken from me again."

Nick didn't hesitate. He stood from his chair and rounded the table. He reached down and put an arm around his father's shoulder. Dad laid his head against Nick's chest, just above his heart. "I'm not going anywhere," Nick said quietly. "I promise. You and me, okay? That's how it's gonna be. It's easier to stand together than it is to struggle apart. And I know I'm getting older, but if you think that means I won't need you as much, you're wrong. You're my dad. No matter where I go or who I'm with, that's not going to change."

Dad chuckled hoarsely. "That so?"

"Yeah. I mean, you break it, you buy it. You're pretty much stuck with me forever."

"I'm okay with that." Then, "She'd be proud of you, you know."

Nick's breath caught in his chest.

"I know . . . I know we don't talk about her as much as we should. And that's my fault. I should—I should have done things differently. I got lost a little, I think. And I'm sorry for that."

"It's okay—"

Dad shook his head as he pulled away. He looked up at Nick. "It's not. You deserve everything, Nicky. And someday I'll tell you everything. But know that she'd be proud of you. Everything you've done. The man you've become. You've done good, kid."

Nick sniffled. "Yeah?"

"Yeah. Now, eat before this gets cold."

Gibby and Jazz were sitting on the bench in the Franklin Street station the next morning. They both jumped up when they saw him, hurrying over. Jazz kissed his cheek and cooed in his ear, and Gibby admired the sling. "You look better than you did at the hospital," she said, ruffling his hair. "It was touch and go there for a moment."

Nick rolled his eyes. "It was a dislocated shoulder."

"Yeah, *we* know that, but you were the one shouting that they were going to have to amputate. It was probably the morphine talking, but still."

"I regret nothing," Nick said grandly.

"All right otherwise?" Jazz asked.

"Yeah. How bad is it going to be?"

Gibby grinned. "Pretty bad. I think almost everyone at school is talking about how you cheated on Seth when you had a threesome with Pyro Storm and Owen."

Nick groaned. High school sucked balls.

"I also heard a rumor that you are actually the evil mastermind behind all of it," Jazz said, flipping her hair. "Because of your manifesto, which is just ridiculous. You're about as evil as a puppy."

Rebecca Firestone was going to get her comeuppance. Nick would make sure of that. "Hey! I could be evil if I wanted to."

"Keep telling yourself that," Gibby said. "There's even a rumor that you're an Extraordinary yourself, and you're keeping it secret."

Nick scoffed. "Yeah, if only they knew what I went through to try and be one. I swear I still smell river water every now and then."

Jazz shrugged. "It doesn't help that you fell off the spire and landed on your feet."

Nick frowned. "Yeah, I haven't quite figured that out yet. Seth thinks I got lucky. I think it was Owen. Cap told me I just . . . stopped before I hit the ground. I mean, it had to be Owen, right? His shadows. Maybe he's not totally bad. I mean, he's still a dick, but . . ."

Gibby eyed him curiously. "What did your dad say? He saw it too, right?"

"Wouldn't talk about it. I think it's still too much for him. He's a softie."

Gabby picked up her backpack, slinging it over her shoulder. "Well, whatever it was, expect lots of people to be staring at you and whispering behind your back, with nothing but wild speculations."

"So, pretty much like normal, then. Cool. Cool, cool, cool."

"Yeah, but think. Now you can tell everyone if they don't shut up, you'll sic your Extraordinaries on them."

That sounded like the best idea ever. "Oh, man. Can you imagine? I'll tell them that they'll be lit on fire if they—"

"Who are we lighting on fire?"

Nick said, "Meep." He whirled around.

There, standing in a pair of chinos and a bright green sweater vest with a pink bow tie, was Seth Gray.

"I want to put my face on your face," Nick breathed.

Seth blushed brightly, looking down at the ground as he shuffled his feet.

"Oh my god," Gibby muttered behind them. "I honestly thought it couldn't be more awkward. I was wrong."

"Young love," Jazz said with a sigh. "Remember when we were like that?"

"We were never like them," Gabby snapped. "We're queer women. We have *some* sense of decency."

Nick ignored them, his heart stumbling all over itself as he watched the boy in front of him.

"Hi," Seth mumbled.

"Hi," Nick managed to say. "Um. It's . . . nice to see you?"

"You too."

"You look good."

Seth blushed harder. "Thanks. So do you." He shuffled his feet some more before saying, "I brought you something."

"You did?"

"It's nothing big," Seth warned, pulling his backpack around to his front. He opened the pocket on the side and pulled out a plastic package. He shoved it into Nick's hand.

Nick looked down to see watermelon-flavored Skwinkles Salsagheti. He didn't know that Mexican candy could make him feel like flying. "I got you something too."

Seth perked up. "What?"

Nick shook his head. "You have to close your eyes."

He did it without hesitation.

Nick stepped forward, his Chucks bumping against Seth's penny loafers. He leaned forward and kissed Seth on his lips.

It was brief, this kiss—barely scraping his lips against Seth's. It wasn't much, but he gave it his all.

He felt Seth's smile.

He decided right then and there that smiling while kissing was the greatest thing in the world.

He pulled away first. Seth's eyes were sparkling. "Thanks."

"You're welcome," Nick said. He wanted to do it again immediately.

But before he could, Gibby said, "Okay, as sickly sweet as this is, we're going to be late. We gotta go."

Nick rolled his eyes. "Yeah, yeah. Way to ruin the moment, Lola."

"Don't make me punch your good arm, Nick. How do you think Seth will feel when you can't use *either* hand?"

Seth squeaked.

Yeah, Nick was pretty sure this was love.

And without even thinking too hard about it, he took Seth's hand in his own. Their fingers interlocked, and Seth smiled so brightly, it felt like fire.

"Let's go," Nick said cheerfully. "I need to get to school in time to tell as many people as possible that some of the rumors going around about me might be somewhat true. Especially the three-some one, because that makes me sound awesome."

"Nicky, *no*," they all groaned at the same time.

"Nicky, *yes*," he crowed, and led Team Pyro Storm toward the stairs.

Fic: A Pleasure to Burn
Author: PyroStormIsBae
Chapter 1 of ?
3,164 words
Pairing: Pyro Storm/Original Male Character
Rated: PG-13 (Rating *will* go up)
Tags: True Love, Pining, Gentle Pyro Storm, Happy Ending, First Kiss, More than First Kiss, Fluffy Like a Cloud, So Much Violence, Evil Shadow Star, Bakery AU, Anti-Rebecca Firestone

---

Chapter 1: Everything Will Be Okay, I Promise

Author's Note: Hi, and welcome to my fic! You're probably wondering who I am. I'm not exactly new to the Extraordinaries fandom, but I've decided to start fresh given . . . certain events that I can't really talk about due to . . . reasons. So, new me, new screen name! I've worked hard on this, and I can't wait for you to see where it goes. I live for comments, so please let me know what you think! Unless you're going to be a jerk, then don't even bother. And MIND THE TAGS. This is hardcore anti-Rebecca Firestone and I won't apologize for it. This is beta read by my awesome boyfriend. YOU ARE THE BEST!!!

Nash Bellin groaned as his alarm went off. Given that he owned his own bakery/detective agency, he was used to the early hours, but some days, it wasn't easy crawling out of bed at three in the morning, even if scones needed baking and crime needed fighting. It didn't help that his ADHD caused his brain to never shut up, but he'd learned that having a disorder didn't make *him* disordered. It was part of him, his very own superpower.

He reached over and slammed his hand against the alarm, cutting it off. He yawned, stretching his arms above his head. He groaned as his back popped deliciously. He was about to push himself out of bed when a crash came from below.

Nash shot upright, heart thundering in his chest. The crash had come from downstairs in his bakery that also served as client intake. He'd lived above his shop for close to a year and had never had a problem. He thought quickly as he climbed out of bed, wincing at the cold floor against his bare feet. If someone was breaking in to steal, they'd quickly realize they'd messed with the wrong baker detective.

He crept toward the door, grabbing the baseball bat his father had given him, even though baseball was the most boring game ever created. He clutched the ash handle, choking up on the grip like Dad showed him. He opened the door.

Silence.

He moved quickly and quietly toward the stairs. He stopped at the top, peering down into the darkness. He thought he heard a low groan, but it could have just been the wind.

He took the steps one at a time, avoiding the next-to-last step that always creaked. When he reached the hallway that led to the storefront, he pressed himself against the wall, sliding down.

He took a deep breath as he reached the end of the hall. He kissed the tip of his bat and whispered his amazing catchphrase: "It's time to take out the trash."

He jumped out from the hallway, bat raised above his head. He looked badass and terrifying.

And there, slumped against the confectionary display case, bloodied and bruised, was a costumed man, his cape in tatters.

The man looked up at him. "Are you Nash Bellin?" he asked in his deep and sexy voice. He was also really muscular, and even though he was hurt, he was very attractive.

Nash lowered the bat. "I am. Who the frick are you? What are you doing in my bakery?"

The man grimaced behind his mask. "I'm not here for the baker. I'm here for the detective. I need your help, Nash Bellin. You're the only one I can trust, even though I've been hurt before." He looked off into nothing, filled with quiet strength and angst. "You're the savior this world needs."

Nash sighed. "I always knew I'd get pulled back in. It was only a matter of time." And with that, he strode forward toward the man, not knowing then that they would soon be in love and having mind-blowing sex in a variety of positions. "You might as well start from the beginning. What's threatening the world this time and how can I help?"

CREDITS

A bunch of awesome people helped to make this book the best it could be.

To my editor, Ali Fisher, you rock, as always. And to the assistant editor, Kristin Temple, you're pretty rad too. Thank you for believing in Nicky.

Christa Désir and her mentee Deborah Oliveir of Tessera Editorial provided invaluable insight to make sure I got things right. Thank you.

To the publisher, Devi Pillai, thank you for championing my work. And also for the cookie.

Lucille Rettino, the associate publisher, you are a rock star. Don't let anyone tell you otherwise.

David Curtis created the cover. He captured Nick and Seth perfectly, and for that, I'm eternally grateful.

Lesley Worrell did the cover design and knocked it out of the park. Thanks, Lesley!

Heather Saunders did the interior design and made it beautiful. Thanks, Heather.

My marketing team—led by Anthony Parisi—includes: Isa Caban, Becky Yeager, Julia Bergen, and Renata Sweeney, all of whom worked tirelessly on my behalf to make this book a success. You're all very, very good for my ego, and also, your work is top-notch. Thank you. And to the VP of marketing, Eileen Lawrence: you are wonderful.

Saraciea Fennell and Lauren Levite are my publicists who put up with me on a daily basis. Thank you for never complaining about the thousands of emails I send you, and for all the hard work you do on my behalf. Without you, I'd be lost.

Thank you to Melanie Sanders, the production editor, and to Jim Kapp, the production manager.

On the audio side of things, thanks to Tom Mis for producing the audio, and thanks to Michael Lesley for bringing the world of *The Extraordinaries* to life. I'm so glad to have a familiar voice joining me on this journey. In addition, thank you to the team at Macmillan Audio and to the Macmillan sales force.

Last, but not least, thank you, reader, for coming this far. I hope this story gave you a bit of the same happiness it gave me while writing it.

Oh, and one more thing . . .

STUNG

Aaron Bell watched the footage for the eighth time. Even though it never changed, he had to see it again.

It was shaky, and slightly blurry, shot from overhead. He'd muted it, because he didn't want to hear the shouts coming from inside the helicopter.

The camera focused on his son.

He knew how it ended, but his heart still leapt to his throat as the platform collapsed underneath Nick's feet, metal crumpling around him.

Nick started to fall twenty-six stories toward the ground below.

Aaron remembered standing helpless on the bridge, screaming his son's name, sure he was about to witness Nick's death right before his very eyes.

He should have.

Nick should have died.

Except—

About twenty feet above the ground, he just *stopped*.

Everything did.

The struts.

The large beams.

Nick.

They hung suspended for one second, two seconds, three—

And then he lowered slowly to the ground.

Cap said it was either Shadow Star or Pyro Storm. They had to have done something to save him. "Does it even matter?" Cap had asked him. "Nick's fine, Aaron. He's fine. And he's a hero."

That was what scared Aaron Bell more than anything in the world.

Because he *knew* what happened to heroes, in the end.

He'd seen it before.

It's easier to stand together than it is to struggle apart, his wife whispered in his head.

The footage ended.

He reached for the mouse to replay it again. One more time.

But before he could, someone knocked on the door to his tiny corner office. He quickly closed the video player. "Yeah," he said roughly.

Officer Rookie stuck his head in. "Sir, I wanted to remind you we have a meeting in ten minutes. You know Cap hates it when we're late. Need to talk budget for the Extraordinary Division."

They really needed to talk about that name. The ED, which Nick had immediately latched onto as Erectile Dysfunction and laughed himself hoarse. "I told you not to call me sir."

"Um. Okay. Detective Bell."

Aaron sighed. "Thanks, Rook. I'll be out in a minute."

Officer Rookie nodded and closed the door. He was a good kid. Overeager, but Aaron could deal with that. His own kid was the same way. He was used to it by now.

He looked down at a framed photograph on his desk. Jennifer Bell grinned up at him, a tiny Nicky slung on her hip. Beautiful, forever beautiful. "I don't know if I'm doing the right thing," he whispered to her. "What if Nick—"

The phone on his desk rang. It startled him, but he recovered quickly. "Bell," he grunted into the receiver as he put it against his ear.

"Mr. Bell?" a woman said. "Hold for Mr. Burke."

Aaron closed his eyes.

"Mr. Bell," a smooth voice said a moment later.

"Burke," Aaron said through gritted teeth. "I'm about to head into a meeting. I don't have time to—"

"Oh, I think you'll want to make time for me, Mr. Bell." The warning was clear.

"What do you want?"

"My security team was going over footage of the break-in at Burke Tower. I was made aware of a curious thing. Would you like to know what that is?"

Aaron didn't take the bait.

"It appears Owen wasn't alone when he broke into the tower that night. Someone was with him. Someone who seems to bear a remarkable resemblance to your son. It's not clear, and whoever it was wore a hood over his head, but there's a moment when he looks at the camera. I suppose an argument could be made that it's Nick. Strange, don't you think?"

"Why don't you ask Owen who he was with?"

"Oh, I have," Burke said. "But he's not speaking to me much these days. He finds the private rehabilitation center he's in rather confining. He's having trouble sleeping, given the lights are always on. Can't be too careful in case he . . . manifests. Tell me, Aaron. If it *was* Nick, and I'm certainly not saying it was, why do you think he'd be breaking into my building?"

"It sounds like you're making an accusation. And if you were, I'd like to do the same. Care to explain about these pills—"

Burke chuckled. "You would know if I were accusing someone of anything, Aaron. We were friends, once. When you and Jenny—"

"Don't you dare say her name."

"When you both came to me, telling me you thought your wife's telekinesis had passed on to your son, did I not do everything I could to help you both? To keep him safe? To *suppress* it? It took many trials to find the right combination before we figured out the correct dosage. After all, given his ADHD in conjunction with his abilities, that could lead to disaster, couldn't it? I know it wasn't enough to keep *her* from eventually being targeted, but Nick . . . he has no idea just how extraordinary he is, does he?"

He could barely breathe. "I don't—"

"Speaking of pills, how is the supply of Concentra, Aaron? Still have enough for your son? Do let me know when you need a refill, won't you?"

Aaron thought the handset was going to shatter with how hard he was gripping it. "What do you want?"

"A favor from an old friend. I heard about your promotion. Congratulations. Now, let me tell you what you can do for me."

Aaron Bell thought, *Jen, I'm sorry. I'm so sorry.*

And then he listened.

FLASH FIRE

**The explosive sequel
to *The Extraordinaries* by *New York Times*
and *USA Today* bestselling author
TJ Klune!**

"Uproariously funny."
SOPHIE GONZALES on *The Extraordinaries*

"The most down-to-earth book about
superheroes I've ever read."
MASON DEAVER on *The Extraordinaries*

"TJ Klune is doing powerful work
that inspires and impresses. He is a gift to our
troubled times, and his novels are a radiant treat
to all who discover them."
LOCUS

TOR TEEN